THE BEND IN THE SKY

THE BEND IN THE SKY

D. S. Morgan

Matador
9 Priory Business Park
Kibworth Beauchamp
Leicestershire LE8 0RX, UK
Tel: (+44) 116 279 2299
Fax: (+44) 116 279 2277
Email: books@troubador.co.uk
Web: www.troubador.co.uk/matador

ISBN:
978 1780881 614 SB
978 1780881 621 HB

British Library Cataloguing in Publication Data.
A catalogue record for this book is available from the British Library.

Typeset in 11 pt Century Schoolbook by Troubador Publishing Ltd, Leicester, UK
Printed and bound in the UK by TJ International, Padstow, Cornwall

Matador is an imprint of Troubador Publishing Ltd

To my friend Robert Van Den Eede

CHAPTER 1

Scents jostled in the warm night, like the creatures moving among them, billions of beings in wild shapes and shades, groping, crashing past – or through – one another.

Batteries of organs, organs of batteries, snouts and feelers, sniffed and jabbed the air, then reported back to their owners, or to partygoers who'd just rented them for the rave.

The scene was all the more eye-poking, as each reveller was made of the same basic stuff. Universes. Trillions, centillions of them. In the larger life-forms, serious overspillions. Those with grades in astro-anatomy knew it, but none of them gave a toss. Here on Level 7c3, with more sexes at the big event than bristles on a bouncer's bodywig, you had a deal else to think about if you wanted to get lucky.

Things were starting on the concert platform. A threatening roar burst from a point above it. Splinters of sound swooped over the audience. A huge cheer bounced off the clouds as two semitones went visual in the act of syncopating.

The sounds spiralled outwards into the distance, leaving behind the menace of the lurking roar.

A creature that was basically a ball of gristle rolled onto centre-stage and unwrapped itself.

"Are you ready?" it rasped.

" **Ready!"** vibed the fans, scrambling for a better view.

"And here they are!... " all nine of the gristle's snouts announced, each slightly after the other.

"Yeah!" screamed the horde.

"It's... "

"Yeah!"

"... It's... "

A gift of this species of gristle was that it could eat anything and convert it into more gristle. Because of this, in rougher places on 7c3, it was greatly sought after by suppliers to fast-food chains. This piece now had a major problem. A bag of nerves at the best of times, it had taken a bite out of its own memory just before coming on.

"... It's... "

The name was on the tip of its stomach.

The gristle began to sweat heavily. It bit its lip. It liked it. It bit its chin. It liked that too. There was only one thing left.

The rest of its body.

It rolled off and chewed itself into oblivion.

The band began anyway, in what, on Earth, would be more or less centillion-centillion time. To the group itself it was nearer four-four.

It wasn't a band in the commonly accepted meaning of the word. But, as a band, it worked. And it played live, in the sense that the instruments were live and played their own bodies, and each other's.

The crowd went crazy. Sections of it pulsed and closed on one another. Areas of it glowed. Ripples of colours and aromas fanned through it, building to waves that exploded in brilliant pheromone sweatbows as they crashed on reefs of entwined beings.

If it had been visible from Earth, a point so far down the scale of Levels that the rave-riders would have rounded it out of time-space altogether, this gig would have been one dango of a mind-melter.

In fact, just being *told* about it would have made Earth's leaders seriously sick. If it had ever got round that countless universes were out till further notice at a cosmic megathrob, it'd have blown the work ethic so far out of the water they'd never have clawed it back.

At the front of the stage, a gang of smells knocked out a line of security guards. For the briefest of moments, barely a billion Earth years, there was chaos. Then, as fast as they'd muscled in, the post-punk pungents were flung back on the convulsing body of the mob.

***

There were two reasons why Joe Alexander Outwood got from the campsite to the village in the same time that it took the group on 7c3 to finish their opening song.

The first was that he was walking slowly. It was a cool, clear evening, and he was thinking. He mentally loosened the straps on life's rucksack and groped around inside.

Though he felt he was "sort of getting along okay", there were some key things he wanted to do. Something inside him was whispering he *could* do them. And something inside *that* was shouting he'd be ace. He drew in a sharp breath. Did he *have* to lead, like, such an *ordinary* life?

His mind's hand felt onwards, and closed on the thing he liked best.

A big raw slice of freedom.

He swung round the corner into the high street. A man lurched towards him.

"Hezzawayee!" said the man.

"Hezzawayee," said Joe, spotting vital knowledge. "What's the best place for a drink here?"

At this key question the man sobered briefly. "Used to be three pubs. Now there's only the two... "

"And which do you think... ?"

"Third one folded last month. Landlord'd tried all kinds of tricks to fill it, but he needn't have bothered."

"What... ?"

"He had a 'Sample the Juice of the Grape' evening. I told him it'd be no good."

"So how... ?"

"A complete taste of wine."

"And ... ?"

"Then he did a fancy cocktail night."

"What... ?"

Bloke next to me had a Screwdriver. I tried the Electric Drill with Sanding Attachment."

"How... ?"

"It took the skin off my tongue!"

"Right... "

"After that he launched a Happy Hour."

"So... "

"Not a soul came! I told him he should've done what the pub in the next village did."

"What... ?"

"They ran a Misery Hour."

"How... ?"

"Brilliant! People *swarmed* in! Place packed! You could hear the whingeing for miles!"

Joe pressed for a clearer answer. "So there are just two pubs now?"

The man turned, nearly fell over, and waved his arm vaguely. "Yup! Over *there*!"

"So, which do you reckon?"

The man paused rockingly. "You can try'em both if yer like," he suggested helpfully, "but there's only one that's any good".

"Okay. Thanks. I'll take a look."

The man continued. "Might seem there's a choice but... "

Joe felt he shouldn't be keeping him from whatever he had to do.

"Fine. Yup."

"Life's often like zshat!" his advisor added liquidly. "You thinks you're free and with all the choices, but there's really shumwun up there workin the strings!"

"Yup. Thanks again!"

Joe watched him slewing home under some kind of miraculous guidance, and thought there might be something in what he'd just said.

"Good luck!" he found himself calling out.

The figure manoeuvred itself round and peered at him briefly. "More's the point, gooluck to *yoo*!" it shouted.

And then it was gone.

Joe walked towards the pub on the right-hand side of the street.

*

The second reason for Joe being more or less in step with the group on Level 7c3 had to do with time itself.

Formula-writers might try to explain it with barbecue-skewers of x's and y's, sprinkled with words about "Temporal Incongruities". But that would be an over-simplification. The gist of the thing was that Time's Winged Chariot was lying overturned in a layby just beyond the Outer Drussocks, with three bent flight feathers and a knackered spoke. And the recovery team was taking for *ever*.

It had been a spectacular multi-dimensional pile-up, leading to a messy temporal spill all over the intersection. And though this had pleased everyone by shambolising the speed traps, it had led to what's best described as a general mixing of the after, the before and the during.

The celestial roadsweeper will push back his cap and has wiped his forehead. He is speaking for many.

"It'll take more than a few bloody theories to sort this lot out!" he muttered.

***

In a different place, Ked Coot's fingers interrupted their restless drubbing on the air, and brushed the hairs on the skin wall of the Urban Fangster.

He could have used the remote, but hands-on was more *live*.

The mech-animal quivered expensively along its full

length, an optional feature that had cost Ked a full month's salary.

Then its taut, furred hide suddenly relaxed, creating folds in its body next to where he stood. They deepened, reformed briefly into shark gill slits (another extra for which he'd paid heavily), then structured themselves ripplingly into driver's door, windows, view-round cameras and personalized traff-nav-aggro accessories.

Ked slid into the driver's seat and felt it yield pulsingly in recognition. He liked that. In fact he liked everything about the mechan that throbbed and purred excitedly around him, ready for a fresh, savage bout of prowling.

He reached for the drive-stick in front of him and whirled it impatiently. A cartilage-belt poked out from the cabin wall, slipped across his body and locked into a socket in the meto-bone drive-casing.

The door of the condominium garage swung open.

The throbbing throated up to a growl, then belched to a turbo-vascular roar. Ked jerked his head, shaking his hair back over his shoulders. He gazed for a moment at the world beyond the driveway. He drank in the thrill of power rising in the genetically-engineered mech-beast as it strained for release.

"Okay Grux," he smoothed with velvet breath, "get into it, you sweet bastard."

***

At the back of the stage, the acoustics specialist checked his connections.

This was normally a straightforward task, made easier by the fact that he'd trimmed his claws, teeth, antennae and other projections into the exact shapes of the one hundred and forty-three tools needed for the job.

But tonight it was proving more difficult. Not only was he suffering from a rough bout spent on the town the night before with the band's lead feeler. He was also trying to prepare something special as a mega-boost for the PA system. This involved arrays of components linked in stunning complexity by a series of inter-spacial vortices which, for lack of anything else available, he'd compressed into an old no-return singularity twelve-pack.

And his schedule was closing on him.

One of his body-tubes itched, then buzzed.

"Where *is* it, Olok?" a voice rumbled in the tube. "I mean *tell* me if it's for the *next* show you're doing this. Then I can make *arrangements*! It's just I thought it was all supposed to be happening, like sometime in the immediate *now*!"

Olok waved his receiver organ around for a moment, plugged it into a communications body-zone that doubled for other uses, and responded.

The manager didn't appreciate it.

"What in Slaksbixin was *that*? Look! Are you *making* with these effects, or do I get Crull Weegpf to fill for you on this and *all future* gigs?"

"Right!... Hey!... *Alright*!" Olok stalled, his five hearts disappearing as his skin turned opaque under the stress. "It's set to go *anytime*, man. I was just waiting for you to call it. You want it, then?"

"Do I *want* it? Do I want a trillion years off in Skoorap Balaronga after this show? Just *do* it!"

Olok shrugged it off as a bad-bristle day. He wasn't sure the system was hooked up the way it should be, but it was too late to change now.

He hung on for a fraction longer, claw poised over the button. It had to be the right moment, not before.

The sound was incredible. It was metamorphosing, ready to burst out of its air-skin, pick up existence and run off with it.

The band was closing on superspasm.

The claw went down...

It wasn't the effect he'd intended, but the audience went mad about the blue flash and the ice-cool blackout.

All it took was a couple of flicks with his tail on the panel behind him, and the Ac-Spesh had the power back on before anyone sussed.

And the show got better and better.

And so, as a matter of fact, did the new-born blue flash.

But that took a while.

***

"This pub does not welcome strangers of any description.

This pub in fact welcomes nobody.

This pub is only here so that it can despise the pub opposite,

its clients and anyone who is passing by.

This pub does not want its air breathed or its beer drunk.

Nobody knows how this pub stays in business,

not even the proprietor or the staff.

If, warned of this, you still wish to step inside,

we will do our utmost to ensure that you are not served."

said the barmaid's expression through the window.

Joe wasn't into her kind of mug-processing, but he faced her a short message.

Then he turned and walked across to the pub on the other side of the road, a pub with a strangely drawn sign above its door, which gave its name as

THE BEND IN THE SKY.

He stopped for a moment in front of the building and glanced briefly at the sign. "Might as well," he suggested to himself casually, as if there were hundreds of pubs around.

If he'd had *the gift*, Joe would have noticed that the only thing keeping this surveyor's nightmare from falling down in a heap of rubble was a collection of ghostly regulars who, in their various ways, buttressed it by leaning, lounging and propping themselves against it.

They did this, in fact, purely for their own support, since they were all drunk. Some had been so for centuries. One, who was particularly heavily spirited, was in the habit of commenting that the only reason they were ghosts at all was that they were simply incapable of moving on anywhere else. Others said it was merely a question of trying to stay ahead of an extremely long hangover.

Joe went inside. The place smelled of congealed time. Assorted laughters and wheezings swirled round him, mixed with sounds of boasting-auctions and beers shoalling down throats.

The pub was long and erratically shaped. Its walls and ceilings went their own ways, veering off unexpectedly, then re-emerging, roughed up by experiences in unseen alcoves and deeper places.

At each end a log fire burned cheerfully. Clutches of people conversed at tables. Odd individuals roosted on bar stools. One even odder-looking inividual was making chanting sounds while kippering himself in the smoke at one of the hearths. Somewhere, unseen, the pendulum of an arrhythmic clock agonized over its next beat.

Joe walked towards the bar.

It wasn't a long way. A matter of a few steps.

He'd taken about half of them when the pub, as he'd just begun to know it, disappeared.

Things went dark. Joe's arms, legs, solar plexus, head and other parts got mixed up with each other and with a small mat he remembered having trodden on. He felt all the bits tumbling around in a confused mass. He crashed onto something. It teetered underneath him for a moment, then gradually stopped moving.

He sat catching his breath. If this was the afterlife, eternity smelled of rotten wood and beer. If the wood was rotten, so be it. But if the beer was crap, this was a serious corner of hell. He looked around for karaoke bars. There had to be karaoke in hell... and junk mail... and...

"Oi! Y'all right down there?"

"Yeah! Great! What d'you think? Maybe you'd like to plunge down here as well for a bit of a laugh, and get some of your friends to come too. We could make an *evening* of it!"

"Look, there's no need to get like that with *me*, sonny!" said the peering head. "I don't own the place. I were just standin' near when the floor fell in."

The head, framed by splintered wood, paused, preparing the next piece of helpful information. " 'S'appened before," he added, as if this would comfort Joe in some way, "at sevral points."

"Is there an easy way out?"

"Landlord's convinced of it, but there ain't. 'E's bin doin' botch repairs for years, but 'e'll 'ave to put a new floor in sooner or later."

Joe stared at the face. "No that wasn't what I meant. I meant -*How can I leave where I am now*?"

"Depends where you wanna go, really, don'it?"

"How about *up*?"

"Uh. Dunno. 'ave to see about that." The man paused for a long time, then gave a start, as if surfing some kind of brainripple.

"Ooh! ... Er... Would you like me to see if we can 'elp you up out of that 'ole? Maybe you'd like to come back into the pub. We could try *that*."

Moments later Joe was standing nursing his right shin. The landlord stared at him anxiously.

"It's not broken, is it?"

"Only bruised, I think," Joe growled.

"I meant the barrel you fell on," said the publican.

***

The K*rargxtko building was less than four miles away from Ked's apartment. But, whenever he managed to get up in time for it, he took what he called "the long route", a major detour three-quarters of the way round Thrarrxgor city, along what the population referred to as "The Blood Run".

It was well named, splattered – as it was – with the haemoglobin of past drivers, passengers and mech-animals. Pieces of crushed meto-bone, fragments of tusk and wheel-claw, sections of shredded hide, with remnants of torn fur attached, littered what was laughingly described by the Thrarrxgor-city authority as the "road surface".

It was along this duelling-track that Ked liked to kick up his existence-awareness level, and to give Grux the freedom of his skull for a deathbrinking clutch of heartbeats before checking in for another day at K*rargxtko.

He was early enough this morning. But before he hit the serious section of his route there was the essential matter of finding a girl to impress. He slowed his mech-animal temporarily, headed into one of the residential zones favoured by newcomers to the city, switched the slide on the beast's 'Pull' facility to '*Musk scent / Sinew-flex*', and cruised ostentatiously.

It didn't take long. It turned out that the girl who flagged him worked for K*rargxtko in the same building. Not that there was anything unusual about being hired by the company. Its owner had taken over the city, and most of the planet, in the last twenty years. But the fact that both of them were at K*rargxtko HQ struck Ked as useful – a chance not just to show off his beast-driver skills but also to brag tantalisingly about his role in 'Proj. K'. Maybe he could even hint at some link with K*rargxt himself.

"... There's a deal you need learn when you cut the beam on the door of *that* joint," he over-sighed. "First is, K*rargxt runs the planet." He reached forward, drew a pair of furred sunglasses from behind a pulsing vein on the dashboard, and slipped them on. He took a different pair from his pocket and offered them to the girl.

They were digital shades that fast-trialled live enhancements of his image, checked the wearer's eye-responses, and defaulted on the one with the biggest turn-on. She pushed them away. He guessed she'd come across that stuff before.

She struggled hard to look at him without laughing. Poser of the day *nothing*! This had to be the biggest slup-blower she'd met since hitting town. The satinized torsoe-sash, the hologrammed finger nails, the chromed nostril air-scoops…

"… And there's a heap else I could tell…" he trailed, begging she'd be curious.

He wasn't disappointed. His co-rider was a good listener. He sensed she knew it paid to keep your ears open when you worked for K*rargxtko, if you wanted to stay working, and *living*.

Her ears, as well as being open, were shaped. It had been diamonds last month. Now it was deltas. As for Ked, his were moulded for the next trend, starfish. He prided himself on staying ahead of the pack.

"… You said you're a 'designer'… " she led, as he paused between bullshits.

"Yup." He wished heavily for her to ask him what he designed.

She asked him what he designed.

"Lives," he said, casually.

"*Lives*?"

They eased onto a wide stretch of highway. Ked glimpsed a K*rargxtko police mech-beast savaging a private one it had ambushed. It was a full year since K*rargxtpolico had stopped feeding their mechans. Now anything with non-K*rargxtko plates was prey on any pretext. Ked watched the last of the 'suspect's' claw-wheels slither down the the enforcer beast's gullet, then glanced back at his passenger.

"Yup. Lives."

"Whose?"

"No-can-say. It's classified at 9+."

He fumbled at a short-cut through the chat, "… Course, 'fyou want some brush-strokes on yours, I'd *look* at the idea… "

"Thanks, but I'll draw the line on my own."

Ked killed a hiss and kept on target. "*Right*… Well

maybe you'd like to know the kind of *perks* you get on grade 47. That's *my* grade. There's the *Exec. Beast Park*, the access to K*rargxtko *hyper-tec goods* at special rates and… "

"Look, just *freeze* it a second, will you! – A moment ago. You didn't finish! This *life-designer* thing. Are you telling me you're some kind of therapist? You can't be in Sect-Franchising. They told me that unit moved out of the building years ago."

Ked's hand twitched the control stick. The beast tensed. Flaps opened. Side breather-pipes deployed. Energy surged through the beast's fire gut, morphed to thrust in the power unit, then burst onto the road in an orgy of clawed wheel-spin. Hot gas flared onto the mechan's tusks till they glowed red against the city's vomiting sky.

The shock pushed their bodies back hard into the Fangster's throbskin seats.

He gave a nervous laugh and looked at the cold outline of the K*rargxtko building in the distance ahead, and at the giant hangar next to it.

"*Therapist*? – Hardly! Just the *opposite*, I'd say!"

***

The blue flash spun and sparked on a large piece of tarpaulin underneath a snack barrow in a corner of the field.

An elderly bi-pedal creature was peering down at it.

"You alright, dear?" asked the bi-ped. "Looks like you've had a bit of a nasty turn. Come for a hot sludgie have you? Got lots of 'em here."

She swung up a lid on her barrow. "What was it you was after? Mucus Special? Enzyme Frothy?"

The flash fizzed around vaguely. The Level-Seven humanoid tried another tack. "You might fancy *this*," she coaxed, dragging out a boiling green gas orb on a stick, "there's free billion galaxies dressin' wivit. Mind you, if you want garlic sauce, it's extra!"

A queue started to form behind the blue buzz of static,

which had taken to spinning round its own axis like a catherine wheel that had gone off in its box.

First to arrive was a particularly nasty odour. It hung about irritably.

The saleslady took a closer look at the spiral and gave a surprised jump. "*Wait a moment*! Aint you that flash what just whizzed across the sky?"

A cloud of multi-functional cells flew in on final approach, arranged themselves into a one-legged mouth, and touched down in the queue. The sludgie-seller ignored the clients and stared at the electric waif. A life of hard cosmic knocks had hammered her heart to a moonscape. But, somewhere, a warm underlayer had survived.

It was the moment to hand out a bit of help.

She spoke to the blob softly.

"Look, you ain't getting far like that dear. You'll be needin' some kind of a... operatin' system for a start. Even a brain, perhaps."

She thought for a moment. "Don't know I can do very much. Still, there's a chance I might just find *something* ... hang on a sec."

She pulled open a drawer at one end of the barrow and rummaged around inside. "Minds... *minds*. Thought I had something here *somewhere*... "

The queue was growing longer and increasingly impatient. The customers watched the flash chase its tail round the barrow-wheels.

The remote head of something unpleasant eared itself to the front of the line and told her, in its own way, to ground the electrical charge.

"... Best, really, lady. Just move your barrow and pull the tarpaulin away. Maybe throw a coil of wire at it too. It won't feel a thing!" Others joined the death-call.

The vendor had no time for them. "Miserable bastards! You can all shut it an' zakin' wait! Look at the poor little mite!" She pulled out a plasticky box, blew the dust off it, and scrutinised the instructions...

*

They watched the blue flash move off. The bipedal followed it with her eyes for a few seconds, then glanced down at the label in her hand, on which was printed:

R58b Mind and Body Pack
With new added shape and sense options

"Got to admit it's a bit up the power scale for a bunch of sparks," she murmured, "but it's the only one I had."

The odour was apalled. It was going to make a stink about *that*!

"A 'bit up the power scale'!" it scathed. "'A '*bit up the power scale*'!

An *R58b* on *that*! It's like installing a *23c47* on a *5t whiff*!"

"Or a Neebik 9 on a 2b blowfly!" sneered another being in the queue behind. "Well it's gorn, anyway", the saleslady said firmly, "an' it ought to be a brilliant bleedin' little flash now. Good Luck to it, *I* say!"

***

Joe was given a pint on the house while a circle of beer crates was built round the gap in the floor. His dive had caused hardly a stir amongst the drinkers. It was as if it was a regular event for people to go crashing into the cellar.

He took a large gulp of the pub's bitter. Perhaps it was because he'd gone close to hell and back for it, but it tasted like the best he'd ever had. He glanced at the fireplace at the far end of the pub, the one where no self-kippering was currently being done, and noticed, on the floor in front of it, five long rows of upturned thimbles.

Something shot downwards through his field of vision and landed in one of them with a ping. A collective shout came out of the rafters above the hearth, followed by a burst of applause and the sound of heavy backslapping.

Joe looked up and saw, inside the roof, about twenty human forms balancing precariously on a dodgy jumble of struts and beams. Some, whom Joe assumed to be the winning team, were lolling about perilously, chanting "*Easee*!" and waving their tankards at what he took to be the opposition.

" 'S'game," said a man standing near him.

"Ah... thought it might be."

" 'Splayed with pebbles. They drop'm, see?"

"Yup," said Joe.

"Into them thimbles. At least, they try to."

"Yup... right. Must take a lot of skill."

"Yup, it do."

Joe ordered a pint for his neighbour, and exchanged info with him on pebbles, beer, life, themselves, and the world generally.

He wouldn't have been surprised to know he was being watched. Strangers who walk into country pubs can expect that to happen sometimes.

But he would have been a good deal more surprised if he'd known that one of the watchers was from a different universe and that another was from a very much higher Level of Existence altogether.

There are those who'll travel a long way for a drink at

THE BEND IN THE SKY.

CHAPTER 2

The blue flash, integrating the new R58b Mind and Body Pack (with added shape and sense options) bobbed about above the field and sniffed reality.

Its mind began explaining things. It had got as far as running through some of the career opportunities in quantum accountancy, when the blue flash decided to set a few priorities. Then it narrowed them down to *one* priority.

It was going to have a *wild* time.

It opted for a variable shape, selected a wide range of senses and, from a huge gamut of gender opportunities, chose to be male.

Then he named himself Boontrak Firefish, and moved on.

Moving on, for something that's from Level 7c3, is fairly uncomplicated. There are plenty of directions to choose. You can stay on the floor you're on, so to speak, or move downwards and drop in on as many points of time and place in the Lower Levels as take your fancy. The travel opportunities are enormous.

Boontrak was interested in all of them.

It should be mentioned here that, despite attempts to standardize them, there are big differences in the regulations applying on different Levels.

Examples are to be found in the laws of physics.

For instance, light born on the cluttered layer shared by Earth's universe (classified currently as Sub-Lamina 2k16, pending appeal for up-grade to full Level status) has to behave in a restricted and unspontaneous way. There is:

No stopping off to rest your particles.

No sparking about with interesting, mysterious phenomena.

No dazzling intercourse with energetic ravers on the same wavelength.

Bright young sparks from the Upper Levels often look on this as particularly boring.

Light on Seven has it parsecs better. No one hassles you, experiments on you, times you, reports on you, or puts you in prisms as they do on lower, upwardly-ambitious parts of Existence, like Earth's.

For this reason, when they go on trips to the lower levels, Seveners, including all light-forms, usually take along their own Level's rules. And, unless they disintegrate or run into other difficulties, they simply stick to these. With the power they can kick in at will, the rides they can cut through Levels 6 to 1 shoot off the far edge of wild. There are wide open regions out there, untamed voids cascading endlessly into each other, begging for action. No organized tours! No fixed trails! Everything off-piste!

Of course, there are other parts of the lower levels which, are more densely populated. These too have their own particular charms for fun-riders. And though some of the lower-level inhabitants moan about the hoo-rays that occasionally drop in and smash things up, there's precious zero they can do, except protest to some of the more enterprising Upper-Levellers who turn up from time to time, pretend to listen sympathetically and then present their bill for consultation fees.

Boontrak headed towards the outer slopes of Seven.

Coming the opposite way, a group of transmuters were funning their way back from a short break. Boontrak watched them whoop their path inwards over the temporal rim, morphing from form to form and colour to colour as they planed through the time-surf. One of them, temporarily a forty-nine-appendaged planetary-ring rider, called out to him.

"Hyer! Flash! *You*, my friend, are pointed somewhere

way cool! Out *there*, my fine starbeam, it's like... like you didn't know it ever *could* be!" He transmuted on through a range of beings, shapes and colours.

Boontrak began trying it out himself. Sweeping through a starter selection of body-options, he gave the group a friendly parting wave, with what he took to be the equivalent of a hand.

***

"C'mon Dewt, it's our team's turn now!"

Joe's neighbour thanked him for the pint, waved to the caller and clambered up into the rafters.

There was a loud attention-seeking cough just behind Joe's ear. He ignored it. Probably someone wanting a refill.

He was beginning to develop a strong liking for the place and its beer. He finished off what was left in his glass and was on the point of ordering another, when it hit him.

The sound, that is, not the glass.

The sound wasn't the cough he'd heard a moment ago. It was quite different. And it came from somewhere else. From the man over at the hearth who, having finished his chant, had just taken up a strange musical instrument and begun to play it. In fact it seemed to Joe he must have taken it up a long time ago, because he played it as if the two of them had grown up together.

He wore it like a coat, and the more Joe looked at it the more he thought it probably served for one too. He could see the man's arms sliding up and down inside its perforated sleeves, his elbows catching in rents and loops in the cloth, stretching, then relaxing the mysterious fabric. Strangely shaped bows darted across and through the material, stroking out sounds from it. Joe saw that they were attached to the man's knees, which moved up and down in a kind of vigorous, seated dance.

The eyes set in the weathered face stared at something a very long way away.

The fingers frolicked over the holes of what looked like a

cross between a set of bagpipes and an elbow-powered vacuum-cleaner, which seemed to form an integral part of the garment.

Through a grin-shaped opening, the device drew gasps of woodsmoke down to its insides, then exhaled them in an extraordinary mixture of changing scents and sounds.

It spoke, too, to other senses known to none there except the player himself.

Nobody in the pub appeared particularly touched by it, apart from Joe. And he was so absorbed that he didn't hear the attention-seeking cough that had been directed at him, just behind his ear, for a second time.

***

For reasons already explained, when Upper-Levellers go down the hill for a bit of fun they tend – understandably – to hold on to their full power-rating. But on the matter of their size (or, put another way, the size of their matter), most prefer to reduce this so that it matches the Level they're travelling on. It makes manoeuvering easier. They then upgrade to their original size when they return.

There are, though, a few lazy Upper Revellers (including those from Seven and higher) for whom all this chopping and changing is a serious drag, and who can't be bothered to scale down at all.

The result is that, when they arrive in a region, they simply fill it up, and those residents who didn't believe that size is important soon realise that size *is*, in fact, everything.

There are also cases where Upper Level travellers forget to switch themselves onto *permeable* setting, an oversight which reduces their collision insurance cover to a blanket of zeros.

Boontrak, being young, energetic and sort-of-responsible, opted for variable volume. But, feeling that enough time had been spent selecting options, he turned off a voice in his superbrain that kept nagging him to go *permeable*, and plunged over the edge of Level Seven.

It was like nothing that, even using his R58b, he could have imagined. Undreamt-of powers surged up from somewhere inside him. New skills sprang into being as he performed seemingly impossible feats. Seemingly impossible feet, together with other seemingly impossible body extensions, appeared on demand, and demonstrated further seemingly impossibler skills.

He became totally absorbed in cosmobatics. For a long time he climbed, rolled and ace-looped, stunt-riding time-scorching turns on the ether – a streak of brilliant blue.

After that he soared back to where he'd been and flew in formation with his earlier selves. This took some getting used to, since he'd morphed about so much that, even with his R58b, he had a job remembering *what* he'd been and *where* he'd been it.

It was during one of these fly-pasts, in which Boontrak's present self was spearheading a squadron of its veteran, vintage and classic versions, watched excitedly by some of its more recent ones, that the globules appeared.

It seemed, at first, there were just a few. But Boontrak realized quickly that they were just some of a mass of droplets that was moving steadily towards him, spreading out, then contracting, like beads of sweat on some strange, invisible, puffing face.

As the mass closed on him, Boontrak began to pick up a chorus of high-pitched twitterings.

The twitterings grew louder.

He flicked his brain up a couple of notches to make some sense of it all, and felt it begin to exchange some kind of technical data with the droplets.

As if responding to a request from his mind, the globules gelled into one deeply harrassed globoid shape, and the twitterings into a wheezy voice.

"Had to split up for a bit, old boy," it wheezed. "Throws 'em off the scent."

It paused, sweatfully, to gather its breath, then resumed.

"Not far to Seven now, is it?" it asked urgently.

Boontrak replied that he wasn't sure, since he'd been having a great deal of fun soaring about recently, and had rather lost track of the lie of the cosmos.

The globoid shrugged roundly. "Oh, well, I'll just have to make do with dead reckoning." It sighed and, with difficulty, cast a glance over its chunky equivalent of a shoulder. "Anyway, looks as if the bounders may have gone after some other poor bastard."

"What bounders?... Who?... Where?... "

The traveller didn't seem to have noticed the question. "Watch out if you're going below Six," it rasped. "They're from *Eight*... Free-loading round the lower levels... *Swarms* of the things! As a matter of fact, if you've been having a good time recently, they could know about you already. Some of them have a tremendous detection range!"

The globoid drew a husky breath and looked at Boontrak more closely, "Anyway," it added, "if that really *is* a complete Level Seven R58b you've got, like it *claims* to be, you'll sense 'em out soon enough. As for me, I'm damned if those yobs are getting to chew on any of *my* kicks!"

A bulky arm emerged into view through an inter-dimensional slit in space and wiped the being's forehead. "Do you know," it spluttered in a hurt kind of way. "Do you know, they actually went for me when I was on my *foie gras*. How ghastly can they *get*?"

There was a brief squishing sound, and the traveller was gone.

Boontrak's mind threw out a telepathic tendril in the hope of making some final contact with it.

"What *are* they?" he projected sensorily.

The last gasp of a signal frailed across the void.

"You don't... *know*?" it whispered hoarsely through the static, "you're telling me you *really don't know*?... You *must* know!... They're Ple... ."

Then all contact was gone.

And Boontrak withdrew the tendril.

***

Joe floated in a bubble filled with the scents and the music.

If anybody had asked him, he wouldn't have been able to say how long he'd been drifting there. Eventually he heard someone cough. He'd heard the cough before, somewheretime. It meant nothing to him.

The cough assembled itself into a voice.

"Twenty-five!"

Joe felt that perhaps his body might be turning round to see who it was. He started tumbling about inside the bubble. Its walls broke.

He found that he had indeed turned round, and that a man who'd been sitting near the door when he'd first come in was now standing within inches of him. He supposed it was the man whose cough had almost intruded on him about a million years ago, before the music and the scents had drawn him away.

The bloke's clothes gave Joe the impression that, a few hours previously, they had been hanging uninspiringly on a shop dummy. This was a good impression because, a few hours previously, they *had*.

Now they hung uninspiringly on the man. He seemed somehow to have a dummy's moulded hairstyle too. The general look was of someone trying hard to be in the general trend of fashion but knowing nothing about it.

"Twenty-five, eh? That's a good age," patronized the man, stabbing at the air in front of him with his forefinger as if this gave him some kind of authority to intrude further. "Couldn't help overhearing it when you were talking earlier to that other bloke. From West London, you said. In between jobs at present, if I heard correctly. Going to begin a new one in some months time, didn't you say? Engineering, wasn't it? Taking a bit of time out before starting work again, isn't that right?"

If Joe had come fully back from the music to himself he

might have given him the two syllables. But, instead, he heard himself murmuring "Yup... that's about it."

And he found himself listening to the man, who told him he was a talent-scout, that he was looking for someone to star in an imminent spectacular, that he could give no details just now, as it was extremely secret, and that, if Joe would tell him more about himself, he'd put him down on his list of possibles.

After a while Joe realised, vaguely, that he'd told the man some more, and that, since the man had pressed him for it, he'd given him his name and address. He sort of recalled, too, that the man had said he didn't really need the address, as he'd have ways of finding people anyway.

More questions were being asked now, but Joe missed most of them. The sound-scents were pulling him away again. He didn't notice that this was making the talent-scout increasingly irritated.

So, when the interviewer slammed his drink down on the bar, stormed over to the hearth and started shouting at the musician, it took Joe totally by surprise.

The playing stopped. Suddenly everything swung into focus.

Joe saw that the man was trying to lift the musician up by his coat, and dragging at it, doing his best to wreck it, and was snarling to him that people should be left to talk in peace. The victim was struggling to defend himself, but his knees and arms kept getting caught up in the various parts of his coat, so that he was definitely coming out worse in the argument.

Two and a half seconds later, the attacker was three feet off the ground and moving rapidly backwards. When he was sufficiently out of the musician's way, Joe deposited the talent scout on the pub floor.

"Leave him alone! Let him play the music! What the *hell* do you think you're at?"

The heaped bloke, who was in no mood to explain anything, scrambled to his feet. He stared furiously at Joe, his face pale with anger, for what seemed a long time. Then suddenly his mouth tightened, as if he'd come to some kind of decision.

He levelled an index finger at Joe, giving the impression it was loaded with something very nasty.

Then he said something that struck Joe as odd.

"*Right*!" the man snapped. "It'll be *you*!"

And he walked out of the pub.

Joe checked to see whether the musician was hurt, found he was okay, and bought him a pint.

And then, shortly afterwards, he received a great honour for a first-timer at THE BEND IN THE SKY.

Dewt climbed down and asked him if he'd like to play pebbles.

***

Ked's fragrance medallions clashed under his shirt as he fidgeted in the drinks-machine queue. Two minutes was all they got for the break, and K*rargxtko only granted *that* for the boost it got in mid-morning effort by selling its staff a body-wrecking range of strange liquid stimulants.

Suddenly his head stopped its compulsive scanning of the corridor, frozen in mid-sweep. On the other side of a group of armed K*rargxtko guards, his early-day passenger was exiting a lift. But not just *any* lift. It was the lift *nobody went near*, at least not without clearance from people so powerful, irritable and deadly that their own shadows had formed a mutual protection group. It was the lift that rose through the organisation's upper storeys to the forbidden floor of *THE MAN HIMSELF*.

Ked felt himself twisting inside. He forced his jaws together and feebled a grin as she came past.

His "*Hi*!" was so high it was a yelp.

He followed it with a squawk. "Didn't realise you had that kind of access… "

She stopped and looked at him, as if musing over

something the floor-cleaning mechan had puked back. She seemed to surprise herself by bothering to speak at all.

"There are a good many things you don't realise, *Ked*! One is that being *new* doesn't mean I'm poorly connected. I promote fast." She glared at him piercingly. "And, of course, working for the *Supreme Security Office* helps... "

Ked felt gastric meltdown approaching.

"... Another thing you should've known, Ked, is that even *humming* about K*rargxtko's activities gets to be terminal. And when you start shout-wondering what's "Powering-up our Intervener Units", your mouth talks you nearer the edge than the *drop itself*! If you hadn't shut it while you watched that gerbil of yours trying to bite-race the Fire-Tiger in the next lane, your warm remains would have been festering in K*rargxt's personnel shredder for the last two hours."

She turned to go, then paused briefly. "And by the way. That Fire-Tiger. You really know how to pick 'em, *don't* you Ked? It belongs to Sculpin. That was his bio-mechanic on a test run. If Squid had been driving it, you'd be wishing you *were* in the shredder."

"Squ... *Squid*?"

"Yes. Squid Sculpin's a close... *friend* of mine," she said casually, and strolled away.

Ked stared into the space she'd occupied, not daring to move. Meltdown beckoned.

*

It took Ked a long time before he could concentrate on his work again. He'd only ever seen K*rargxt and Sculpin at a distance, or in holographic messages to K*rargxtko employees, but ghastly images of them kept rushing through his mind.

His colleagues in Life-Planning weren't used to him being so quiet. Most days, if they wanted to whisper-check a rumour, or speculate on some staff change, he was as ready to join in as anyone.

Ked's silence hit Juncus hardest of all. Working in Minor

Events Manip kept Juncus out on the fringe, and he relied heavily on Ked for updates on the Big Project.

Eventually he decided to try where higher-ranking members of the team had failed.

He tugged on a control hair at the edge of his orange syntho-moustache, deploying a fashion mouth-awning to hide his lip movements. He leaned forward at his desk and murmured into a hole cut in a dummy cable-tube the team used for whisper talk, to avoid the bugs and cameras that Security often planted.

"Ked, is Hepkin Dangle back yet?"

"No idea."

Juncus paused and toyed distractedly with the Wind-Gust icon on his screen. He just *knew* he could do something big with it if they'd only let him. Once the team's Intervenor was up and running, he'd show them just how well he, too, could create events. Maybe they'd let him hit a place in another world with one of his squally showers. He turned back to Ked, and tried again to draw him out. "It's just you said, yesterday, that you were *pleased* you hadn't seen Dangle for a long time."

Ked stared at the screen in front of him, his hands covering the lower part of his face. "I am, Juncus, but I guess, sadly, that he's back here on Thrarrxgor now."

"You sure, Ked?"

Ked glared at Juncus, "Of *course* I'm not sure. Since the Earth trip, he's travelled to a heap of other places. *I* haven't been tracking him."

"I heard a rumour he'll be spending more time here and have some kind of job in the management… "

"Look, Juncus, the more he's out of Thrarrxgor the more I like it. He's a *creep*. But if he's going to be here so be it, so long as he stays out of *my* hair!" Reminded, Ked reached to the back of his neck, and switched on the follicle-wave-generator embedded in his scalp. "Dangle's given us a Main Character, and that's all *I'll* ever want from him. Now just let me get *on*… "

Juncus watched the peaks and furrows surging through

Ked's hair. "Anyway, Ked, if he's not moving around, I suppose it'll give the tech team a chance to do a maintenance on the Transporter beam system." He paused and thought for a moment. "By the way, what about the *Viewer*, Ked? Couldn't they have been able to watch Dangle on *that*?"

The question struck Ked as so stunningly stupid, he broke his silence. "Look, Juncus, they've known well enough from the Transporter data *where* he's been while he's been travelling, and as for the *Viewer*, you have to be *joking*! Have you seen where they *are* on their work schedule with *that*?" His eyes narrowed impatiently. "And has it *occurred* to you, Juncus, that if our *Viewer* system had already been working all sweet and humdingy, we wouldn't have *needed* to send a scout. We'd have been able to see everything we wanted, and choose our characters from *here*, wouldn't we?"

"That'll happen soon, Ked… "

Ked could feel his stress level mounting further. His nose-hairs were starting to un-perm under his nostril airscoops. "Juncus, I *know* it'll happen soon. But not till the tech team's through it's work schedule!"

"Same for the Intervenor, I suppose."

"That's it. Same for the *Intervenor* Juncus. Now, if you'd just… "

"Can't understand why they sent *Dangle* as a scout, Ked. He's hardly the easy, patient type."

"Say, Juncus… "

"Yes, Ked?"

"Juncus… Why don't you keep your profile sort of *minimum* right now. I've a lot on my mind."

"Wouldn't you like to hear about the robot I've been building in my spare time, Ked? I'm going to bring it into work sometime soon."

"*No*, Juncus!"

"Or my collection of artistically stained lavatory-seats? It nearly won an award… "

"*Juncus*!"

"Yeah. Right. Sorry, Ked."

***

Pleasure-Filchers are part-being, part non-being. Even Upper Levellers avoid defining them too closely. Lower Levellers are, for the most part, unaware of their existence. But not *blissfully* unaware. The Filchers make sure of that.

Although their name might imply that they are more or less human in size, individually they are so infinitesimally small as to be completely undetectable to man-made devices. But their effect is felt clearly enough wherever they strike.

If, when you're splashing through the rollers of a good time, you ever manage to stay ahead of the Pleasure-Filchers, each wave's as much of a thrill as the last. But, even for the ablest beings, staying ahead of the P-Fs is a tough run.

Pleasure-Filchers do just what their name suggests – as soon, that is, as they've found a chunk of pleasure to steal. Their motto is a simple question. "Why work fixing fun for yourself when you can spin a ride on *someone else's*?"

While Upper-Level philosophers have had varying amounts of inner joy probing this question, P-Fs don't give a toss as to the answer. But they go *crazy* about the inner joy that's been generated, and will do whatever they can to get their teeth into *large* slabs of it.

Pleasure-Filchers are responsible for the second round of a good experience not being quite up to the first, and for the next rounds sliding further below the mark. Forget economists' theories about diminishing marginal utility and all that stuff. Though we never have time to realise what's happening, it's the P-Fs who end up with close to 99% of the fun in existence.

They go after all forms of enjoyment in the cosmos, starting with the kicks from the exchanging of variably coloured breath, so relished by the Sproornagrs of Preet, to the ectasy of synchronised trunk-picking widely practised by the elephantine Itch-Hunters of Thrarb-Mult. Hard and merciless, Pleasure-Filchers don't even spare the thrills experienced by the accountants on Sub-Lam.2k16t as they check their trial balances. Wherever the fun comes from, P-Fs go for it like it was the last rodeo on the Wusk-Grablik Continuum before its authorities adopted the gravitational constant.

They roam in swarms, each with a band of outriders, whose role is to seek out traces of any nearby joy.

The mechanism works as follows:

One P-F outrider passes an area where a fun experience is being had, and picks up the happiness-waves generated. It infiltrates the being that's having the experience, and chews on the delight.

Other P-Fs catch on to what's happening and move in, tapping off increasing amounts of pleasure as more of them join.

After a while the victim gives up doing whatever it was doing, as the P-F swarm is now slurping up any further joy that its 'host' can get. It's at this point that the Multi-Faceted She-Dronne rolls over and sighs to her nine hundred and and sixty-seven partners, 'that's enough for now, boys,' that the bishop turns away the fifteenth cucumber sandwich, and that the hyper-gargic black hole belches inwardly and retires to spend the remainder of its days as a paperweight on a higher Level of Existence.

The swarm then moves on.

Attempts at studying the behaviour of P-Fs are occasionally made by those academics with funding big enough to try to build equipment capable of doing the job. But, so far, all such work has run into the sand well before the study's begun. This is because, every time the researchers have had a wave of joy on getting a grant to fund their project, the P-Fs have snaffled it straight away. The academics have been left wondering how the hell they ever thought they'd get a kick out of doing the job in the first place, and have set off swiftly for the nearest pub to discuss not doing much at all for a very long time ahead.

Fun-lovers who know about P-Fs clearly do their best to stay well out of their way. This is easier in the higher reaches of the Upper Levels, where there's more to move around in by way of space and other dimensions, and where the population, with the exception of those attending music gigs, tends to be spread a bit thinner over the vastness.

As you travel downwards, however, the chances of meeting P-Fs increase sharply. Even in apparently empty stretches of the cosmos they can be encountered in large numbers, migrating from one region to another in harmony with the ebb and flow of pleasure between universes.

Boontrak came across them in a very big way on the fringes of Level Five. Just before they got to *him*.

It was a strange feeling, his early warning signals to himself. They were part buzzing sensation in the fingernails of the humanoid body he was currently in, and part a series of coded tremors running round the edges of his ears.

Then, switching to a body-form with clearer vision, he saw what looked, at first, like a thin vapoury line some fifty billion parsecs away.

As he watched it he noticed that the line seemed to be moving towards him at an incredible speed. He asked his R58b brain about it.

It told him that the line was moving towards him at an incredible speed. It added that it would be with him shortly.

In an instant, Boontrak realized that the line was in fact the leading edge of just about everything he could see, and that what he'd thought of as a vast empty background piece of the cosmos was enthusiastically coming to join him. As it neared, he began to make out some of the individual dots among the centillions in the swarm. And each of them had its hungry eye focussed on *him*.

***

Carefully, Joe separated his thumb and forefinger.

The pebble spun slowly as it fell. He kept his hand motionless, in a line between his eye and the thimble, as if half hoping that this would still somehow guide the stone to its target.

In the rafters there was silence. Twenty people gazed at the small, rounded piece of granite. The contest and half a barrel of beer rode precariously on it. A mouse quivered nervously. A death-watch beetle looked away, mortified...

Joe had not yet seen the young woman watching from below.

He'd been concentrating on the game when she'd come into the pub.

But soon he would see her.

Light from an alcove lamp played on her face and splashed about in the long strands of her dark hair. Life danced in her eyes. She and it seemed to get on extraordinarily well together.

The corners of her mouth had bobbed up into a smile as she contemplated the outcome of the game.

The pebble closed on the thimble...

... and landed spot-on in the centre.

The inebriate phantoms were impressed. Some boasted they'd have done even better. This was a blatant lie, as they all suffered from a ghastly, ghostly version of delirium tremens.

A living local, who hadn't been playing, swung a glance at the row of thimbles, then turned back to his drinking partner. "It's all very well having them kinduv skills," he muttered, "but there ain't no one that's goin' to save the world that way, *is* there?"

Joe politely declined his team's offer of a place in the next game, swung himself down from a beam and landed in a shambling way on the pub floor.

"Was that your first time?"

He started to answer the question as a sort of

conversational reflex, before he turned round. "Er… yes, as a mat… "

He saw her.

He stopped.

He tried again.

"Er… yes, as a m… "

He stopped again.

He stood there, his mouth half open, for what he took to be a hundred and twelve years. He assumed this amount of time had passed because he felt as if he'd seen the sun rise on each day of them.

It was surprising, he thought, that, after that amount of time, she still only looked about twenty. It also occurred to him she must be a very patient person to wait that long for him to finish his sentence.

Suddenly he realized she was speaking to him again.

"You must have got a bit of dust in your throat while you were up in the roof. Would you like a drink?"

"Y… "

"Pint of the local stuff?"

"Y… "

"Right."

Joe's hand took the beer unsteadily.

"Ch… "

"Cheers."

He felt her smile reaching inside his being, gently nudging a dial from **GIBBERING**, past **UNSURE AND DEFINITELY A BIT SHAKY**, on past **MAYBE BEGINNING TO FEEL SORT OF ALRIGHT**, then past **QUITE A LOT BETTER, REALLY**, and onwards up the scale till it set itself firmly on "**HAPPY WITH THE WORLD ! HOW ABOUT YOU?"**

"Are you a regular here?" he would probably have asked, if he'd been on a different setting.

"No. I'm not from this part of the world – just staying in the village for a while," she might have replied.

And the talk would have gone for a long walk sideways.

But he said,

"You have the most beautiful eyes I have ever seen."

And they looked back at him.

And said nothing...

... and everything.

At the other end of the pub the man with the far-travelled face gathered his musical coat around him and moved towards the door.

They didn't notice him leave.

In the words between the spaces, they finally got round to their names.

Joe found he was saying his rather breathlessly.

"I'm Riska," she said. "Maybe it seems a bit unusual, but I'm happy with it, and my friends say it suits me fairly well."

It didn't surprise them that their hands were touching. They'd been touching for longer than they could remember.

After a while Riska said, "Have you ever done any hang-gliding?"

Joe said he hadn't but that he'd always wanted to.

"There's a course starting tomorrow, Joe, and they've still got a few places. Do you want to come along?"

***

Boontrak's brain told him he should try to kid himself that the fun-waves from his recent astrobatics had completely gone. But it was no good. The pleasure was still surging through him. He tried out the idea of getting worried about the huge swarm that was heading straight for him. But it simply brought him out in whoops of laughter.

A brief telepathic crackle scratched through the skin of space.

"Well, don't say I didn't tell you, old boy. By the way, that really is an *awfully* big bunch of Pleasure-Filchers out there, and they all seem to be taking a great interest in you!"

"Gee! *Thanks*!" Boontrak tele-sarcked.

"My... er... *pleasure*! Hope you manage to hang on to *yours*, eh? Ha ha! Good luck!"

The voice faded for a moment, then struggled back through the jagged static with a perforated afterthought.

"Just one thing you... bear... mind. Before... start... really fast... whatever... do... make sure... meable"

Space zipped itself up.

"Say again?" Boontrak minded into the nothingness.

But there was only silence, a silence which, unlike the relaxed Boontrak, grew tense. It became tenser, then moved beyond tense... till it was past tense... and simply was.

Then, a few moments later, it was no more.

Boontrak realized his R58b brain was picking up something new.

The hum. The grinding hum of the P-F swarm that was close to a micro-breath away.

All in all, Boontrak thought, it would be better not to hang about. Gathering up every volt he had, he threw himself into fast-forward. He burned through ultra-speed and out beyond it, blasting the marks off the scale. Even more than before, hyper-thrill took over his designer senses. His body and accessories cavorted with joy, spreading huge pleasure waves in all directions.

Cavorting with joy at a thrilling time is definitely *okay*. Only a few disapprove of it, amongst them BWDLOBHAGTs (Beings Who Don't Like Other Beings Having A Good Time).

The other main objectors are AOHTGAFPFs (Advisers On How To Get Away From Pleasure-Filchers). Their advice, in a nutshell, is 'Act the undertaker, better still, one who's just lost his wallet.'

It's good advice because, when Pleasure-Filchers are around in hordes, the more pleasure waves you're making, the faster they come after you.

Which is what they did.

And that meant Boontrak had to go still faster.

Leading to more cavorting with even more joy.

etc.

It was the cavorting and the chase that kept Boontrak's mind away from any thoughts about having left his option-switch set on *non-permeable.* He was too busy showing himself how well he could outrun the P-Fs. He hurtled along, happy in the belief that nothing that might be around, that might happen to get in his way... could ever...

... Thwppp!

It was then he had a nasty shock.

The normal procedure for many Upper-Levellers when they bump into things is to look back at the receding cloud of diffused energy that has been the other party, to wave aside enquiries from local law enforcers, and to press on.

Boontrak, being a decent inter-level citizen, would in fact have stopped to help out, have done what he could, and have left his name and contact details.

But behind him there was no cloud of diffused energy.

Instead, there was an intensely intact and very large something.

And Boontrak was feeling...

How was he feeling? he tried to ask himself.

After a while he came up with some sort of answer.

Yup. That was it, he thought.

That was, as far as he could make out, how he was feeling.

Like a cloud of diffused energy.

***

Sprawled across Existential Levels 9 to 1, Shloomger Shoon lounged with (what had best be thought of as) his feet perched on a plushly upholstered multi-time-space continuum and (what had best *not* be thought of as) the head and torso of his body in a great many other places. One of these, not that it has anything to do with the events that follow, happened to be a doormat outside the house of Mrs. Kloris Tring, at Number Five Muir Gardens, Lower Scratchley, Kent.

Here, as at a good many other sites where parts of his body rested, he was completely undetectable.

Being undetectable had clear plusses. No hassle from inquisitive beings, however weaker than Shoon they might be. No embarrassing books about him by scientists. No pressure for him to become the centrepiece of a new religious chat show.

But, on the other grasper, it wasn't endless excellence either. Though, to Level-Dwellers 1-6, Shloomger was invisible and completely permeable, as far as those from 7 and above were concerned, he *wasn't*.

For reasons which Shloomger hadn't bothered to check out, beings which came from the Upper Levels, and which hadn't changed their *own* settings to permeable, sometimes collided with him.

So far, Shloomger's major ranking as a Level-Elevener had meant these other beings had come off worse. Often very unpleasantly for them. But he'd still picked up a few scars from some of the splattings. There had been that encounter with a precocious ball of light a while back, which had left him with a faint mark on (what it would *definitely* be better *not* to think of as) his thigh.

"A while back" for Shloomger was a vague term. In an Earthly sense it could mean a few years or a couple of aeons. One of the reasons he had such a loose idea of time was that he'd spent so much of his life half-in and half-out of it.

Shoon had been around for an extremely long 'while' and, though he still wanted to stick around, the general ease of his life had made it feel tedious.

Shloomger was bored to a degree not fathomable on Earth.

He shifted his head on Mrs.Tring's doormat. He yawned as he watched her cat walk into the immeasurable immensity of his being, mutate into a foot-soldier in the United Army Of The Benign Galaxies, rise through its ranks to Cosmic Chief of Staff in a mere sixty-million eras, seize power from the Weavers of the Threads of Existence, crown itself Argg the Tyrant of the Seven Universes, rule for two thousand and twelve Infinities, suffer banishment in perpetuity by the Golden Knights of Orryk, and then stroll out on the other side of him in search of its Crunchy Chunks.

No, he thought (scratching himself somewhere it would be better not to think about *at all*), things just didn't have the kind of buzz they used to have.

Maybe it was time to pay a call on the gypsy.

CHAPTER 3

In the zone of time, space and other dimensions where he was, Boontrak struggled to pull himself together. It was about as easy as trying to persuade the jailbirds back into the penitentiary after the mass break-out on 7b12 to discuss successful escape techniques. But in the end he got himself down to three clusters of semi-diffused energy.

There was a very large one, a much smaller one, and a fragment which, compared with the others, was more of a turbo-charged flicker. The smaller piece and the flicker, though a short distance apart, found themselves travelling along in the same general direction.

But the biggest was on a slightly different course.

The zones of Sub-Lamina 2k16, where the collision had happened, are stuffed with universes, and it wasn't long before Boontrak's remnants met a couple of them.

Cosmic travellers find, when they get close to them, that universes have a habit of tugging at them and *pressing* their hospitality on them. Seveners have no problem in politely refusing such offers if they wish. As long, that is, as they're not drifting along in three separate, seriously concussed pieces.

The largest clump of energy was pulled into one universe. The other two were drawn into one nearby.

The reason why these two universes were so close to each other was that they had once, in fact, been the same universe. Though they were still nearly identical, they were gently mutating away from each other, rather like the East and West Lothian recipes for chocolate nut sundaes.

When asked why universes reproduce and then slowly change into different versions of their original self, some beings shake their heads, or their alternatives, and mutter that *nothing is simple.*

Nothing, however, is *very complicated*, and for this reason Nature tries to avoid *nothing* by keeping things *simple* or, to put it another way, by simply *keeping* things.

The explanation goes something like this:

If universes disappear, Nature has to go through the equivalent of a range of long and intensely boring procedures (such as rummaging around to find creation certificates, registering the exact moment of annihilation, examining claims for compensation, dealing with requests for reconstruction grants etc.).

On top of this there are other chores, one of which is AOE, or the Adjustment Of Eternity, a time-consuming process.

But, for Nature to do nothing when a universe folds up its galaxies, or gets terminally spaced out, isn't much of an option either, since, as has just been mentioned, *nothing* is very complicated.

Preferring the easy life, Nature plumps for a much softer alternative, which is to make duplicate universes before anything awkward happens. So, if a universe disappears, there's still a marker in the file, which says it *exists*, even if the copy's mutated a bit. In fact sometimes Nature decides to make multiple copies of an original universe, just to be on the safe side.

Beings who like arguing over this explanation usually end up agreeing on at least *one* thing about it. *Nothing* could be simpler.

The reception arrangements provided by universes on Sub-Lamina 2k16 are more or less standardised, and generally helpful. Newcomers pass through a series of 'auto-download' zones which help them to absorb, with no effort, some universal working rules, such as the local light-speed restrictions, and enough thermo-dynamics to get them by.

There are often a few other handy info-fields around as well, though these can sometimes be patchy. Among them are the language fields. Simply brushing up against one of these provides the incomer with all the necessary codes to be able to communicate with anyone/thing else in the District (an administrative division of a universe, normally covering about half a billion galaxies) that they are entering.

The distribution of language fields in universes on Sub-Lamina 2k16, though, is haphazard. This is because the being responsible for installing them is doing it as part of a court-imposed community service order, and no one's been checking the work. Some universes have been missed altogether. Here, tourists have the thrill of actually learning the local languages themselves.

This, in fact, didn't concern Boontrak's fragments since, even in their present knackered state, they were still able to use the special language codes that had been factory embedded in his R58b brain.

The fragments' new courses were taking them to different places, and within each of these, they were heading for the rocks. Not the unpleasant sort that spoil the captain's darts game, but friendlier kinds of stones.

They fell into worlds which, like their universes, had once been the same but were now merely very similar.

On its way the largest chunk of energy was whisked about by a piece of time-turbulence, and arrived in its host-world about twelve years before Joe had his first pint in THE BEND IN THE SKY, which was situated in the world to which the other two fragments were travelling.

In the spot in the host-world where the first and largest piece of energy fell, a world its inhabitants mostly called Thrarrxgor, night fell at more or less the same time as the chunk. But unlike night, which soon picked itself up and moved on, the energy remained stuck where it was.

It stayed inside the stones of a cave in the wild, isolated place where it had landed, and imbued the stones with its power.

The largest lump of Boontrak had come to rest.

And it did just that.

Until, that is, someone discovered the cave and its stones, and found out about their power.

Twelve years afterwards – as measured in the times of both Earth and Thrarrxgor – the smaller pieces of energy reached Earth. They also arrived under cover of darkness, and touched down fairly close to one another in a large city.

The first of them slipped quietly into a gallery that contained many carefully displayed and labelled rocks. It settled into one of these.

The fragment-wisp, which was the other piece, landed some miles away in a house in a street of terraced homes. It slipped into the half-open drawer of a desk, and took refuge in the gem of a dusty antique ring.

And each of these two stones also received its own dose of Boontrak's power.

***

Unaware of just how close it was to extreme horribleness, a mouse wandered unseen through the shadow of the figure standing on the terrace outside the laboratory.

Squid Sculpin, looking as if he was on day-release from a cemetery, wiped the sweat from his forehead and cursed the air-conditioning inside the converted mansion he'd just come out of. Though he'd introduced some extraordinary technology to Thrarrxgor, many other items which he hadn't had time to 'modernise' were seriously sub-standard.

Trying to turn his thoughts towards an unmanipulated piece of nature, he glanced at a large pink-flowering bush near the edge of the terrace. It was a pleasant summer shrub. But the gardener had warned him the plant could turn very nasty in the winter.

From his pocket Squid drew a comb so foul no flea dared land on it, and forced it through his hair. Next he took a small hand mirror from his pocket and watched his reflection corrugate into even intenser horribleness as he stared at it.

Though he was a man almost totally swamped by viciousness and greed, there was one tiny corner of his personality that remained afloat, supported by the buoyancy of a secret self-loathing.

Squid knew he needed the corner, not because he had any feelings of guilt, but because seeing himself as a grim little man made it easier to understand the ever-growing collection of nasty things he did. While he sniggered at the rest of existence, his tiny watching corner included him in it too, and marked him down comfortingly as just plain rotten.

He lit a cigarette, and allowed himself a glance into the distance, towards the hills that formed the boundary between Thrarrxgor city and the world outside.

It was in the mountains beyond those hills that, quite by accident, he'd come across the source of what people believed to be his own genius, a profitable genius for making strange and incredible machines, and for doing much else.

His mind drifted back some twelve years, to a crucial event in his life...

It had been during desperate days, just before the 'Great Reform', while Sculpin had been camping out in the mountains, hiding from 'business rivals'. He was checking out some escape routes he might need for getting to even remoter areas, when suddenly he was strangely drawn by the idea of wandering through a gap between two largish rocks. Behind the rocks was an equally largish cave...

*

Squid had pulled out some food from his rucksack, eaten it, and settled down for a rest.

Somewhere between sleeping and waking he had found himself in what seemed to be a conversation with the walls of the cave. It had kicked off more or less as follows:

Cave walls: "Hello. Glad you've come in. I can't seem to communicate well with anyone outside here. You know, I'd really like to get these 'spread-about' stones more joined up. Get back to my old self, if you see what I mean. I suppose you wouldn't by any chance be able to get your hands on a set of pneumatic drills, a mechanical digger, one very large shaping-mould, a fair amount of adhesive, and a reasonably-sized workforce?"

Sculpin: "What's in it?"

Cave walls: "Well, nothing, really. You see, the shaping mould would have to be *empty* first. The idea is that it would hold the adhesive and the newly-mined stones once they'd been poured into it. So that I could sort of re-unify myself just a bit."

Sculpin: "I meant what's in it for me?"

Cave walls (after pausing for a while): "Ah, I see what you mean. You'd like a small arrangement fee for organising it."

Sculpin: "No."

Cave walls: "Sorry, don't quite follow... "

Sculpin: "I want a *very large* arrangement fee."

Cave walls: "Ah... yes... I see... Well, unfortunately, the fact is that... at the moment... I'm not really in a position to... nothing to hand exactly... you understand... no local currency... or anything like that... "

Sculpin: "Then the very large shaping mould and other items will remain a distant dream."

At his use of the word *dream*, Sculpin assumed this was what he was in, and decided he should try and wake up.

But the walls pressed on...

Cave walls: "What I *could* do, perhaps, would be to offer you a kind of audio-visual show in lieu of payment. For example... "

A zone of space inside the cave turned itself into a three-dimensional travelogue of Sculpin's recent journey, complete with moving, miniaturized images of him at different points along the way.

Squid shifted uneasily. It was clearly a con, probably leading on to an assassination attempt. A film, with a smoke-and-mirrors job, set up by a business rival who'd followed him.

He pulled a pistol from his rucksack and fired through the audio-visual display. The bullet narrowly missed Squid's image, thwapped into the wall beyond, split some stones from it, and ricocheted into the depths of the cave.

"Ah!... " the walls said in a surprised and rather hurt kind of way "... What happened there?"

Then, after a moment, they added: "... Well, I suppose it explains the landslide. Sort of self-inflicted, you might say, eh?"

Squid looked back at the display, and found himself watching a replay of a hairy incident during the trip, when he'd come close to being wiped out by a shower of boulders from the rockface above.

"And, from a more specific viewpoint... " said the walls...

Squid knew this was no camera-work. The scene that now played in front of him was a re-run of the events seen through his own eyes. The ground coming up to hit him as he dived out of the way, the dust surging into his face...

*

"Yeah," Squid said slowly, "I'll kinduv think about it. But I'll need some *samples* if I'm to get the right sort of adhesive for the stones, you see."

He gathered up some of the pieces he'd shot from the wall.

"I don't really like to see them go," the walls commented. "It'll be like...sort of...getting even more spaced out than I am already. But I suppose it'll be in a good cause. The walls fell silent for a moment in a cavernous kind of way, then resumed thoughtfully, "By the way, those pieces should be able to help you a bit."

"What do you mean?"

"To find the right adhesive. They can help you do a lot of other things too. Even very small parts of an R58b brain are incredibly powerful, you know. Anyway, you'll find they'll sort of explain what they can do."

"How? What do you mean?"

"Oh, they'll provide some illustrations and instruction details and all that. The pieces are pretty well clued up. I hope you'll find them useful in planning my re-integration and my escape from here… "

Sculpin looked at the stones in his hand, and thought for a moment.

"I may be back for more."

"I can't see why you'd *need* any more but, if it helps, I suppose you could come back for a few extra ones. Anyway, be careful."

"What?… Why?"

"They're extremely powerful. They could be very dangerous if they got into the wrong hands."

"Er… Right. Yes. I see. I'll be off, then."

"Goodbye."

"Er, yes. See you."

A while later, Sculpin had returned to Thrarrxgor's controlling city, which had taken the planet's name as its own. He'd found himself a safe, anonymous bolt-hole and had almost thrown the stones away, convinced he'd had some kind of stress-related, psychotic experience in the cave. But, just to make sure, he'd decided to do a bit of experimenting.

And now, as far as he was concerned, the rest was history. But a very secret, personal history.

*

Sculpin glanced back towards the laboratory. He *had* been back for more stones from the cave, spieling stories about needing more time and about having to get some practical experience at mining the stones. The pieces he'd brought with him were a miniscule fraction of the rocks that lined the cave walls, but they'd been more than enough to get his work to where it was now.

The lone figure turned and walked back into the building. The unfortunate mouse, which, for want of anywhere else particular to go, had scurried ahead of him, was already inside. It squeezed itself under a locked door, climbed onto a laboratory bench, stepped onto one of Squid's experiments...

... and fell off the edge of the universe.

CHAPTER 4

The forefinger and thumb closed on opposite sides of the small wheel and began to turn it slowly, precisely. After a moment they ceased the rotation and opened gradually, with the deliberation of petals just touched by sunlight.

Then they displaced themselves carefully a few inches to the right, moved downwards, and closed on the handle of a tiny screwdriver lying on the surface of the table.

On the floor, in a corner of the room near the door, a hairy ensemble of dog and rug heaved and twitched a sleepy journey through the current hour.

The screwdriver rose, reached inside the apparatus, adjusted here, twiddled there, tapped very gently somewhere else, then adjusted the twiddle, twiddled the adjustment, and returned to the table.

A short distance from it, like objects randomly grouped for a memory game at a children's party, various bits and pieces lay close to the mouth of an open leather pouch.

A sharp eye would have noticed that among them was a ring with a large setting-cup from which the stone had been removed.

The thumb and forefinger caressed the wheel again, and were met shortly afterwards by the hairs of a descending white beard.

The head carrying the beard lowered itself a little further and moved forward, its bespectacled eyes fixing on something just in front of it. It mumbled quietly to itself a couple of times, then whispered a gentle "Aha!"

After that it smiled, said softly, “I think we’ve done it, Spanger”, and moved carefully away from the apparatus to contemplate the result.

***

The sunlight edged round Ked’s bedroom curtains. The curtains weren’t essential. The apartment’s windows were of voco-glass, responding to speech commands as to the strength and colour of the rays they should let in. They were, in fact, up-market versions which could also create images, on demand, of things the user wanted to see happening outside.

But Ked had disabled the system with nose-gum. He preferred natural light. And he liked the softness of the textiles in the curtains. They seemed to add a touch of something-or-other to his surroundings. He’d asked himself once what it was, and whether it might have to do with ‘warmth’. He wasn’t sure. He’d not come across that word very much, beyond instructions on thermostats.

Consciousness was up there somewhere. Ked drifted beneath it, like a diver in decompression. Fathoms above, the control board beside his bed warbled. A button on the panel began to glow in a pulsing, comforting, way.

His mind rose gently towards it...

He broke the surface, and basked for a moment.

Once awake, Ked liked to linger before starting things, to take time to say hello to himself, to muse on life generally and to make a slightly paranoid mental count of his toes and other body parts.

He finished his inventory and moved to the next stage of his early-morning preparations. Since he’d started using this new item of bedroom hardware, he’d come to look on the procedure as a piece of proverbial.

He made sure he was lying inside the span of the body-length arch that hung above him. Then he reached out a finger and touched the pulsing button marked ‘Glide’. Ked preferred buttons to voice controls. One or two people he knew had talked in their sleep, with bizarre results.

A pre-programmed pause gave him time to bring his hand back under the arch. The module checked that he was ready. Then, in one surge of power, it launched him sweat-free into his day. A brief squishy sensation, and there he was, shaved, quantitatively eased, showered, and sitting in front of breakfast.

Ked's morning meal was a simple machine-delivered bowl of Goodtime-Re-Run. Today's offering was a muesli, with synthetic versions of aromas that had been machine-recorded at the only breakfast he'd ever shared with a golden-haired woman called Spatula Sprag. Sensing a general souring in the second part of the rendezvous, the mixer had thrown out the last ten minutes of data. The result was a rather uncertain taste, with hints of industrially-polluted air and body oil. But it somehow reminded Ked of a vague feeling of optimism he'd once had.

He was half-way through breakfast when the hologram gnome appeared in front of him. He swore at it. He was proud of his cursor-curser. His hologphone was one of the few devices he trusted to voice-control. He'd programmed it to name the caller when he swore once.

Despite his use of expletives for commands, he liked the gnome. Most people simply had a stock hologram, but this one was the work of a laser craftsman, and Ked valued its features, its *user* features rather than its *visual* ones.

It named Hepkin Dangle.

Ked nearly swore again, so that it would say he was out. But he stopped himself in time. When Hepkin called him at home it could be a sign of some imminent crisis and, if there *was* one, it made sense to know about it.

He took the call by telling the gnome exactly what it could do with it. The hologphone thanked him politely and put Hepkin through. Ked watched the gnome mute into Hepkin's head.

"Hey! Success! At *last*!" sarked the 'gram, "I've been

trying to find you for the last *hour*! Why aren't you at K*rargxtko? Have you given up work?" The face grew even more unpleasant, "I don't think *Sculpin*'d be at *all* pleased to hear *that*."

Ked stared back angrily at the grim head floating in front of him.

"If you'd bothered to enquire, Dangle, you'd know I got six extra hours sleep-recovery after working *two nights* solid to finish the script!" He picked up a spoon and flung it through the image. "And that's only to stop me folding totally, in case they need changes after Sculpin's seen it!"

He sensed Hepkin was set to loose off more vocal shrapnel, and pre-empted, "Anyway, when are *you* ever around Dangle? Haven't seen you at K*rargxtko since I can remember! Been out univ-jumping on expenses again, eh? Or picking more fights the way you like to? Or both, maybe?... Or what else?... "

The spectre seemed ready to explode, "Look, Coot, do you wanna make something of it?" A warning holog-finger appeared to the left of the face and aimed itself threateningly at Ked. "And keep that sparkle-toothed gaper you call a mouth *tightly locked*! Have you forgotten the secrecy rating of those trips?"

He warmed to the theme of his own importance. "*Sure*, I travelled a good deal. They sent *me* cos I took *care* of myself *and* of K*rargxtko's interests. If you want to launch a fluffy duck that some other world's gonna send back *inside-out*, then go ahead and *arrange* it, Coot. An' you'll see how K*rargxt and Sculpin will love you for *that*!"

The head erupted with holog-sweat. "Maybe you'd like me to *call* Sculpin about it, eh? I'm in touch with his office daily now. You want me to tell him *you're* volunteering instead?"

Ked fingered a control on his wristband and morphed Dangle's face to a toad's. "Look, if that scout-work you did's not out-of-date, Hepkin, it soon *will* be. The *Viewer*'ll replace you once its running properly." He saw the toad gulp angrily, as if it was about to leap straight at him. "... Okay! *Okay*, Hepkin. If you knew just how happy I am to see you right now... So, tell me, *why* exactly are you calling?"

The toad's face calmed slightly. "It's about the life-script you've done on Outwood. Have you been playing around with it?"

" '*Playing around*' with it? What do you mean, '*playing around*', you boss-eyed skrantakiyster? I *wrote* it!"

"That's not what I meant, you *dinch-prutt*! Quit the slide-spieling and *give*! Did you, or did you *not* play with the script after you finished work on it?"

Ked fought back an urge to use hand-signals. "Dangle, it'd help if you'd say what you mean. I've not the *saddest hint* what you're on about! I came straight back here to my apartment right after I'd closed the script and sent it to Sculpin's team!"

The toad's eyes fixed furiously on Ked. "I'm not so much concerned *where* you've been since you closed your secure terminal in K*rargxtko. I just want to know if you did anything else on that terminal *after* you fired off the script and *before* you closed it."

"I don't know what business it is of yours, Dangle, but I did nothing else."

"You're *sure*?"

"As the complete failure of your wrinkle-remover, Dangle! Now, *maybe* you can tell me why you've been making with these questions. What's *happening*?"

The toad's mouth twitched in hesitation, then opened reluctantly. "Security scare. Bernie told me to check the whole team – *informally* – to see if there's any basis to it. You're the last."

"And what does Bernie think might have happened?"

Well... he reckons there probably *hasn't* been a breach. That's why he hasn't contacted K*rargxtko Security. The last thing he wants is an interrogation from *them*."

"Dangle, I still haven't a clue what you're on about. Be *specific*. What *happened*? Or, at least, what did Bernie think *might* have happened?"

"There was a very slight power loss on the network around the time you wired the script."

"Power loss? *And*? Is that so unusual?"

"No, it happens from time to time, but the system-checker showed this one had a pattern."

Searching for clarity, Ked re-morphed to a straight view of Hepkin's face, and winced as it re-emerged. "What do you mean? What *sort* of *pattern*?"

"Apparently it had a kind of tech 'footprint' to it, like some of the recent power losses there have been on other parts of the network. The system checker's building a profile of all similar cases where it's happened."

"So what's so wildly special about all *that*, Hepkin?"

"Well, it's hard to believe, but it could just mean someone's *cracked* into the entire system."

Ked stared incredulously at the Dangle horror-gram. "*Gritts*! You have to be *joking*, man! A *data* leak?... ". He paused for a moment and considered how it could affect his interests. "... A data and a *script* leak? Does Sculpin know? I don't care to think how he'd react!"

"He may suspect there's been some kind of intrusion. He's the top-whizz on all that kind of stuff. But, as you know, he keeps things to himself, and he's said nothing about it to us. And Bernie hasn't spoken with him about it. Like I told you, Bernie doesn't think there's enough yet to show it's happened. But any more events like it, and the auto-checker will bang off a high-level alert... ". Hepkin's face became even grimmer. "... And, if he doesn't know about it already, Sculpin's likely to be *extremely* upset!" Dangle's expression self-importanced itself away from the conversation. "In any case, Kedrin Coot, I'm far too busy to waste time with *you*!"

There was a designer-engineered click, and he hung up.

The zone of space in front of Ked cleared itself.

He pushed away his bowl of cereal. Even allowing for the stress from his talk with Dangle, he was feeling strange. It had often seemed to him these days that he felt odd. He wondered vaguely if it could have anything to do with that new piece of bedroom hardware he was using.

***

The tanned, weathered face scanned the crystal ball. Suddenly its eyes gleamed with inner vision.

"Well, I'll be *bugg*... !"

"Can you leave *your* horoscope out of it, Eelag? It's *my* future you're supposed to be telling."

"Ah!... Yes! Sorry, Shloomger. It's just I've remembered where I left something."

"What?"

"My analogiser."

"Don't like the sound of that at all, Eelag! Do you have some sort of medical condition?"

The gypsy turned his attention away from the ball, gazed across the beach, and watched a giant two-way roller bring a surfer landwards, then twist-turn and take her round for another run. His hand reached up and toyed with the hairs of his right sideburn.

He wasn't a real gypsy. They called him that because he'd travelled more than most. In view of the huge number of trips made by other Level-Eleveners, including Shloomger, it meant he'd seriously moved around.

Eelag focussed back on the subject. "No Shloomger. It's just something I've been testing out recently. I'll tell you about it later if you want."

He paused, and gave the laid-back figure a long, searching look. "But, first, tell me more about this boredom thing."

During the times when Eelag was back from his travels, a good many Eleveners, especially frustrated or perplexed ones, liked to drop in on him for a spot of personal advice and prediction. However, since – under most conditions – Eleveners were immortal, there were some who laughed at these consultations when they heard about them, and who made disparaging comments about the size and adequacy of Eelag's ball.

As his Elevener visitors turned up in a wide variety of forms, it wasn't always easy to distinguish them from run-of-the-mill items washed into his garden from the shore or blown in by the wind. Two fluffy and rather lethargic beings that had drifted round recently for a bit of counselling had had to spend several days doubling up as handy insulation round Eelag's hot water tank before being identified and consoled.

Those who came back on follow-up visits, like Shloomger Shoon, tended to turn up in broadly humanoid form, since – as well as making them more recognisable – it meant they could fit more easily into Eelag's outdoor furniture.

Shoon glanced idly at the old smoke-stained music-coat draped over a nearby chair. "Look, the thing is, Eelag, *you* may still get a kick out of this travel thing, but to *me* it's as gripping as a lecture on u-bend attachments."

"Why, Shloomger? I remember how, when we used to bump into each other at the Trans-Level Currency Exchange Counter, you were always leaping about at the idea of going off somewhere new."

"Maybe that's it. Nowhere much *new* left to head for." Shloomger threw a mega-yawn, anaesthetising a couple of seagulls straight out of the sky. Even Eelag struggled to stay conscious. He shook himself and pressed on, "Look, Shoon, maybe it's got something to do with the *kind* of travelling you've been doing?"

"How so?"

The gypsy ran his hand through his hair thoughtfully. "Well, from what you've told me, it's been *easy* stuff. Not much scaling down to Lower Levels. No risk-taking. That's a very superficial kind of tourism, Shloomger."

"Don't follow you."

"If you'd done just *that*, you might see what I mean. *Real* travel's about being a part of the action, mixing with the inhabitants, living the kind of life *they* live, taking *chances*, making yourself... well... *vulnerable*."

Shloomger felt uneasy. It wasn't the sort of advice he'd come for. Maybe he'd better check around, find something more suitable.

"Look, Eelag, if I go *anywhere*, then right-side-up's the way I want to come back. I've got a vast collection of stings and bumps from just *relaxing* in places. That's all the adventure *I* need!"

"Okay Shloomger, it's your choice. I can't live your life for you."

"Well, isn't there anything *else* you can suggest? What about that analogiser-thingummy you were talking about? Is it one of those suppositories of all wisdom I've heard of? Sounds like a drastic approach to the problem, but maybe at least I should try it."

Eelag drew a long breath and reflected on just how sub-serious some of his consultees had become in recent aeons. "It's *nothing* like *that*, Shloomger. If you're *really* interested, I can tell you about it. But you'll need to *concentrate* if you want to get an idea of how it might help you see things more clearly."

***

Capias K*rargxt stared at the stars. Their light passed through the transparent dome of his orbiting shooting-lodge and surrendered to the eyes of the man who had spread terror across the world that spun silently beneath him.

Those on that world who'd have dared guess at his mental state might have thought his ambitions were fully satisfied. But, if they'd wagered their life on it, they'd have been terminally wrong. Beyond the grip he already had on the planet, ideas of vastly greater power beckoned to the menagerie that was his mind.

Behind the eyes, prowling the labyrinths of a multi-schizoid brain, seventy-three 'personalities', mostly non-human, savaged each other in the struggle for control of his head, and soon – they hoped – of all else in existence.

Most people would have felt a sense of wonder at the blaze of stars that stretched above and around. Not K*rargxt. To him the shining dots, and all things between and beyond, were already his personal property, to do with as he wished. It was simply a matter of making sure they knew. And, judging from what Sculpin had promised him recently, it would only be a short time before they *did*.

He stabbed a button on a console. A flap opened in his desktop. A clawed, unbodied mech-limb reached outwards, clutching a transparent sphere, inside which was a small plump mammal. K*rargxt looked at the creature appreciatively. He paused for a moment.

"No, I'll eat it later."

The mech-limb withdrew the snack.

The president's current mind-ruler caused his body to spin its chair and turn its eyes on Sculpin. Though K*rargxt had already given the man the title of Chief Engineer, he'd decided a short time ago to boost his loyalty by calling him his "Deputy". He gazed in disbelief at the fashion balloonlets tethered to Sculpin's earlobes. It had been K*rargxt's own idea to replace real freedom on Thrarrxgor with a cosmetic substitute that he'd sloganed 'Fashion Freedom'. But *this* get-up was close to insurrection!

He felt one of his *turns* coming on. A rival 'personality' attacked the one currently piloting his brain. K*rargxt's body stiffened further against the artificial gravity of the lodge. It rose, as though to strike out. At last the challenger gave up and slunk to its brainlobe-lair. It would be back.

K*rargxt resumed his position and fixed his attention on a transparent box fixed to the top of his desk.

"So this is *it*?"

The Chief Engineer straight-eyed the psychopath.

Sculpin was one of the few surviving people who knew K*rargxt's background, and who'd survived the fact he knew.

As a relief from the current eyeballing, he suddenly found himself reviewing the tyrant's history in super-fast flashback.

It was the early part of K*rargxt's life that fascinated him most, the 'sociological experiment' run by his mad stepfather. Being passed, cage by cage, to a collection of mentally-disturbed animals, as part of a study on trans-species childcare, had already been enough to unhinge him. But being put into a major follow-up test, that took in the big cats' enclosure and a seriously dysfunctional reptile-house, had blown the doors off sanity completely.

One thing that had helped K*rargxt along his path to power had been his observations of visits made to the zoo by a broom-salesman, from whom he'd picked up the art of being cunningly charming when it suited. It was a skill which in earlier days, in-between killing opponents, he'd used a lot, but which he rarely needed now.

The maniac's eyes were narrowing impatiently. K*rargxt banged the box with his fist, making it glow eerily.

"Yes, Sir," said Sculpin.

"So I'll see it all in *there*?"

"The '*human entertainment*' action shows? Yes, Sir. But you can see it all in a giant holog-cube too, if you prefer… "

"*And* the annihilations?"

"You mean the Cosmic Reforms, Sir?"

"Don't namby, Sculpin, *I know* what I mean!"

"Yes, Sir. Those too, once the next Intervenor development phase is through."

"And when's 'Once' ?"

"*Soon*, Mr. K*rargxt."

There was a silence. The Chief Engineer waited nervously.

The supremo suddenly resumed. "And the '*human entertainment*'? That starts soon?"

Sculpin had long since realised that K*rargxt enjoyed watching human agony as much as planning the extinction of universes. He didn't ask why. He'd long since known the best thing was to play along with his boss's tastes and whims, whatever they were. There were some urgent organisational details to be finalised. He took the discussion forward quickly. "Yes, Sir. But, before it does, we'll need a temporary planetary-destruction-exemption order from you."

"*Exemption?*"

"For planet K*rargxt 3b22c4R."

"What's *that* ?"

Sculpin toyed with one of his balloonlets and checked his eyelid data-screen. "A world known to some of its inhabitants as 'Earth', Sir."

"Not for much longer, eh?"

"No Sir. It's a temporary exemption. Once we've got what we want from the planet and its population, we'll vaporize it."

***

Shloomger swivelled the chair that contained the bronzed human body he'd selected for his visit to the beach.

It was, he thought, a fine place to laze around. Warm sun, beautiful skies, user-friendly waves. You could stay here a long time. But then he already *had*. On *long* holidays. So long they'd almost joined up. A million years here, an intervening break of a mere hundred millenia somewhere else, then back for another million or so.

He'd often thought it might be an interesting pastime to watch the fish evolve during the time he'd spent here. But, as far as he could tell, they were all immortal too, and – though he hadn't looked particularly closely – he'd never noticed any changes. Even the unfittest seemed to survive. Looking at the ocean in front of him, he imagined it must be crammed with vast numbers of biologically-challenged creatures.

There was a lot he didn't understand about the natural order of things on this part of Eleven. When it came to the workings of the food chain, he was totally mystified. After all, there were plenty of fish served at Luigi's Ocean Diner, and clearly *they* weren't immortal. He'd eaten enough of them himself. Someone had once told him the food was all brought in fresh from the lower Levels. He supposed all the predatory species here had some similar kind of arrangement.

Eelag emerged from his bungalow carrying a bundle of strange items, two of which were fixed on tall tripods and looked rather like a film-maker's spotlights. The rest of the stuff seemed to be some kind of control system.

He set up the tripods several yards apart, on either side of Shloomger, and put the control module on the table.

"Here it is," he said proudly.

"Here's what?"

"The Analogiser."

Shloomger wasn't impressed.

"Doesn't look particularly special to me. What's it supposed to do?"

Eelag squinted in the general direction of Shloomger and adjusted the positioning of the tripods slightly. "This device", he said confidently, "presents problems in a new and different way."

"So what's the use of *that*? I mean, you've still got the problem you started off with, haven't you?"

"Well... yes, but it can give you a new insight into solving it. That's the joy of the analogiser, you see. You get another version of the problem, a kind of *analogy*, and if you can see a general sort of solution to the analogy, you may be able to transfer that solution to your original problem."

Shloomger wiped away some sea spray that had landed on his forehead.

"What do you mean – '*may*'? Supposing it just *adds* to the difficulty I had in the *first* place? Remember that time I got stuck in Gina's jacuzzi and was too tired to change my body shape? Well, with that contraption of yours, I might find myself in the same sort of fix, and up to my neck in something a lot *worse*, such as... "

"Unlikely!" said Eelag. "It'd probably present you with *another* kind of problem. Sort of move you sideways, so to speak."

"Well, if I were lying *sideways*, I'd be head-under in it, and *then*... "

"No, Shoon. What I mean is it presents a new example of your kind of difficulty. *That* way you might see a clearer solution... "

"... *How* much clearer? I've seen some 'clear' solutions in my time that I wouldn't want to pour on the ground, let alone use for anything else!"

"*You'll* see," Eelag said encouragingly, feeling the need to move the imagery along. "You'll really find it quite helpful. I mean, let's suppose it presented you as a wreck... "

"Thanks a *gigabillion*!"

"No, I mean a *ship* wreck, like when you were jammed in that jacuzzi. For example, *one* way you can get a ship off the bottom is by putting bags round it and pumping air into them. Maybe *that*'d have worked."

"Instead of the eight-day starvation diet, you mean?"

"Spot on!"

Shloomger began to sense some value in the idea.

Eelag tinkered around with the control unit. "Come on, I'll do a demo. Let's suppose you've got some sort of difficulty."

"I've already told you I *have*. I'm giga-gargantually *bored* with this eternity thing."

"Alright. We'll talk about that later. But just for the demo, let's take another problem. A hypothetical one. Let's suppose you've got a massive debt that's come up for payment, and you haven't got the cash to meet it."

Shloomger began to pay careful attention. The sun still glinted off the sea. The reassuring mother's-heartbeat-boom of the surf was still there in the background.

But somewhere, deep in his psyche, a memory stirred, one that had slept undisturbed for mega-aeons, anaesthetised by his boredom.

The memory stretched, then shook itself, and out of it fell a creepy, unspeakable fear. It climbed out of its niche at the back of his mind and abseiled round to the front.

“Ah... yes... I see,” Shloomger said as casually as he could. “A massive debt, eh? No cash to meet it, you say? Well, maybe I could spare a little time to look at that. All highly hypothecatory... I mean *hypothetical*, of course.”

***

Sculpin looked at his boss who, since they’d last spoken, had lapsed into a long silence. The tyrant’s eyes were fixed in a grim stillness, like two billiard balls frozen into an English village pond after a disputed winter pub-match.

K*rargxt suddenly snapped back to his previous self, and grimaced at the Chief Engineer. “We were speaking, amongst other things, about the *entertainment*.”

“Yes, Sir, the *action shows*. And would you like to talk about the two focussed destruction tests as well?”

A snarl did a jig around the corners of K*rargxt’s mouth, “*Not now* Sculpin. We spoke about them *days back*! I’m asking you about the *entertainment*!”

Sculpin spotted a nervous twitch building half-way up K*rargxt’s forehead. K*rargxt’s twitches didn’t bode well.

“Right, Sir. The *first* human action shows are extremely short. They’re a *preliminary* test.” He twiddled an ear-balloonlet with false modesty. “In fact I wrote the very first one myself. That’ll take place around the same time as the two focussed destruction tests.”

“And the *second* show?”

“That’s the next development stage Sir. It’s the *Outwood* show. If you recall, I told you about it at a previous meeting. It’ll be a bit longer, but still quite short. And *very* nasty.”

“Who wrote *that* one?”

“Man called Kedrin Coot. He wrote it under my instructions. But he doesn’t know about the first shows. I thought, if he did, he’d get distracted from his work... ”

“Cut the detail, Sculpin. When does all this *start*?”

“As I said, *soon* Sir.”

"You haven't forgotten the more important purpose of this 'entertainment'? "

"How *could* I, Sir? It was *I* who proposed the plan. As I said, the human action shows are preliminary tests, mere rehearsals of our techniques for mind-manipulating Earth's population and enslaving it, ready for its transportation as forced labour to wherever we wish". Sculpin saw an expression of reptilian approval pass across his boss's face. "But, as a matter of fact, I think you'll find the focussed destruction tests – flood and fire – quite entertaining too, though of course they won't have the kind of heavy-handed bang of our cosmic annihilations."

K*rargxt stared icily in front of him. Then, distracted by some impulse, he jabbed another button on his desk and interrogated an inter-com to find out if '*they*' were there.

A sugary voice said 'they' *were*, and that they would like to come and see him if he could grant them a few seconds of his precious time.

The visit was short. The group of K*rargxtnauts sang the company song. They enthused over the logo on their spacecraft, a circle of inward-pointing arrows with a dot at its centre. They thanked K*rargxt for the bonus they would receive on their return, told him how proud they'd be to tell their grandchildren one day that they'd met him, and left to start their mission.

K*rargxt lapsed into yet another of his long silences.

There was a slight shudder as the K*rargxtnauts' vessel undocked from the shooting lodge and moved off further into space.

Sculpin tried to take up the conversation. "As I mentioned earlier, Sir, in order to proceed with the *entertainment*, we need to have a temporary destruction-exemption order from you... "

The Head of K*rargxtko abruptly struck another button. A giant monitor screen slid silently into view. On it was a crisp image of the K*rargxtnauts' space vessel. A triggered joystick swung up from the desk. On the screen, a virtual rifle-sight imposed itself over the image.

"*Keeeoorargh*!"

His screech over, K*rargxt glanced away from the screen and through the dome into space. The glow from the direct hit faded to darkness. An underling came in, fixed another trophy-plaque to the wall, and left. The tyrant settled back in his chair.

Sculpin reached into his file and handed him a piece of paper. "That temporary exemption for K*rargxt3b22c4r, Sir... "

K*rargxt scrawled his signature and handed it back. "About those action shows... "

"Sir?"

"How much does the production team know about our plans?"

"Nothing. Only what they need to run the shows."

"And that man you've selected for the *longer* show."

"The *slightly* longer show, Sir? That's *Outwood*, Sir... "

"When do you start brain-controlling *him*?"

"Very soon, Mr. K*rargxt."

The reptilian pilot driving the tyrant's mind moulded K*rargxt's expression closely to its own. His deputy cringed as the face focussed on him.

"Sculpin."

"Yes, Sir?"

" If Outwood gives you any trouble, the *slightest* difficulty, *destroy* him."

"Yes, Mr. K*rargxt."

"And then, forget the enslavement programme. We'll find enough slaves elsewhere. Simply destroy that planet."

"Yes, Sir."

CHAPTER 5

The birds soared above the beach, as they had done before. The heavy-husked trans-dimensionally-dispersing coconuts swung gently on the palm-trees, minus one or two that had just vanished with the whistle-pop sound so loved by the locals that, with clever use of repeats, it makes up the first sixteen bars of their regional anthem. The colour-and-scent-changing tone-weed went on playing variations up and down its scales of hues and smells, as it had earlier. But Shloomger Shoon's thoughts, now, were elsewhere.

A large debt. More than a large debt. A debt so huge that other debts were indebted to it. For it was a debt that had blazed a trail through a wilderness of balanced budgets that lenders and borrowers could but follow on padded and threadbare knee.

It was a debt that knew how to grow. It had been bred to do that. By a cunning and extraordinarily nasty creature.

Many business-beings try to choose names for themselves that not only hit the customer's eye easily but grab hold of it before it gets further down the trade-directory. (Some lexi-biologists claim certain *species* also do this by attracting names that conservationists will latch onto early, and have proposed DNA research on the Aardvark and Abalone in this respect).

But this business-being had positioned itself carefully on the Trans-Level Lenders' List by choosing a name beginning with a symbol that showed up just below the last letters of any of the billions of alphabets used by advertisers and subscribers across the cosmos.

The other advertisers who, for one reason or another, were situated in this rarely visited zone at the bottom of the directory, were honest and well-intentioned. Not so the creature that Shloomger would later come to call 'Zunddertokk'. Here, spider-like, this lender placed himself in waiting for the 'Clever-Dicks', the ones who thought no one else would ever contact him, and that he'd be desperate to do business on any terms.

And Shoon had gone straight for the web. The amount Shloomger had borrowed from Zunddertokk had been small, just enough to fund him into an 'unlosable' poker game with a bunch of drifters from the Eleven-Twelve Borderzones. Shoon had assumed it was the trivial nature of the sum, together with his negotiating skill, that had caused him to be offered an interest rate so low it bordered on complete indifference.

He'd looked at the number on the paper Zunddertokk had handed him. It had started with a nought, followed, in a way Shloomger found mathematically challenging, by a decimal point. But, as he began to recall his maths, things had quickly brightened when he realized that, between this dot and the only positive number to its right, he'd counted more zeros than he'd seen surging into the Level Five Super-Long-Drink Bar at the start of a 30-aeon bank holiday.

So, when Shloomger had heard Zunddertokk muttering something about a '*trans-level contract*', he'd let the term drift right past him. It was probably, he'd thought, just a way of making things easy for cosmic itinerants who'd run a bit short of ready cash far from home.

Inter-laminate lawyers would have clucked their tongues, or whatevers, when told that Shloomger hadn't read the small print. But in fact, since the contract stretched out of the window of Zunddertokk's office to infinity, most of the relevant clauses were already a very long way out of sight.

So Shoon, Eleventh-Leveller that he was, had missed the bit about the time on Level *One* being the reference-time used for clocking up his annual interest.

This was a pity. For, in the short, Eleventh-Level, time it took Shloomger to loop out his signature on the document, Zunddertokk had acquired not only the right to everything Shoon currently possessed but, in the event of Shloomger ever happening to own all the sub-particles in Levels One to Eleven, the right to send the bailiffs round for those too.

The fact that Shloomger was wiped out in the next day's poker-game shrank to a detail when, two hours after that, he received the demand for his first billion-billion years' interest, compounded by a surcharge of a decillion percent per second for his delay in repaying the capital.

Making money, of course, involves *collecting* it, and it might seem surprising that Zunddertokk hadn't rushed round to grab his gains straight away. However, because he took care to stay informed of his debtors' whereabouts, and since Shloomger's life expectancy was open-ended, Zunddertokk simply got on with the business of taking every other smart punter he could find on a long trip to the cosmic launderette.

Zunddertokk would be *back*. Something in Shoon's mind told him he would be. The only question was: *When*?

Shloomger kicked at the sand with his boot and tried to remember exactly when he'd signed the contract. He couldn't be sure. A couple of trillion years ago? Maybe more? Thinking about it was making him feel increasingly queasy.

He rummaged around in his memory. It wasn't giving him dates, but he recalled having once asked some people in the Elders and Betters' Arms whether they knew anyone else who'd come across Zunddertokk.

"Why not ask *him*?" someone had said, pointing to a picture on the wall next to the lavatory door. The shrunken humanoid in the appliqué 'miniature' seemed to have suffered some apalling accident, and Shloomger saw it wasn't just his wristwatch that was floppy. The rest of him looked like a packet of dried figs that had been under the steam hammer seconds before framing.

"Wot' are *you* staring at?" the portrait squeaked, moving its tiny surreal-like foot just enough to show the lender's signature underneath it.

Shloomger apologized, and in an attempt at polite conversation with the cameo'd bloke, he learned that Zunddertokk, whilst taking his time over collecting, *always* came, and that hard luck stories upset him terribly. This was apparently because he had some kind of allergy to them, which made him extraordinarily violent.

Another way of looking at it, the picture had suggested, was that it was the *tellers* of the hard-luck stories that were allergic to them, and that Zunddertokk was simply delivering the symptoms.

Bidding the picture a fatuous good evening, Shoon had glanced at an inscription that looked as if it had been burned into the bottom of the frame by a hot claw.

"*Clever Dick*", it had read.

Shloomger watched Eelag tinker gently with the analogiser.

If, he thought to himself, *if* there was just the faintest chance it could help him out on the matter of a debt, then it should be tried.

***

Joe gave a sigh. There was definitely something tailor-made about the way Riska's back and his arm fitted each other. Why couldn't they spend *more* time like this? The day had zoomed away somehow. He'd have to set off soon. He should be on the road already.

A tickling sensation ran up his other arm. He glanced casually at a beetle as it set off on an evening stroll towards his biceps.

Riska ran her fingers through a grass-tuft on the tiny lawn where they were sitting, and looked at the lengthening shadow cast by Joe's travel bag. "It's lucky to have got a ground floor flat with a garden, Joe, even though it's a small one. You've got quite a good view from here."

"Yup, it's not bad." He tried to straighten his foot, and stopped after an inch of movement, as it hit the fence. "Could do with more space, though. If we invite anyone to have drinks in the garden, we'll all have to have contortionist lessons first." He paused for a moment. "But at least I don't need a lawnmower. A throw-away razor does the job fine."

The beetle tried swinging round one of Joe's arm-hairs, ballsed up the manoeuvre and fell to the ground on its back. Joe reached down and turned it right way up.

Riska smiled. "I'm really pleased about your new job. You'll be able to walk to work."

"Yup. You can just see the corner of the office building through the trees over there, though I'm not crazy about focussing on it right now."

"I remember how those trees were when I first came, said Riska. They weren't in leaf yet. You said they'd been waiting around for something to happen."

"Like before I met you," Joe mused silently.

He looked down at the bulging travel bag. All in all, he thought, his packing *was* getting better. While the bag wasn't anywhere near symmetrical, it wasn't as grotesque as some of his past efforts. A left-luggage official had once refused to have the bag on his shelves, claiming it would upset the staff.

Hang-gliding, he realised, had improved him. You had to get yourself organised to do it. But it wasn't just *that* that had caused the change. Riska, in her fuss-free way, was bringing out the best in him.

She was leaning back now, watching a flotilla of pinkening clouds cruising above them. "I wish I could come flying with you Joe. The only free time I could get is next Saturday morning, and I'll need that for the job interview."

"Hope you get *that* one. Anything has to be better than the outfit you're with now!"

She looked down at the beetle, which was making for the last patch of sunlight on the grass. "Yup, they're really difficult. To get *that* time off I had to agree to work late every weekday next week. But I'll try and get away early enough on Saturday to come and see you fly on Sunday."

Joe stirred at the injustice of it. He knew aerobics teaching was vigorous stuff but, the way *that* place was working her, he was worried she'd come home one day minus an arm or leg.

"Can't you get at least a *few* more free days?"

"Not yet. They've got four new course-groups starting, and Tibia needs all the staff there for the time being."

"*Tibia*?"

"Yes. Why?"

"Seems sort of humorous."

"Sound like you've gone off on the wrong limb, Joe!" She turned her head and smiled him ten feet off the ground.

They sat and watched the pink in the clouds turn to grey. After a long time Riska said, "Look, I don't like to say this, Joe, but I think you'd better be making a start soon."

***

Though Eelag's choice of debt as an example had been completely random, he was beginning to sense some unmentioned fear behind Shloomger's bravado.

Shoon pushed back his chair and eyed the analogiser with a mix of doubt and last-chance optimism.

"So take it away, Eelag. Let's ride this woooowa *out of town*!"

The gypsy gave him a long-suffering look and toyed with the portable control panel. Problem-fix-trippers were a *pain*.

"Well, before we do that, you can start by telling me what kind of a debt we're riding out to meet. I've got to feed that to the machine, so that it gives us a good *analogy*."

"You mean... something of a kinduv... comparable amount, if I get your gist?"

"Yup. So, how *much* ?"

Shloomger shuffled his feet. He didn't like lying to Eelag. But the real debt was unmentionable for two reasons. Firstly, the general range it was *in* was too embarassing to talk about. And, secondly, the actual figure was unreachable. Even if he *had* known the exact amount, as soon as he'd mouthed the sum it'd be dust in cosmic history. He shrug-waggled his shoulders. "You're *sure* this'll get me, er... *someone*, out of a cash-fix?"

"No, Shloomger, it won't. But it'll give you an *insight* into how to deal with it."

"Okay! Let's *see* one of these *insights*, then. I mean... can this baby show me how to bust a *big* lump of debt?" He wiped his reddening forehead. "I mean, like something *really* knobbly. Just to *test* it, of course."

Eelag cupped his face in his hands, "Look, *golden droplets of splain*, Shoon! *Stop stalling*! Just tell me how much!"

"... How about... say... a gindaspillion Spiraks?" Shloomger's lower lip lost contact with reality as he breathed the sum over it. He wasn't particularly good with figures at the best of times, but the mere *idea* of this one chilled him like a freeze-pack of black holes. Worst of all, the figure he'd given was so *way under*, it wouldn't have bought the ink to print out a centi-centillionth of what Zunddertokk had down next to his name.

Eelag snatched a breath and stared at him. His hands hovered in a dazed kind of way over the controls.

He re-assembled his poise. "A *gindaspillion Spiraks*, you said?"

"Yup."

The gypsy adjusted the device. "Well *maybe* it'll take it. I'll try feeding it in and see what it does. But I'll need to reset the scale... "

Shoon watched Eelag fiddle with the settings and start his inputting marathon. At last the gypsy stopped, and gestured towards the floodlight-type contraptions.

"Right. That's it." He checked that he and Shloomger were correctly positioned. "But hang on to everything you've got, Shloomger. This could be a wild ride. Here we go!"

He took the analogiser's portable control unit from his pocket, and flicked a switch.

Shloomger had seen and done a huge number of things during his existence, but in spite of all his experiences he was totally unprepared for what happened.

There was no gentle introduction, just a horrible shaking. He waited for it to stop. He supposed that, wherever it was they'd arrive at, they'd get there soon. He also supposed that, once they'd *got* there, things would get gentler.

They didn't. And soon the horrible realisation came to him that they *had* arrived. The only thing that had just changed was the *style* of shaking. Instead of feeling he'd been picked up by the skin and hung underneath a mechanical rock-shute, through which stones were crashing onto his body, it was clear now that the action was driving upwards through his feet.

He was suddenly hit by the potent smell of large animal. The sort of animal that *likes* to smell, that takes a *pride* in it.

The smell rammed itself up Eelag's and Shloomger's nostrils and gleefully kicked-in the linings. It was clear it came from no single beast, but from a successful species, one that had multiplied in a big way, that was *going* places in an *extremely* big way, and going there *rapidly*.

Shloomger and Eelag both had the feeling they were standing spot-on one of those places.

The smell was also the smell of an animal that loves to grunt, that grunts gratuitously and loudly, even though the smell already grunts for it. The grunt was sinister, *communal*. It alternated with another sound, the horrible joint wheeze of lungs processing dust, mixed with what passed for oxygen here – wherever here *was*.

The next thing to hit them was visual.

It was the fact that they saw nothing.

And the effect was terrifying.

More exactly, they saw nothing ahead but a vast, swirling bank of dust rushing towards them, that seemed ready to burst at any moment.

Shloomger realised that, every second, it was somehow becoming even darker. The vibes coming up his legs were focussing into a single rhythm. A rhythm you don't ask questions about, because *it's* the kind of rhythm that asks the questions, not *you*.

It was synced hooves. Trillions, he guessed, though – thinking about it – a gindaspillion was more of a ball park figure. At least, it was for any fool thinking of playing ball in *that* park.

Shoon turned to Eelag, who was stabbing excitedly at the control panel.

"Okay," he sighed, "that'll do. I get the picture. Very interesting. Yes. But that'll do. I think it's time to break for a little drink now. An Overbrim Pinkelsnapper, maybe. The mouth gets very dry in these conditions. So, if you'd like to switch us back and out of here, Eelag, I'll just wander off and freshen up under the shower before we settle down over our cocktails and discuss the day."

Eelag gave him a look that said a great deal. In written form it could have filled volumes. In a nutshell, it said:

"I'd really like to, but I *can't*."

For a few seconds Eelag struggled to find the best way to put it concisely into words. And then he said:

"I'd really like to, but I *can't*."

CHAPTER 6

In a place tucked into a slot between Levels, her feet immersed in the time-pool of Larb, the soothsayer finished her sandwich, took a swig of throat-scorcher, checked her watch against the pool, and prepared to meet other creatures' dooms and her afternoon quota of sooths.

It wasn't *all* doom. In fact many of her visions turned out to have reasonably satisfactory endings, though it often depended whose viewpoint you took.

She wiggled her toe, sending time-ripples across the surface of the pool, turning a patch of dried petals back into budding water-irises.

All in all, she reflected, the job wasn't too bad. Better than in the transdimensional mines of Grarvoid. Here, at least, you could plan your own lunch schedule, and the pension scheme was okay. Her mother had always told her it paid to think ahead.

A shadow darted across her perceptionscape. In thirty-eight minutes fifty-three seconds, the Predictions Manager would exit the rear door of the Trans-Laminate Commodity Futures Corporation. Tensely and hurriedly he would pretend to amble through the synth-stone mockery of a rockery. He'd then make out that he'd just happened to see her. Next, he'd ask what she'd come up with that afternoon.

She shifted her attention urgently back to the pool and eye-trawled a mixed batch of pre-sooths. Sometimes, she mused, she could surprise herself with what she could find at short notice.

*

"They're just first inklings, Proyn." She handed her boss some sheets of paper with jotted notes. "I could maybe give you more on some of them if you want."

Proyn started scanning the Sooth-Report Sheets. "Any floods, crop infestations, labour unrest, Ora? *Cereals* are short. They have to forecast tomorrow. Thruke says he's close to wetting himself... "

"He *will*, but I've nothing much more than a flash-flood on non-farming land and a gas depot explosion on a small planet. As for the rest, it's mostly star-births and the odd supernova." She twiddled her lizard-bone brooch distractedly. "Ah... there *was one* that might click with you. I think it's on sheet 5." She watched him flick nervously to the page. "Sorry it's a bit short. I ran out of inklings."

The manager screwed up his eyes and struggled to decipher the writing. "A... *script* ? A *script to turn someone's current life into a short, extremely nasty one?*"

"Yup, that's it."

"Well that's not relevant to *us*." He brightened suddenly. "Not unless it's... "

"No, *not* Head of Forecasting, sweetie! It's not about *here*. It's a trans-universe job, between two dupli-univs in Sub-Lamina 2k16. As a matter of fact it's to do with the same planet as the flood and the gas explosion."

"That's not in *our* patch."

"No, but it *could* get kind of super-relevant to us here if it goes to its next planning stages."

Proyn scooped some water and bathed his face in the hope of a freebie facelift. "In that case Ora, you'd better tell me about it... "

*

The Predictions Manager supported his chin thoughtfully on his right knuckle. "Just to get this clear," he mumbled, "you've seen a script that's set to become a *man's life...* "

"Yup, a *manipulated* life. Man called Joe."

"Right. And his scripted life, and death, are *grim*?"

"Yup. I'll not go into those details again – the mind control and the programmed bouts of madness, the break-in at the laboratory, the theft of the deadly substances, the take-over of government installations, the kidnappings, the dismembering… "

"That's enough, Ora!" Proyn got to his feet and swayed over the edge of the pool. Puking in it wouldn't be a good idea, he decided. Somehow it would remember. He sat down, held his hand to his chin again, and tried to calm his stomach. Ora was still speaking.

"… Or his death in the saw-mill… the blood… the intestines festooning the wood-racks… "

"Okay, *right*! I *got* it. Cut – I mean *leave* – that out!" Proyn thought for a while, "Look, I'm sort of *interested* in what those people on Thrarrxgor are up to, if it might affect *us*." He glanced again at the report sheet, and then at the soothsayer. "And you've written here that this Outwood action show's to be part of an *Earth test* of some *long-distance manipulation and focussed destruction system* that'll make use of Thrarrxgor's new 'Special Precision Intervenor' "

Ora opened her bag and took out a thermos flask and a few other items. "That's the plan. And then, after that, their aim is to use the system to take over Earth and… "

"Yeah, you said… *manipulate its population into slavery*, then *transport them to another universe* where they'll make *more and bigger machines for Thrarrxgor's boss… K*rargxt*. After which Earth will be destroyed?"

"Yup, that's the plan, Proyn."

He waved away her offer of tea. "And you said the teams in charge of the shows are in the dark on that. They think it's just *entertainment* for K*rargxt?"

"Well K*rargxt does *like* that kind of stuff anyway, but you're right about him keeping his later plans under wraps. By the way, there's a short first manip-test before the

Outwood one. A mad axeman. She stared into the pool again. "Hang on. Ah! It's all starting to gel!"

Proyn sighed. "Not *again*?"

"Yup. Third time this week! Must be the sodding weather!"

After a few moments, just as suddenly as it had begun to solidify, the pool cleared. Ora concentrated again. "... Yup, K*rargxt and his deputy are both *paranoid*. They've already told the teams they carry cards that neutralise the effect of the Intervenor and the Transporter, just in case anyone turns those machines on *them*, and... "

"And I suppose they don't want their staff to know about their *real* plans in case any of them get ideas about taking over Earth and Thrarrxgor themselves... "

"That's it, and maybe places like *here* too."

Proyn shifted uneasily. "And K*rargxt, you say, likes the idea of blowing up worlds, star clusters, and a heap more, with his machines... "

She poured a cup of what seemed to be tea, "*Likes* the idea? He's *crazy* about it. And his deputy's working on some new slam-bammy heavy hardware for *that*!" She took out another cup, filled it and put it down next to hers.

"So, when's the *first* action planned, Ora, if that's measurable in *our* time? By the way, I *will* have a tea... "

She handed him the cup and looked into the pool for a moment. "Yup, it's measurable. It's due to start *soon*". She glanced into the depths again. "It's that *mad axeman* show." She paused for a moment, shifting focus slightly. "Oh, yeah, and there are those two other things as well, the gas depot explosion and the flash flood."

"And you say those Intervenors could be upgraded to reach us *here*?"

"Yup, very likely, I should think. Still, that's all I can pick up, dearie. And I don't suppose there's anything we could do about it anyway."

Proyn moved his hands away from his face. "You wouldn't happen to have a shot of throat-scorcher to hand?... "

"It's in the tea," she murmured casually. "And now I want to complain about my performance report... "

He took a swig and stared at her, "But I haven't *written* it yet... "

***

For the thirty-odd years that had marked his span so far, the life of Approbrius Thwuckwaite had been broadly blameless. He hadn't much aspired to fame or power, his only, very cautious, moves towards them having been an entry for the parish Geranium-of-the-Year competition and a once-only, over-hesitant role as replacement line-judge in the first round of his local tennis club's tournament.

To those in the neighbourhood who knew him, he was a mild-mannered man who smiled at cats and helped old ladies across roads that often they had merely been contemplating.

One example, among many, of his kindly nature had been the way he'd spontaneously given a lift, during one of his rare holidays in the countryside, to a testy man called Hepkin Dangle. Whilst many would have found the man repulsive, App had done his best to get along with him during the journey, and had even tried to entertain and amuse him by speaking about himself, where he lived, and about the progress he'd been making with his stamp collection.

The odd feeling that came over him now, as he sat in his armchair, reading a newspaper article on vegetarianism, was therefore entirely new.

But, once he had got up from the chair, App found that the feeling no longer seemed odd or new. It was clear to him that he had always intended to go out and buy a large axe.

In fact he found himself wondering how he could possibly have put it off for so long.

He looked guiltily at his watch. The local ironmongers would be closed. He'd have to take a bus to the big DIY store two miles away. It would still be open. As a matter of fact it was closer to the town hall. It was there, he recalled, that the local council's public consultation on crime-control was to take place that evening.

He asked himself why people didn't think the same way as *he* did, and then he realized it was because they were all mad. That was why he was going to have to *deal* with them, or at least as many as he could manage.

He looked carefully at the bus timetable and considered his schedule. He might arrive a bit early for the meeting. But, if he did, he could wait in the bushes behind the car park.

***

It was a kind of drainy-itchy feeling. It had been bugging Boontrak more often recently. It was as if small amounts of energy were being drawn out of him.

Just after his crash he'd known he wasn't altogether himself. A bit later, he'd realised that he, himself, wasn't together at all. But his mind had improved a bit since then. He'd been able to chat some years ago with that visitor, and to show him a tiny fraction of what he could do. But he understood that he was still seriously spaced out.

The strange thing was that not much space separated the parts of him that were spread around the cave. Those parts, he could tell, made up most of him. But there was some more of him that seemed to be in two stones in another universe, and the rest was in the rocks the visitor had been taking away.

As for *that* bloke, he'd been as useful as a sat-nav to a statue. He'd often been back for more 'samples', but he'd never got the cave's 'host-stones' into anything more joined-up.

It was a great pity, Boontrak thought. Maybe one day, *if* he could find more energy and get himself organised, he'd be able to zoom off somewhere else.

Well, he told himself, he could *dream*. After all, he didn't have a lot else to do at the moment...

***

"What do you mean, '*Can't*'?"

The words, which had taken a long time to get ready in Shloomger's throat, got a short way past his lips, froze at the oncoming roar, and fled back into his mouth.

The gypsy guessed his drift. He felt he owed Shloomger some kind of explanation.

"It's the dust! In the controls! It's jammed them!"

Shloomger's mind flicked him an ace. He grabbed it. His voice grew bolder, "Well – dust or no dust – Eelag, at least it's not for *real*. I mean, after all, ha! ha! we're *immortal*!"

"Not *here*, we aren't!"

"What do you mean, 'Not *here*'?"

"This analogiser. It's just the basic version. Got it cheap from a dealer on 4a. There's no IM facility on it. They *die* where we are now, you see!"

"But we're on Level Eleven, not *there*!"

"Tell that to the analogiser. As far as it's concerned, the here and now's *there* and now, wherever *there* is!"

"You mean '*Deathland*' ?"

"As good as!"

"What do you mean 'As *good* as'? What's *good* about... "

Eelag wiped his face on the inside of his arm. "Look, Shoon, cut the quibbling! You wanted an *insight* into your problem! Now you've *got* one!"

Shloomger struggled to free a clod of soil from his molars. "Well if this is one of your *insights*, I'll take a *million problems* any day!"

The dirt-clouds swirled down and in. Here and there, in vaguely clearer gaps, Shloomger made out huge, horrible shapes. Eelag caught sight of them too. It was the first time he'd had live contact with the Level Four Dagger-toothed Dusthog. The only specimen he'd ever seen before had been dead and chained to the floor of its cage. And even then the museum staff had had to tranquilize it every thirty minutes.

Shloomger dropped his arms to his sides. "What in *splain* do we do?"

"We leave!" Eelag's words just made it through the dust.

"An *intriguing* idea! But *how*, exactly?"

"We jump."

"What? Sort of *hop about*? *Dance* our way out, you mean? Like that cabaret act we did with sexy Lola last year at the Purple Potato?"

"No. We go over the cliff."

"*What* cliff?"

"Look behind you, Shloomger!"

***

It was an odd feeling, hurtling down the side of an immense precipice, having just been de-immortalised. Shloomger rolled over on his back and noticed, some way above him, that a large and stubborn part of the herd was up there, free-falling through a zone where his stomach had been a few seconds before.

Eelag was looking down, his eyes on the analogiser's control unit, which he'd let slip from his grasp as they'd jumped over the edge, and which was wobbling about in the air tantalisingly close below his foot. As the wind-pressure played funny expressions with his face, Eelag wondered whether, by any chance, it might blow the dust out of the unit. If it did, and if he could get his foot over the Escape button just as the unit – and he – hit the ground, then maybe the device would finally activate. But then maybe, very finally, it *wouldn't*.

He aimed his foot.

CHAPTER 7

It was like the meeting hall for a cablers' festival, the night after the party. The wires that festooned the place clearly felt no need to justify their existence by even hinting at what they might be connecting. They simply hung there, as if the Intervenor Preparations Room was a collection of random electrical decisions.

The machines looked no better organised, scrawled, as they were, with hand-written operating instructions and splattered with paint-droppings from the ceilings of the rushed-up workshops where they'd been assembled.

But the equipment, which was used to direct all K*rargxtko's Intervenor operations, *worked*. Viewed by those in charge of it, it was 'neat'. But considered from the angle of those in the galaxies and universes it had destroyed, and the people who'd fallen foul of Approbrius Thwuckwaite, it needed serious demolition.

Ked looked at the technicians seated around the room. They seemed more smug than he'd usually found them when he'd come down here on his trips from LIFE PLANNING. He guessed it had to do with the 'success' of their recent work.

He drubbed the air with his new brushed-platinum index-finger extension. He felt awkward, and strangely angry. Up to a few moments ago, until his boss Bernie had told him what had actually been 'achieved' by the Intervenor machines, none of what they had been doing had seemed *real*. Working for K*rargxtko had simply been something that had given him a sense of importance, and that had joined up the weird, mutated pieces of his life.

He felt confused about his anger. Though he was upset about the mass cosmic destructions, part of him was also annoyed at not being consulted on the mad axeman script, the gas-depot blast and the freak flood. But he realised he was furious that those had happened too. His only relief was that he'd been well out of it.

His eyes fell on the thick column of cable leading, through a wall arch, to the Intervenor Desk in the giant hangar nearby.

He drew a long in-hissing breath, making his tooth-pendants dance against the inside of his cheek. What kind of mind would want to blow away spreads of galaxies and whole universes? Its owner would need to be a seriously professional looney. He squinted thoughtfully at the K*rargxtko identity bar on the ridge of his nose. Well, from the rumours he'd heard about K*rargxt and what he did to K*rargxtnauts, it seemed to fit the picture.

Bernie had been moving around manically between work-stations, engaged in what he considered to be the motivation of the staff. He suddenly stopped, and beckoned to Ked.

Ked wandered over. The electro-pulse fashion skewers in Bernie's eyebrows were on *hyper* setting, sending spasms through the bristled flesh.

Bernie greeted him with his usual canon-fodder fanaticism.

"Waheey, Ked. – Wahooobee! – In fact, *Superwababaray*!"

"As you say, Bernie."

"Say, Ked, about the script for that bloke – *what's* his name?"

"Outwood, you mean?"

"Yup, that's it, Joe Outwood."

Ked's face began to feel hot. "Look, Bernie, the way you say *Joe*, you're making it sound as if he's a *friend* of yours, not… "

"Sorry, Ked, don't follow you." Bernie thumbed the band of variable smile-inducing magnetic lip-studs to the left of his mouth, producing a grinning slit that came close to unzipping his face completely. "Anyway, I've been thinking about your script."

"And... "

"Well, you know that *other* script – the short one we ran on the axeman... "

Ked felt his blood pressure rising, "I wouldn't *know* about that, Bernie. I had no hand in it. I didn't even know it was going to *happen*!"

"Sure, of course, but... "

"But *what?*"

"Well, it went off so well, it led me to thinking maybe we could blood-up the Joe script a lot earlier... "

"What kind of *grintz* are you giving me here, Bernie? *How* the *boonag* are you proposing we do *that*?"

"Like he could get kinduv... maimed earlier. In the first episode for example... "

"Maimed *earlier*?" Ked felt a part of him standing outside the argument, watching himself. "*What* ... ?"

"Something spectacular, but of course not so much that it'll bollocks up our control of him."

"Ked knew the argument was dragging him back into his job. He felt the stress welling up in his body. An old, dormant beach-poser's tattoo began to show and spread, in all its horribleness, across his face. "You have to be *joking*, Bernie! How the *sluck* do I deliver a serial that's been written for a bloke with two hands – well for *most* of the show anyway – if his arms are chopped off in the opening scene? Tell me just *how* I'm going to do *that* ?"

Bernie thought for a moment. "I was thinking more of *one* arm, really." He paused and reflected further. "Well, maybe you've got a point there, Ked. I suppose, like, it *could* be kind of tricky... "

"Look... *Bernie*, it gets *bloody* enough *soon* enough! Even in the *first* episode, he stabs five people!"

"Well, yup, I guess maybe he'll sort of need one arm to do the stabbing and the other arm to balance himself while he's doing it... " Bernie fell silent and stared for a moment at the rampant ghastliness moving over Ked's features. "*Stagg me*! Where *did* you get that tatt?"

Ked glanced at his reflection in a nearby glass partition. "Flockted *Grintz*! I thought *that* had gone for good. It's an old one, from a beach-holiday years back," he scowled, " in the days when I *had* holidays!" He checked his image more closely. "It was supposed to be just a *tempo*, but it seems to be rebuilding!"

"More like a full-scale *urbanisation, I'd* say!" Bernie peered at the hideous rendering. "Seems to have taken on a life of its own. Like, it's sort of *evolving*!"

Ked changed subjects. "So what's next on the action? When'll the Serial roll? That is, *if* you've dropped your idea for those changes you just told me about?"

Bernie turned his eyes away from the tattoo and gave his reply to the wall. "It'll roll once we've done more checks on the Intervenor and re-tested the Viewer. But Sculpin will give the order." He ran his tongue around the inside of his teeth, opened an inter-molar store, drew out a wedge of gum and chewed on it frenetically. "Anyway, as well as the work for *that*, I've a heap of other stuff he's given me..."

"Like... ?"

"It's kinduv secret. So this stays *inside* your throat, *right*? It's to do with what Sculpin says are *contingency plans*."

"What for?"

Bernie drew a second gum wedge, from the other side of his mouth, and began chewing in stereo. "Like – for a *hugely bigger* serial. Apparently it's got a mega-cast. Can't give more detail, but I have to make technical plans for brain-controlling vast numbers of people, and for inter-planetary mass transportation too... " He turned his head slightly and winced again at the sight of Ked's face reflected in the glass partition. "... Say, that *temporary* body-art's getting like...

seriously *sub-optimal,* man! Maybe you picked up one of those digital tattoo viruses? Ever fallen asleep on the beach?"

"Nodded off a couple of times, maybe. Look, how the *spurgk* am I supposed to remember?"

Bernie shifted position and talked back to the wall. "Well, *whatever*, Ked, I'd get it fixed *fast*! Gotta think of the other people in the teams here. Can't have them traumatised. Like, it'll affect their *output*!"

***

Shloomger was surprised the handset wasn't covered in dust anymore. He was even more surprised that – apart from a heavily impacted Escape button – it seemed in generally good condition. But what surprised him most was that it was on the table and that he and Eelag were sitting in Eelag's garden staring at it and listening to the sound of the surf hitting the beach. It was... well, *surprising*. He wasn't dead. At least, not as far as he could tell.

"Like a pizza?" The gypsy enquired, reaching for his mobile.

"Yup, nearly *was*! Oh, I see! Well, yes, now you mention it, Eelag, I don't mind if I do."

"Seafood... or Four Levels?"

"Make it Seafood, and a churn of Margarita, superchilled."

Eelag reeled off the order and closed the phone. He turned towards the crystal ball and looked into it for a while. Suddenly he gave a short unexplained gasp, peered at the ball for a little longer, and then turned his chair back again, with studied casualness, in the direction of Shloomger.

The two stared at each other reflectively in a strange kind of syncopated silence. Shloomger was the first to manage more than a dry raucous surge of air across his throat.

"Close," he murmured, "*very* close. I was just rolling over to say a last hello to the ground when I saw you do that pinpoint landing on the handset. You must've done it before."

"Never," said Eelag.

There was another very long silence.

"I think I'd be a bit careful about using that machine," Shloomger said softly. "Maybe best take it back, trade it in for something else... "

"Well, look, Shloomger, it worked for *you*! Maybe it's just that you didn't want to get the message."

Shoon's mind was already deep inside the Margarita travelling towards him in Luigi's van. Talk of messages was unwelcome. All he could manage was a vague grunt.

Eelag's hand moved to his forehead to brush away the sweat. "Well, it couldn't be much clearer, could it Shloomger?"

"*Clearer*? *It* ? *Clearer*? *What*?"

The gypsy let out a long sigh. He was used to it, trying to get his visitors to see slightly further than the end of a cocktail stick.

"It couldn't be clearer *what you have to do*!"

"Sorry, don't follow... "

"The debt, Shloomger, the *debt*! I *know* about the debt. I just saw it in the ball. And I *know* about Zunddertokk!"

Shoon dragged his brain from the approaching drink churn. Why did things have to be so *difficult*? That debt business had been such an amazingly long time ago.

"You've got to leave, Shloomger."

"*Leave*?"

"Slip away – over the cliff, so to speak. Somewhere he won't find you. Somewhere he'll never even begin to look."

"*He*?"

"Get your act together, Shloomger! *He – Zunddertokk*!"

"What do you mean, Eelag, Somewhere he'll never even begin to..?" The Margarita arrived. Shoon grasped for it. "Begin to *look*... ? What d'you *mean*?"

The gypsy eyed him seriously. "Of course, you realise, Shloomger, it'll mean mortality. For a while, at least... " Eelag pushed the churn away to the far end of the table, "till we've come up with some long-term way of handling the problem."

"*Mortality*?... What, *like we've just*... ?" Shoon's mouth opened and closed like an empty polystyrene hamburger box in front of an air conditioner outlet. "A... *while* ? How long a *while*? I mean, you can't be mortal for a very *long* while, can you? *Otherwise*... "

"I know, Shloomger. But I think it's a risk worth taking."

"Worth *me* taking, you mean!"

"Well, yes. It'll *never* occur to him you've downgraded."

A ghastly shivering fear ran through Shloomger.

"Hey! Just a moment! By '*him*', you mean *Zundddertokk*, don't you? Well, I haven't caught sight of him in what seems like a billion years. And, when I *did*, it was through a moth-hole from the inside of Allinka Maythrop's massage tent. What *now* makes you think he's about to appear on the scene? I mean it's likely I'd have ended my new mortal lifespan before he ever turned up. *That's* no solution!"

The gypsy glanced across to the crystal ball.

"Look, I wasn't going to tell you this, Shloomger, but I've got the very clear impression he's on his way already!"

"On his... *Where* is it that you think I should I go?"

"It's a fairly easy ride down to it. Well, there *are* a fair number of levels to drop through, not to speak of a few time warps too, but the trip's nothing really uncomfortable. All the same, you'll need to get used to the scaling-down."

"*And* the mortality."

"Yup, that could be trickier. Particularly with the job I want you to do."

"*Job*?"

"Ah, yes. I was going to mention that later. It might be a bit... sort of dangerous," Eelag's eyes moved back again briefly to the crystal ball. "You see, I came across your destination place in the crystal ball a few days back. Someone there is planning to do something particularly nasty to someone who's somewhere else... "

"You're being as clear to me as the mud on the waste-dump planet of Groid, Eelag."

"Sorry, I'll give you more on that shortly. In a nutshell, there's someone on *Earth* who helped me out of a tricky situation, and now *he's* in one himself. So I'd like you to help *him* out if you can. I only got a brief glance of what's being planned against him, and then the ball clouded over."

"I hope that ball of yours is *reliable*, Eelag."

"It's fairly much spot-on most of the time. Anyway, about that bloke. It's a question of keeping him out of something nasty and extremely terminal, if you can. You see, as I say, he did me a bit of a favour... "

"Er... Eelag... do you think you could pass... "

"Oh, right. Sorry," Eelag slid Shloomger the churn of Margarita. "Of course, the aim will be to get you back here safe and sound once you've sorted things out for that bloke... "

"... And once Zunddertokk has gone on his way."

"Yup, that's it. And, you know *what* Shoon?"

"No. *What*?"

"It's just possible it might help solve your first problem, the *boredom* thing, too. So, you see, *that* way we'll have sorted out the debt difficulty, the threat to that bloke's future, and your boredom, all in *one*. It'd be like killing three birds with one stone."

Shloomger frowned. "That's not a term one normally uses on this level, Eelag. As you well know, the birds here are as immortal as we are. And, as you also well know, I've quite often opted for their body shape and done some soaring myself... ". A thought whooshed across Shloomger's mind. "You don't think, perhaps Eelag that if... "

"No, don't even *think* of it Shloomger. Even if you stayed here and morphed to a bird, or whatever else, Zunddertokk would find you. He'll be used to debtors trying those kinds of tricks."

Shloomger poured himself a goldfishbowlful of Margarita and reflected. If staying here wasn't an option, then Eelag's idea probably *was* the best one going.

He began thinking about the risks in it. Oddly, the more he thought about them the less unpleasant the prospect of the trip seemed.

A new body-tremor surged through him. He couldn't tell exactly why, but the sensation was a bit like the one he'd had after they'd gone over the cliff.

He had to admit it. He was starting to feel... a little bit more *alive.*

***

"Good. ... Seventeen." Frank Squirt could just read the number in the light from the lamppost across the street. This was it.

He pulled his car into a gap opposite the door and rummaged on the shelf in front of him for his wallet, notepad, and his ancient cassette recorder.

The inside of the car looked like an ashtray. That was because it *was* an ashtray. Dog ends in a thousand hideous variations of stubbed death lay twisted and crumpled at his feet.

All the 'seats', including the threadbare fabric that kept his buttocks off the floor, were covered, and in some places completely buried, by layers of litter. The thick film of tobacco smoke that lined the inside of the car was matched on the outside by a heavy coat of grime.

It would have been hard to imagine that the vehicle in which the grunting man sat had once, fragrant with newness, graced a showroom. Few would have believed it could ever have been anything but the rattling, perforated bin that squatted at the kerb of Clackley Close.

Frank switched off the engine, opened the door and eased himself out of the car, nearly crushing the camera that lurked in the pocket of the rag he called his 'raincoat', a laughing stock of the elements.

He steadied himself and headed for the front door.

He pondered. Maybe, just *maybe*, his luck was about to change. It needed to. Out of the country on booze-buying ferry trip when axeman had gone beserk, then still coming back on boat when gas depot had blown. And, to cap it all, three hours after he'd driven off boat, ferry port hit by mysterious freak flood!

He scratched one of his many chins. But, if this story was *right*, it'd more than make up for the others he'd missed. The question was, *could* there be any truth in the rumour?

Arnold, his source, had been right on an earlier story. Said he'd been tipped off by a female friend on that one. He'd probably added in a bit of guesswork, but he'd been right all the same. About politician. Politician in public eye, but with tattoos on private parts.

What special about *that*? Slogans for another party, *that* was what! And more than just *slogans*. A fully erected *campaign platform*! Man had been miss-handled by Pristine Cringe, a blonde, petite twenty-six-year-old who, as Frank had put it, had *designs* on the man. All this had been done while man had been in drunken state at her flat in Flaxton Terrace. When first questioned, politician had refused to comment. Then said he thought it'd been acupuncture to cure squint.

Frank ran a hand through his hair, scratched another chin and considered further. Same source now. Arnold the milkman had been gathering gossip for years. Mostly no use, but he'd been pure gold about those non-deleti graffitti. It was another kind of story now, but maybe he was onto something.

He reached the door, rang the bell and waited, one hand holding his press card, the other a part-open wallet. He attempted a smile. The effect was ghastly.

There was the brief sound of barking somewhere inside the house, then a shout and a long silence. Finally the door swung inwards. In its place stood an elderly man with round rimless glasses and a white beard resembling the hairs of a knackered broom. His hand ruffled through its tufts and chasms as if searching for some lost item. Then, seeming to recall why he'd come to the door, he looked down at the figure on the step in front of him.

"Press! Squirt!" said the journalist.

"No thanks!" said the man, and slammed the door.

Frank rang again and waited for the figure to re-emerge.

"Squirt! Press!" he clarified.

"Now look here,"! said the man, "why don't you... "

"I do it for all the big ones."

"I'm sure you do, but if you think ... "

"Freelance. For all the big papers."

The old man looked at him carefully.

"I've come about the machine," Frank continued, "the *time* machine."

CHAPTER 8

"Yeah! In *one* this time, Grux! And *no* use of mirror-cams!"

Ked stared through the Fangster's screen and fingered along the last lane of the face-puzzle and into home base. This latest male cosmetic touch-maze was grades ahead of anything he'd tried before, and just two stages below competition level. He'd come a long way since he'd first drifted into skin-navigation.

It had started with a shoulder-to-erogenous zones version he'd once bought, aiming to draw Threegla Bleem, a wary conversationless girl, beyond giggle and into serious interact. The attempt had failed hopelessly. She'd lost the trail just below Ked's collarbone, and all interest well before that.

He wince-ripped the sticker from his cheek, glanced at his face in the mirror-cam to make sure his tattoo hadn't re-surged under the puzzle, and checked the route ahead. If there were no louse-ups through 'The Pits', a vast zone of box-flats K*rargxtko exorbi-let as 'Compact Dwelling Cells', he'd be home soon. All he had to do was cut through a part of that warren that jutted across his track.

Grux took the first batch of bends easily, then clawed a 360 stop that carved a strap-weal in Ked's ribs.

Ahead, two K*rargxtko police mechans straddled the street, blocking it. There seemed to be more beyond them.

Ked was on the point of pulling Grux back to another route when he heard a scream. He peered between the mech-beasts. Suddenly he caught sight of what looked like a rag doll being thrown around by some other police mechans.

He knew it was no rag doll. Beyond his own sightings of transport mechans being torn apart by K*rargxtko mech-beasts, he'd heard stories of things like this happening to kids, but had only half-believed them. Or, rather, he'd half-suspected they were true, but had chosen not to think about them.

He stared at the scene in front of him. From what he could see, the kid had only a few seconds to live. The thought came to him that, if he didn't clear off rapidly, he and Grux would be the next items on the menu. He twitched the joystick and part-turned the Fangster in a first-stage to a fast exit.

Something hit the sidescreen and landed on one of Grux's shoulder-plates. It was a child's shoe.

He didn't ask himself what made him do it. He sprang open the doors of the Fangster's luggage trunk, then opened his own door and got out.

He didn't ask himself why he said, 'Sorry Grux, I'll get you some more stuff tomorrow,' and swung the first of the K*rargxtko Luxury Mech-food bags up into the air towards the mechbeasts. And he didn't bother to wonder why he kept on heaving new bags at them till they had all lost interest in the child, and were fighting themselves for the fodder. Nor did he think about the gut-clutching risk of running round the edge of the snarling mech-beast pack, picking up the child and taking him to safety.

*

"Just round the next corner, Mister, on the right."

Ked looked at the boy in the passenger seat and wondered how he'd cope with memories of those mechans. He glared angrily at him. "That was more blocks from home than you should *ever* have been, sonny! *Never* go so far on your own around here! Do you *hear* me?"

He regretted he'd near-shouted the words. It'd been to hide that he cared about the kid's welfare. But maybe he'd frightened him.

The Fangster slowed and turned down yet another dark slit between concrete cliffs. To Ked's relief the boy didn't seem upset by the scolding he'd given him. The lad pointed to a steel grating in the wall a few yards ahead. "See that, Mister? We live a bit further on from there. We're on the same side."

Ked pulled the Fangster over, reached into a pouch under the control panel, pulled out a pack of mixed-sounds musical gum and flicked it into the boy's hands. He took him to the building and up to his door.

"My mum's out", said the kid. "She works at the K*rargxtko drinks factory on the other side of town. My dad's away at work too. Pity you can't meet him either. He wants to go on a special training course", the boy added brightly. "If he gets onto the course, then, in two years time, he's going to be a K*rargxtnaut! We're going to be very proud of him!"

"Tell him not even to *think* about it!" Ked looked straight at the kid and told him about the rumours he'd heard.

He watched the boy's dreams die in his eyes.

He turned and walked away.

*

Ked looked back through Grux's mirror-cam at the walls of the block behind him, and thought for a moment. It was something the child had said. He searched for it in his memory. What *was* it?

Yup, *that* was it. He'd said "*We're on the same side.*"

Suddenly Ked found himself murmuring:

"Yup, sonny. *Now* we are."

***

"Are you sure *this* one's going to work, Eelag?"

Shoon looked at the device suspiciously. He couldn't see

why this machine was needed. After all, there were other ways to move around between Levels. But Eelag had explained something about having to use a 'pure downgrade' system, and had also mentioned, rather hurtfully, Shloomger thought, that it would be faster and more accurate than Shoon's 'casual navigation methods'. He supposed he'd just have to go along with what Eelag said, mortality and all.

The gypsy pulled the last of the plastic wrapping from the device, wiped off the polystyrene gravel, and filled in the product registration card.

"No problem at all, Shloomger. It's guaranteed for..." Eelag glanced at the brochure and did a quick mental calculation of time-rate differences between Levels 11 and 4a. "It's guaranteed for... "

"How long, precisely, Eelag?"

"Oh... er... a billion-billionth of a second."

"Well, that's *brilliant*! Of course, I know those guarantees don't mean much at the *best* of times, and we got the *worst* of times out of that *last* device of yours!"

"Come on, Shloomger, it'll be alright. This is a seriously designed machine."

"Never mind about 'seriously *designed*'. Does it seriously *work*?"

"Don't worry, everything'll be fine. I've run through the video-nodule they sent with the pack. It seems all very straightforward... "

Shoon counted the tremors running through his abdomen, "*Straightforward*, Eelag, is the *outward* part of the trip. When this business is all done, it's *straightback* I want, *right*?"

"It'll be okay, Shloomger. The system should be able to focus on you and pull you back directly to the inside of the launch-and-receive capsule here." Eelag paused and looked at the device thoughtfully. "Of course, I'll have to make sure its auto-system can *aim* at you correctly. I'll maybe do a few practice sends-and-returns of various items between here and other Levels, just to get used to it while you're away. But don't worry. I'll keep a good eye on things at this end... "

Shoon was looking unconvinced. Eelag sensed the need to lift his friend's morale. "... And, of course, you can take this mini text-module with you. It'll enable us to send messages to each other. It's ultra compact, so you should be able to use it discreetly without problems."

The gypsy handed Shloomger an extremely small, flat device. Then suddenly remembering something, he turned to a side table and picked up some coin-sized wafer-thin packets. "Ah! And as a special extra, I've managed to super-compress a few cocktail mixes into inter-level portable form."

Shloomger took the packets and brightened visibly.

"But go easy on them," Eelag advised, "there aren't many, and there'll probably be only a few occasions when you'll be able to enjoy them." He gave Shloomger a serious look. "And, remember, this voyage is *important*! I'm sure I don't need to remind you about the specific purpose of your trip... "

Though he'd been fully and repeatedly briefed by Eelag, Shoon felt he could still do with a revision session. But he knew it would be too embarrassing to ask for another complete run-through. His friend was looking at him, expecting a reply. Shloomger attempted a summary of his mission.

"Well, yes, of course. In a nutshell Eelag, it's to help that bloke, the one you met... "

"The one who got *me* out of a bit of trouble."

"Yes, that's it. Er... *Joe*, isn't it? The one who you found out – in your crystal ball – they're going to be horrible to."

"And horrible *with* if they get the chance."

"Yup, that's it."

The gypsy looked at him hopefully. "And who are *they*, Shloomger?"

Shoon paused for a moment and scanned his memory. He'd thought Eelag would be pleased enough that he'd recalled Joe's name reasonably quickly. But now he seemed to want more. Why was it always *names* that were the most difficult things to remember? Those were the things people got most upset about if you forgot them, particularly when it came to *their* names.

He realised time was ticking along. His friend was waiting. Suddenly it all came to him. "Ah yes! K*rargxt and Sculpin, and a bunch of other people. But they're in a *different* universe from the one Joe's in."

Eelag relaxed visibly. He moved on to the next question. "And how are you going to try to help… Shloomger?"

"I'm not going to try to help Shloomger. That's *my* name."

The gypsy pushed the side table over into the sand and cupped his head in his hands. Was it *any use* going ahead with this? He tried a few of the relaxing breathing exercises he sometimes taught to visitors, and was surprised to find they seemed to work. He pressed on with exaggerated calm. "So, tell me, Shloomger. *Who* is it that you're going to help, and *how*?"

"*I told* you already! It's *Joe*. Weren't you listening then?"

Eelag gave him a long, pained look. "Alright, and *how*, exactly, Shloomger, are you going to try to help?"

"I insinuate myself into Thrarrxgor society."

"More precisely?… "

"Into K*rargxtko, if possible."

"And by what means do you do that?"

"I use my initative."

Eelag suddenly had a sinking feeling. The idea of Shloomger using his initiative was central to the whole plan, but it could, he feared, be the point when the plan ceased to have any centre at all and collapsed in a heap.

The gypsy fought off his doubts. He knew deep down, like many on Eleven did, that Shloomger was really a *bright* being. It was just a question of him snapping out of his lethargy and using his brain. And he'd need to start *soon*. There was little time to lose. He pushed ahead. "For *example*, Shloomger?"

" I try to get a job… "

Eelag groaned inwardly. "Yes, Shloomger, such *as*?"

"A staff member of K*rargxtko, as high up the hierarchy as I can get in at."

"And, failing *that*, Shloomger?"

"Well, the odd temporary job somewhere else, till I manage to get into K*rargxtko… "

Their talk moved on to some of the more practical details, including the fact that, on his mission, Shloomger would be unable to change from his human body-shape and, once there, would have to kit himself out in appropriate clothes for whatever he had to do. After a while Eelag realised that his inner groans were beginning to deafen him.

*

Dressed in what he hoped would be a suitable starter get-up for Thrarrxgor, Shloomger strolled, with slightly overdone casualness, out of the bungalow's back door, and towards what looked like a total-enclosure sunbed.

"I prefer to use this launch-and-receive capsule to send you off," Eelag muttered, "rather than target the swift-beam facility at you. I'd need a lot of practice with that, even at close range. You see, if I missed, and aimed it between the palm trees by mistake, I might end up sending the entire contents of the Balagooga beach bar instead."

"Well, if we *are* what we drink, Eelag, there's probably a fair amount of that in me anyway. But I get your drift. Let's get on with it and use *this* thing, shall we?"

Shloomger settled himself into the apparatus. "So, was there anything else I need to know?"

Eelag reflected for a moment. "Ah, yes, Shloomger, there was one other thing I forgot to mention. Something I saw in the crystal ball. I think it's possible someone else, who's not on Thrarrxgor, may soon find out what's being planned for Joe, and that he may also try to help him."

"Someone not on Thrarrxgor, you say."

"That's it. Someone in the same universe as Joe's. On the same planet as Joe, as a matter of fact. But the ball clouded, and I couldn't see any more. Just thought I'd let you know."

Shloomger stared at the inside of the roof of the apparatus just above his head. "Well, yup, I suppose it could be handy to know that." He took a few slow deep breaths. "So... *See you* Eelag. I'll do what I *can*."

His friend reached for the instruction leaflet, checked some dials on the control panel, and activated the machine.

***

Frank's legs were aching. They often did in these doorstep jobs. It was the sheer tedium of talking his way in.

Some visits were tougher than others, and this was no pushover. The old boy had been playing difficult. Still, he seemed to be weakening at last.

"You'd like to *see* it? Don't know. I'll have to *think* about it. Better if you'd made an appointment, really. Well, anyway, I suppose you might as well come in for a minute... "

Frank surged into the hallway. The two men part-circled each other in a 'pas-de-deux' as they manoeuvred to open the inner hall door. In the end they gave up. Frank went out of the house while the inner door was opened, then returned and followed his host inside.

He was led down a corridor, past some stairs, through a junked-up room, which seemed to double as library and lab-store, and into a back annexe that looked like something cobbled together from the remains of a Wild West film set. Frank sniffed damp and chemicals.

His host gestured him to a balding settee, then pointed to a curtained-off area in a corner of the shack.

"I've been working on it for quite a while, Mr. Squirt. It's still a prototype of course", but I'm getting my first results."

Frank draped his 'raincoat' on the arm of the settee, wiped his forehead, and extracted his recorder from its default site in the folds of his armpit. He snorted at it, by way of test.

"Right, a few details first then. I'll need your full name

and age. Plus info on any partners, live-in or other."

"*Live-in ...* ?"

"Ones with whom you share the... more *intimate* aspects of your life."

"Don't follow... "

Frank held out a battered pack of cigarettes. "Want one? Mind if I... ?"

The old man frowned. "Better not. Safety, you see... *chemicals*."

"Course. Slipped my mind. Now, can I have your full name and age?"

"Quilldragon. *Marlin* Quilldragon. Does the age mat... "

"I'll put you as a young seventy."

The old man brightened. "Er... right. Fine."

"Now, your... *device...* " Frank edged into the story casually. Raise an eyebrow these days and they were phone-auctioning exclusive rights round the world, like Etheldreda Goatrider and her unusual brassicas.

"... So what's this machine *do*, Mr. Quilldragon? I'm told by an unrevealable source that it can transport people to the past and the future. *Can* it ?"

"Ah, well... it's not yet possible to go *back* in time with it, but I'm hoping sometime in the *future*, to be able to travel back to the past... if you see what I mean."

Squirt was becoming confused. "Er... right. Well, what exactly can the thing – the *invention* – do for the *present*, so to speak?"

"Well, as I say, I'm still developing it, but I've already had some success with my work. " He looked at the reporter carefully. "I don't know how you found out about it. I've done my best to keep all the elements secret... "

"Can you show it me ?"

"Don't know about *that*. No, I don't think so. It's got a lot of potential, my machine, you see. I wouldn't want crowds of people coming poking round its workings."

Frank had an approach to dealing with such replies. He took out his wallet and waved it just below the old man's beard, like a vet luring a tom cat into the surgery with a pilchard.

"We can come to a financial arrangement on this, Mr. Quilldragon. Shall we say a tenner? That'd be for exclusive rights."

The beard recoiled. "No! It's not a question of money. It's a matter of professional secrets, and intellectual property, and all that kind of thing."

Squirt cast his eyes around the shanty structure. "No, I understand, of course, it's not just about money, Mr. Quilldragon. But there are *facilities* as well."

"Facil... ?"

"Your *equipment*. Can't be easy taking your research forward in these... er... premises." He stabbed a finger at the planking. "Maybe I could put you in touch with a *well-endowed* alma mater, heh heh! A scientific institute that'd give you free run of a laboratory, and perhaps some kind of academic title to go with it." He leaned forwards into the old man's face. "And, of course, Marlin – *may* I call you Marlin? – There'd be travel... invited to lecture on your device at scientific conventions... luxury hotels... pretty girls... You'd develop a following of, how shall I put it? *Academic groupies* very quickly. Not just a *time* machine, Marlin, more of a *bloody-good-time-machine*, eh? He gave the old man a heavy nudge."

"Use of laboratory facilities, you say?"

"*Full* use. With access to libraries... and to the research assistants... young, *nubile* research assistants... "

"Well, I must say it would be easier to pursue my work with the support of a scientific establishment." Marlin glanced at the bulge behind the curtain in the corner. "You see, there's so much more I could do. Are you sure an institute might offer help?"

"*Certain*! I've got contacts, *friends* in the scientific community, *colleagues* in the specialist journals." Frank tapped an assuring finger on the side of his nose, "they know *me* alright. Just mention Squirt, and you're as good as fixed up with a research budget and your pick of pretty Ph.D students. Useful for test-bed operations, eh… eh?"

"As I was saying, Mr. Squirt, if only I could have access to the right kind of facilities, I'm sure I could take my machine to a much more advanced stage… "

"But you'll have to let me *see* it first," said Frank," and we'd better start *now*."

CHAPTER 9

Ked managed to catch the waiter's eye. Just before it fell into the consommé.

The man took the glass marble back gratefully.

"Thank you, Sir, very kind. It's happened a few times before. Some poor fellow broke his tooth on it once. Bloke was worse off than me, really, Sir. You see, it was the last tooth he had. At least I've got one good eye. And I got the false one back when he spat it out with the tooth!" His voice took on a boastful tone, "I lost the real eye in the *Great Reform*, you know."

The man shook his hair from his shoulders, glanced behind him, then leaned forward confidentially.

"The boss's been really good to me, Sir. He let me have this job 'cos I fought with him on the right side." His voice fell to a whisper. "Well, on the *winning* one, anyway." He looked carefully around him again. "*These* days, as you know, most of the waitering's done by mechans, stupid things! They don't realise it, but half the time they're serving up recycled bits of themselves!"

There was a hiatus while Ked choked on his soup.

The waiter waited, then turned again towards Ked obsequiously.

"Is there anything else you wish to have before your main dish, Sir? A little... smoked... er... *lobster* meat is quite often a good adjunct to the Madrilène."

"No, I'll skip it."

"Then your luncheon companion, perhaps?"

The man sitting opposite Ked waved the idea away with a sweep of his hand and said, "Just bring us what we ordered for the next course."

The waiter moved off.

Trying to tell someone's future from the lines on their hands had always struck Ked as a dubious exercise. But he reckoned that guessing at a person's past from the lines on their face might be more revealing, though it'd still only be *guessing*.

The face of Ked's lunch companion gave him the impression of someone who'd once cared a lot about a great many people, but who'd afterwards come to the conclusion that he'd cared too much. The furrows on his brow and the smile-lines under his eyes were still perceptible, but they looked like the relics of another life.

Now, Ked thought, the appearance the man wanted to convey was that he cared little for anyone or anything except his own survival. He laughed sometimes, but it was a laugh that seemed designed to turn away questions and deter attempts at deepening discussion.

With the exception of Ked and a few others, he rarely spoke to people in K*rargxtko by their name, and details of his precise role and position were sketchy. Ked didn't really know him well at all. In fact he couldn't remember exactly how and when they'd first met. Too embarrassed to admit the fact, Ked usually feigned a sort of heartiness at the start of their conversations. The man was known to Ked, and recorded on his phone's memory list, only as 'JT'.

They met occasionally for lunch or dinner, mainly at Ked's suggestion, and chose places which, because of their dreadful food, were reasonably snoop-safe. Although Ked often had difficulty making time for these breaks, he saw them as a chance to scrape away a flake or two of the fear that coated K*rargxtko, and to ask discreetly for advice. It was clear to Ked that JT knew more about the organisation than he could ever imagine.

The surface heartiness with which Ked had begun the

conversation was long since past. He pushed away the soup bowl and resumed their interrupted talk.

"So that's the nub of it, JT. I don't like what's been happening, and I don't want to be a part of what's *about* to happen."

There was a longish silence. The other man looked at him carefully and said, "I think, from the way you've been talking, that *that* is putting it *mildly*."

Ked's hands drubbed at the air nervily. "But, you see, I don't have any choice."

"You *do* have a choice," his companion commented casually. It's more a question of whether you're willing to *face up* to it."

Ked distractedly peeled away his right eyebrow-trim, stared at its black-and-yellow zed-stripes, then fumble-replaced it at a wonky angle. "So what do you think I should do? What would *you* do in *my* place?"

JT looked through the window at a drain-laying mechan working on the pavement outside, and watched it bite sections of pipe to length, stamp them into the trench, and spit at passers-by. "It's *your* decision, Ked. I'm not in your place." He turned his attention back from the window, and stared quizzically at the head of the 'chef' as it peered at them round the half-open door of the kitchen. "Well," he murmured, "I wonder what delights the next course will bring!"

***

Shloom to Eela: Hop ths thng yu gav me's workig ek. Had bite of trub gitteen osed to… oh boll!…

Eelag 2 Shloomger: Received your message (garbled). Push 2nd button on left of back of device (as you look at thing when you've turned it over). This releases fold-out instructions leaflet. Read carefully B4 sending again. End message.

Shlomgr to Eolig: No section B4 to read, but have gone thru hole of instrictions anywaa. Soom to hgave got hing uf it mere or loss. Here is mi furst repeaort (apallgees for spilling. (-sevril butonz just stunck);

1) Arruved oakay but nott used too trivilling via yore devyce aza mortal. sugest u modifie macheen. ride ear was bumpy!

2).This v. odd plase. Straingely... ...

Eelag 2 Shloomger: Your message tailed off. Hope all OK. Think programming of your set is duff. Press green-spotted button so I can try & correct it from this end. May take some time.

*

Shloomger 2 Eelag: Thanks. Yes, it took a while, but that seems to have sorted it out. Now, where was I? Ah yes, as I was saying, this is a very odd place, and – strangely enough – I've never visited it before, at least not as far as I can remember, not even on that 'Grand Tour' which, if you recall, a group of us organised after we'd been to that talk by Borker Spline, the one he gave about the outer reaches of Level... Just a moment, there's a weird kind of buzzing coming from this set...

Eelag 2 Shloomger: The buzzing's from *me*! Get *on* with it! Use shorter style & stick to facts.

Shloomger 2 Eelag: Ok. No need get shirty. This odd place. Some surprisingly advanced technology alongside very basic stuff. Many parts of Thrarrxgor city in fact greatly run down. Unpleasant feeling here. Very dangerous. Whole planet run by that organisation called K*rargxtko you told me about. Very nasty man at top, I overheard someone say.

Eelag 2 Shloomger: Thanks, now please inform of progress in getting yourself into K*rargxtko as we discussed or – if not been able to do that – of infiltrating Thrarrxgor society generally.

Shloomger 2 Eelag: Not much success so far. But have only been here short time. My results to date with various disguises definitely sub-optimal (putting mildly!). This perhaps because not up with latest fashion trends, or maybe cos using wrong get-up for particular occasions. (eg: laughed-out of interview for bouncer's job when turned up without pink inflatable biceps-boosters)...

Eelag 2 Shloomger: Suggest keep eyes widely open and look in newspapers 2c trends & what people wearing in different jobs. In N E case, bouncer's job not right one for your mission. Not likely 2 get much info that way, only black eye.

Shloomger 2 Eelag: Sarc thanks for *valuable advice*!

Eelag 2 Shloomger: Sorry. Only trying to help. Fully understand task not easy. Wish U good luck. Please report on progress – or whatever – soon. Regards, E.

***

"That's... *it*?" Frank eyed the contraption warily as the old man tied back the parted curtains.

"Yes, this is the apparatus, Mr. Squirt. You'll notice I haven't paid much attention to the finish. I think it's more important to concentrate on the functional elements. The aesthetic aspects can be left to a later stage."

Frank wasn't sure about that. To him, the device looked like an assembly of decrepit wooden boxes with rubber tubes leaving and re-entering them at various points. There was a crudely built, hinged door on the top of the main box, which he took to be some kind of cockpit hatch. As far as he could see, it had all been nailed together in one rushed botch-job. Still, it was the inner workings that counted. And Arnold from the dairy had been right so far. Frank decided to leave the photos till later. Maybe his contacts at the art college could do a makeover on the outside of the machine.

"Do you have it working at the moment?"

"It is in fact ready to accept a subject wishing to proceed into the future, Mr. Squirt. Would you like to try?"

Frank had been part wanting, part dreading this. But

the newshound's instinct won. If he could come back with some kind of proof that the thing worked, it'd be Mega Money, *container* trucks of it.

"Okay, Marlin. I'm game for a go."

Saying it was one thing, stuffing himself inside the machine another. The two weren't designed for mutual ease of operation.

Ten minutes later, hideously contorted, Frank was in the passenger compartment.

"How far do you want to go into the future, Mr. Squirt? One day, perhaps, just to start with?"

The reporter bit his lip, not out of nervousness, but simply because he couldn't move his mouth without doing it. He paused, while he struggled to a more speakable position, and agonized over the options.

Maybe better not get too far ahead on the first trip. Might get out of touch. And, after all, could the old git bring him back? But, on the other hand, if this thing *did* work he could use his scoop-experience with it to collect a whole batch of *other* scoops from the future. *All* the stories would be winners. He'd be ahead of the world's news. All he'd have to do would be to come back and write up each story before it broke. After that, if he got exclusive rights to the machine, no one would beat Frank Squirt to it again. *Ever*!

An idea clutched at him. The *horses*! The punter's *dream*! The more he thought about it, the bigger this thing was getting. If only the bloody machine's passenger compartment would *too*!

He mulled the options. One day into the future. *Maybe*. But a *couple* of days'd give him more chance to arrange things properly when he got back. He mumbled into his right armpit.

"Make it a couple."

"Sorry, Mr. Squirt didn't catch that."

"Two days!"

"Right ho. The doorlock of the machine will auto-release when you've progressed that far, and you may then leave the compartment. After you've done that, and found out what you want to find out, you simply re-enter the machine and close the door. When you leave again, you'll find yourself here."

Frank listened to the sound of Marlin closing some handles on the contraption. Somehow the reporter managed to work his hand onto the switch of the recorder lodged in his other armpit. Even though, in his own interests, he might have to keep quiet about the owner and the exact location of the machine, there could be money to be made from a vague story about an eccentric inventor.

"Oh, by the way, *Marlin*, just for background information," the newshound muttered, "do you have any unusual *habits*?"

The question was lost on the old man. He was too busy sealing the hatch.

There was a loud click, and Frank felt himself cut off from the world.

***

The waiter lifted the plates from the table, "I expect you enjoyed the... *steak*. It was from one of a group of obsolete mechans that broke out of a K*rargxtko warehouse a few weeks ago." His face took on the expression of someone doing his customers a great favour. "And you'll be pleased to know we may have some more in soon. There are still a few around in the dealers' yards. They haven't all been culled completely... "

JT's face took on a greenish shade. "*Killed*, you mean!"

"Er, yes, I suppose that's the word Sir. Anyway, they don't do that till they've got a buyer, you see. And then they strip the flesh off the meta-bone... "

"Just take the plates *away*!" JT shouted. The man shrugged and returned to the kitchen.

"It's one of Sculpin's rackets, along with his illicit sales of new cosmetic technology around Thrarrxgor," JT said.

"K*rargxt doesn't know about it, but Sculpin's been cross-breeding mechans for ages, and flogging them off to his own contacts."

Ked took a couple of deep breaths to ease the nausea. "Is that why there are so many feral ones around?"

"Mainly. There have been thousands of break-outs each year, but it's hushed up every time." JT joined his finger-spread hands, touched them thoughtfully against his chin, and changed the subject back to Ked's dilemma. "Now, you were trying to work out what to do… "

Ked unscrewed the whoopee-whistle attachment from his left-nostril air-scoop and toyed with it shakily. "Look, JT – that *choice* you were talking about. The way *I* see it, it's between going on working for K*rargxtko, or leaving without their agreement and then finding that it's not just my *contract* that's being terminated!"

JT gave him a long, straight look, "You don't *have* to end up dead. It's a *risk*, but not a certainty."

Ked dropped the nose-attachment, snatched it from the floor, wiped it on his sweating palm, and then tried to insert it into the wrong nostril. He winced as it pushed a hog-call simulator further up his nose,

"And how, exactly, *am* I supposed to play all this, then?"

"You said you're *uneasy* with the whole setup, right? So the question is: Do you want to try and stop it or *not*? Face it, Ked! Simply leaving K*rargxtko now would be walking away from the chance to stop this grim business, *whatever* happened to you later."

Ked fumbled the whistle back to the vacant nostril and stared at JT. "You mean I should stay in K*rargxtko and try to *louse it up from the inside*?"

The man leaned back in his chair. "Well I think *that's* probably how you could be most effective. For the time being at least."

Ked's fingers started drumming the air wildly. "But what about K*rargxtko's security spooks? They cling tighter than a mermaid's T shirt?"

JT gazed into the distance. “I might be able to help a bit there. I’ve heard they’ll be moving some of the security staff around soon. It could be – because you’ve finished the life-script now – that you’ll be offered some kind of short-term local security role yourself.”

“Local? You mean control of surveillance of the Life-Planning section? And of the *hangar*?”

“Not *that* senior. You *might* be given some security work there, but there’s no way they’ll give you a major control post. Still,” JT paused, “it’s possible they might also put you on Security Admin… organising watchers’ shifts, filling staffing gaps, checking workers’ credentials. You might just find a way of playing it so you can snarl up K*rargxt’s gameplan.”

The words set off a scream of panic in Coot’s head. He sat rigidly for a while, gulping, like some species of frog. He suddenly remembered his stress-sensitive tattoo, and wondered if it had started another break-out. JT hadn’t mentioned anything, but then he’d be too discreet to comment.

Somehow he calmed himself a little. He decided not to look at anything that might throw back his reflection. When he finally spoke again, it was in a considered, careful way.

“Look, JT, *insider-sabotage* is *so* high-risk that just *thinking* about it seems like a terminal experience!”

His luncheon companion gave him a resigned smile. “Like I said, it doesn’t *have* to be fatal Ked, but *yes,* it’s dangerous. And, like I also said, it’s up to *you* .”

“Right, I’ll think about it.”

JT nodded, and looked into the distance again for a while. Then he pulled a small key-holder from his pocket. It had a short chain of round beads attached to it. He threw it onto the table in front of Ked.

Ked glanced at it. “What’s that?”

“Oh, just a key fob with some worry-beads. You can take it if you like.” JT seemed to look again into a far away somewhere. “They’re not for continuous use but, if you get really stressed, you can try squeezing them.”

Ked picked up the key-fob and slid it discreetly into his wrist-wallet.

"By the way," JT added, "those squeeze-beads can deter feral mechans quite well. Your Fangster's immune, but the ferals don't seem to like them at all."

"Thanks. Look, if you don't mind my asking. -You don't have access to our security zone but, from a number of things you've been saying, you seem to know a lot about the project I'm on, and a heap about Sculpin too. Isn't that *also* very kinduv *dangerous*?"

JT's eyes were still far away.

"It *is*. But there's a chance it may not be *quite* so dangerous, if you've arranged for some of your knowledge to escape if anything happens to you."

"And you have... ?"

"Don't ask!"

"... Right!" Ked's hands stopped moving about. His face took on a slightly puzzled expression. "Say, JT, I know the guy's a genius, but it kinduv *surprises* me that Sculpin's got so *far* so *fast* with developing all the stuff he's done. I mean, not just the Viewer, the Intervenor and the Transporter. There are the mechans, and there's all the hardware you can get from K*rargxtko now. He's done that in just a few years. I mean... *okay* ... he's *brilliant*. But to have done it on his *own*... ?"

"Who *says* he did it exactly on his own?"

"You mean he got help from someone?"

JT seemed to be reading the tiny letters on some very distant eye-check card. He finished, and glanced back at Ked. "*Maybe* – in a manner of speaking."

Ked sensed he was getting out of his depth fast. And he was also starting to feel slightly dizzy. He was pleased when his companion, who'd seemed to notice it, changed the subject slightly.

"By the way," JT said casually, "as you say, it's true that most of the technology Sculpin's developed *is* brilliant. But *some* of the things K*rargxtko sells for the home, such as

'Morning Launchers', are less marvellous than they seem."

"What do you mean?"

JT grinned discreetly. "Look, it's supposed to be secret, but those things don't do the chores *themselves*. They simply put the users into a trance and get *them* to do all the work without realising it. Then they wake them up, and when the users come out of the trance, "Whahay!" They think the job's been done for them!"

Ked looked at him in amazement. "Isn't that kind of *harmful*?"

"Well, being stunned regularly that way doesn't do anyone any good. People get to feel very strange."

"How do you know about all thi... ?" Ked stopped himself in his tracks.

And after that, for the rest of their conversation, his companion would only make small-talk.

***

Frank had expected some sort of loud humming noise in his ears, and a dizzy sensation as he accelerated through the time-barrier.

But there was none of that. In fact, in-between his wheezings inside the capsule, he could still make out muffled sounds from elsewhere in the house.

It seemed a long time ago that he'd heard Quilldragon close the door of the room and wander off upstairs. There had been various floorboard creaks and domestic noises since then. Now he heard the sound of a teacup being rattled, and the renewed barking of a dog.

He waited. Presumably the process would take a while to get under way. Perhaps there were chemicals that had to mix and react.

He waited.

Upstairs the man with the white beard settled into his armchair.

*

Frank stirred suddenly. He couldn't feel his right foot. It must have gone to sleep. He realised the rest of him probably had too, at least for a while.

His sense of a faint ticking he'd heard earlier seemed to be becoming more focussed, more intense.

The ticking continued… .

And continued… …

There was a cascade of chimes, followed by a series of dings. Frank counted ten of them..

A horrible feeling spread through those parts of his body he could still feel. He struggled to bang the side of the capsule, but his arms were pinned. He tried twisting himself round so he could find the release-catch on the inside of the door, if there *was* one. But he couldn't move far enough. He realised, in fact, that he couldn't move at all. There was only one thing for it.

He bellowed.

Upstairs, the white-haired man poured himself another cup of tea, handed the dog a biscuit, leaned back again in his chair and contemplated a technical sketch that he had just pencilled. Then, for a few moments, he mused gently on the fact that, busy though he was these days, there were still occasions when time could pass by in an unhurried way.

*

The clock struck eleven.

Frank had managed to move his armpit just a fraction to make his cries for help more audible. But his voice was weakening. The sounds coming from the capsule were more like a feeble braying.

Marlin patted the dog, rose from his chair, and made his way slowly downstairs.

He stood by the box for some moments, listening.

"Is there some kind of a problem, Mr. Squirt?" he asked.

"Get me out!"

"I don't understand. Is your time-journey proving unsatisfactory?"

"Of *course* it's bloo... ". Frank stopped. It wasn't the moment to get awkward. "Look... er... I've been in here for a *while* now, Mr. Quilldragon, and nothing's happened."

"Well, it takes a certain amount of time to get two days into the future."

"How much time?"

"Forty-eight hours, Mr. Squirt."

*

"I did say the device was very much in its early developmental stages... "

Frank didn't bother to turn and answer Marlin. He staggered out of the house and into the night.

The old man watched him go. Then he stood on the doorstep for a few seconds more. A smile spread across his lips. It was less likely he'd be troubled by nosey journalists from now on.

Then he went upstairs to the attic and took the covers off the *real* machine.

CHAPTER 10

Joe unpegged his sleeping bag from the clothes line, threw it into the tent, and told the fleas to take care of it. He was feeling tired, but it was worth it. The day's flying had been the best so far. He'd turn in soon after dinner and start off for the hill again early in the morning.

The smell of his concocted stew drifted across from the fire. He went over and served himself a helping. A moth landed on the side of his plate, edged towards the food, then took off hurriedly.

He looked around him at the dusk-covered landscape. He liked the open country. But the fact that Riska wasn't there was grinding away inside him. He sat and thought about the difference she'd made to his life.

A spark cracked from the fire. Joe prodded a smoking log with his boot. It shifted, opening a cave that pulsed from silver to red. Strange, he thought to himself, how you could sometimes make out faces in the embers. There was one there now, staring at him. It seemed to be the face of a man with a sort of reptilian expression.

And it wasn't smiling.

***

Marlin Quilldragon reached gently into the unfinished, *real* prototype of the inter-universal transporter, and removed a gemstone from the nest of switches and wires to which it had been linked.

He peered at the stone briefly, slipped it into a pocket in his antique sports jacket, and set off down the attic stairs to his small study on the floor below.

Skirting round his slumbering dog, he sat down at his desk, took the gem from his pocket, and inserted it into a different device that looked like a very 'alternative' kind of computer.

"And now, Spanger," he murmured, "Let's have a *closer* look at that mass of information I, er, *acquired* a while ago."

The dog slept on, for a long time too deep in his dreams to notice the changes in his owner's voice. The man's tone, which had been casual to start with, grew more serious, then urgent. The dog opened an eye. Something special was happening.

"There's so *much*, Spanger! I hadn't realised how *important* any of this would be. I need more on that place, *Thrarrxgor*. But I can see it's *grim*!"

Marlin moved away from his home-made 'screen' and glanced at the dog. "It's not just that life *there* is terrible, Spanger. The people running Thrarrxgor are a threat to planets in their own universe and *others* too, including *ours*!" He turned back to the device. "But let's get on with the run-through. Now, where *was* I?"

Spanger forgot about the excitement and went back to sleep. At one point, when Marlin shouted the name 'Joe Outwood', the dog woke again with a jump. But, as the name was repeated more and more, followed by other words that meant nothing to him, he lapsed into his snooze.

Quilldragon's voice grew hushed as he read on, then it edged gradually into silence as he took in the enormity of what he'd learned.

He reached to a pack of paper and fed a thick wad into the stack of electronic jumble that served as a printer. Then he moved his hands quickly around a strange 'keyboard', and pushed a button.

***

Eelag 2 Shloomger: Any progress? How goes?

*

Shloomger 2 Eelag: Sorry about delay in replying. Have not had great deal of free time recently as have had to get series of survival jobs all of which extremely brief and ghastly. One was stacking mechan parts at scrap site. Another, assembling robot, which seemed to know more about the job than I did...

Eelag 2 Shloomger: Thanks. V. interesting, but have you managed to get any kind of contact with K*rargxtko?

Shloomger 2 Eelag: None, apart from K*rargxtko police. They claimed I had to pay for breathing what they call air here. Said nothing's free. Extremely nasty lot. Was only set free after pay-offs amounting to all my earnings.

Have heard vague rumours, though, that K*rargxt has domesday device or even worse. Is said to be absolutely horrible and no one able to stop him doing what he wants. Have you managed to get any further info about Thrarrxgor yourself from crystal ball?

Eelag 2 Shloomger: No. Ball cloudy on that. Relying on you for updates and action. Keep trying. All the best, Eelag.

***

The dog stirred at the rattle of his lead in the hall, yawned, stretched, and rushed down the stairs barking loudly.

"Quiet Spanger! We don't want to wake the whole neighbourhood."

The sky was growing lighter. Somewhere in the distance the tap of stiletto heels on a pavement perforated the edge between night and day.

The dog and its owner turned out of the gate and headed towards the main road.

"Easy Spanger. I know we're in a hurry, but it's a fair stride yet." Marlin weighed the risks. Maybe he'd be seen when he got there. Maybe he was being watched *now*. But probably not. As far as he could make out, the Thrarrxgor Viewer wasn't quite powerful enough yet.

But he couldn't be sure. They'd better get there, deliver the script, and move off fast.

There weren't many people about. One or two on their way to the underground, a few speeding cars. He was surprised he wasn't more tired. All night he'd mulled things over in his mind, building the picture as best he could.

Of course, it would have been nice to have turned in and slept till late morning, or at least till Spanger woke him. But there was no time for that. Scarcely any time left at all. He had to fulfill the errand he'd set himself.

Suddenly the dog-lead swung round, dragged Marlin back a few feet, and held him anchored. He flicked on the lead but Spanger wouldn't budge. There was an urgent smell to check.

Marlin knew the best thing was to humour him. The more you tried to pull him away, the more he'd resist. "Like his *owner*!" Marlin muttered to the air between them.

They set off again. Marlin thought for a moment. If he tried to tell the authorities about this they'd have him in a funny farm before anyone could say 'Looney old git!' But then, if most people knew what *he* did, they'd probably be rushing to find a padded cell where they could head-bang themselves to terms with it, or else they'd just sit around helplessly waiting for it to start. And that would turn Earth into even more of a sitting target for *K*rargxt* and *Sculpin*.

That was why it was essential, for the moment, that only a few people should know about this. He called Spanger to heel as they came to a pedestrian crossing. Then he started to move forwards.

The car came round the corner fast. Its driver didn't expect him, didn't see him till he was a few feet away. He had no time to brake.

The smell saved the old man. The exact order of factors was: post supporting crossing-beacon; smell at base of post; dog; taut dog-lead.

The car missed Marlin by a fraction of an inch. His raincoat belt, which had been hanging unfastened, bounced off the nearside wing. The buckle hit him in the chest. He saw the driver shrug as he sped on.

Marlin gave the dog a fur-ruffling pat, then felt his own chest. It was okay. Maybe there'd be a small bruise, but that was all. "Come on Spanger!" he shouted, "It'll take more than *that*!"

His mind raced back to the threads of his thoughts. – Yes, as few people as possible should find out. But, if there was to be any hope of preventing this world-terminal disaster, there *was* one person who had to know *now*!

And he'd have to be prepared to work with him, to trust him, to take risks. To use his wits.

Marlin plucked at his beard. Could he convince him of the danger he and the planet were in? The best way was to deliver the envelope now without any message. The man would have to read the script and see the danger for himself. But then maybe he'd treat it as a hoax. The old man took in sharp breaths of morning air, hoping the person wouldn't make the mistake of interpreting the whole thing that way. What chance would he stand without him? Would he help? Was he *up* to the job? He had to know soon. *Very* soon!

He quickened his stride.

*

As his master slipped open the gatecatch, Spanger added the hedge to his trail of widdled waypoints, then followed Marlin up the short path to the door.

The old man quietly lifted the flap on the letterbox, slid the large envelope inwards, and waited till he heard it land. Then he turned quickly back towards the gate.

Spanger, who – a couple of streets back – had already sniff-located an odd sock lying in this particular garden, gathered it in his teeth and followed his master back.

Marlin glanced at him behind, and saw the sock.

"Silly dog! It's amazing what you pick up! Let's get on home!"

***

The breeze pushed steady and straight into the cliff. Fifty feet above its edge, Joe flew the liftband, the wind roaring in his ears, the wires and the gliderframe adding their music as they cut through the rising air.

Sheep were grazing below on a stretch of turf between the hillcliff and the shore. The wind brought up scents from the nibbled grass and, now and then, a taste of saltspray snatched from the sea-roar.

Further along the ridge, to the north west, two buzzards were riding the glass wave, calling to each other.

Joe pulled strong deep breaths of it all into his lungs.

This was it! This was what he liked!

That big, raw, slice of freedom.

On the other side of the hill, a blue motorbike throated its way towards him, up a thread-road through the grassland. Beneath the rider's helmet, a torrent of black hair played over shoulders encased in a dark leather jacket.

A cloth bag attached to a small luggage-rack on the bike contained food and drink for a picnic for two. A plastic bag, also fixed to the rack, contained a couple of credit-card sales letters, and a newspaper with stories about a mad axeman, a gas-depot explosion and a freak flood.

The plastic bag contained something else.

It contained an envelope with a script inside it that set out the past and very short future life of Joe Alexander Outwood.

CHAPTER 11

Shloomger 2 Eelag: Thought you might like another progress report. But first, how goes with you?

*

Shloomger 2 Eelag: Are you there?

*

Eelag 2 Shloomger: Yes, sorry for delay in reply. Was working on upgrade of ball. They sent the wrong patch.

Shloomger 2 Eelag: Why need patch?

Eelag 2 Shloomger: Don't like to tell you this, but ball got brief full picture of Zunddertokk (only caught sight of shadow before). Full picture nearly wiped out ball (cloud of nasties always round Z's image). Had to put in anti-viral sub-ball. But that insufficient, hence patch.

Shloomger 2 Eelag: Have you right patch now?

Eelag 2 Shloomger: Yes. After much messing they sent right one. Zunddertokk not re-appeared since, but concerned he may do so in ball fairly soon, and then sometime after that in person. Anyway, how goes?

Shloomger 2 Eelag: Had more short job-tests. Would you like to hear about them?

Eelag 2 Shloomger: Perhaps not relevant, but please describe very briefly, to give idea of your situation.

Shloomger 2 Eelag: Failed first job-test for assistant wino.

Eelag 2 Shloomger: Sounds horrible. What did job involve?

Shloomger 2 Eelag: Fortunately, job did not involve me drinking, seeing what the winos are swigging round here. Work was to fetch bottles, open them, be sworn at, and have empties thrown at me.

Eelag 2 Shloomger: Why failed test?

Shloomger 2 Eelag: Dropped bottle-opener down drain. Worse thing could have done, apparently. Had to leave test area fast.

Eelag 2 Shloomger: Have you tried job vacancies further up scale?

Shloomger 2 Eelag: Yes. Did test-morning at dry cleaning shop.

Eelag 2 Shloomger: How was?

Shloomger 2 Eelag: Business was racket. *Two* shops really. D-C shop took in clothes, fast-cleaned them and 'lent' them to short-rental dress-hire shop on other side of town. Ages before clients got them back.

Eelag 2 Shloomger: Why didn't get job?

Shloomger 2 Eelag: Made mistake. Took clothes to wrong dress-hire shop. Were running same racket but wouldn't hand clothes back to me. Were immensely unpleasant. I did not return to D-C shop. Thought it unwise.

Eelag 2 Shloomger: Anything else re job-hunt?

Shloomger 2 Eelag: Yes, have tried others.

Eelag 2 Shloomger: Fast-forward to the last two, then.

Shloomger 2 Eelag: Last-but-one was a job for sweeper in hairdresser's. Quite a fancy place. Even the broom had highlights.

Eelag 2 Shloomger: And?

Shloomger 2 Eelag: Swept customer's long-haired mechan lapdog into rubbish chute. Easy mistake to make. Was bred to be flat. Looked like discarded ponytail.

Eelag 2 Shloomger: And the last attempt?

Shloomger 2 Eelag: Was sales job.

Eelag 2 Shloomger: Any joy?

Shloomger 2 Eelag: No. Sold nothing. Job was for back-street inventor launching new breakthrough private network phone device.

Eelag 2 Shloomger: Why no sales?

Shloomger 2 Eelag: Nobody wanted to buy first one. No one they could call. Difficult to get thing started, really.

Eelag 2 Shloomger: Let's move on quickly. What your current plans?

Shloomger 2 Eelag: Will keep trying. Intend to go on new search for work this evening around night-life area. Parts of it very seedy, but hope may get some kind of starter job there.

Eelag 2 Shloomger: This all proving more difficult than we thought. Good luck, and take care of yourself. Remember you now mortal.

Shloomger 2 Eelag: Becoming increasingly aware of it. Will do my best. Keep smiling Eelag. C U sometime I hope.

***

"They didn't kick up about you having Sunday off, then?"

"They couldn't this time, Joe. I've done way over the maximum hours this month."

The wind pushed ripples through the grass and tugged at the paper napkins under the sandwiches. A mile or so out to sea, a blue hole opened in the cloud. Light fell onto the water, making a patch of bright waves that danced like a childhood memory.

Riska could see clumps of seaweed below them, left by the falling tide. Its scent came up on the breeze. She put her hand on Joe's.

"Anyway, even if they hadn't agreed, I'd *still* have come."

They stared at the bright waves for a long time. Then Joe looked at Riska. Her face was as fresh and unworried as it always seemed to be.

"Aren't you tired from the trip?"

No. I got a really early train down to my aunt's this

morning. But I had a couple of hours sleep there. Good of her to lend me the bike."

"Is that the aunt with the vintage submarine in her driveway?"

" No, that's Horteellia. I stayed at Rye's this time. She's the one with the giant flugelhorn. She tows it around behind that ice-cream tricycle of hers."

"Bloody hard work, I should think".

"She manages. It's got a sort of trolley under it. And it works a lot better than the usual jingles. "Brings 'em all out," she says. Anyway, she does good business." The wind ruffled Riska's hair. She shook it back over her shoulders. "Oh by the way, Joe, I got you a paper... "

She brought over the plastic bag and handed the paper to Joe. "It's one from a few days back. Some grisly news. A bloke went crazy with an axe. There was a big gas explosion at a depot, and a flash seaport flood somewhere. They're saying no one predicted it."

Joe glanced at the paper. "Yup, looks grim."

Riska thought for a moment. "Oh, and there's a bit of post, and something else too. *That's* it. A large envelope marked 'URGENT', with your name hand-written on it. It was on the mat with the letters when I went round to water your plants yesterday."

"Right... Thanks... I'll put it all in my bag and check it later."

Riska looked at the waves the wind was making through the grass on the hill. "The breeze is really good, Joe. Are you going to fly again in a while? I've got my camera. I could take some pictures."

"Okay. But let's finish the sandwiches first, eh? And then... "

*

It's difficult to get inside the mind of a bird, unless you're an Upper-Leveller with the right kind of technique. But, from the sounds the buzzards were making, they didn't seem impressed, even though Joe was soaring well.

Maybe they felt creatures of his size should have been lifting sheep clean out of the fields at one swoop, rather than hanging around all day.

The motorbike had gone from the hill below. On the grass, near where it had been, was a holdall. Inside that, next to some clothes, a newspaper, a pile of letters and a pot of yoghurt, was a future with Joe's name on it.

Ever had the feeling there was something you meant to do... but... ?

CHAPTER 12

Ked knew the stress was getting to him. Grux sensed it too as they headed home through a network of dark side-streets.

To add to Ked's worries, some K*rargxtko food he'd eaten earlier was disagreeing with him, and the food was winning the argument. On top of that he could see, from his reflection in the control panel, that his tattoo, which had eased off some time ago, was starting to make a horrible comeback.

He glanced through the Fangster's screens at the narrow pavements. After his encounters with the K*rargxtko police mechans he'd decided to try other routes home. Fears of meeting Sculpin's Fire-Tiger had kept him from riding the main rat-races again, but the problem was that every new backway he tried seemed even grimmer than the last.

Along the streets, small groups of people dawdled from bar to bar. Here and there, drifters – most of them already seriously pixellated – negotiated with bouncers in dark doorways to get into places that would break them up completely.

Ked asked himself if he was in any more control of his life than they were of theirs. He turned down a dark street. Suddenly, for no clear reason, Grux slowed. The Fangster's body stiffened. Bristles rose on its outer walls. It let out a low growl, horribly shaking the cabin, and Ked's gut.

"What the gritts *is* it Grux? What the… ?"

The mechan went silent, cut its lights and moved slowly backwards till it was level with a narrow gap between two buildings, then edged quickly into it.

The cabin lights faded. A nasal-sounding advisory whisper, installed by the breed-builder, told Ken to 'Click L 2R7L4 for Camouflo-smell option.' He fumbled with the stick, nearly setting off Aggro-Shriek.

Anyone close to the mechan, with strong night-vision, would have noticed thousands of tiny holes opening in its skin.

There was a series of low hisses as the mechan spread scents that matched the smells around it. Ked gagged on his next breath and cursed the Fangster's designers. *Yeah*! They'd thought of everything. Except, of course, stopping the smell seeping into the cabin!

He tried dealing with the stench by guessing what was in it. Maybe three parts dead and very close coypu-mechan, two parts fractured sewer, one part sleeping wino.

There was a brief noise from somewhere further along the street, then silence. Ked took a chance and deployed an infrar side-scope that jutted from the Fangster just far enough to get a view of what was happening.

For what seemed ages things were completely still.

Then he saw them, moving slowly towards him.

It was a large group. And they were big and ugly.

He'd heard of feral mechan-packs, but not *seen* any before. And before his conversation with JT he'd not understood how they'd formed. All mechans, even special models, were supposed to be K*rargxtko-approved.

After what JT had told him about the breeding-rackets, he'd discreetly asked some of his colleagues if they knew anything about it. Some of them had said they'd heard rumours of back-street body-tuning, rapid in-breeding, even full gen-tech re-makes. If this had happened big-time, it would explain how the packs had grown so fast.

All he could do was wait, and hope the gang would pass by.

He suddenly remembered the 'special features' blast-pistol that he'd bought from a stranger one night outside the K*rargxtko beast park. He could see its multi-control handle poking out from a skin-fold in the dashpanel. The problem was he'd no idea how to use it without blowing him and Grux away with the whole street.

Best thing was to stay quiet and completely still.

It wasn't easy. His fingers were itching to work the Fangter's control stick. He peered carefully through the front screen.

The gang was getting nearer.

***

In the Intervenor Preparations Room the Operations Manager gazed boredly at the small cube of space in front of him. Bernie didn't care much for his staff even at the best of times, but he tried to hide it by faking an interest in their lives.

He was glad, at least, that Juncus had called him on the cube rather than coming to see him personally. Even so, listening to him was becoming more and more of a pain.

"Did I tell you about that great crap I had three weeks ago, Bernie?... "

"No. I don't think we need ... "

"Of course it wasn't what I'd describe as *life*-changing, like the one I told you about last year, but I feel I should have given it a better write-up in my journal... "

"Juncus... "

"Which reminds me, Bernie, I've been meaning to *show* you those write-ups. It's not *everyone* I'd let see them. Only people who really appreciate... "

"That's enough, Juncus... "

"And, by the way, Bernie. Do you know some people have actually been whispering that I've got a *bowel* obsession!"

"You don't *say*!"

"Yes, I know. It's a *terrible* thing for anyone to suggest! It's *not* an obsession, it's the *real thing*. I *love* my bowels. I'm *crazy* about them!"

"Sure seems so, Juncus. And I hope you and them will be very happy. Now, as I've got you in the cube, let's talk about your *immediate job-content upgrade...* "

"You mean the extra work you've dropped on me? The stuff Glype's supposed to do?"

"He's called in sick, Juncus. Some feeble story about stress, but... " Bernie waved a hand frantically towards the giant schedule hologram that stretched down from the hangar ceiling. "*Now's* your big chance to show just", he almost winced at his own hype, "what you're *made* of."

"I'd prefer it if Ked could show me what to do first... "

"It's *not* his area, Juncus. Anyway, he's gone home."

"But It'll be hard doing Glype's job all on my own... "

Bernie glared at the back-lit syntho-dewdrop hanging from Juncus's left nostril. "*Look*, once Sculpin gives the order, we have to start the show *big-time*! That'll mean Intervenor switch-on, brain control of that bloke... Joe, and *action*. In fact, the *full works*!" He watched the underling's dewdrop mute from silver through to pale green. "So we're testing the Viewer *Now*! *Without* Glype! And *you're* going to do it Juncus!

"Er... right, Bernie, *right*."

*

Juncus walked through the Intervenor Preparations Room, down some stairs, and onto the floor of the hangar. He had the feeling the Intervenor was somehow *leering* at him as he walked past it. He was glad, at least, he'd be working on the Viewer and not on *that*.

The Intervenor was immense. Not as huge as the hangar that housed it, but massive, all the same. It was a creepy machine. Looking like a collection of giant, oddly-shaped boxes, it towered over Juncus and the staff scattered at their work stations around the hangar floor.

Juncus jumped as a scavenger mechan brushed past his foot, scurrying to beat another mech-rat to a food scrap dropped by one of the workmen.

The Intervenor had been assembled by Bernie and the technical staff using instructions sent by Sculpin. None of them dared admit it, but they hadn't the slightest clue as to how it really worked. Putting it together had given them enough headaches. While Ked had asked them questions about it, the last thing anyone in the tech team wanted to do was to probe into what lay at the heart of its power.

To the left of the Intervenor was the Viewer. Above it, bounded only by the walls and roof of the building, was a vast space into which it projected 3-D image-cubes of scenes from other universes.

It was in this space that Sculpin's horrible image also appeared occasionally to give orders.

Juncus installed himself at the Viewer Desk's control panel. It was mind-blowingly more complex than his work-station at Minor Events Manip. Rows of lights winked at him. Buzzing noises came and went. More ominously, some stayed.

He could vaguely hear Bernie, over at his central control desk, mumbling about being messed around with the countdown. He looked over towards him and saw him jabbing angrily at various keys and switches on an enormous panel.

Juncus turned his attention back to his own control desk.

The buzzing above him grew louder. It was nagging him to do *something*. He tried desperately to recall what he'd noticed Glype doing a few days before in what he guessed must have been a trial-run. He couldn't be certain, but maybe if he pushed... was it the *third* button from the right?... Oh, what the gritts... He'd do it *anyway*...

***

Ked felt he'd been there far longer than the current flavour of his time-lapse lozenge was telling him.

It seemed like hours ago that the mechan gang had switched direction and headed off somewhere else. Off up another side-street, Ked guessed. But he couldn't be sure. Maybe they were planning a surprise attack. Grux was showing no signs of wanting to move on. He wondered whether he should flick the control-stick and start shifting him out.

A full body tremor shook the Fangster. Suddenly Ked saw that the mechan gang had split into two groups which, having temporarily withdrawn, were now closing on them from the front and behind. This pincer tactic was much liked by the group. Besides tearing prey to pieces, it was one of the few things the ferals liked at all.

A horrible thought ran through Ked's mind. Maybe all his past life had been leading to him finishing as a heap of mechan-droppings. Worse still, since they'd mug him before they ate him, he'd die *broke*.

Something else surged into the whistling panic that had begun to swirl through his brain. The *screech*. The oil-belching screech of feral mechans as they prepared to charge.

***

Juncus stared at the giant cube carved out of the space above him. Pouring from it, the sunlight of a late afternoon played across the faces of the staff below. The rustle of leaves, a blackbird's call, the distant sounds of buses and shouts of kids echoed round the hangar walls. He wasn't awed that the scene was happening live in another world in another universe. He was amazed that he'd hit the right buttons to get the thing working at all.

The smell of a freshly weeded flower bed filled the hangar. The scene within the space began to shift. The scents too. Juncus pushed aside the fashion nasal-dewdrop and sniffed. There was something else in the air now. The smell of soap, maybe shampoo, drifting from a half-open window.

A door was opening, a beautiful girl in a dressing-gown stood just inside. Bernie's voice cut across the hangar. "Who's *she*? Does *Ked* know about her?" No one answered.

Juncus saw a man with a large travel bag walking up to the open door. He threw the bag down and put his arms round the girl.

Two blinding beams of light shot from the Intervenor Memory-Register Unit near Bernie and stabbed the cube. At the points where they struck, two targeting icons locked onto the embracing figures.

"*Wooee*!" Bernie shouted. "We got 'em. They're *ours*!"

***

Ked recalled having seen an ad somewhere for a virtual cemetery where you could book a plot with a giant tombstone on which, before snuffing it, you could record in letters of gold what a tremendous bloke you'd been. He wondered whether to call up his holognome and dictate a text. The problem was he'd have to pay for it upfront. And even if they really *did* craft it out after he'd gone, he couldn't be sure it would last. There were thousands of viruses out there that re-wrote stuff. He might end up memorialised as a total *proot*.

His mind was pulled back fast to the savagery breaking out around him.

Grux wasn't going down any mechan's gullet without a fight. The Fangster was struggling to ward off the ferals with a combo of acid-spitting from his front release-valves and huge jets of flame from his exhaust vents. At the same time he was countering attacks to his flanks by spinning up his wheel-claws to max revs and shoving them into the ferals' teeth.

The gang-members had encircled the Fangster and were hyping themselves up with some pre-kill ritual roaring.

Ked clung to a hand-grip, peered through a view-slit in the shield Grux had drawn over the screen, and found himself looking straight down the leader's throat into the fire of its gut. He'd been hoping at least to get some kind of revenge by giving it heartburn, but that was clearly a non-starter.

A claw reached round the side of the Fangster and tore its way into the cabin. It snapped around within a hairsbreadth of Ked's face, then finally withdrew, ripping away one of Grux's wing-scopes and hurling it into the feral's mouth as an appetiser.

Grux made a desperate thrust at the mechan. The jolt shook Ked's body and made his arm flail out, shaking JT's gift from his wrist-wallet and shooting it out through the gash in the Fangster's side.

In the instant he saw it go, Ked remembered what JT had told him about the beads on the key fob. He watched the fob spin around on the ground and come to a stop well out of recovery-range. Then a new contortion from Grux sent his head crashing against the Fangster's meto-bone drive-casing.

***

E 2 S: Have thought about your plans and am concerned about your safety in area you currently in, as you described parts of it as 'very seedy'. How goes?

*

E 2 S AGAIN: Please let know if alright. Await reply.

*

S 2 E: When you say 'Await reply', are you telling me to await a further reply from you, or do you mean 'I await reply' (ie: from me) ?
E 2 S: I was expecting reply from *you*, of course.
S 2 E: Well, at this end, things somewhat below okay level. In fact place here awful. Very run-down area, with gangs of mechans (which I'll tell you more about sometime if get chance) roaming streets.
E 2 S: Suggest you move on. Very unlikely will get significant job or make useful K*rargxtko contacts where are.
S 2 E: Just moment... Terrible noise coming from somewhere nearby. Will go and investigate.

E 2 S: Advise you not to. From what you say, you are in a place of considerable danger.

*

E 2 S: AGAIN: Are you there? Please let me know if you alright. *I* await *your* reply.

***

A short distance from the fight, next to a large broken bottle of K*rargxtko gin, in the debris of a demolished house, a reeking blanket stirred. The one thing going for it was that its reek kept the ferals away. From the folds of the blanket the head of a senior wino emerged.

He was a wino who'd dropped out from other wino-zones in Thrarrxgor city to this particular one, considered by many to be the piss-artists' finishing-school. The head – surprised it had emerged at all – turned and, in the glow from the mechans' fire-guts, watched the action unrolling on the nearby street.

The wino had already witnessed many of these incidents. Mechan gangs formed and re-formed continually, as their leaders were challenged, overthrown and eaten. But, apart from these 'family squabbles', their day-to-day, night-to-night, role of carving up anything that took their fancy was fairly straightforward. So the wino wasn't surprised when he saw the nastiest of the local gangs preparing its evening meal.

What *did* surprise him, a moment later, was the sight of someone walking up to the action, swiftly sussing out who was doing what to whom, and stepping in between the mechan leader and its victim.

It surprised the mechan leader too. Its metabone jaw fell open and hung gaping for what to the wino – who judged all time by the length of pauses between gulps of hooch – seemed a seriously long double-take.

From their different places, dazed for different reasons, the wino and Ked watched the newcomer profit from the mechan's moment of disbelief by taking off his jacket and shoving it into its air intake.

The mechan was even more astonished by this, but for less long. Before the other gang members had sidled round to see if they could eat their choking leader prior to moving on to the newcomer and then to the Fangster and its contents, the mechan coughed out the clothing with a sheet of flame that lit the night sky.

Shloomger recalled that the last time he'd jumped sideways to dodge a fireball like that had been during a premature ignition at the all-lunar-night fireworks party on Kragular 16.

As he speed-reviewed the happy landing he'd made next to the hostess that night, he saw his foot was coming down on a bolt that looked as if it had once held a wing-scope on the Fangster behind him.

His foot careered away sideways.

As he fell to the ground and watched the mechans move in, he had to admit to himself that this mortality thing was just too short-term to recommend.

CHAPTER 13

"Could you find the smoked trout, and put it on some kind of dish?"

It was funny, Joe thought, how Riska could excite him with such simple things. It was the *way* she'd said it. In fact it was the way she said or did *anything.*

He glanced round his flat. It had a strange air of tidiness. But he could live with it. And he could live very happily with its cause.

"In the fridge", she pre-answered through a trial mouthful of lettuce.

"Er... Right."

He headed for the dump-salvaged steel wreck he'd shared various places with. He loved the way it gurgled and belched, and how it startled visitors with its sudden shaking spasms.

Before Riska had cleared it, some of the stuff inside had been a part of his life almost as long as the fridge had. When he'd brought it back from the tip it had had a box of eggs stuck to its middle shelf. He'd never got to opening it, but it had been a good land-mark to where he'd stored stuff. Soon a lot of other things had gained fixed 'founder' status. When she'd first opened the fridge door, Riska had suggested he hire it out as a rotting shock-horror-show. He'd pointed out that, though the food had best-by deadlines, none of it had worst-by dates. Now, it had been emptied, sterilised and carefully re-stocked. But he wondered how much longer she'd put up with the ancient piece of equipment.

He made towards it, then swerved round the wood-and-metal contraption he thought of as a kitchen table, and kissed her.

"Thanks for coming here before I got back, and... breathing life into the place."

She stopped conjuring the salad and laughed, "I'm no miracle-worker Joe, but I thought it needed some help."

He headed back to the fridge and took out the shrink-wrapped fish.

"Ninety per cent of success now is getting stuff out of the pack", he murmured, jabbing the plastic with his thumbnail. It resisted. He jabbed again. It still wasn't playing. He tried a doomed slitting movement with a blunt knife along a top edge.

Curious, he thought, how certain things were trickier when someone was watching you. Drop-aiming pebbles in pubs wasn't a problem when there were spectators around, not even cliff take-offs with a hang glider. But for some reason, with things like this, it was different.

"You'd better stop looking at me while I'm doing this", he said. "I'm getting stage-fri... "

Then he realised Riska wasn't there. She'd gone into the living room. He could hear her starting to draw the curtains.

He still had a feeling he was being watched.

He struggled on with his task. He dropped the packet, picked it up, pinned it to a chair with his knee, tried again with a sharper knife, and slit his thumb instead of the plastic.

"You okay?" Riska shouted.

"Yup. Fine. No trouble."

"It's just the swearing made me think maybe... "

"Nope. Fine." He clutched his hand under the cold tap.

"Well that's alright then, Joe. Now, let's see... I think that's nearly sorted things out... "

She came in, picked up a vase of flowers and went back to the living room. "Right", she called to him, "I'll go back and finish my shower now."

***

Ked hit the door-release. There was a chance he could drag the bloke into the Fangster before the Mechans ripped into him, but it'd probably just win them both a few more terror-filled instants.

It seemed to Shloomger that the rest of his life was being fed to him in shrinking fragments of a second. He had a strong feeling the next minute was far away in a sealed jar marked 'Unused.'

As he shifted, to find out whether his ankle was broken or just twisted, he saw Ked's exit start well but fail, as the Fangster, rammed by a feral mechan, rolled over on the side Ked had been getting out of.

Shloomger guessed the forebears of the feral Mechan nearest him had dug roads. A prong punched a deep hole in the place he'd just moved from. He saw the arm re-aim its metal point for a terminal shot, and – in the corner of his eye – glimpsed the shadows of other mechans moving in with even sharper things.

Using the seatbelt to drag himself upright again, Ked watched from the Fangster. It was just a matter of which of the next moments would be the bloke's last. And, after that, the gang weren't going to break off for sorbets and light chat before turning on him and Grux.

Shoon, for escape ideas, tried speed-recalling tricky spots he'd been in that were a bit like this one. There had been that time he'd drawn the short straw and stood in for the wounded Fleeber Skrang as a strapped-to-the-spinning-board-assistant to a knife-thrower on a rowdy night at the Stag and Proton. But *then* the thrower – incompetent though he was – had at least tried to *miss* him. And the fact that Shloomger had been immortal had rather taken away the thrill for the audience.

His mind raced across other events to his recent adventure with Eelag and the analogiser. It wasn't exactly the same scenario but there were similarities. And for that brief time he'd been mortal too. "We jump," Eelag had said.

Though there was no cliff-edge visible, it occurred to Shloomger that maybe, if he put everything into launching himself sideways with his good foot, he'd win a few more micro-secs to come up with a better idea.

In a slowed-down kind of viewing of what he knew was happening fast, Shloomger watched the re-raised prong poise itself, then turn slightly till it was directly above him.

He gave the moment his best available leap, and wondered if, during his short time in the air, the mechan would skewer him in one. Pity there was no analogiser stop-button to land on. If he fell on anything, it'd probably be another painful piece of stuff from the Fangster.

It *was*. Shloomger's right shoulder-blade came down hard on something just as the feral's prong pierced another hole an inch to his left. And in the same moment, as well as the crash of the hole-punch, he heard another noise, a brief, high-pitched shrieking sound underneath him.

He dragged his mind from the stabbing-pain in his shoulder, and was surprised to see that the mechan, instead of raising its prong again, was keeling over sideways.

By way of an afterthought, Shloomger twisted himself around and felt along the ground for what he'd landed on.

*

As the Fangster heaved itself upright, Ked kept his grip on the strap. For a while he didn't realise what was happening outside.

Then, like the afterglow of a Bung Rat sun-downer, a warm feeling began to run through him. It started somewhere in his middle, moved outwards, and bounced off the edges of his body. The feeling roared to him that he was *alive*! It was the din outside his head that had died.

In its place there were faint whimpering sounds. They weren't coming from Grux. Ked peered through the

Fangster's screens and focussed back on the gang. The place looked like a mechan-knacker's yard. Crawling across the ground, as if they'd been hit by some multi-targeting lightning strike, the ferals were an almost pathetic sight. He watched them drag themselves away.

He suddenly realised he'd forgotten the bloke, who was now sitting on the ground looking curiously at a key-fob in his hand.

He got out and walked over to him.

***

Juncus watched carefully as the picture in the cube of space above him changed from Joe's kitchen to the interior of a bathroom. The Viewer-eye moved around the room, focussing on various objects. Juncus's nose began to quiver. It quivered rarely, but when it did it could out-vibe any hamster's. He hoped the others wouldn't notice. No, probably not. They were too busy at their workstations.

The sound of running water stopped.

The shower-curtains parted.

Three of Juncus's colleagues fainted. One of them grabbed a nearby length of cable as he fell, and dragged it down.

Juncus had the impression, in the instant before the whole system crashed, that a beautiful woman had been stepping out of the shower.

But he hadn't really been paying attention. His mind had been somewhere else. His whole body quivered as he recalled what he'd seen.

A design of bidet unknown to him, with a *mahogany surround* to it!

***

"*Waywahwayee*, team! Are *you* lucky! *No comeback* on the breakdown!"

The staff in the hangar stopped throwing cable off-cuts at the mechan rats, and listened to Bernie.

"Sculpin's *passed* the first Viewer-run, and just wants checks on the wiring. He'd been called away to K*rargxt when the power blew, and he *missed* when you grintzters blew it! So, blow-outs or *no* blow-outs, that was a *winner*! We *tracked* them! We *focussed* on them!"

Juncus looked up from his private journal and heard someone ask Bernie boot-lickingly about the future work programme.

It pushed the Ops manager to a new peak of hype. He spun round and pointed wildly at the man. "Say, that's a *wow* enquiry, friend! Sculpin says to hold off Viewer ops till the wiring checks are through. Then, once they *are*, we start when we're told. And I reckon that'll be in a *big* kind of *soon*! Then, we go full on with the Viewer. *And* with the Intervenor too!"

*

Riska came out of the bathroom and began loosely tying her dressing gown belt. Joe put his head out of the kitchen doorway. "We've heaps of time", he said, "can lunch wait?"

She stopped, and looked at the dressing gown.

"Why knot?" she said.

***

"How's that ankle?"

Shloomger waggled his foot around on the floor of the Fangster.

"Sort of okay. I think it's just a bit twisted."

Ked eyed the sprawled shambles of mechans, and kept a firm grip on the joystick. Astonishingly, apart from the gash in his side, Grux seemed to have survived the fight without serious damage. But Coot knew he needed to stop the Fangster having a go at them. He'd heard wounded ferals could sometimes find strength from somewhere deep inside them and turn even more vicious than usual if they were attacked.

He glanced at Shloomger again. "How long do you reckon they'll stay like that?"

"No idea. I'm sort of new round here."

Ked tried not to gape."Oh, right... It's just that, from the way you were operating, you seemed kind of well clued-up about them."

"Not really."

"Oh, I see... Right."

There was a short silence.

Ked drew in a slow breath, "There's no guarantee that key fob thing'll work again. It looks knackered now. It might just be a one-time gizmo. I think we'd better pull out fast."

"Yup. Good idea. "Shloomger thought for a moment. "By the way, you wouldn't know of any jobs going in Thrarrxgor, I suppose?"

"Odd time to ask, but I *might* be able to help. Looking for something in security, by any chance? I reckon you'd be ace at that." Ked looked around, chose a suitable out-route and set Grux on it.

The Fangster shot a burst of back-flame at the ferals. Then the faithful mechan, its tattoo-saturated master and its new passenger were gone.

***

Boontrak stirred briefly back into something nearer consciousness. He tried to focus his mind. The part of it that he *could* vaguely focus told him the rest of his mind was on hold. It also reminded itself that being spread around the stones of a cave was a crazy state to be in, and that having some of the stones regularly taken away by that strange bloke wasn't helping.

What was more, Boontrak had a stronger feeling that two of the stones he was in really *were* in another universe.

It occurred to him that it might be a good idea to do a kind of run-through of where all his various pieces were.

It wasn't easy. Turning around inside the stones gave

him a strange, dizzy sensation. It was a huge pity, he thought, that no one was around to re-build his super brain. The more he thought about the strange bloke who sometimes came to see him, the less he trusted him.

He went on with the next stages of his test, working his way through the rocks that had been taken away, and then groping into the two remote pieces. They were so tiny, it was a bit like checking two of your finger tips to find out if you could still feel them. He sensed that he was still fairly well connected with them. But he thought it would be good if those two far-out stones could somehow get *nearer* to each other, so that one of them could boost the other by transferring its power into it.

He wasn't up to any super-communications job, but he found he could just manage to send the smaller of the two remote stones a vague squeezed-together message about his idea.

Then, drowsy from the effort of the whole exercise, he fell asleep again.

***

"S'pose I'd better sort this bag out before it goes critical", Joe murmured.

He knew, despite his generally improved self-organizing, that he'd been kind of lagging with the sorting-out-the-bag thing. There were waftings from inside. Staleness and mystic rotting. It couldn't be left. Well, it *could*, in fact. It was a tempting option.

He'd done it before. But bags he'd ignored had taunted him. They'd dared him not to open them, and ripened steadily for months, raising the stakes till, sometimes, he'd thrown in the towel. At least, he would have done if it hadn't still been in the bag. Other sadder, unopened, cases had ended up on the local tip.

This bag caught his glance and somehow offered him ten quid to leave it closed. He tensed, wondering how sacks could will themselves to the dump. He met its call and raised it ten again. The bag doubled it.

He paused. He could walk away. There were bigger, more urgent things. Like a football match to be skillfully watched, a paper to be scanned yawningly.

The bag doubled again. Bags' rules allowed it to call twice.

Joe countered by double-pausing.

Even outside the bag the atmosphere was unbearable.

"I'll see you!"

The bag tried the jammed-zip trick, but it was no good.

*

Riska paused in her efforts at giving intensive care to one of Joe's house-plants. "I *did* give you the big envelope that came while you were away, *didn't* I Joe?"

"Yup, you gave it me at the flying site."

"Ah, yes, I remember now," she said diplomatically. "I thought I'd better give it you there in case it was something important. It had '*URGENT*' written on it, I think."

Joe stared at the yoghurt-stained envelope he'd taken from the defeated bag.

"As a matter of fact I haven't got round to looking at it yet. It's probably not important." He picked it up. "Still, I suppose I'd better check it anyway… "

***

The figure under the quilt rolled over onto one side and finally stopped snoring. For a short moment, apart from the sound of his gentle breathing, there was silence. In his downstairs basket on the ground floor below, Spanger slept soundly, oblivious to what was about to happen.

A tomcat, which had been waiting by a wall on the opposite side of the street, recognised the change in the man's sleeping pattern, and moved to a point below his bedroom window.

One of the tom's ginger relatives jumped down from a

gatepost and landed in the small front garden of the house. It fixed its eyes and ears on the inside of the upstairs room that lay behind the breeze-rippled curtains.

Within a minute and a half, ten cats had gathered in or around the garden of the house, while – from further away – others were breaking off their night patrols and heading over.

It's a rare gift for a stomach, by digestive wailing noises, to be able to draw cats into large groups and to convince each group-member that it's being spoken to individually. For the stomach to do this without its owner's knowledge is an added feature. But being capable of persuading animals that it's been sent to dish them the goods on the meaning of life itself puts it right at the top of the gastric league.

Marlin – if he'd had time to take a break from saving humanity, the Earth and countless universes from destruction – would have been intrigued to know about it, and all the more surprised to learn that the sounds from his insides had spawned a cat-rap cult. And he'd also have been really proud to know that they had triggered the first primitive scratchings of a feline alphabet.

If his stomach had been into time-telepathy it might have swapped notes with the belly of an ancient rhinoceros that had once addressed a small group of primates gathered outside the slumbering animal's cave, with remarkable consequences.

*

Marlin stirred, looked for a moment at the sunshine coming through the bedroom curtains, and got up. After a quick walk with the dog and a short breakfast, he went to his desk and looked at the pile of salvaged bits and pieces that, in his chats with Spanger, he often called 'The Device'.

Despite his early results with the equipment, he knew it needed an urgent upgrade.

He reflected briefly on the machine's history. Some

design stages had been easier than others. He'd definitely had lucky moments.

The first, of course, had been when he'd taken the ring out of his desk drawer, while rummaging around for some old photographs. But he'd only put it aside on the desk while he got on with what he was doing. No, the *really* lucky break, he recalled, had come just as he was about to put the ring back into the drawer. He'd put it down on a photo for a moment. He'd thought it might have been his imagination, but he had felt sure that, looking through the gem at the picture of his grandmother and his great aunt as children, he'd seen them chatting and laughing just before they stood still for the camera.

But what he'd been really certain about was the interesting pattern that the gem had cast on the top of the desk as the sunlight shone through it. Turning the ring slowly, he'd found that the stone projected a range of different images. Marlin had gone on turning the jewel until he'd come across a picture that looked like some kind of construction diagram.

To get through the first stages of building the core unit of the machine shown in the diagram, he'd used pieces from an old radio, parts from a camera, items from a dumped fairground organ and the gemstone itself. After that, things had got a bit easier. Instead of a computer screen, he'd set up a framed piece of card on which, with the help of a small lightbulb, he could project the diagram and other images from the gem.

Then, using the jewel in his core unit, he'd discovered, half-hidden underneath the diagram, something that claimed to be a user handbook for a 'Mini-Fragment of a R58b Mind and Body Pack with new added shape and sense options'.

The rest had been ups and downs and trials and errors. But at least, Marlin reflected, the device worked in its own kind of way. If doom *could* be avoided, he might one day use bits of the device for the spatial/temporal transporter he was working on in the attic. But, for now, the machine on his desk had a job to do and, if he could somehow give it a power-boost that would certainly increase its chances of doing it.

In fact, even at its present power level, it had had some intriguing successes. The chief one, which had seemed a purely chance discovery, had been to get him into the network of that place, Thrarrxgor.

Once he'd got in, he'd managed to find out how the network operated, and to get more details about the place.

Marlin pushed back his chair and reflected on just how grim Thrarrxgor had turned out to be, and how great a threat K*rargxt and Sculpin posed to Earth, its universe, and other universes.

He snapped out of his muse, pulled his chair forward again, and turned to the matter in hand. He reached to the far edge of his desk and picked up what he called the 'revised keyboard' he'd been working on the night before.

It brought together components from a variety of sources. A protruding section of old gumshield (a relic from Marlin's sporting days) provided a range of short-cut options. Also integrated into the keyboard were a set of glued-in poker dice, a dozen or so whittled acorns, some old typewriter keys and three adapted seashells from Jersey. Supporting the metal frame of the keyboard were some pieces from an old steel bottle-crate begged from the local milkman.

On the floor underneath the desk, linked to the machine by a length of cloth-covered flex, was what Marlin, in his chats to Spanger, called 'The Mole', a foot-operated cursor-control system, which featured a threadbare slipper, part of an early roller-skate, an old ostrich egg, a bed-spring and a discarded turntable from an indoor miniature railway.

To its left – worked by Marlin's other foot – was the machine's power supply, designed to avoid dependence on mains power or batteries. So far, the round, antique grindstone above the sewing-machine treadle had worked well enough as a flywheel, and the spinning assembly of billiard balls and geometry-set dividers had kept the supply of power even enough for working purposes.

Marlin got ready for his next intrusion into Thrarrxgor. He linked the keyboard to the device, then gently worked the power-treadle. The thought came to him that maybe, before he'd started his morning's work, he should have got in touch with that young couple, to tell them how very pressing the danger was.

He shrugged. It would have to wait till he'd finished. This intrusion shouldn't take long. Just enough to search for any new developments in Thrarrxgor's plans. He turned a small adjusting-wheel to trim the angle of the gemstone, placed his hands onto the metallic frame of the keyboard...

... and crashed to the floor as a massive charge surged into him from the machine.

***

Squid Sculpin scrutinised the holographic data display in the cube of space in front of him, and allowed himself a few quiet seconds of self-satisfaction.

After that he looked up at an array of terminals connected to a large stone about the size of a fist, then at a power discharge-unit linked to the system of cables he'd installed.

Whoever it was who'd cracked into the network, *that* should have sorted them out, *and* their equipment. There'd been no further sign of activity from them after he'd delivered the power-pulse.

His hands resumed work on the controls, then stopped while he scanned the cube again.

He scowled. The data was inconclusive. There was nothing on *where* the intruder was. They could have been somewhere on Thrarrxgor or maybe even in another universe. And he had no idea what they'd looked like.

Anyway, he told himself, they'd been dealt with.

And *now* there were other things to be done, and done *quickly*.

CHAPTER 14

S 2 E: Have job.

E 2 S: Glad to hear that. Even gladder to hear you're still around. What kind of job?

S 2 E: Real one this time. Job in K*rargxtko. Security officer.

E 2 S: Whereabouts? Anywhere near our area of interest?

S 2 E: Almost spot-on. Had lucky break. Well, more than one in fact. By way, your crystal ball right about danger to Joe. Have learned more on that.

E 2 S: Please say if you now in position to influence events.

S 2 E: Hope to be soon. Not yet exactly sure how. Have to find out more about K*rargxtko technology and other things. Not always easy to get info, but will keep trying. How goes at your end?

E 2 S: Okay… sort of. Yes, in fact, fine.

S 2 E: Good. Right. Well, we'll be in touch then.

E 2 S: Yup… That's it. We'll speak again soon… I hope.

S 2 E: You sure all okay?

E 2 S: Yup… Don't worry.

S 2 E : Right. Fine then.

E 2 S: Yup… Fine. Cheerio.

***

It was the persistent nuzzling of the dog's wet nose on the back of Marlin's neck that finally woke him. He had the feeling he'd drifted in and out of consciousness a good many times, and that the day had been hot.

From his place on the floor he glanced up at the window of his study. It was getting dark. He realised he must have been lying in the room all day.

Though the floor was hard, he didn't feel much like moving yet. He gathered his thoughts, or – more exactly – hunted around for thoughts to gather. The fact that his painfully twisted foot was still inside The Mole helped him begin recalling events.

A short while later, when he'd made some progress, he began trying to remember what he'd been meaning to do after he'd taken his quick look at the K*rargxtko network.

Whatever it was, it had been urgent. In fact, Marlin remembered asking himself if he should have started the day with it.

Some minutes later, after much rubbing of his sore head, it came back to him. Yup, it had to do with that young couple. He half-raised himself, reached up to the top of his desk, grabbed a piece of paper and scrawled a message.

Then, half-lying, half-sitting, he worked his way out onto the landing, down the stairs and into the hall. He found the sock Spanger had brought back, gave it to the dog, tucked the message in his collar, told him what to do, and let him out of the front door.

Exhausted by the effort, he lay back. His head was beginning to swim again. He just hoped they had read the script. If they *had*, they ought to understand how dreadful the danger was!

***

Eelag put aside his empty coffee cup and looked again into the crystal ball. It was even cloudier than it had been a few moments before. In fact the clouds inside were forming themselves into one large, intensely dark one.

He watched closely as it expanded to fill most of the ball.

It swirled around, throwing out leg-like extensions that kicked viciously against the inside surface of the crystal. Then it grew even angrier, developing shoulders, with which it buffeted the ball, jolting Eelag's view.

After a while it stabilized itself. Its front part morphed through a range of foul features until it had selected the most horrible. The features seemed to be able to see Elag through the crystal. They leered at him briefly, then zoomed back a fraction into the middle-ground, revealing a ghastly body.

The whole thing swung itself round to one side for an instant, then turned fully into view again, holding the end of what looked like an infinitely long piece of paper. It waved it furiously at Eelag.

Eelag wondered why his prediction system hadn't crashed under the strain. Maybe the viruses that usually travelled with Zunddertokk's image had been suppressed to make sure the grim message would get through.

The picture zoomed further out, to show a wider field of view. Shapes on either side of Zunddertokk sharpened into focus, clear challengers in the hideousness stakes.

From their general look, Eelag assumed them to be assistant debt-collectors. One of them raised what Eelag took to be a horrible set of talons, shook them threateningly and began advancing towards him. The picture in the ball grew ever more horrible, then exploded, blotting out everything.

Eelag threw a piece of fire-resistant cloth over the ball and headed back into his bungalow. This was the fourth time in as many days that the ball's short-range forecast system had thrown up Zunddertokk. More accurately, it was the fourth time the ball had thrown up while Zunddertokk's image had been inside it. And this had been the nastiest warning yet.

Though he was normally a light drinker, Eelag felt this called for a fast, large, Prodder's Prancer, and some careful thought.

***

It was a warm West London evening, one of those evenings that nudges you with the smell of moist soil from places that still have soil to be moist, that sends you distant sounds of people going to interesting places, and that whispers that you should make the most of it.

Joe couldn't put into words exactly why he felt restless. Nor could the wasp that had flown in through the window and was circling Joe's head. The insect tried tightening the circle, cocked up the geometry and crashed into Joe's ear. It buzzed around inside it for a few seconds.

"The last time I heard you say *that* was when your team missed the equaliser!" Riska shouted from the box-cupboard that doubled as a study.

Joe reached for something to drive off the wasp, which had quit his ear and gone back to its circling attempts. His hand fell on the document he'd read earlier, the one he'd been meaning to run through again. He picked it up and swung it around wildly, missing the wasp but knocking over the travel clock that he'd taken out of the bag with the document. The wasp retreated to the top of a cupboard.

Riska left her computer and wandered into the living room. She glanced at the wad of papers in his hand.

"Something in it upset you, Joe?"

"That? No. Oh, no. Not at all. At least, not much. I flicked through the pages a bit, but there were a whole lot of other things I had to do, so I haven't really had a chance to look at it properly."

"What's it about?"

"Er, at a glance I reckon it could be some kind of spoof life-story which those colleagues of mine, Geoff and Dale made up as a farewell from the crowd at my old job."

"Are you *sure* it came from them? It's been quite a while since you left that place."

"No, not exactly sure, but they're the most likely ones, I reckon."

"No clues from the envelope it came in?"

The wasp launched itself back down from the cupboard. Joe swung at it again. "No. There was no stamp or postmark on the envelope. So I reckon Geoff, or Dale, must have dropped it through the door."

He put the papers on the table. "I'll read it properly sometime. They'll expect me to get in touch about it. Decent of them to go to the trouble, really."

"Mind if I take a look? I mean, if it's a spoof, there won't be anything true-to-life about it."

Joe looked out from the flat through a gap in the curtains at the softly darkening sky.

"Er... no... That's fine. I mean... as long as you don't take any of it seriously."

She picked up the papers.

Joe admitted to himself that it was that script thing that had been making him uneasy. Was it the trail of violence, or the gruesome ending? But why should he worry? The whole thing was bogus.

He could imagine Geoff and Dale maybe dreaming up that kind of thing for a laugh. All the same, they were busy people, and it *was* a very intensive piece of work.

He ran through the script in his memory, searching for what it was that jarred about his Geoff-and-Dale theory.

He looked through the window again. His eyes picked out the light of the first stars just managing to break into the night sky against the glow of the city. He stared at one, then another, then on to the next ones, drawing imaginary lines between them as he'd often done in the past.

He had to admit that the mental sketch he'd made between them was very basic, just made up from a few points he could see. He paused for a moment. It was as if his mind was trying to tell him something.

Yup, *that* was it! *That* was what had bugged him about the script thing! Those points in the introduction to the script. About his past life.

He took a mental step back and considered. There

weren't many of them, and they weren't *superfine* details, but they were fairly personal. The sort of things you might run through in a frank chat with a close friend or perhaps in an unguarded moment with someone you didn't know well at all, like a person you'd met while travelling, or while you were briefly in a new place.

He stopped and thought carefully about his former colleagues. He'd got on fine with them all, but there were things in that lead-in description that he'd never mentioned to any of them.

Riska had gone into the hallway. He realised she was speaking to him from there.

"Sorry. Say again, Riska?"

"Joe, there's a woofy-scratching sound outside the door. Can you come here for a moment?"

*

Riska gave the dog a drink of water while Joe read the piece of paper it had brought with his sock.

He looked at the paper for a long while, handed it to Riska and sat down beside her while she read it.

On the note, in shaky pencil, were the words:

DANGER GREATER THAN YOU COULD EVER IMAGINE !
PROBABLY TOO RISKY TO PHONE.
COME WITH THE DOG ASAP.
IT'S ALREADY VERY LATE

P.S. IT MAY BE TOO LATE ANYWAY

P.P.S. IF YOU REALLY CAN'T MAKE IT, TOO BAD.
IT WAS A NICE WORLD.
M Q.

***

"Do you think it's safe to talk here?" Shloomger looked carefully around the one-room bar. The place had a sort of studied basicness about it. The only light was an oil lamp hanging from a concrete beam above them. The furniture was limited to three tables and a few battered chairs.

Apart from Shloomger and Ked, the only occupant was the mechan bartender behind the counter, which – from the way it was leaning on the beertaps – looked as if it had been welded to them. Shloomger had been intrigued at the way it had managed to draw off the beers and take the money with an almost total absence of movement.

"Probably the safest in town," Ked murmured, "outside Grux, you can never be sure of anywhere in Thrarrxgor city. But this place is difficult to bug." He swung his head in the general direction of the heavy steel door. "As you saw, this building's an island in a rubble wasteland, and the roads outside were dug up years ago, and all the cables severed."

"What about wireless bugs?" Shloomger asked.

"Well, with the static that's kicking from that old electricity sub-station beyond the rubble, the one that powers up the mechan recycling plant, anyone eavesdropping here'll have to work their tail off trying to send our sweet voices anywhere." Ked looked around instinctively. "All the same, we should still be careful."

Shloomger took a taste of his beer and was surprised to find it a shade less grim than it looked. But he felt he could get by without ever repeating the experience.

"Then maybe," he suggested, "I could ask you a bit more about K*rargxtko, and that place called Life-Planning and Intervenor Operations that you mentioned earlier. It sounds, er... interesting."

*

Ked broke off his chat with Shloomger while, with what seemed impossible slowness, the mechan disengaged itself from the counter, moved across to their table, unhooked the gasping pressure-lamp above them, tiredly re-pumped it, and returned to its default position behind the bar.

"Probably a scrap-survivor," Ked commented, "there was a mass crawl-out from the mechan recycling plant one night. They rounded most of them up, but a few got away."

Shoon looked at the mechan. "I suppose you could call this one lucky, then."

Ked shrugged. "I don't think it'd answer to that".

Shloomger read the shrug carefully. It had a resignation about it. But what kind? Was the man in front of him just going along with Thrarrxgor's grim state? Or had he decided his only choice was to fight it?

He took a chance. "Is there anything you can do about the way K*rargxtko works, Ked?"

Coot gave a short, coughing laugh. "You mean... go up to K*rargxt – as if I'd get anywhere *near* him – and tell him to change the whole set-up on Thrarrxgor to how *I* want it?"

"Not exactly."

"Glad to hear it. I'm pleased that, having saved my life, you're not suggesting I hand myself in for shredding!"

"Far from it... "

"*How* far?"

"Look, I know it won't be *easy*, but I was simply thinking that maybe we could manage to do a little bit ourselves, very discreetly of course, to... sort of reduce the general amount of nastiness here -and *elsewhere*, if you see what I mean." Shloomger gave Ked a long, careful look. "As a matter of fact, to start off with, there's one area in particular where you could help me. About that *script* thing you mentioned a while ago, the one about the bloke who's 'elsewhere', as you put it. It'd be kind of useful if you could fill me in on that... "

***

"Would you like another glass of water?"

"I'd rather have a whisky, but better not. Maybe some

tea. There's an electric kettle on the fridge."

Joe searched for the items. The trickiest was the tea itself. Eventually he found a teabag wedging a cupboard-door from falling open, and replaced it with a dog-biscuit.

Riska finished bathing the back of Marlin's head, and dabbed it dry. "You must have given yourself one hell of a bang when you hit the floor."

The old man shifted uncomfortably on the kitchen chair. "You think – from what I've been telling you – that I'm either concussed or mad."

"No I don't think that."

"Which? Not *concussed* or not *mad*?"

"*Neither*. It's clear you thumped your head when you fell, but to me you seem highly switched-on. It's more Joe and I who are confused."

The beard quivered. "You've every right... " He stopped and looked round. "The *dog*! What about the *dog*? Has Spanger had a drink?"

"Yup. We gave him some water before we set out, and some more just now."

"Right. Where *was* I?"

Joe handed him a mug of tea.

Marlin stared at the tabletop for some seconds. "Ah yes, as I was saying, it all came out of the blue, you see."

Joe looked at him carefully. "That business about the ring, and the script of my life, you mean?"

"Yes, and the network I got it from. The one I... "

"Hacked into?"

" *Unwittingly accessed* is how I prefer to put it. But, as I said, it's not just any... "

"*Ordinary* network?... "

"*Exactly*. As I said, it's based somewhere *else*." The old man drew a long, contemplative breath. "And, as I was trying to explain to you earlier, it's somewhere else that's physically *like* Earth." His beard quivered again. "But it must be... *has* to be... " he gave them a look that was part-pleading, part take-it-or-leave-it, "... in another *universe*."

In a matter-of-fact kind of way, Joe and Riska looked at him and said simultaneously,

"Well yes. Why *not*?"

*

Marlin waved away Joe's offer of help, and positioned himself in front of the device.

"It's possible I can get it working again, but the problem is it's desperately underpowered anyway. It needs some kind of... "

"Up-grade?" Joe suggested.

"Yes, that's one way of describing it."

The three of them stared at the device. It occurred to Riska that, burnt-out and oddball as the machine seemed, there was something strangely attractive about it.

"Can it work as a time-machine too?" she murmured.

Marlin knitted his brows together as he looked at it. "No," he said, "but I'm building a spatial/temporal transporter in another room that might work in tandem with this one day." He sighed. "I'm afraid the 'time machine', as you put it, is for the future... "

"Well, if it's only for that, it would *halve* its workload, I suppose," said Riska. She looked back at the singed machine sitting on Marlin's desk. "But, about your present plans for up-grading *this* device? How are you going to do *that*?"

Marlin hesitated a moment. "It's guesswork... I've been thinking about it a good deal, but it's still *guesswork*."

"*What* is?"

"This is going to sound ridiculous... "

Joe grinned. "That's a word people often use to stay away from something that's very *possible* !"

"... Well, the thing is I think the stone gave me some kind of up-date on its status."

"An extra piece of programme, you mean?"

"Not exactly. I'm guessing, but I think it's more something about there being another power-source not far away, one that may be able to transfer its powers into this one." The old man put his hands together thoughtfully. "You see, I often go back to look at its 'instructions' when I want to check the system-layout for any reason."

"And... ?"

"I found a *new* message, a kind of add-on."

"What did it say?"

"Well it started off by saying, a bit vaguely, that power might be transferred from one source to another by bringing the two sources close to each other. But then, right at the end, the message got really difficult to understand. It said: 'NEAREST BOOST' BR BLIJSP NHM'."

Joe reached into his pocket, pulled out a pen and an old shop receipt he'd meant to throw away, and jotted down the last part of the message. "What's it mean Marlin?"

"Don't know. At first I thought it might be a misprint about a local chemist, but I don't think it's that. I'm convinced it's something about an extra power-source somewhere."

Quilldragon paused thoughtfully for some moments, then went on nervously. "I'm afraid that if we *don't* find a boost for the machine it won't be strong enough to survive for long on that network. And then there's no chance of our doing *anything* about those other... unfortunate matters we spoke about earlier."

Joe looked at him. "About me and those other people being killed off in that script and then... ?"

"Yes and, after that, about dreadful things happening to mankind, and the Earth being destroyed."

The old man suddenly seemed very tired. He looked at them both intently, "You see, the problem is we have *very little* time left!"

CHAPTER 15

On 7c3, the band had cut for a time-out, and was wowing itself off-podium in the performers' refreshments lounge. On the field, the collective body-mass of the crowd writhed in sync with an on-stage inter-lewd act featuring a distortion of transdimensioners beamed in at vast expanse from Plarnac 7b.

In a shed on the rim of the field, the Visual Effects Team were training their solar-flare-seeder guns on the Sploglelard twin sun system, to prepare aurora effects for the grand finale several days ahead.

On the other side of the ground, lines of live discarded drink-containers shuffled and rolled themselves to flush-and-refill stations, hoping they'd make it back to the central sales areas in time for the band to play The Six Wild Moons of Glondor.

Closer in, a team of security agents were muscling their way towards an embarrassed thief who'd mistaken another being's organs for a snatchable cash-bag.

And, like the drink-containers, the thief, the being, its organs and the security agents were all seriously hoping to be back and ready before the band played

The Six Wild Moons of Glondor.

***

"Do you think he'll be okay on his own, Joe? I wish he'd agreed to come and stay, at least overnight."

"Can't force him if he doesn't want to. He's an independent old boy." Joe stopped for a moment and looked back at Marlin's gatepost. "You know, I've never seen graffiti like *that* before, or so close to the ground."

They were silent for the first minute of their walk home.

Then Riska said, "What do you make of all this?"

Joe stopped and gave her a long, thoughtful look. "I think it's for real."

"So do I."

Joe pulled the scrap of paper from his pocket and read out loud his jotting of the last part of the message Marlin had discovered, " 'NEAREST BOOST BR BLIJSP NHM'. Anyway, solving what *this* means and chasing it up is one way to find out."

"It is", said Riska, and we need to do it fast, Joe."

*

The breath of the warm night drifted in under the curtains. Joe tried to concentrate. Riska lay on the sofa, staring thoughtfully at the ceiling. It wasn't inspiring her much. Apart from a cobweb or two it had an unhelpfully blank look about it.

Joe was finding her seriously distracting. She was wearing very little, which made it difficult for him to focus on his jotted message.

He dragged his attention away from her and tried, with great difficulty, aiming it onto a saggy inflatable globe that lay slumped in a corner of the room.

Riska followed his gaze. "What happened to that, Joe? It's gone pear-shaped."

"Quite a history to it, really. Got it from an aunt when I was seven, after I'd told her I'd like to see the world. And it did travel with me a lot later. But one day... you know how it *is*. I'd sort of packed a fair amount into my bag... "

"*Crammed* it, you mean?"

"Well, yes, a bit. I'd been collecting a load of stuff. And, inside the bag, the globe brushed up against the tail of a hand-made model pterosaurus I'd bought." He pointed to a shelf. "That's it, there."

Riska walked over and picked up the model. "It's well made. Lots of detail. So *this* did it?"

"Yup, punctured the globe."

"Where?"

"Somewhere near the Azores, I think. Knackered it." He got up, took the soggy sphere from Riska and peered at an area around a grubby bike-puncture patch.

She watched as he put it carefully back in the corner. "Well, maybe sometime we can sort it out, Joe." She looked at the model in her hand. "And was *this* damaged? It seems okay. Anyway, I wouldn't know how to fix it. I'd have to take it to an expert, or find one like it."

Joe yawned. "No, I think it's alright." He settled on the sofa again. "Now, about the letters in that message. I can understand the *first* bit, '*NEAREST BOOST*,' but I haven't a clue what the rest means."

"Nor me. And why's that last part in code. From what Marlin said the message he found was fairly understandable, at least till that *last* bit."

Joe thought for a while. "Well, I really don't know. I reckon I haven't got the energy to go into that now... "

"Maybe that's *it*, Joe! Maybe it's *not* code! It might have been cut or squeezed because the sender, whoever it was, was running low on *battery energy* or text space or whatever."

Joe shrugged. "For all I know, you could be spot-on right, but I still can't make head nor tail of it."

Riska stared at the model in her hand, "head nor tail of it" she murmured. And, looking at Joe again, she saw he'd fallen asleep.

***

"Need any more help on that?"

"No, fine for the moment Ked. I think I'll just sort of think about it all for a bit."

Shloomger switched the desktop machine into standby mode, touch-closed the holographic display that had been suspended in the air in front of him, and sat back to contemplate the results of his first entries into the K*rargxtko network as a new recruit of the company.

It had been a long time since he'd had much to do with networks of this type. His mind drifted back to his last experience of them. He tried to work out how long ago it had been, and guessed it was about five billion years back, as measured by the planet he was currently on.

It had been a frustrating experience. He'd been roped into helping a female friend, Vandolia Varsterbroom, launch a cosmic discussion about why reality re-establishes itself – with a few changes – at each level of existence. Whilst it was a subject Shloomger would have been happy to skip right past, it clearly interested Vandolia, who'd exercised a good deal of influence over him at the time.

Shloomger's task had been to run an interactive article about the subject on the Inter-Level-Net. Vandolia had told him to launch it as an on-going question-and-answer session.

He'd hit his first problem when he found that, rather than coming up with a few basic questions for the participants to try and answer, *he* was supposed to reply to *theirs*. It had turned out to be a real klonker of a problem too because, a very short time (in Eleveners' terms) after its launch, he'd received some 900 billion enquiries.

A random look at six of them had been enough to put him off the whole project. The first four were on issues he'd never heard of. The fifth started with a sentence so complicated that Shloomger reckoned the being who'd sent it had simply been testing all the buttons on its keyboard. And the sixth one asked why the article didn't have its own fluffy-looking logo at the top of each page, and made a few suggestions about what kind of shape it should be.

Not wanting to spend any more time on the whole thing, he'd announced that, as knowledge on the subject was moving ahead so fast, it would be better for participants to answer each others' questions. Then he'd quietly distanced himself from the whole exercise, and from Vandolia Varsterbroom.

When he'd chanced to bump into her a good deal later, he'd learned that the on-going article was in fact a roaring success. In the case of the mortal participants, the correspondence was well into the hundred-millionth generation. Some species had out-evolved the ones that had been providing the early answers, and were now replying to *their* questions. He'd also noticed that a fair number of the originally brighter species had dropped down to discussing the fluffiness of the logo.

Shloomger had often been lectured by tut-tutting friends, Eelag among them, about his having lots of intelligence but not using it enough. Now, he supposed, was one of those moments when he'd better start focussing his wits pretty sharply. He dragged his mind back to the K*rargxtko network and to what he'd learned from it.

The first thing was that, after a certain amount of faffing about, he'd been able to find his way around the network quite easily. This was mainly because Ked had given him a lot of information that he shouldn't have had at all, including a pile of passwords and entry-codes.

The second thing he'd learned had been how to get details on some of the technical procedures used to work the Viewer and the Intervenor. There were still gaps in his knowledge, which Ked hadn't been able to fill, but he thought there was a chance he could get some more information on those subjects.

The third thing he'd learned had been particularly intriguing.

Ked had told him about a scare over an intrusion into the K*rargxtko network, and of rumours about other system break-ins.

Maybe, Shloomger thought, it'd be worth trying to find out a bit more about that. After all, if someone had been hacking into the network, it might be useful to get in touch with them. Assuming, of course, that they hadn't been wiped out by now.

***

"Would you like some coffee, Joe?"

Riska was drawing the curtains slightly to one side. Joe stirred on the couch, then suddenly realised he must have been sleeping there all night.

"Yup. Thanks".

She put the cup down beside him. "How are you feeling?"

"A few aches, but they'll go quickly. In fact I had a great sleep. Sorry I nodded off like that."

"You don't have to be sorry Joe. You were worn out."

"How about you? Did you get some sleep?"

"Yes, but I did a bit of research first."

"On the internet?"

"Yes, and in some of your reference books."

"Any luck?"

"I think so. At least, I've had an idea. It's about the last three letters of the message. In fact it's that model of yours that sparked it. But I could be wrong. As for the rest of the code-type part of the jotting, I still haven't a clue what that means. Anyway, let's get over and see the old boy fast."

*

Marlin got up from his chair, flexed his right leg a few times, and sat down again. "Well, it's a lot better, but I don't think I'm up to the trip."

Joe tried to hide his relief. "Best not to go, really. Nope. Not worth pushing your luck. And anyway, you need time here to prepare the machine thing."

Quilldragon's beard quivered. "You mean the *Device*?"

"Yes, sorry. The Device."

Marlin glanced at it, then turned to Riska encouragingly.

"I think you're probably on the right track, but the two of you are going to have to play it by ear once you get there."

He reached into the apparatus, tweezered the gem from its scorched interior, and held it under the lamp. "If your hunch is right and you manage to get to the other source, then the sooner we get its power into this stone, the more chance we stand... " he paused for a long thoughtful moment.

"... *Assuming...* "

"*Assuming...* ?" Riska and Joe asked together.

"*Assuming...* " Marlin paused again, and stared at the gemstone thoughtfully. "... Assuming it's *this* stone that'll get the power-boost."

Riska looked carefully at the jewel. "You make it sound a heartstopper of an "*if*!" You mean it could work the *other* way?"

Marlin finger-scanned his hair-roots, and stopped quickly as he reached the bruise on the back of his head. "You see, there were some rather vague instructions early on in the message about how to programme a stone so it can receive a power transfer from another source. Anyway, I managed to get the gist of what they meant, and I've programmed the gem for that." He gave a fatalistic sigh. "But there's no way of knowing it'll work. I'm just hoping my programming was right and that, as it's been used in The Device, the jewel will be the default-receiver for the boost."

He stared at the stone intently. "But I could be wrong. For all we know, it could turn out the other way round. If so, this gem will empty all its power into the other source."

Joe looked at him. "And then we'd be... "

"Yes, *deep* in it. So far down we'd never come up. I'm guessing, but I think the other source is probably something that's a fair bit bigger than the gem. So, even if we managed to borrow it, which would probably be difficult to arrange, there'd be no chance of adapting The Device in time to make use of it."

"So this *has* to work."

"Exactly."

"Yup, I see," Riska said.

"Yup... er... well... Yup," Joe added.

Marlin resumed briskly. "Now, as to the *trip,* I think it'd be best to use public transport. The Thrarrxgor people will be preparing to take over your mind, Joe. We don't know whether anyone on Thrarrxgor will be watching you in the next few hours, but the last thing we want is for them to know we're onto them, let alone that we're trying to upgrade The Device."

He took a bus timetable from the shelf and handed it to Joe. "So to be absolutely safe, it's best to make it look as if you're just out on a run-of-the-mill journey."

Joe looked around the room uneasily. "And how do we know they haven't tracked us here with that 'Viewer' you told us about?"

"We don't. But I'm gambling on what little I know about those tech people on Thrarrxgor, and I'm hoping they haven't used their 'Viewer' much yet. My guess, from what I've hack... – er *discovered* – is that they've tested it a bit, but that it's not working all the time yet."

"So we're in with a chance?"

"Yup, but only just. And I think they'll use their Viewer *and their Intervenor* sometime soon."

Riska glanced at her watch. "So we'd best get there fast."

The old man gave them both an intensely serious look. "*Very*. But, before you go I've got to check you both for gem-portability... "

Joe felt some detail of reasoning had just slid right past him. "... Gem – *what*?"

"In case the stone has any effect on you. You see, I've noticed it seems to be the case with certain people."

"What? You mean you've already sort of... *handed the gem round* generally for people to *look at*?"

"No, nothing like that, exactly. But some time ago I decided to get a special setting made for it, so that I could take it out of the ring and replace it easily without damaging it. I thought it'd be a good thing if it could be kept in the ring while I wasn't using the stone in *The Device*." That way, if anyone broke in and saw *The Device*, they wouldn't know what its core unit is and – even if they stole the ring as well – they wouldn't realise the two went together, so to speak… "

Joe felt the need to push things forward. "Right. So, the people who changed the ring-setting handled the ring and the gem, and it had an effect on them?"

"Well, not *all* of them. In fact, really only on *one* of them, as far as I could see."

"What happened?"

"Well, one of the ladies reacted quite noticeably."

"How do you mean?"

Marlin hesitated, slightly embarrassed. "… Well, her breathing sort of speeded up and… well… fluctuated a bit… and she… well, went pink rather a lot."

"Maybe she just had a cold and was trying not to sneeze," Riska suggested.

"Or maybe she was thinking about something totally unrelated," Joe added.

"Yes, perhaps. But, when I asked how long the work would take, the other ladies said I could pick it up in the afternoon, while the pink-faced lady didn't want to let go of the ring, and said she'd need to keep it for at least a month, maybe more. They had quite an argument about it. In the end I managed to get one of the other ladies to do the work on the counter while I waited."

"So you want to check us both, to make sure," Riska murmured, looking at the ring and the gem more closely.

"Yup, that's it," Marlin said airily, "and, while the gem's out of The Device, I want to get on and check a few of the other components. But first," he carefully inserted the stone into its gem-setting and handed the ring to Joe, "you'd better put it on your little finger for a moment. The ring's far too small to go on any of the others." He turned back to the Device. "Now, let's see… the condenser-linkage should be just behind here… "

Joe slipped the ring onto his outermost finger. He thought he might have felt a slight tingling for a second or so. But he couldn't be sure, and simply put it down to his imagination.

Marlin took the ring back and put it on the desk distractedly. "Just a second, Joe, your eyes are better than mine. Can you have a look inside the Device... *there...* and tell me if the linkage-pins behind the condenser-platform are properly aligned? Tell you what, if I push the retaining-spring to one side, it should be a bit easier... "

*

Joe found the general rule – about technical things which are only supposed to take a jiffy taking *ninety* of them – was applying to the current work. When he'd finally been able to see the pins properly, he'd found them as aligned as a scarecrows' symposium. "It must have been seriously shaken when the shock came through it," Marlin murmured thoughtfully.

"Talking of shaking," Joe said, "I didn't realise you were so close to the underground. The house's floorboards have been heaving around a good deal."

"Yup," Marlin said matter-of-factly, staring into the apparatus, "but it doesn't usually happen so often. Probably a lot of trains passing underneath us in the tunnel."

*

"Well, that's got them sorted out at last, Joe." Marlin looked at his watch. "Gracious! Is that the time? We really must get on. Now, where *were* we?"

"The gem-portability check," Joe reminded him. "Riska just has to try on the ring... "

"It's okay," Riska said from behind them, "I took it out to the landing and put it on while you two were working on the machine. "You know, it's *really* nice... very comfortable... seems a pity to take it off, really... "

"If you could pass it to me, then... " Marlin muttered, still peering at the condenser-platform, "I'll just make sure the whole shebang fits back together again correctly."

"Right ho... Oh, I'm afraid it's not coming off very easily... Ah!... *that's* it." She handed the ring back to Marlin.

"Thanks," the old man muttered, still looking at the machine. "... You know," he said in a matter-of-fact way, "if it doesn't come off too easily, it's probably best for Joe to carry it on this trip." He smiled at Riska. "But if you'd like to wear the ring for a while at some time in the future, as long as it's not needed for the machine, that'll be fine."

"Thanks," Riska said, "yes, I'd very, very much like to do that sometime, assuming, of course, that the wheels haven't come off the world."

Marlin went on adjusting the machine for a few moments, giving them some pieces of advice about the power transfer. Then he turned away from it, handed the ring to Joe, and gave them both another of his long, serious looks. "*Right*," he said quickly. "We don't know what access Thrarrxgor might have to our communications, so – to keep them secure – I suggest *no* use of telephones, mobile or other. And, though your computer was excellent for the research, I think we'd better skip using it, at least for the time being."

"Okay!" Riska breezed, "best be getting along, then!" She gave Joe a powerful slap on the bottom. "Come on, we've got to hurry!"

*

"It's okay, don't come downstairs, we'll let ourselves out," Riska called up to Marlin.

"Goodbye," the old man called to them, "and I hope it's not going to be too dangerous, particularly the power transfer." He hand-ruffled his beard. "There might be a lot of energy surging about. Remember what I told you when you bring the gem close to the other power-source." He gave them an encouraging wave. "Good luck!" he shouted.

CHAPTER 16

S 2 E: How goes?

E 2 S: Fine. Yes, all currently fine. Nothing to worry about. All highly okay at present.

S 2 E: You sure?

E 2 S: Yes. Why?

S 2 E: You going on about it a lot.

E 2 S: No, all fine.

S 2 E: Good. Pleased to hear it. Thought you'd like some news from this end.

E 2 S: Yes, very much. Fire away.

S 2 E: Have informed myself about K*rargxtko network.

E 2 S: Fine. Please inform me too.

S 2 E: Fairly basic, as networks go, but has large amount of info on Thrarrxgor and what's happening here. Lots about K*rargxtko. And have found more about what you glimpsed in ball.

E 2 S: What... *recently*?

S 2 E: I mean what you glimpsed before I came here, about the script for that bloke, Joe.

E 2 S: Oh, Yes... of course.

S 2 E: Well, that's what I'm here for isn't it?

E 2 S: Quite right. Sorry. Was getting bit sidetracked in thinking. Anyway, what have you found?

S 2 E: It's all going to happen very soon. But not sure I can do anything about it.

E 2 S: When you say 'it', you mean the nastiness involving Joe?

S 2 E: Yes. Extreme *n*. Worked way into K*rargxtko files and found secret plans. Found out that the serial script you saw in ball – though grim and lethal for Joe and some others – is in fact only cover?

E 2 S: You mean... sort of intro 'front-page' for set of other serials?

S 2 E: No. Cover for plans to take over Earth, turn population into slaves for K*rargxtko, transport them elsewhere, then wipe out planet. Surprised your ball didn't spot that. Is ball okay?

E 2 S: Has ups and downs. But please say what you hoping to do on Thrarrxgor as of now.

S 2 E: Would like to find out how Viewer and Intervenor you told me about *work*. May *possibly* get access to them, though difficult. But can you get details from ball on how they're operated?

E 2 S: Unlikely to get stuff on that with ball. Do you have tech contacts there?

S 2 E: Have a contact. Believe or not, bloke who wrote script for Joe's life. Okay guy as matter of fact, and v. helpful. But not actual tech specialist.

E 2 S: How will get know-how then? Sounds desperate.

S 2 E: Is. But have found that someone hacked into K*rargxtko network. Think intruder could be useful source of info for us. Think that, because they *wanted* to hack, they may not like K*rargxtko. Also think that, since they *managed* to hack, may be tech wiz on other things too. If I can make contact, wherever is, maybe hacker could help. Probably our only chance. But possible serious problem about hacker.

E 2 S: What's that?

S 2 E: May be dead. Have found, from v. secret file, that Sculpin knocked out his hacking device and possib. hacker too.

E 2 S: If so, most unfortunate for hacker, Joe and Earth.

S 2 E: Yes. But will try to make contact with them, whoever hacker is/was.

E 2 S: Fine. Good luck.

***

Brushed by leaf-shadows, sunlight and the sounds and smells of town in mid-afternoon, the bus moved, unflustered, towards South Kensington.

To Joe, the best way of observing life in London was to be on the top floor of a double-decker. You watched it swirl and splash past outside, while people brought in samples of it and discussed them.

Riska looked at a clock in a passing window. "I think we've got enough time," she said, "but not a vast amount. Let's hope I got the meaning of NHM right, otherwise this is all useless."

Joe pointed to a fold-and-run stall on the pavement below them. "That's where I bought those bargain gloves I was telling you about."

"The ones with only three fingers?"

"Well, I didn't notice till I got home and opened the pack. But they were incredibly cheap."

"I imagine they would be. Did you take them back?"

Joe re-arranged his feet slightly. "Well, I did *think* of it. In fact, I phoned the man who sold them to me. Amazingly his mobile number was on the receipt. Nice bloke, very amusing, full of good stories. It was worth buying them just for that."

He noticed Riska was grinning broadly at him. "Anyway," he added, "I took his advice and tried one glove as a wintertime prong cover for a barbecue fork I'd bought from him a week earlier."

"Did it work?"

"It sort of fitted but as it wasn't really essential, I gave the gloves to the zoo."

"What for?"

"Three-toed sloth. The bloke who sold them to me had suggested that too. He said it might get chilly there during the cold nights, even in their special quarters."

"What did they say?"
"Not much. Sloths don't talk a lot."
"Very funny. And the zoo?"
"They said thanks and they'd keep them in reserve."
"Why?"
"They'd already been given stacks of them."
"Right."

The bus reached a stop. Joe looked into the see-around mirror near him and watched the passengers getting on and off. He edged his thumb gently against the ring on his little finger. He thought about the new tingling sensation he'd felt when he'd put it on for a second time, and wondered if the gem might also have an effect on the people around him.

With many passengers and much to do, the bus driver, eyeing into the chain of mirrors, didn't focus his attention particularly on the young couple on the top deck. But he did spot his Auntie Millie, which surprised him, since – as far as he knew – she was currently living in Brazil.

Peering more closely, he saw that *that* was exactly where she was. In fact she was sitting at a table near her favourite beach, the one she'd often taken him to, and was sipping coffee.

He looked into the mirror again and noticed, just behind the stairs, a sizeable part of Paris. Indeed, the more he looked, the more he realised he could see the entire city, Seine, Eiffel tower, Louvre, the lot. Then, reflected from another part of the bus, he caught sight of the city of Melbourne, and there was more beyond that...

He turned his attention quickly to the rear-view mirror, pulled back into the traffic and got on with the journey which, for the next few minutes seemed normal enough.

It was only after he'd pulled into the next stop and when a young couple were moving through the exit door near him, that he noticed the oxcarts, the powered rickshaws on the other side of the street and, a bit further on, the in-gate to what looked like some kind of wild rock festival.

He closed his eyes and took a series of long, deep breaths...

*

Joe and Riska entered the great hall of the Natural History Museum and looked around them. It had an echoey hugeness that put even the great dinosaur skeleton into perspective.

Riska said, "I often think when I come here that it's like the station hall of some gigantic railway junction," she paused for a second, "except, instead of trains, it's people's lives meeting up with the past, and with explorers' journeys, and with the things they brought back."

Joe pulled the scrap of paper from his pocket and scrutinised for the hundreth time the squash of letters he'd jotted down just in front of 'NHM'. He looked at Riska. "Well, if we get through this stage, at least we should be going *somewhere*." He stared again at the huge hall around him and then at the letters again, "But what we're trying to do seems just crazy. Bloody *impossible*!"

Riska pointed to an academic-looking person standing near an exhibit-case, holding a large reference book. "Look, there's someone who might be able to help us. Let's ask them what *they* think."

*

"You say you've got a heavily abbreviated text from someone and can't get back to them to ask about it?"

"Yup." Joe handed over the paper scrap. "Sorry, I er... sort of scrawled it down. Can't show you it on my phone... "

The person looked at it. "Is it for a rendez-vous?"

Joe hesitated. "Well I don't know, er, if you could call it exactly... "

"*Yes,"* said Riska,"it's for a *rendez-vous*".

"Well, the NHM part would make sense then. Just a moment. I've got an idea! There's a friend of mine here today who has known the museum for most of his life. Four heads are better than three. Could you come this way?"

Joe took back the paper. They were led to an area near a large staircase. "John, maybe you can help. This lady and gentleman are trying to fathom out a text message… "

Joe started to hand over the text, then stopped. The tall man had not turned towards him to take it but, through his dark glasses, seemed to be looking straight ahead.

"Fine," the man replied, "can you just read it out to me?"

"Er… right," Joe murmured, "yes, okay." He wasn't sure how to read the whole thing out. After the first two words, maybe he should read it letter by letter, but that might make it even more difficult to work out. Best try and *pronounce* the squashed-up bit.

"Er… 'NEAREST BOOST BR … BLI… JSP… er… NHM'."

The man considered for a moment. Then Joe saw his expression change. If, behind his dark glasses, the blind man's eyes had lit up with recognition, Joe wished he could have seen it.

"Just before 'NHM', you said 'JSPER'. Is that right?"

"Well not really. I was just sort of hesitating."

"Because, if you *did*, that would make sense of it."

Joe felt as if the museum floor had started to spin under his feet.

Riska recovered first. "Sorry, don't follow you."

The blind man stood for a moment, listening to the echoes of voices and footsteps in the hall. Then he turned his body about a quarter-circle and pointed in the direction of a floor above them.

"Over *there*", he said, "you may need to ask again when you get nearer. They might have moved it since I saw it. That was quite a long time ago. But my guess is it's probably still where it used to be."

"What *is* it?" said Joe.

The man smiled.

"Bright Blue in Jasper," he said.

*

They climbed the staircase. Riska laughed. "Sometimes he who hesitates is lots lucky."

"Yup!" said Joe.

They'd almost reached the entrance of the room they wanted, when something hit them both hard.

It hadn't been travelling fast, but even at low speeds it was more than enough to knock them sideways. Joe lost his balance and briefly went down on all fours. The mass that had hit them began to sway, staggered slightly and just stopped itself falling over. It let out a few grunts, which could have been faint apologies, sounds of bewilderment, or just samples of its *regular* grunts. When Riska had got her breath back, and had managed to stop herself pointing him to the Whale section, she asked if he was alright. He said he *would* be if she'd hold his hand for a moment while he steadied himself. Once she had, he recovered instantly.

"Thanks," he muttered. "Squirt's the name. Freelance. Been doing a bit of research for an article I might sell." He pointed to the room he'd come from. "Thought I'd do one on minerals. Sex it up a bit." He brought his face close to Riska's and leered confidentially, "I think '*Bedrock*' would be a good title… "

"Well, Mr. Squirt, I'm pleased to see… "

"And *I'm delighted* to see *you*, my dear!"

"… that you haven't damaged anything."

"Well, not as can be seen without more *intimate* examination. I suppose you're not in the medical profession?"

"No, and if I were… "

"Pity. Never mind."

Joe, who'd been badly winded by the collision, was waving to the museum staff that all was okay.

Then he realised he could no longer feel the ring on his finger. Maybe his hand had been numbed by the fall. He looked at it.

The ring had gone.

He stared at his finger in a dazed kind of way.

Then, he looked beyond it, and saw the ring lying on the floor near Riska's foot.

The problem was that Frank Squirt had seen it too, and was bending down to pick it up.

***

The core of the storm was on the beach. At its centre was a water-filled column that was no ordinary high-street cosmeticologist's essence-of-darkness, but something a lot stronger.

The rain was so heavy the drops had joined themselves into a single drenching slab. The downside end of the slab was doing its best, needlessly, to press Eelag's head sideways into the sand. Needlessly, because a very large, ugly boot was doing the job perfectly well.

A voice designed to cut through the din of any storm, including the storm the voice's owner always carried round with him, was speaking grimly.

"Where *is* he, Eelag? You're his *friend*, Eelag! He wasn't home. But then I found out he'd gone to see *you*, Eelag! That's why I'm *here*, Eelag! You know where he is, *don't* you Eelag?"

Though this creature might have a good memory for names, the gypsy reflected, everything else about him was foul. If this was Zunddertokk's henchman, he never wanted to meet the boss.

Eelag watched the torrent of rainwater surge over the fragments of the crystal ball. He searched round the edges of his mind for an escape plan. Maybe the henchman would hold off re-arranging his body long enough for him to work *something* out. But things weren't looking good right now.

He was expecting the question to be put to him yet again. But, instead, the vile being took his boot away, placed the heavy base of a sunshade on Eelag's head, and began a bout of persuasive damage on and around the bungalow.

By the time the creature returned, Eelag had managed to move his head just enough to see it show a sudden interest in the transporter device.

"No! *Whatever* you do, you musn't touch *that* !" Eelag shouted, "Or Shloomger will *never* come back!"

***

Finding a ring close to his own feet would have been a non-starter for Frank, since his view of the area around them was blocked out by his paunch. But, as the ring was on the floor behind *Riska's* feet, spotting it had been a lot easier. And he'd decided that picking it up, though difficult, was definitely worth trying.

Riska, who hadn't noticed it yet, was trying to work out why Squirt had moved alongside her. She'd seen him go into some kind of grovelling posture.

Though he was further away, Joe would probably have got to the ring before Frank, if it had stayed where it was. But, as it turned out, neither of them reached it in time.

Joe thought the young woman who picked up the ring was exceptionally rare, because, although she was different, she was as beautiful as Riska.

"Here you are!" she said, holding the ring out towards Frank, "it'd be a pity for you to lose that... "

Joe got as far as "No, it's not hi... "

"Young lady!" an out-of-breath man cut in, closing on Riska from the right, and waving a business card, "I couldn't help seeing that you were the victim of a collision caused by the negligence of this... person."

The man pointed at Frank, and then turned back to Riska. "As a lawyer specialising in personal injury claims, I can assist you in suing for compensation... "

He stopped to deal with some kind of digestive twinge, then lowered his voice, "... And of course you needn't worry about the costs of my services. My fee will only be payable if... "

"I see you like cryptic crosswords", said Riska, glancing at a half-filled puzzle in the newspaper the man was holding. "Here's a clue from me: ' Travel order reported to cancel intimate reciprocation', *four* and *three*, and make it *snappy*!"

The man seemed upset by the clue, and left hurriedly.

Frank looked at Riska. "It's obvious that someone as beautiful as *you*, my dear, would never even *think* of taking legal proceedings." Then, turning round and looking closely at the other young woman, he added, "... nor indeed *you*, my dear."

The young woman who, during this time, had been holding the ring, looked at it closely and warmly, and said, "I think it would be really *terrible* if this were lost... "

"Too *right*," said Joe, "but it's okay. I'll make sure it isn't."

"Oh, I see, you're this man's bodyguard," she said. She closed her eyes as if going through some kind of internal struggle, then re-opened them and handed the ring to Frank.

"Look, that's not *yours*!" Joe snarled at Squirt, "Give it... "

"Just a sec," Riska whispered, "if there's a brawl in here, the security people and the police'll have us out of the building like a shot. Leave this to me."

Squirt peered at the ring, bounced it up and down a few times in the palm of his hand, and then made a ridiculous attempt at putting it on the smallest of his fingers. Having given that up, he slipped it into his jacket pocket.

"Yes, very nice," he said, grinning at Riska, "I could *see* you find it very attractive." He paused "And, speaking of attractiveness, I know a bit about that too. You see, I do *photography* as well as articles. The two often go together ... " He looked at her thoughtfully. "But sometimes I just do pictures on their own, to sell to certain... *quality*, upper shelf magazines. Only the most tasteful ones of course. And I'm always on the look out for new... er... *talent*... ".

"And I hope you find some soon, Mr. Squirt."

"As a matter of fact, I just *have*." Frank made one of his

horrible attempts at a smile. "Now, about the jewellery. I'd like to make sure it's returned to its rightful owner."

He took the ring out and held it in front of him. "And, while I suppose this *might* be yours, I don't *know* it is. I'd need to be *convinced*, and, you could convince me, young lady. Some photos could do that." He returned the ring to his pocket.

"But I thought it was *yours*!" the other beautiful woman said to Squirt, "otherwise I'd never have given it to you in the first place! If it's *hers*, you should give it back to her straight away!" She turned to Riska. "I'm so sorry, I didn't realise... "

"How do you know it's *hers*?" Frank asked. "It was on the floor when *you* saw it."

The woman hesitated for a moment. "...Well... I suppose... if we handed it in to lost property, this lady could come back tomorrow with the receipt, or something to prove it's hers, and that would sort the whole thing out... "

"There's no time for that," Riska said firmly, "I'll have to do it *his* way. The ring *is* ours. Well, in fact it's somebody else's, but we're taking care of it for him, and he needs it back *today* ... "

"Anything special he's about to do with it?" Frank chipped in. "Connected with *rituals* or *strange practices*, perhaps? I suppose you wouldn't have any *unusual habits*? The public have a right to know about unusual habits. I could add a piece about that below the photographs."

"Photo... *graph*!" Riska clarified, "Only *one*!"

Frank considered for a moment. "No, my dear! Two nude full frontals now, in the park, or *no ring*. It's my *last* offer." He turned to go.

"How about *one* photograph of *two*?" the other woman suggested.

"I don't want a man in the picture," Frank said, glancing at Joe.

"No, I meant her and *me*, the woman said."

"It's a deal," Frank said quickly. "*Come on* then! I haven't got *all day*. But first I need to get my cameras. I left them at the reception place here."

The group headed for the exit. Riska squeezed Joe's arm.

"Well… " she whispered, "… If it's to save the world."

*

The taxi made a sharp turn. Joe lunged for the grab-handle. He watched the reporter grip his camera bags to stop them shooting across the floor, and wished he could do the same with his life.

"I *owe* this to you," the other young woman whispered to Riska, "I shouldn't have given him the ring. If this helps you get it back then it'll be worth it."

They scanned the passing park for a quiet, reasonably suitable place. Parts of it were crowded, but a few areas were surprisingly empty. "That place beyond the trees'll do," Riska said. "There are some bushes around, and they might give a bit of cover."

*

Joe stood on the spot that Riska had assigned him, and felt his mind slip out of gear. The only thing he was sure of was that Riska was in command of the situation.

She was speaking to Frank, who was getting his camera equipment ready near a large tree. After what looked like some brief negotiation, she went back to join her companion photo-model behind the tree. Frank took the ring out of his pocket, put it on the grass at a point just too far for Joe to be able to get to it before him, and resumed his position.

There seemed to be a lot of chatting and laughing going on behind the tree. After a while Riska's voice shouted, "Okay, Mr. Squirt. You wanted this! We're on our way!"

When two stunning women step out stark naked from behind a tree on a summer's afternoon in central London, words leave them to it, and stare.

Frank had been preparing to take the picture, but wasn't quite ready. Then he looked up. He saw them both. He took a picture. But it was a picture of a summer sky, which was exactly where his camera was pointing. That was because he had fainted.

*

"There's some water in my bag. I'll go and get it," Riska said. Her companion carefully re-packed the cameras. Joe gave them to Frank and helped him to his feet. "I think it's best if we walk to that seat over there on the other side of those trees," he said to him.

After a few rather shaky steps Frank got into what, for him, was his stride, and revived quite quickly. "Just a giddy spell," he muttered, "no need for a park bench. I'll get on my way now." He walked out of the park, waving away Joe's offers of help, and hailed a cab.

Joe turned back towards the wide green space. He'd been expecting Riska and her companion to have dressed again and to have caught him up by now. So he was surprised to see they were still completely naked.

There was still no one else around, but – from the way the two were cavorting – it looked as if they'd have been perfectly happy for the entire audience of the Albert Hall to drop by.

Perfectly happy, Joe saw, was exactly what they were. He stood and watched them laughing and throwing the ring backwards and forwards to each other in a rhythmic dance that made them seem to be half-floating, half-flying above the grass.

*

It wasn't any distant clock-chime or other sound that closed their dance, but the dance itself, which – in its own natural way – gradually changed until it merged back into the time outside it. Invisible to Joe, the first Pleasure-Filcher arrived, and veered away, furious that the dance had beaten him to it.

Riska and her companion walked to the tree and disappeared behind it. After a while they came back. Joe saw they'd swapped clothes.

Then the other beautiful woman mentioned that she had to go and get ready to catch a plane, and said goodbye.

"You'd better have this, Joe," Riska said. He wondered if he'd just imagined it, but he sensed she'd been having some kind of personal battle about giving him the ring.

"Now," she said firmly, "we have to move fast if we're going to get back to the museum before it shuts."

*

Joe got ready for some new crisis as they neared the spot where they'd collided with Squirt. But nothing happened. They went into the gallery and stood for a moment, looking at the rows of display cases, each with its sample of minerals.

Riska pointed to a part of the room. "I think it should be in that section." She saw Joe was holding his ring-bearing hand in front of him, rather like a water diviner who'd lost his stick. His arm swayed slightly, then fixed itself on a line between his head and one of the display cases.

"It's *there*," he whispered.

He recalled what Quilldragon had said to them. The old man had thought about the power transfer as carefully as he could, given that his head had still been very sore. He'd used his common sense and a fair amount of guesswork. "Whatever the source of the power-boost is, only the one of you who has the ring should go up to it at first," he'd said. "It could be very dangerous if there's an energy surge. No point in you both chancing it."

Joe moved slowly forwards. The ring had begun to tingle when they'd come into the gallery. Now it was buzzing. He came level with the case. Something seemed to tug at his hand. He glanced at the display inside, trying to find the rock, and realised his finger was pointing straight at it. He read the label:

"Bright Blue in Jasper".

He stared, fascinated, at the streak of blue in the rock. It seemed to pull his eyes towards it. Then he noticed, in the space between the ring and the rock, a slow swirl of images.

He watched them swim in and out of view. There were various cities and islands, a long-distance shot of what looked like a wild kind of rock concert, Spanger asleep in his basket, the living body of the giant dinosaur skeleton they had just walked past, then Riska and the other beautiful woman dancing naked in the park, some strange beings who seemed to be surfing on space-waves, a very confused bus driver, and a burnt-out office building.

His hand was being dragged at so violently, he felt that in seconds it would smash the display case.

Suddenly the power-transfer happened. There was no bang or splintering of glass, just two simultaneous blip-noises that sounded rather friendly. The ring buzzed so intensely, he thought the tip of his finger would fly off and end up somewhere as an unofficial exhibit. But after a few seconds the buzzing calmed to a tingle and stopped.

He signalled to Riska to come over.

They stood staring at the blue in the piece of stone.

"Well, it's free to be a rock like the others," Joe murmured, "and a beautiful one, too."

"And now," Riska said, "we have to get back to Marlin *fast*!"

CHAPTER 17

Even when only two tiny fragments of a disintegrated Upper-Leveller have started to work together, it boosts morale. And though it might seem like a drop in the cosmic ocean, when those fragments are from a highly active area of a R58b brain, it's even more encouraging.

This sort of miniature success, Boontrak told himself, meant there was just a vague chance that one day he might get to be himself again.

And, floating on this light-headed eddy of optimism, Boontrak drifted back to sleep.

***

Marlin removed the gem from the ring and placed it carefully into the machine.

"You didn't have any problems, then?"

"Nothing we couldn't handle," Riska said.

"Good. Now, as you can see, while you were away I rebuilt and revised the Device… "

Joe looked at the machine. Most of its components were now housed in a large white box, which had a hinged flap so they could be reached easily. The whole machine seemed a good deal bigger than before.

Marlin was clearly pleased with it. "It'll work faster now, and do more. Oh, and I've added a signal-surge deflector…" he gestured towards a large cable leading out of the room and into the cistern of the lavatory across the landing,"... by the way, if you're in there while the *Device* is working, *don't* pull the chain. You never know... "

"Right, I'll give it a miss," Joe muttered.

The beard quivered, "Steady on! I try to keep that place *presentable...* "

Riska looked at the spread of tools and food plates on the desk next to Marlin's device, and realised he must have been working flat out since they'd left him. "Don't you think you'd better stop for a bit?" she said quietly. "I know it's vital to get back into the Thrarrxgor network fast, but shouldn't you be getting some rest?"

Marlin shook his head. "If I stop now, it'll probably be too late ever to start again." He shifted his chair and peered into the Device's 'screen'. "Ah, I don't think I told you about the extra piece of programming I finished just before you came... "

Joe was beginning to feel slightly fuzzy about Marlin's tech work, but he tried to keep focussed. "What's it for?"

Quilldragon sprang round and looked at him with pleasant surprise, "You're very *close.* Actually, I call it 'WHAT'SIT *FIVE.'* It's my latest piece of software. It's designed to throw off intruder-chasers when I'm in the Thrarrxgor network."

"Well that's a *must-have* after what happened before," said Riska.

"Yes, I'd be wiped out without it!" Marlin looked at her. "I hope it'll work, but if there's someone there who's really bright, they might see through the camouflage and find me."

The room fell silent for a moment.

"So, what's the next step?" Joe asked.

Quilldragon toyed distractedly with an old bedspring he'd been using as a paperweight. "You mean from *our* point of view, or from *their* point of view?"

"*Both*, I suppose," Joe and Riska found themselves saying together.

The old man lifted the bedspring a little further from

the table, squinted down it lengthways and said in a matter-of-fact tone, "Well... from *their* point of view, they're probably going to unleash the Viewer soon. And then they'll be able to see -and hear – everything you're doing."

Joe felt a strange squashing feeling coming over him. "*Everything*?"

"Yup. If I'm right, their Viewer will be able to track you, *wherever* you are."

"So, how soon will they start?"

"Could be any time." Marlin paused, turned the bedspring round and inspected it from the other end. "I only hope it hasn't started already. If it has, they're listening to every word we're saying."

He put the bedspring back on the desk and picked up an old telephone dial he'd been keeping as a possible part for the upgrade.

"And what about their... " Joe thought for a moment, recalling the word, "... their *Intervenor*?"

"Anytime too, I should think," Marlin said, looking at the dial. "Though I imagine it'll probably be after they start using the Viewer. And when the *Intervenor* starts up... " he paused for a moment "your free will goes straight down the Swannee, and *you* won't be with *us* any longer!"

Joe eyed him steadily. "So, what's the next step from *our* point of view?"

Quilldragon put the dial back on the desk and looked at him thoughtfully. "Well, I'm assuming the Intervenor hasn't started up yet, and that *your* point of view hasn't turned into *theirs*. If, of course, it *has* been switched on, then it's already game set and match to them."

"And the *start* of that script for Joe!" Riska said.

"Precisely." Marlin took in a slow, contemplative breath. "Well, let's not be paranoid about all this, just *very* careful."

He glanced back at the machine. "The next thing *I* have to do is to try and hack... er... obtain *access* to the Thrarrxgor network again. It's just possible I might be able to break into their Viewer and Intervenor control systems, but... "

He fell silent. It was the first time Joe and Riska had seen Marlin look near to defeat. At last he resumed, "... But I'm afraid, with no one on Thrarrxgor to work with, the odds are heavily stacked against us."

"So, what should Riska and I do now, Marlin?"

"I think the best thing is for you to stay here just long enough to watch how I start up the Device, and see how to break into the Thrarrxgor network. That's just in case anything happened to me again and you needed to take over in my place... "

"And then?" Riska asked.

"Best thing then is to get the hell out of here. If the Viewer system tracks you to this room and sees you both next to the Device, then we're up the proverbial without a thingy! And we don't want *that* to happen, *do* we?"

"No," said Riska, "we *don't*!"

***

The cube of space in front of Sculpin's head suddenly emptied itself of data. An alert sounded from a point somewhere inside it.

Sculpin touched a small pad in the middle of his forehead to switch off his skin-throb music accessory. He needed to work without distractions.

The alert had turned into an alarm, and was screaming crazily. The system was filling the cube with new information. He silenced the alarm, and scanned the contents.

He couldn't be sure, but this looked seriously like a repeat of the first break-in by the intruder he thought he'd burned away.

He reached to a cabinet at the side of his desk and took out a flask of Spewk's Delight. The trouble was, this incursion was much *subtler* than the first. He poured himself a tumblerful of the liquid to steady his nerves, and thought for a moment. The intriguing thing was that, though he'd managed to discover it, the new intrusion had covered its tracks well.

He began to feel uneasy. He still had no idea where the intruder was based or what they were like. But, whoever it was, it looked as though they were bright and dangerous, and probably not on Thrarrxgor.

Sculpin took a gulp of Spewk's, stared at his ghastly image in the glass, and considered. The enemy must have some kind of advanced shock-shield by now. But he could reach them another way. He hadn't bothered to use it last time because the fast wipe-out method had seemed a better idea.

He looked at the settings on his machine and concentrated on what he needed to do. If it was done stealthily, his victim would have no idea anything was happening.

***

The alert that Shloomger had set was playing his improvised version of 'The Crescent Dustcloud of Cludnarp' from a point somewhere in the small screen-space that K*rargxtko allowed security staff of his grade.

It had taken him a good deal of secret work to programme an intrusion-detection system that would, itself, be undetectable by the Thrarrxgor network. He was pleased to find it operated well.

Shloomger turned the tune off to avoid attracting the attention of other staff in the Hangar. In his mind he ran through what he'd just found out. Although the intruder had hidden himself fairly well, he'd used a system similar to one Shloomger had come across by chance about thirty million years before, when playing a slightly up-market version of Spot the Spaceship with Frondella Fragg, while waiting for her swimming pool to fill up.

This was handy, since – by adapting a technique Frondella had shown him, which she'd called 'Fragg's

Finesse' – he'd discovered another thing about the hacker, which was that he didn't come from Thrarrxgor.

Using an advanced ploy that he'd mastered all that time ago, just before he and Fragg had jumped into the pool (a method she'd named Frondella's Fly-Net), he'd narrowed things down so that he knew both how to get in touch with the intruder and precisely *where* he lived.

Frondella had tried to explain the theory behind her technique, some strange mix of trial, error and infinity. But Shloomger had treated her talk a bit like his only-ever lesson in self-motivation, and had slept through most of it.

All the same, he'd been able to take the ploy further, and been slightly interested to find that the intruder, one Marlin Quilldragon, happened to live within walking distance of Joe Outwood.

For Upper Level beings like Shloomger, coincidences often have less surprise-power than for beings further down the cosmic pecking-order, and so they create only the *slight interest* Shloomger had felt.

This is mainly because many Upper-Levellers have been in such a range of places and events that there's not much left by way of coincidences to surprise them. But one set of places with an endless supply are the Incomprehensible Events of Splard, flocked-to by all Upper-Levellers wanting to tick the last box on the *Must-Go List-Of-Wild-And-Crazy-Places*.

Friends of beings who've got back from the IEs of S see such huge changes in them they often have to touch them for a quick loan to confirm they really are their old buddies.

The cause of the changes is that these travellers have moved on from no-longer-very-surprisable to a new state, where they believe the wildest things *must* currently be happening – and *have* happened – simultaneously at all points of existence. One payback is it saves a huge amount on newspaper bills.

The Incomprehensible Events of Splard are called that because no one has been able to call them anything else.

When asked to give a brief run-through of their trips to the region, travellers have usually – in the equivalent of human behaviour – made humphing sounds, shrugged their shoulders, and ordered a large Bison's Bodybuilder.

Anyone pressing them further is usually rewarded with details such as "Er... *Yeah... Like... It's... Well... Yeah...* Sort of *has* to be... *Doesn't it?... Well... That's* how things kind'uv *are. Aren't* they?... *Yeah.*"

One of the things about the IEs of S is that the comforting laws of cause and effect have, for their own comfort, steered right past them. And so everything that happens there does so by sheer coincidence. In fact, unlike what is often understood in other places to be the general gist of the concept, there don't even have to be two things involved for there to be a coincidence at all.

Beings that *inhabit* the IEs of S, however, are so used to coincidences that they can't be bothered to *call* everything that happens there a coincidence. But the word does sometimes appear at random in Incomprehensible Eventish dictionaries, which themselves tend to materialise and disappear without warning.

The long and the short of it is that those who *have* visited the IEs of S are unlikely, when the conversation turns to the fact that someone's auntie is living near the inner edge of the rotating Island of Thryggrketagrok, to say "*Well, call me a nebula's nightcap! My uncle brought me a dried fish and a spraggett shell from the beach there only a couple of trillion aeons ago!*"

Though Shloomger had travelled a fair amount, he – like his extremely well travelled friend Eelag – had in fact never got round to visiting the IEs of S. So he was still able to be surprised, even sometimes stunned and amazed, by a good many things. But he knew certain Upper Levellers who *had* journeyed there, and some of their attitude to coincidences had rubbed off on *him*.

So, whilst he'd been *lightly fascinated* to find the Intruder lived within walking distance of Joe Outwood, Shloomger hadn't gone into a *swoon* about it. In fact, he'd rather hoped the hacker would be someone on Thrarrxgor who knew about K*rargxtko's tech systems, including the Viewer, the Intervenor and the Transporter. He had an instinct he might need to do something with that stuff fairly soon.

He suddenly had a cheering thought. Maybe Quilldragon *had* found some tech details. If he could contact him, there was always a chance he'd have some useful advice.

Shloomger's hands worked on the keyboard for a while. When he'd finished, he looked into the screenspace again, studied some new data that had just appeared in it, and touched one of the machine's controls. After that he sat back thoughtfully.

One new and disturbing thing he'd just discovered was that *Sculpin* was onto the Intruder too.

***

Marlin finished his demonstration of the Device, put it into standby mode, and turned to Joe and Riska. "That seemed to go well enough. The power boost's made a huge difference!"

"I think we'd better be off now," Joe said.

In his corner, Spanger stood up and stretched, then came over and nuzzled them both.

Riska saw the dog was walking oddly. "Hold it, Joe, I think he's got something in his paw!"

Spanger clearly enjoyed the attention, and held up the paw meekly as Riska fussed over it. She glanced at Marlin. "It's a splinter. If you've got a needle, I can take it out now."

The old man thought for a second. "I think there's one in the attic. But we'll have to be quick."

He got up, paused for a moment, and settled the dog on the chair in front of the 'Device'. "Might as well", he murmured, "you never *know*." Then he went off to look for a needle.

***

Sculpin ran his hand over his grim head. Getting into the intruder's machine undetected had been quicker than he'd thought. His new data showed the machine had been proofed against another shock attack, and that it was more powerful than before. All the same, it was no match for *his* one. He considered. Yes, this would be a good time to launch a spy-view operation.

He changed his settings. He needed to get the appropriate part in the other machine to change to visual transmission mode. Then it would work as a camera.

If the enemy wasn't on Thrarrxgor, where the hell *were* they? What did they look like?

He waited for the image to appear.

The rocks he'd mined had given him vast amounts of information, including data on mind-blowing numbers of species across huge varieties of universes. But he wasn't ready for the image when it came. He knew some dogs were more intelligent than others, but this was a real turn-up.

There was a bleep. A message from Bernie appeared above the image.

It said the Viewer had just been activated and was searching for the Principal Male character of the serial. It added that, as soon as it had homed onto them, a live picture would be sent to Sculpin, for viewing in the corner of his screen-space.

Sculpin reflected for a moment, closed the picture, and decided to do a little more work on the controls of his machine.

***

From where he was standing in the doorway of the room, Marlin beckoned to Spanger to get down from the chair. The dog gave a slight yelp as he landed.

Joe and Riska started work quickly on the paw.

***

Sculpin finished his work on the control settings, then ran some data checks. Yes, his work confirmed the dog was a hoax. But where exactly *was* that machine?

He called the picture back to the screen space.

The dog had moved away, and Sculpin had a clear view of the background it had been blocking out. The décor of the place didn't look like the current trend on Thrarrxgor, though he remembered seeing something resembling it long before the Great Reform.

He could just make out two people on one side of the room, bent over the dog he'd seen earlier. He tuned his controls to see more clearly.

There was a new bleep from the screen-space. A message appeared, offering to show – in a corner of it – the picture coming in from the re-started Viewer.

Sculpin opened the picture, glanced at it, then looked back at the other image. He paused, did a double-take, and bounced his eyes back and forth between the two images like a mega-lottery player realising he's hit some kind of a big number.

After more checks to make sure he couldn't be wrong, he closed the screen-space, pressed a button and told Bernie to switch off the Viewer and come and see him immediately.

While he waited, Sculpin reached into a pocket, took out his voice-recorder, and replayed the order K*rargxt had given him at their meeting. The engineer smiled as the recorder confirmed that he'd remembered correctly.

The canned words couldn't have been clearer.

" If Outwood gives you any trouble, the *slightest* difficulty, *destroy* him."

"Yes, Mr. K*rargxt."

"And then, forget the enslavement programme. We'll find enough slaves elsewhere. Simply destroy that planet."

"Yes, Sir."

***

Quilldragon patted the dog gently. "He seems a lot happier now. Thanks for your help." He held out his hand to Joe and Riska. "And now, I think the best thing is for you to get on your way quickly. Take care, both of you."

Joe and Riska could see Marlin was trying hard not to show his feelings. He shook Joe's hand and kissed Riska.

"Goodbye," he said as brightly as he could, "I hope very much that we will meet again."

***

Shloomger watched the blades of the jewelled windmills on Ked's earlobes change speed in sync with his voice-tension. Ked had been whispering to him, faking a state of calm, but the blades had been spinning wildly most of the time.

"... So that's *it*, Shloomger. Those are the orders. It's a wipe-out! At least it's *about* to be, unless Bernie persuades Sculpin to hold off for a bit longer so he can do those equipment precision-tests he's so keen about."

Shoon stared into his empty screen space thoughtfully. "Yup, looks like it. Well, thanks anyway."

Ked started to move off, but Shloomger suddenly gestured him back. "You couldn't maybe get hold of some of the more secret technical details on those thingummies... the *Viewer, Intervenor*, and *Transporter Beam*? I mean, *how they're worked* and all that? Perhaps some details on the Switching System between them too? It's just on the off-chance."

Ked tried to hide his amazement at the question. "I think that's going to be kinduv difficult, Shloomger, as people who aren't supposed to know those kind of details tend to disappear as soon as they ask about them."

"Well... " Shloomger paused "... Tell you what. Maybe each of us could very soon, like *now*, happen to walk past the Switching Desk, take a look at the way it's configured, for as long we can without being noticed, and then meet back here."

***

Marlin gave Spanger another biscuit and settled himself in front of the Device. As part of his start-up routine, he touched the hacker-alert button, then switched it off quickly. The shriek was hurting Spanger's ears.

His hands darted around the keyboard. He stared at the data in front of him, then turned away and stared at the wallpaper instead, while he tried to think.

"Oh, *bugger* !" he muttered. Then he went back to the controls and worked them rapidly again. He paused, and then said "Ah!... But *this* is very interesting!"

He turned to Spanger, who was drifting back to sleep.

"Odd, in the same day," he said, "in fact, within *minutes* of each other. *Two* hacker-trackers! Both Thrarrxgor-based. One *friendly*, as far as I can make out, and who's actually sent me a message. And one who doesn't even bear *thinking* about. Except that I *have* to think about him a lot now!"

He stared again at the wallpaper for some moments, then looked back at the dog. "But first I need to get in touch with the *friendly* hacker. In fact, Spanger, I think it's our *only chance*."

CHAPTER 18

S 2 E: How goes?

… ..

… ..

… ..

S 2 E: Go ahead please.

… ..

… ..

… ..

S 2 E: Am contacting you on action needed to stop forthcoming annihilation. Reply as matter of urgency please.

… ..

… ..

… ..

S 2 E: Please inform asap that all okay. Cheers.

*

Zunddertokk's henchman reflected, as far as he could reflect about *anything,* on the words Eelag had shouted at him earlier. He moved away from the control panel of what he guessed was the transport equipment that had sent Shloomger to wherever he was.

He suddenly realised a bleeping noise was coming from what looked like a small message-machine lying on the ground nearby.

He fiddled around with the messager, trying to kill the bleep. After a bout of random jabs at its keys he finally switched off the noise. Then, as Eelag hadn't thought he needed to build in any safety codes, the device automatically flicked up Shloomger's message.

The creature stared at the text, pulling gruesome expressions as it scanned it, but failed to find any hint of where its target was.

It grew impatient. It put the messager between its teeth, then into one of its seventeen nostrils. After that it pushed it into other body areas. Then it hit the device, vomited on it and jumped on it before looking at it again to see if this had pursuaded it to come up with anything.

The machine disappointed it.

The henchman turned to the gypsy, whom he'd recently trussed and hung upside-down from the flagpole.

"What's it *mean* Eelag, and *where's* it from?"

"What's *what* mean?"

"Don't come the funny one with *me*, Eelag!"

The package swinging from the halyard writhed frustratedly.

"Look, how do you expect me to tell you while I'm up this flagpole?"

"I can swap those positions round for you, Eelag. Maybe you'd tell me sooner!"

"Er... *No thanks*. But perhaps you could lower me down... just a bit, so I can see what you mean... "

The henchman reached to the halyard on the pole and lowered Eelag joltingly till he was dangling at around shoulder height. It put on an insulated glove and picked up an electrical cable, the bare end of which was sparking brightly in the rain. To make sure there were no misunderstandings, it re-stated its quest.

"I want Shloomger back here *now*, Eelag! So, make with the answers! – *Fast*!"

***

Shloomger looked into his K*rargxtko screen space, read Marlin's reply to his message, encrypted it for safety, and then closed it. He thought carefully for a few moments, something many people had suggested he should do more often.

He already knew a little of what Marlin had just told him, such as that Sculpin had tracked down the Device. But he was pleased to learn Marlin had just built a *new* Sculpin-dodging programme. Above all, he was delighted that Marlin had *contacted* him and wanted to work with him.

And he was also delighted to have learned that Earth had at least a momentary stay of execution. He'd been surprised to hear from Ked that Sculpin had agreed to it. Ked thought it must be because Bernie had persuaded Sculpin to spare the planet until they'd done the precision blast-tests that he'd wanted.

Shloomger glanced at the swirl of activity going on around him in the hangar, and tried to look as if he was thinking about some deep security question rather than how to nobble K*rargxtko. He didn't know whether he and Ked would succeed, but it was worth a try.

A senior female engineer, in a sleek body-net and black boots, brushed past Shloomger's chair on her way to give orders to the Intervenor team.

Shloomger thought the male staff would need a lot of discipline not to be distracted by her, but concluded she'd probably be happy to provide that herself, as she was now threatening them with a steel antenna broken off from a redundant machine. He assumed she was one of the 'Results-Drivers' Sculpin had sent to beef-up Bernie's gentler, '*Woweey'* style motivation.

He re-focussed his thoughts, and wondered if Marlin could give him any technical advice, particularly on what he and Ked had seen on their trips past the Switcher Desk.

It was asking a lot, bearing in mind the man was in another universe. But, after all, he was enough of a whizz to have cracked Thrarrxgor's network and to have got so much from it already.

He turned to the keyboard, and prepared a message and

some questions for Marlin. It was a pity, he thought as he checked the screen space, that Eelag hadn't come back on *his* message yet. Maybe the gypsy could have sent him some useful information too. But then again, maybe not.

*

Shloomger to Marlin.

Am sending this via my work-holo-cube, as don't yet know how to contact you with my messager. But will stick to general format I use for messager texts if that all right with you.

Thanks for offer of help. Things getting pretty tight at this end. Despite very temporary reprieve, situation threatening to be seriously terminal at yours shortly.

Though Viewer homed in on your place earlier, it's currently switched off for urgent technical work. But could re-start anytime.

Have series of questions about operation of Viewer, Intervenor, Transporter, etc.

These are:

Q.1. Ked (a colleague of mine who's *with* us) and I have noticed a row of rather trendy pink and yellow buttons at top of Switching-Desk array. Any idea what they do?

Q.2. There's also a large 'switch' there, a bit like a fancy version of the lever on the manual gear-change cars you have on Earth. It seems to have several possible positions. Any clue what it's about?

Q.3. Have you been able to hack any understandable instruction details on Viewer, Intervenor or Transporter from Thrarrxgor Network? These would be most helpful. Anything on how to disable the security surveillance systems here would also be welcome.

Q.4. As far as you know, is your new Sculpin-dodging programme still working? (Hope it *is*, otherwise, if Sculpin reads this message on your machine, he'll be sending someone round to see me).

Would appreciate reply asap, if you still alive.
Here's to courage etc.
Shloomger.

*

Marlin to Shloomger.
Thanks yr message.
Answers to questions as follows.

A.to Q.1. Ignore row of pink and yellow buttons. Have found, from design document I dredged out of K*rargxtko network, that they're post-modem design accessories. ie: dummies that serve no purpose.

A.to Q.2. The large switch is the one to look at carefully. Have hunch you may be able to come up with way of using it to our advantage. But have found there is secret locking system for switch. This requires special key. You'll have to get one somehow.

A.to Q.3. Have decrypted some instructions on Viewer, Intervenor, Transporter, and Switching system from Thrarrxgor Network, and enclose these. Hope helpful. Also enclose some details on possible temporary nobbling of surveillance systems.

A.to Q.4. As far as I can tell, new Sculpin-dodging programme still working okay. But suggest you keep eye on his activities at your end if possib.

Good luck. Everything now depends on you. M.

***

"So they'll put off destroying that planet while they fine-test the Intervenor's blaster?"

Ked nodded at JT. "Yup, Bernie says the Intervenor's great for blowing away big stuff like worlds and star systems, but when it comes to close-up work, like setting light to buildings or taking out individuals, he says the team needs more practice. Plek, the targetting man, is *amazing,* but some of the others have to bone up fast on *their* stuff."

"You're sounding like you *used* to, Ked!" JT turned and looked towards the kitchen of the 'restaurant'. "I didn't think this place could be as bad as the last one, but it's got right past it already!" He checked his watch. "Are they *ever* coming with the food?"

Ked was embarrassed. He hadn't meant to seem hyped about the team's work. Now he felt tired and tense. If he was missing when the action at the Hangar began, it could mean big trouble. The Viewer technical shutdown was the only reason he'd made it to this rendez-vous. But the thing could re-start anytime.

He looked at his lunch companion. "Yup, JT, I hope it comes fast too. I have to get back soon."

"So what kind of precision tests will they do, Ked?"

"Oh, they'll pick some target they know of already. Probably the office block where Joe was going to start work again, as that's already script-programmed into the Intervenor. And they'll do some kind of precision beam-blast on it, likely a firelighter job, and then move on to Joe and waste *him*. After that they'll take out the entire world."

There was a crash at the exit from the kitchen. The waiter's normal habit was to open the flip-doors by powering into them with his paunch. But this time the man's stomach had knocked one of them straight onto the floor.

The man stepped over it and delivered the meal.

"I think you chose wisely, Sir," he said, handing JT a quiche with a bite out of it. "And, if I may say so, Sir," he said, serving Ked a fishcake minus a tooth-edged crescent, "I think *your* selection places you among the leading gourmets of Thrarrxgor… "

"So what specifically do you need?" JT asked as they walked out of the pukery.

"Besides a meal, anything that can tell us about the Switcher system and procedures for working it. And, of course, the key I mentioned in my message to you." Ked frowned. "You don't think K*rargxtko could have cracked the code I used when I sent you that message?"

"Since it was in the cipher I gave you earlier, you've no worries on that," JT said quietly, "and anyway, Sculpin's team are probably too busy even to read your stuff." He thought for a moment. "I've nothing on the Switcher procedures, but the *second* thing... " He put his hand into his pocket, then took it out again quickly. Something fell out. "Pretend you saw it fall and that *I* didn't," he said casually, "then pick it up and pretend to hand it back to me."

"What *is* it?"

JT walked on, as if reading an eye-test card suspended in the distance. "What you asked for in your message," he said softly. "It's the key to the secret lock on the Switcher system."

***

"You *know* where he is! *Don't* you, Eelag? *Coz* you *sent* him there, *didn't* you Eelag? And *that's* the machine you used to *send* him with, *isn't* it, Eelag?"

The gypsy wondered what motivated Zunddertokk's henchman. Was he working on a percentage basis? If so, he'd be an enormously *rich* being if Shloomger ever paid up. But, if he *was* on a share of the rake-in, why hadn't he stashed enough to retire on by now? Either it was his first big case, or else – so far – he hadn't been much good at his job.

Eelag realised there could be another reason why the being did this work, which was that making things nasty for other beings was his only source of pleasure.

But he could see the creature was getting increasingly upset at not getting an answer. Maybe if he tried the old long-words ploy it would hold him off for a bit more.

"Look," he said in a muffled way from inside the trusswork of ropes, "without entering into a long digression on inter-cosmic cross-cultural communication, my experience is that it *generally* makes me more forthcoming if people can sort of... *edge gradually* into the kind of enquiring conversation that you appear to be attempting to conduct. For example, an appropriate way of... *breaking the_ice*, so to speak, can be for the parties concerned to begin by introducing themselves more extensively."

He shifted slightly, trying to ease the pain of the ropes and to look the being as nearly into its horrible features as he could, "Now, it's clear to me that you are already apprised of *my* name, but -up to now- I don't believe I've had the er... *pleasure* of obtaining *yours*. So, if perhaps you could *elucidate* me on that matter firstly, then maybe... "

The being came from a different school of etiquette.

"Cut the crap and quit stalling, *oven-ready pre-pack! I'm* the one that asks the questions! Get Shloomger here *now*! Or I'll *spark you real good*!"

To clarify the second option, he brought the crackling wires to a spark's jump of Eelag's rain-drenched body and moved them in non-healing circles round it. "One thing I really *don't like, Eelag*," the being hissed, "is having my *time wasted*. And *you're* not going to do that anymore, *are* you Eelag?"

***

It was going like a dream. The tip-off about the security-lights being down for repairs had been gold-standard. And now the job was getting even easier.

The burglar tightened his left hand on the metal, and reached upwards through the darkness with his right arm, feeling for the tube-joint above him.

Nice. Galvanised... Maybe it was old, but it *seemed* okay.

Now – one fluid movement...

Oooph... ..

Oh... Bol... ai... ah... .!

Bill 'Dancing Paws' Groat dangled over black nothing, one hundred and twenty feet from the ground, his heels swinging like a hanged man's, his hands clutching and slithering on a bent, half-severed pipe.

That was the trouble these days. No quality anymore! He thought for a moment. Maybe he was getting too nostalgic. Perhaps those new thieves were right after all, and he really *was* past it. Maybe he *was* losing his... oa... ooah... ah...

His left arm came full away and caught him across the side of the face. A stab of cramp ran through the muscles of the one hand still grasping the pipe. His grip began to open. The hand started to slide along downwards.

Was this *it*, he asked. A couple more ticks and he'd be a pathologist's jigsaw.

He crooked his free arm round the tube to take weight off the other one, concentrated, and grabbed at the pipe again.

The cramped fingers slipped, then held on the hard surface.

He had to get his body back onto the tube fast, or his arms would give out. He went for it straight away, like a trapeze artist, swinging his hips and legs back, building up for a full leap to get his feet back round the piping.

There was a sharp, grating sound further down the wall. He knew he was levering the fixing plate out of the brickwork. If that came out, the length of pipe leaning into space – with *him* on it – would double. And then, most uncaringly, it would buckle and dump him like a vulture's leftover.

But he was going to *have* to get his body on the pipe anyway. Maybe there was a chance he could do it...

***

"So, what *now*?"

Joe wondered whether Riska was the only person who could hear him. Was that 'Viewer' thing onto them? If it *was*, then probably – as well as viewing – it would be *listening*.

He shifted on the sofa and glanced around the room at the things he'd collected over the years. One of them, an

African fertility figure, seemed to be looking very pointedly at Riska. His eyes moved onto a pair of basic candlesticks. Had they somehow been taken over remotely, as extra listening-bugs for the Viewer? Likely not. From what Marlin had told him, it was powerful enough on its own.

His eyes wandered on around the objects in the room, as if they were all life-markers leading to the present moment.

Then the full creepiness of it all hit him. Once he'd accepted the script was real he'd known that, one way or another, things were going to change. But now it was about to happen. And, with that Intervenor thing due to switch on any time, each next second could be his last free one, maybe his last altogether.

He realised Riska hadn't replied.

"What do you reckon?" he said.

She looked up from the magazine she'd been reading, and switched off the table lamp. "*Tell* you what, Joe," she said, "why don't we go for a *walk*?"

***

Bill was back on the pipe and working his way towards the next fixing plate on the wall above him, his hands in a knuckle grip that locked them round the tube, the soles of his trainers pressed hard against it further down.

Com'on! Push gently with forearms… arch body… Don't slip an' roll round pipe… Now push knees back… Like toy monkey goin' up stick…

Somewhere far below him in the darkness there was a snarl and two quick barks. He paused. Not a deep enough bark for a guard dog. Probably a mongrel after a cat.

The thief got to the wall and shifted himself round the pipe till he had his back against the brickwork. He rested for a moment and drew air into his lungs. Suddenly a weird feeling ran up through his spine to the back of his brain. It was as if, close by, some massive force was about to move onto him, and onto the building itself.

He felt a flash of giddiness, and told himself to get it together. The faintness passed. He swung his body round, and edged his foot onto a ventilation brick that protruded slightly from the wall.

Moments later his body was on the sill of an office window. A few more seconds, and he was inside.

He switched on his torch and scanned the interior.

***

"Further *in*. *Closer*! Now, right *onto* the building! *Now*!"

At their separate workstations, on opposite sides of the hangar, Shloomger and Ked listened to Bernie leading the Intervenor team onto the test-target. They watched a huge hologram, thrown into the roof space by the re-started Viewer, rotate slightly and gradually re-focus.

Ked knew the team were a few seconds away from the fire-strike. He gripped the edge of the desk and stared at the image.

A gruesome metal face edged slowly forwards till it was level with Ked's. It paused to scan him in profile, then moved in still closer, its 'mouth' suddenly falling open in a shower of rancid oil. Its 'body' stretched out a dented arm holding a grease-stained beaker. The head turned and spoke tinnily into Ked's left ear.

"Cup of K*rargxtr-Hyper, Sir?"

Ked leapt off his chair, knocking the mug from the 'robot's' huge hand. The droid shed its steel fist from its forearm, lowered it to the floor on wire tendons, locked it on the empty beaker and, with a ghastly screeching sound, wound it back into its arm socket.

Ked hadn't seen the robot before, but he'd heard about it from colleagues. He bellowed to Juncus, wherever he was.

"Get that oversized *tin*bot away from here! There are mechans that can do those jobs ten times better! Why do you need to botch out a droid like *that*?"

"Sorry, Ked. It was just trying to help. Do you know, it

can actually *learn*? I've set it to adapt to the rules of the place where it's working... "

"Get it *out* of here, Juncus!"

The droid shambled off to the other side of the hangar, and loitered in its pathetic version of standby mode somewhere near Shloomger. Ked's eyes went back to the action unfolding in the space above them.

The image rotated again, making Ked feel sick. But he could make out details clearly. He saw that an upper floor window was open. Near it, a section of damaged pipe curved out from the side of the building.

Shloomger had noticed it too, but now he was checking to see if anyone was looking at the Switcher Desk.

A silence fell over the hangar. A rifle-sight symbol appeared at the edge of the giant holog-cube and moved into the centre of the image. Then Bernie's amplified voice slipped through the silence in a creepy, coaxing tone.

"*Cool... nice*! Now... *precision.* It's a *fire*-strike. Go in steadily... "

CHAPTER 19

The thief stepped into the main office corridor and set about disabling the alarm system.

He thought for a few moments. The cash should be in a safe in the Accounts Section. He finished his electrical work, reached to his back pocket, and pulled out the crude map his source had rush-sketched for him. He moved down the corridor and shone his torch on the first likely-looking door. Someone had stuck a picture of one of his favourite sports cars on it, in debt red, with black interior trim. This was encouraging.

He tried the door handle. It was stiff. If it was locked he'd have to use a piece of the professional expertise he'd brought in his backpack, probably the one with the size-twelve steel claws on the end of it. No, the handle was starting to turn...

***

Ked had to hand it to Plek. The Lead Manipulator might be an arrogant bastard with poorly permed eyebrows but, considering he'd not done much of this close-up stuff before, he was a master.

You could see it from the way he'd steered the Intervenor beam onto the office block, synced it with the Viewer, and then joy-sticked both beams into the core of the building. Ked saw the ace ripple his biceps and pass the controls temporarily to his deputy.

At floor level, some mechan rats were squabbling near the wiring that linked Plek's workstation with the Switcher Desk. Ked's eyes followed the cables. Could Shloomger really do anything with the desk? Would he be seen? He looked up at the image above him. Everyone's attention was probably on that now.

Juncus wasn't looking at it. He felt moody. With the rush to get the Intervenor ready he'd scarcely slept in the last two days. His right buttock was sore from some corrective action by one of the new female supervisors, and he was annoyed at Ked's comments about his robot.

He shifted uncomfortably on his seat. His robot was a *fine* machine. It just needed to show what it could do! What the skrat did Ked know? *Boolags* to that slupster!

Impulsively he grabbed the droid's remote and changed the setting from 'standby' to 'patrol'. Then, pleased with his burst of self-assertiveness, he relaxed, and fell asleep.

As Bernie announced a micro-pause, Shloomger slid across to see Ked. He needed anything he'd found on the team's destruction techniques. And maybe, too, Ked could fill him in fast on any news he'd picked up from colleagues around him.

***

The door opened a couple of inches, then refused to budge. Bill kicked its bottom edge. Maybe it had gone wonky on its hinges and was catching on the floor.

His torch started to flicker. He swore under his breath. The batteries from that market trader were crap. Probably stolen goods. A bloody disgrace! Last time he'd buy anything from *him*.

He switched off the torch and slid it away from his feet. He put his shoulder against the door and heaved.

It held stuck. He took a couple of steps back, and charged at it through the dark. It gave in with a bang, then jammed again, half-open. Something sounding like a heavy tin of liquid crashed onto the floor inside.

Bill knew he'd bust into a storeroom by mistake. There was a heady smell, as if from some sort of solvent. It was time to quit. The faintest spark, and that stuff would burn him away.

The fumes were spreading out from the room, making him giddy. He tried to pull the door closed, but it was jammed. Best leave it. Other cans might have lodged against it, and could fall. He looked down. Liquid was starting to leak out along the corridor.

Yup. Definitely time to clear off.

***

Plek was back at the Intervenor controls, ready for the close-up work. Ked watched his eyes follow the image, as the Viewer focussed on the inside of the building, moving in and out of offices, along corridors, up and down stairways.

Ked was intrigued at how some things in the offices were different from those in K*rargxtko, while others were similar. One main difference was that, *there*, no one seemed to have to work through the night. As far as he could see, the place was empty.

The image moved up another stairway. Ked caught sight of something. *No*! It was some*one*. The place wasn't empty…

Bernie's voice cut in. "So, Plek, we do it *now*!"

Ked shouted across to Bernie, "*No! Hold it*! There's a man in the corridor! You *can't*!"

He was sure Bernie had heard him, and seen the man too. He shouted again. Bernie waved an angry arm at him.

Ked stared at the image above them. A white, crackling ball of energy appeared in one of the hallways. Moving along the corridor, it became a band of orange flame that seared the floor, walls and ceiling as it went, leaving them ablaze behind it.

Ked saw the man break into a run.

An instant later there was a roar as the fire-line hit something flammable. The man, who was some way ahead of it, tripped and fell. Ked thought he saw him get up and stagger on, clutching his knee. But suddenly a cloud of dense smoke cut across the image in the Viewer.

***

Bill limped towards the door of the nearest office and tried it. It opened. He got to the window and climbed through it just as the flame-front reached the door. A swirl of air inside the office slammed the window shut.

He crouched on the ledge outside, clutched his knee, and looked for the drainpipe he'd expected. There was nothing. Only bare brickwork. The nearest pipe was on the other side of the next window, and it was too big a single jump to that ledge.

He could see a ventilation brick, like the one he'd used before, jutting out slightly from the wall between the two windows. He thought for a moment. If his knee had been okay, maybe the airbrick could have been a land-and-take-off point in a chancy leap across. But no way now!

He glanced sideways and down into the night below and felt the heat through the windowpane hit the side of his face.

*

"What the hell's *that*!" As he spoke, Joe saw Riska had her mobile in her hand.

She gave the details calmly, and closed the call. "It's spreading fast, Joe! Isn't that where your new job's going to be?"

Joe spotted something on the side of the building. "There's a man up there! I think he's injured. He'll fall before the firecrew gets here!"

He sprinted to the building, got to the foot of the drainpipe that ran up the wall nearest to where the man was standing, and climbed.

*

Bill watched Joe and Riska clamber onto the window-ledge next to his. He was impressed when, a second later, the young bloke launched himself towards him, using the same land-and-jump-from-the-airbrick idea that he had. And he was even more impressed when, having nearly missed his footing, Joe landed next to him. But, as they hairily swapped positions on the ledge, Bill couldn't help thinking about a sharp crack he'd heard as Joe had jumped away from the airbrick.

His knee was still aching, but he steadied himself, ready for an assisted reverse-version of Joe's trip across the void. With the right kind of help from outstretched hands on each side he might be able to do it, but the timing of the release-and-grasp, and the leg-work, had to be spot-on. If not he'd go straight down.

*

As he pushed away from his foothold towards Riska, Bill didn't see the airbrick snap off flush with the wall. But Joe did. And he saw the fire raging at the window behind Riska, and the glow of its heating frame.

Riska was nearly pulled off balance by Bill's weight as she pulled him towards the ledge, but she just managed to keep her footing. A micro-instant later she was stepping sharply sideways to make room for him as he landed. Then, in a repeat of Bill's dicey swop-around with Joe, they changed places.

Joe watched the man climb painfully onto the pipe and make his way downwards and out of sight.

"Go down with him, Riska. Then I'll get over," he shouted, begging she wouldn't look at the wall.

"No. I'll go down with you Joe."

He knew she was leaving enough space for him to do a flying landing after a step-jump off the airbrick. He begged she wouldn't look at the wall.

He tried again. "I'll be fine, Riska. You go on down, now, *please*!"

Her eyes glanced at the stretch of wall between the two ledges.

And Joe knew from her face that she'd seen the foothold had gone.

***

During one of the Viewer's short panoramic"zoom-outs", Plek, like the other team members, had briefly seen three people on the outside of the building, one of them the bloke who'd been in it earlier. But he'd been too busy, trying to gut the whole building, to pay attention. He heard Bernie tell the team to close the fire-test, zoom out, and find Joe and his girlfriend wherever they were. He got off his chair and handed over to his deputy.

Bernie couldn't understand why, every time the team tried to pull the image away from the building to look for its targets, it swirled around and zoomed back onto it. There had to be a technical fault somewhere. He ordered a pause for checks.

Shloomger took his chance, slipped over to the controls of the Switcher Desk, and inserted the key Ked had given him.

As soon as it was found that the Viewer had been right all along, and that the two figures on the building were the *targets*, Bernie's voice suddenly boomed round the hangar. "Look, I haven't a clue how they got there, but blast them away *now* Plek!"

***

The vile features sniggered at the gypsy. "I'm glad you're coming to your senses Eelag, it would have been a pity to cause you more *unpleasantness*."

Eelag saw the storm around Zunddertokk's henchman was fading. The rain that had been hammering the gypsy's face had eased. He wondered if the creature could mood-control the weather, or if its storm had wrung all moisture from the air. Probably the first, he thought, since the storm had been so focussed.

Now he'd been untrussed and could look around more, he saw what seemed like bright daylight cutting through at the edges. Still, this was no time to think about the weather. He had to decide what to do.

The debt-collector kicked away Eelag's battered text module, banged the transporter device with a large claw, and turned on the gypsy. "I want *results*, Eelag! This has to be *more* than quick, Eelag! This has to be *immediate!* I want him back here *now*!"

***

Plek ignored the figure making its way down the pipe. It didn't feature in his instructions. Instead, he waited for the Viewer to zoom onto a close-up of Joe. He adjusted a couple of control-settings, and moved his hand onto the joystick.

Somewhere in the hangar, far from the Viewer, Intervenor and Switcher Desks and shaded by machine-crates, a hand moved, unnoticed.

The index finger of the hand moved past a sign with words on it such as UNDER NO CIRCUMSTANCES, WITHOUT PRIOR AUTHORISATION and EXTREME PENALTY.

The finger applied pressure to a large and very red switch.

After that, for a short time, no one noticed much at all in the hangar, because the lights – and everything else – had stopped working.

Ked put on the night-vision glasses he'd brought with him. He was particularly pleased about the darkness, since – as well as winning a fraction more time – it meant he could sneak back to his workstation unobserved.

*

Riska moved carefully along her ledge towards Joe's, reaching out her hand as far as she could, ready to try and catch him if he jumped over. But they both knew there was no chance he'd get across in a single leap.

Joe saw her suddenly lose her balance and clutch at the brickwork. For a moment she swayed on the edge, then managed to steady herself. He shouted to her again.

"Go down the pipe, Riska! No point you staying there! I'll be okay. Firemen'll be here soon!"

If Riska had heard him over the roar of the fire and the din of things falling and breaking inside the building, it was clear she wasn't leaving. A couple of storeys above them, windows were blowing out. Joe was amazed the one behind him hadn't gone already. It was just a matter of time.

A shower of glass whizzed down past him, followed by what he reckoned to be about a hundred blazing box files in very unalphabetical order.

He was beginning to feel encouraged at their having missed him, when a set of metal shelves did a part-landing next to him on the ledge. It rated no higher than a part-landing because the length of ledge underneath the shelves broke and fell on down with them.

Thoughts started rushing through Joe's mind about options dwindling, about it being better not to look down and about a lot of other things that seemed to be getting muddled up together.

All in all, he thought, the best and only thing he could do was to stay exactly where he was and move as little as possible.

***

The side lamps next to the desk panels flickered, then settled to a steady glow. Moments later the staff in the hangar blinked and turned their eyes towards the floor, as they tried to re-adjust to the brightness from the renewed cube-image above them.

Plek slipped on his shades, returned his hand to the Intervenor's joystick and waited gum-chewingly for the Viewer to resume homing onto Joe and Riska.

On the Switcher desk, Shloomger pulled some notes out of his pocket, looked at them carefully, and moved his hands around on some controls.

Then, powerfully pulled away, he left the Switcher Desk altogether.

CHAPTER 20

A tremor ran through Plek's stomach ulcer. This was *nothing* like he'd wanted! The Intervenor wasn't back on full power, and that bloke would *burn* to death before he'd got him in the cross-hairs. What sort of cruel snatch-away was *this*? His cred as Top Manip would *blow*! He plucked his permed nose-hairs and waited for the 'RE-START' signal.

***

Joe could hear sirens, but doubted the firemen would reach him in time.

A voice in his head pointed out to him that people in the area around were sitting comfortably at home, listening to the sirens and wondering if anyone was caught up in whatever terrible thing was happening. Then it upped the volume, and told him he was currently in 'Pole Position For Death'. Joe muttered a few short expletives at the voice and, seriously offended, it lapsed into silence.

There was a massive bang from the window behind Joe. He was glad the shards of glass had missed him. He wondered briefly if it was due to the way the window had shattered, or whether it was because he'd instinctively stepped to one side.

And then he realised the question didn't matter much anymore, as the piece of ledge he'd been on was well above him and getting smaller.

He tried to wave goodbye to Riska as he fell. But his body began to spin.

When he'd spun fully around once, he saw Riska again. Just long enough to catch sight of her before she saw him, fainted, and fell off the building herself.

***

One of the things that had made Plek K*rargxtko's Top Manip was his gift for super-fast-think. He might be one of the biggest worriers in the hangar but, when trouble *did* come, he had a record for delivering the goods before most people had even thought of loading them into the van.

That didn't stop him being furious when his target fell out of the cross-hairs a micro-second before he'd been set to blast him. But it *did* make him change his style instantly from fixed-shot to moving-target mode.

And, as he switched modes, Plek realised that blasting a falling figure in another universe with a single beam-shot would be high-cred.

He zoomed the image out slightly, watched the bloke accelerate, and waited. It'd look good if he blew him away him when he was further down... maybe twenty feet from the ground.

As he was about to zoom back in, he saw another body fall into the top edge of the screen-space. He ignored it and re-zoomed as planned. But he knew the distraction had cost him a huge amount of free-fall. If the ground took the bloke before *he* did, he'd *never* live it down!

If Plek had had time to sweat, it would have hung in droplets from every skin-stud in his forehead. All eyes in the hangar were on this. He swung the joystick in a sweeping curve, caught the bloke's body at what he guessed was seven feet from the concrete, and squeezed the trigger.

For an instant a bright flash-ball fixed the point where he'd blown his target away. Then his ego shouted to him there was just a chance to make it a double. *Unlikely*, but worth a go. He twitched the stick sharply, fired when he saw something cut across the moving sight, and hoped.

He was really shocked to find he'd done it, and even more that the second flash-ball was as high as twelve feet from impact.

He switched himself to nonchalance mode, moved away from the controls, and acknowledged the wild applause around the hangar.

***

Behind some boxes, unseen by the hangar staff, a brawl writhed to an end.

The robot thought it had followed Juncus's orders to do all it could to help Bernie and the teams. This was why it had dragged the intruder as far from the Switcher-Desk as it could, and was trying to keep him pinned to the floor.

Doing all it could didn't include stopping a plate being unscrewed from its back by a piece of scrap metal that the intruder had picked up with his free hand. The robot knew that, once its hobby-welded wiring was dragged from its terminals, it would be able to do nothing at all.

But to the droid this was not a problem. Its *designer* had a problem. *It* only had a difficulty. The robot considered its mission had been a complete success, because it had done all it *could*.

Shloomger was peeved that a body-change wasn't an option. It felt as if he'd pulled twenty muscles in his arm, and the pain was slowing the business of getting into the robot's workings.

"Need some help?"

Shloomger would have liked to turn his head and thank Ked more fully for his interest, but simply mumbled "Yes."

Ked finished disabling the droid. "Saw your scrape-trail in the dust when I came looking for you at the Desk."

"Ah, Yup. Thanks for the help, Ked. Now I have to get back to that Switcher Desk ultra-quick! You see… "

"It's too late, Shloomger. They've been blasted... "

"No, you see... the Desk, the *controls*... "

"Look, I'm really sorry Shloomger. You don't realise. There's *nothing* we can do... "

"But *you* don't realise, Ked. We've *got* to get there". Shoon got to his feet.

Ked began to feel part embarrassed, part angry, "*Shloomger*! You can't *do* anything for them. It's *over*! They're *blown away*!"

***

Sculpin looked at Bernie's image in the hologphone, poured himself a large glass of Baboon's Buttock, and listened to the report with mixed feelings.

He was pleased the pair had been eliminated, but annoyed about the blackout that had taken place just before that.

Breakdowns weren't the sort of thing he liked explaining to K*rargxt. This one had been short. But when The Supremo got into serious cosmic destruction, the last thing he'd want would be an early lights-out while he had a set of universes in the crosshairs. He let Bernie finish his spiel, then ordered him to shut the Intervenor and run a complete check on it.

Bernie was disappointed. "So, we leave that planet... er... *Earth*... to spin on its way till the checks are through?"

Sculpin stared at the man with contempt. "From what I've just said, it's obvious you'll *have* to, until I tell you otherwise!" The Deputy-Supremo closed the call and leaned back in his chair to reflect.

***

Ked checked the time display on the inside of his eyelid. "Look, you can't keep the Switcher team bluffed away from this desk much longer. It's the *second* time you've come here, remember? Why are you taking pointless risks?"

Shoon didn't look up. He kept his eyes fixed on the display, then flicked some controls. "Well, Ked, I wouldn't say there's anything pointless about what I've just done. In fact I'd say that it was rather *important*."

Coot looked at Shloomger as if he was mad. He fought to keep cool. "Look, Shloomger, I'm not getting you on *any* of this!"

"The switches, Ked. I was putting them back to their previous setting... "

"I don't understand. *Which* setting?"

"Back to *annihilate* mode."

Coot stared at him. "You mean they *weren't* on that when Plek... ? ... You mean ... you'd had time to *change* them before that droid pulled you away?"

"Yes. To *transporter* mode. And now they're back on annihilate, no one will be any the wiser."

"And those flash-balls... ?"

"Just Switcher-generated marker-traces Ked. I set them that way. I used the same marker-traces as for annihilation. I found how to do it from the details Marlin sent me."

"Well you *crafty*... " Coot lowered his voice "... So the bloke and the girl are still alive, somewhere?"

Shloomger paused for a moment. "*Should* be, I think. But there's good news and bad news on that."

"Give me the good news first."

"Well, I've got a broad idea of Joe's route. There's quite a lot of flex in the system on that, but the destination'll be the same."

"Same as *what*, Shloomger ?"

"The same as the last one that 'scout' went to, the one you told me about."

"Hepkin Dangle?"

"Yes. They used the same beam system to send him off from the hangar."

Coot thought for a moment. "Ah... right. But the *last* place he visited wasn't Earth. He went to other places later."

"Yes, and Joe's destination's the last one he went to. It

was the only thing I could do, Ked. You see, I didn't have any data to put in, so I just copied in where Dangle went last time."

"When will he get there?"

"Not straight away. I didn't manage to put it on fast setting."

"And the girl?"

"Well, that's the bad news. You see, when I tried to do the same for the other despatching job, *her* one, I didn't have time to set the destination the same way. The robot got me before I could... "

"So where's *she* headed for, Shloomger?"

"That's the problem, Ked. I don't know."

"You don't *know*?"

"No. You see, if no setting's entered, the transporter sets the itinerary as 'No Destination', and sends the subject off anyway."

"To... nowhere?"

Ked saw that Shloomger was very upset about it.

"That's it Ked," Shloomger said quietly, "to nowhere."

CHAPTER 21

Joe couldn't understand why he hadn't hit the ground yet.

The voice he'd heard before he fell off the building started talking to him again.

It whispered, in a sort of mock sympathy, that it was very possible he *had* hit the ground, and that this was what being dead was like. It went on to point out what people who'd died could expect when they went downwards.

Joe ignored it, and tried to focus on what was happening.

And that was the odd thing. Though he felt he was still falling, it seemed as if everything beyond a short distance around him, like the sirens, the blazing building, the night, the world itself, had moved away.

It was as if he was still in a tiny piece of where he'd been, one that had been cut out from everything else.

In fact Joe was about spot-on right. For ease of operation, nearly all inter-universal transporter systems on Sub-Lamina 2k16 work on what's best described as the '*Cut-and-Paste*' principle, a simpler version of the much vaster '*Copy-and-Paste*' principle used by nature to duplicate universes.

In systems using Cut-and-Paste, creatures or objects are cropped from their surroundings and sealed in a 'skin' that's really a compressed chunk of the environment they've just left, so that they can survive in transit and in the places where they arrive.

This is great for outward-going types tripping off for thrills such as ice-jumping on the intertwining rings of the twin-planets of Flarrf, or who go on guided tours to the centres of giant stars. It's popular, too, with some visitors to the Trans-Nebula Blind-Date Programme on the Scrarnik Islands, since they can meet some really way-out beings while still feeling they're in the safety and comfort of their own home environment.

Like most good and useful things, such systems are of course open to abuse. As well as sheer theft, one widely condemned practice is parents' remote-lifting of objects and creatures from distant universes for their children to use in the next show-and-tell class. Another trend is the cosmic transfer of items for inclusion in multi-dimensional college essays. In fact it was thanks only to the quick thinking of a 9D Systems operator that the Venus de Milo was dragged out of an art thesis and got back on its stand within the instant that it was snaffled.

There are, of course, different varieties of inter-universal transporters. At the top end are the deluxe models that can take huge numbers of guests just about anywhere. Further down the scale are the '*Hey-Lets-Party-Travel!*' smaller group versions. And, at the 'starter' end, there are basic ones such as the one Sculpin had set up, and in which Joe was now travelling.

*

After a while, Joe felt that, though he was still moving, the *falling* part had gone. He seemed to have eased into more of a fast drifting.

And then he realised his eyes were closed. He decided to open them gradually, as he'd no idea what he'd see.

He was glad he hadn't rushed things, because it was all so amazingly… He tried to find a word to describe it. Then he realised he couldn't. It was just so amazingly… *different.*

***

The dawn broke to reveal an apalling sight. Passers-by stopped, then turned away, sickened by the experience.

Against the brightening sky the dreadful, smoking silhouette stood out in all its horribleness.

It called out in a beery rasp to the back of the departing fire officer.

"Sorry. Forgot to ask you. Any unusual habits?"

Squirt's question fell on the charred air. The interview was over.

He looked at the results of last night's blaze. The building was one hell of a mess, but so far no bodies had been found. At present it was assumed the place had been empty.

Safety officers and police were going through the block to trace the cause, but had found nothing definite yet. They'd ignored Frank's suggestion that, in some secret, torrid scene, a couple had ignited the place by body-friction.

***

Visible from only three points in existence, a product of strange and unpredictable contortions in a large number of things, including the fabric of time, a man lived in scrambled space.

In his more thoughtful moments he wondered how, in such a self-organising way, his body had begun continuously re-assembling itself from 'borrowed' and shared parts, most of which were still being used by their owners in places and moments across eternity.

One which wasn't, a freshly cut-off ear, lying unclaimed on a battlefield in northern medieval England, was temporarily serving as the left one on the man's head, which itself was on short 'loan-share' from a live one-eared space-pirate lurking in the remoter regions of Grooderketh on Level Five during the early Salacious period.

In this process of on-going regeneration, a continuous relay of chests and abdomens was itself supplemented by a series of new arms and hands cadged from upper limbs in service all around the cosmos. Legs and feet, joint-operated with owners from widely differing walks of life, switched into and out of view in a kind of part-bodied 'excuse-me' dance.

The man's organs were also replaced on a shift basis. Usually the new substitutes adapted well, though differences in the size and state of their real owners led to occasional twinges, or startling bouts of flatulence.

But, despite the occasional drawbacks, the man felt, generally speaking, that he was happy.

He looked on himself as an all-rounder. He revelled in being involved in a vast, exciting spread of events. And, though he didn't have a finger in every pie, he was pleased to have a lively involvement in a good many other things.

And he told himself that, though he often had only a small part in certain pieces of the action (sometimes a lot smaller than he'd have liked) and, though he wasn't *where it was all happening*, at least *all* his pieces were where *something* was going on.

The man had never felt the need to give himself a name. This was because, despite his many fleeting part-contacts, he had never yet, in his partially entire existence, completely *met* anyone.

As far as he was concerned, he was just a man in scrambled space.

So, when by chance a beam flashed across a piece of space and gently deposited a beautiful, radiant girl in front of him, he was delighted.

He was also at a brief loss as to how to introduce himself.

Riska's journey had been different from Joe's, and she'd begun it by fainting. So, unlike Joe, she'd no recollection that, when it had started, she'd been hurtling towards a set of no-quibble concrete flagstones. All the same, memories of something very worrying happening to Joe were starting to creep back into her mind.

But, at present, all Riska knew was that a man with an unusual appearance was smiling at her.

After a few seconds he grew more usual, since his head became a London traffic policeman's who, though still smiling at her, had his mind on some vital piece of duty.

The voice that spoke to her via the policeman's mouth came from the chest of an operatic baritone between rehearsals in Post-Nebulic Thrargor, and struck Riska as a bit over-throaty. But it cut well through the heavy vehicle noise that surrounded the policeman's head.

"I think the word is *Hello*," he boomed in a pitch some ocean rollers use when bumping the edges of tropical lagoons.

"Yes, I suppose it is," Riska said. And, not being sure what exactly to say next, she added: "You certainly seem busy. I hadn't realised there was so much traffic around here... or," she added, glancing at his left leg, "so much of a market in stilt-walking acts."

"There isn't. Well, not around here anyway."

He did his best to explain his personal facts of life.

"It's okay," Riska said after a very short time, rescuing him from the task, "you don't need to justify your existence. And anyway, it's obvious you know a huge deal more about things here than I do. As a matter of fact, I haven't got a clue what I'm doing in this place, if '*place*' is the right word."

The man's expression changed. So did his head. The ape-man's face from the Pleiadean swamps smiled at her even more benignly than its predecessor.

"Perhaps I can help," he said gently. "I mean, if you're lost, or trying to find someone, maybe I can get some info for you. I mean, without wanting to boast, I've got... well... *connections* in a reasonable number of places. Where are you from?"

"West London. And my name's Riska, by the way."

They stretched out their arms towards each other. Riska grasped what felt like the trusting handshake of a free-fall parachutist in mid-dive.

"Pity," the ape-man said, "not about your name, I mean. But my last head might have given you a few directions straight away." He looked at her thoughtfully. "I suppose I could always see if my body could sort of call him back, but I don't think it likes to keep any of the bits for too long. It gets too distracting for the owners, you see." The ape looked down at its parachutist forearm. "As a matter of fact, I imagine this hand will soon… "

Riska felt her companion's grip ease. In its place was a moister, chubbier handclasp. From the chunky jewels in what looked like tubes of rings on its fingers, she guessed it came from a spoiled twit somewhere in a well-to-do part of the cosmos.

The hand's thumb reached forward and touched Riska's palm in a foppish way. The effect was cancelled out by the *other* hand's index finger being up the ape's left nostril.

"By the way," she said, "what's *your* name?"

"Haven't got one. It'd be difficult, really. I mean people like to put a *face* to a name, and… well… "

"Yes, I see what you mean, but – as far as I can tell – you seem to have the same character, more or less," she paused as his chest morphed to a new one covered by a white coat with a stethoscope in its front pocket, "despite the changes in your, er *parts*."

"Well, somehow or other, I do manage to stay… sort of… consistent, I suppose," a clown's face replied. "I think I must have some sort of spiritual core, or inner *being* or whatever, that keeps on kind of *going*, if you see what I mean… "

There was a burst of flatulence. The clown continued, looking slightly embarrassed. "… But, you see, even if people *could* get used to changes in the way I look, there's not much point in my having a name anyway, if no one's around long enough to get to *know* me. As a matter of fact, you're the first person who's ever… well… *been* down this way at all. Would you, perhaps, like to stay?"

Riska felt the need to explain to a part of her mind, the part that whispers to girls about strange men who invite them into their places, that there didn't seem to be a thousand other options. She added that, from what she'd seen so far, the man -though he had some quirky transient habits – did seem able to keep more or less in character.

"It's very kind of you," she said, "but, as far as I can see, you don't seem to have any particular... *living* quarters. I suppose I could maybe try and sort of... camp nearby." She paused. "What about food? I'd forgotten about that."

"That's no problem," the man replied, "I've got fridges full of the stuff. It gets left quite often, you see. Sometimes I get the odd Tarzan-type arm cradling a pile of mangoes, but mostly it's stuff in the hands of pizza delivery people or else on waiters' trays. And as I usually get a fairly good selection of full stomachs, I don't really have much need for food or drink."

He stepped to one side, and Riska noticed that the piece of space that had been behind him shimmered slightly round to the left. As she followed it with her eyes she began to make out what looked like the corridor of an apartment, with doors leading off it at various points.

The man blew some sawdust from what appeared to be a carpenter's hand, and used its fingers to tweak the edge of the shimmer. Riska watched him pull the kitchen into sight. It was a reasonable size, and equipped with a collection of tools and gadgets from, as far as she could make out, past, present and future.

"How did you get all this?" she asked into the visor of an astronaut's helmet.

"Mostly came with the arms of fitters and installation people. I suppose quite a lot of stuff *does* actually get mislaid in other places too. I look upon it as being here sort of... on approval," a gloved hand rubbed the side of the helmet thoughtfully with a riding crop, "I mean none of it's actually stolen. They can come and take it whenever they want. It's just that, so far, no one's been back for any of it. It's the same with the stuff in the other rooms."

"Other rooms?"

"Yes, I don't remember exactly how many there were at the last count, but I think there were about eighteen bathrooms and six bedrooms… "

"Sounds a bit off-balance to me… "

"I had a whole series of plumbers' arms and hands, you see. One after the other, for some reason. A sort of spatial swarm of them."

"That explains a lot. You can't get them for love nor money where I come come from."

"Love… nor… money… ?"

"A manner of speaking."

"… Oh yes, I see. Well, as for the main structural work on the whole apartment, that's mostly been bricklayers' hands – with a reasonable turnout of other trades too. Of course the styles tend to differ a bit as you go round."

The rugged, scarred face of a fire-bison hunter from Krorvak-Thfrintchz, looked at her with an almost timid expression.

"Would you *like* to stay?" the man asked again. He paused briefly. "Oh, by the way, I think I should tell you… " he stopped for a few more seconds, looking rather embarrassed, "… I know about your boyfriend, Joe… ".

Riska stared at him, "*How…* ?"

From deep within a fur hat, the eyes of a spatial troika-racer from the ice-crater of Sarpienstor Sirot peered at her gently. "Well, you see, with so many heads coming and going, I get this enormous amount of information. Eye-witnesses to things, people gossiping, travellers' tales… "

"No, I meant how *is* he."

"The voice from the fur-wrapped face sounded embarrassed again. "Oh, I'm so sorry! I should have told you what I know… "

"*And…* "

"He's okay."

Riska felt as if she was about to faint again. "But where *is* he?"

“Rather difficult to say exactly.” He paused for a moment, trying to draw together details from his collective memory. “The last I heard was that he was on the move, in a transporter beam. Anyway, there’s always a chance he’ll end up safe and sound back where he started from. It’s not certain, mind you. But, anyway, the latest I’ve got on him is that he’s okay.”

He held out his arm again towards his living-accommodation. “If you *would* like to lodge here... it’d be separate rooms of course, all very respectable. By the way, there are plenty of clothes in the wardrobes, if you’d like to try them.”

***

Shloomger to Marlin.

Thanks for advice, and for tech details on how to contact you with my messager. To put things briefly, J & R not dead, at least, not as far as I know. Think they’re currently travelling via Transporter beam that I replaced Intervenor beam with.

No idea how to retrieve R, but think J returnable to Earth if we can work out how. Would appreciate suggestions on this.

Good news about Earth, at least for very short term, as Intervenor, Viewer and Transporter (whole shebang) currently down for tech checks.

Bad news is: When Transporter comes on again – making it possible to bring Joe back – Intervenor will also come on, and is likely to be used to annihilate Earth. Will try to prevent this unfortunate event happening, but cannot promise anything. Any info and suggestions on this also appreciated.

Cheers. And try keep smiling as long as able. S.

*

Marlin to Shloomger.

Thanks. Have looked at tech data in K*rargxtko network files. Have some ideas on how to return Joe using T-beam. (See enclosed details). Sadly have nothing on how to retrieve Riska.

Re. annihilation of Earth, glad this at least postponed, but have no clue re. stopping this technically. Can only suggest trying various ploys to avoid final decision being taken (see short note below on one possible approach). If all this fails, please inform me asap, so can cancel order for new greenhouse.

Good luck.

M.

Short note on one possible approach.

While trawling through secret batch of files in K*rargxtko network, saw memo about K*rargxt having signed some kind of temporary destruction-exemption for a planet called K*rargxtus3b22c4r.

Having got other information on their plans, and put two and two together, think planet is Earth.

Have recently found later electronic note from Sculpin to K*rargxt's office requesting that exemption document be cancelled and shredded. As far as could see in network, this request had not been acted on yet. Managed to remote-delete the request, so hope exemption document has not been been cancelled. Suggest you try and find document, as it may be useful. Realise this probably next-to-impossible, but it's all I could come up with.

M.

***

Spanger tugged on the lead. Though not a large dog, he was well up on power-weight ratio.

To him the best thing about these walks was the freedom it gave his nose. His home, a place he loved dearly, was crammed with smells, but by now these were mainly sniffed-out and classified.

This was the second visit he'd made here with his master in quite a short time. He liked it. Out here a dog could read the air. He eased back on the leash and sniff-zoomed forward in the hope of cat or largish rodent. Nothing yet. Only scents from cola empties scattered in the long grass.

His nose probed onwards.

Now, *there* was something more interesting. Under that tree in the middle-distance...

*

Bill shifted his sleep-stiff legs and held out the plastic cup to the thermos for a third refill while he finished off the last sandwich from the old man's lunchbox.

This bloke, he thought, was the right kind of stuff. Not asking too many questions. There was just a decent, respectful quietness about him. He took a closer look at the man and wondered if he'd sussed what he'd been up to recently. Anyway, if he had, he wasn't showing any sign.

He got onto his feet, made his excuses and wandered off. Whether anyone sussed or not, sticking around wasn't an option.

CHAPTER 22

It hadn't occurred to Joe that some regions of space might be coloured, let alone able to change to other colours. Maybe, he thought, this wasn't space at all, but something else. If so, things probably *would* be different from the way he'd expect them to be. In any case, everything here seemed to be *real* enough in its own way.

This was probably why the strings-and-planets player Joe was drifting past didn't seem unusual. And the player wasn't surprised to see Joe either. But then, he *was* concentrating on his music.

To Joe, the fact that the musician was a kind of super-giant also seemed normal. He was in just the right proportion to the instrument he was playing, which consisted of two self-orbiting planets and what looked like a a set of changing strands running between them. Joe saw he was playing it rather like a double-double-bass. But how he made his music, and how he could hear it through space wasn't clear. From time to time there seemed to be some sort of shift in the space-scape around him, which made Joe think the player might really be in a bigger place somewhere else, and reaching down to the planets to play them. To Joe, it didn't matter anyway. The music was beautiful.

It took a bit more time for Joe to get his mind round the idea that, as well as making music, the giant was changing the colour of the space – or whatever it was – around him, by his playing. After a while he wondered if this was because the space was vibrating with the music or whether it was somehow changing colour at the pleasure of hearing it. And then he thought that perhaps, from the space's point of view, the two things were the same anyway.

When the musician finished his piece, Joe sensed intense applause, in the form of sounds and colours, streaming towards the player from points around him. He joined in, and thought he saw his own applause mix with the ring-waves converging on the player.

Joe had already moved quite a long way past the musician before he began playing again. He raised his hand to wish him goodbye. The player was so involved with his music that it seemed unlikely he would notice. But suddenly he looked up from the strings and smiled a smile that seemed to gather up Joe, the music and the space around him. Joe went on looking at him till he was a point in the distance. Then, even after the musician had disappeard from sight, it was clear that distance didn't matter at all. Joe, space, and everything in it, knew he was still there.

***

On a podium of empty machine-crates, standing in front of a huge image of K*rargxt, Bernie stared down at the tired faces of the teams on the hangar floor, raved to them about the powers of the revised Intervenor, and hyped himself on to the climax of his speech.

He punched at the air, and somehow missed. He struggled to re-gain his balance.

"... I'm talking about what our teams *have* that sets us above the herd. I'm talking *drive*! I'm talking *grit*! I'm talking the difference between men and eunuchs. I'm talking *bollocks*!"

There was much agreement and clapping.

From his position near the back of the audience, Shloomger mulled over the current state of affairs. Whilst some things in this outfit had been botched, the fact was they had a machine which worked, and which was horribly destructive.

And the earlier part of Bernie's talk had made clear that the machine was intended to be heavily used. Sculpin would be appearing shortly and, after a brief drink to mark the relaunch of the Intervenor, a planet would be annihilated as part of the celebrations.

Shoon watched the staff busy themselves with the final preparations for Sculpin's arrival. Maybe, he thought, it was because there were so many targets lined up for destruction by the Intervenor that it had slipped Bernie's mind to mention that the name of the planet to be annihilated that evening was Earth.

***

A good deal of time seemed to have gone by when Joe saw the first of the odd socks. It passed so close to him that he could have reached out and touched it. But it was so grim to look at that it was the last thing he felt like doing. The sock was soon followed by others, and it became clear that the first one had simply marked the edge of a huge cloud of them.

None of the socks looked like a team player. Joe thought there must be some physical law stopping any two of them getting nearer to each other than a distance more or less the square of their footsize. It also looked as if the law was based on some principle of mutual repulsion. As far as Joe could tell, none of them had been washed for a very long time.

He expected a putrid smell to hit him but, looking more carefully, he saw that space itself was shrinking back from the edge of each sock, leaving a no-go gap, unjumpable by smells, fleas or anything else.

Joe's mind was casting about to get some understanding of the background to it all, when a being with a weary seen-it-all face emerged from a spatial slit nearby.

"*Don't ask*!" it said, and disappeared.

*

After the sock cloud, so much space, or whatever it was, passed that Joe began wondering if anything that had taken place up to now had ever happened at all.

A shape materialised near him, sank back, and then partly re-appeared. As much as it *could*, the shape looked at Joe briefly, then asked, "... And how about *you*? Do *you* think we actually *are*?" after which it lapsed back into a smudgy sort of outline.

"Not sure!" Joe shouted at the outline, assuming its faintness meant it was somehow deaf or distant, "I've been wondering about that myself, as a matter of fact."

"I suppose," the entity said, crisping its edges slightly, "you couldn't drop me a few ideas on it? You see, I've got this urgent college essay to finish. It's on whether we exist or not and, as I skipped the last couple of lectures, I don't know if we actually *do*. The thing is, I've got to read the essay out at the next seminar... "

Joe was beginning to find the entity irritating.

"Why", he suggested, "don't you answer the question by simply not turning up?"

The shape let out an exhausted sigh. "Now why didn't I think of that myself?" it murmured, and relaxed out of view completely.

Joe sensed that some different sounds were coming from another zone of space in front of him. But, in the same way as the ones he'd just heard, they morphed into a voice as they came through his cling-wrap shell.

"Want something very special, Ducks?" the zone asked.

"Well, now you mention it," Joe said, as if talking to a hands-free phone, "I couldn't half do with a... "

"... *Massage*, dear? Hands-through-being treatment in discreet surroundings, with total invisibility, no questions asked... ?"

"No I want... "

"... A kinky time-ride with the lascivious quantity of your choice?"

"No thanks. What I need... "

"Perhaps you're too busy at the moment. Well, we can always switch to yesterday if you had space in your diary then. In that case, it'll have given you something to remember, dear... "

"No, not yesterday either. But, as for *now*, at least, as for *incredibly soon*, I want a... "

Whatever was behind the sounds stopped for a moment, as if reading Joe's expression, and said, "Ah, a *pee*, dear! Why didn't you say so in the *first* place?"

The zone of space fell briefly silent again, then said, "Well, you'll be looking for *somewhere* for that... "

"Yup, you got it in one... "

"Let's see... " there was a long pause which Joe found increasingly painful, "... the nearest cosmic convenience is a long way from here dearie... ". The being began to take on features. It started on a series of directions that Joe thought likely to last longer than the journey itself, then paused. "... Well, if you ever make it past Voinkg-the-Grim, Eater of Beings and Phenomena, which is unlikely, you turn *left* after the second... No, I tell a lie, after the *third* Startling Turbulence of Breelginar... "

Joe's eyes scanned around for something else to distract him from the pressure, but there was nothing. The being, who had firmed into an elderly humanoid lady, seemed to have moved a fraction further along her mind-route.

"... After that you go straight for a bit – well, *quite* a bit, in fact. And then, just before you reach the Shifting Temporal Tunnel – of course, I can't say exactly *when* you'll get to it – you make a sharp turn to the left into a kind of spatial alley... "

Joe hoped she'd get there soon.

"Well, go down that alley dear. Right to the end... " she fixed Joe with a doubting stare, "I mean *right* to the end... "

"Yes, *and*... ?"

"And then *at* the end you turn left into an even narrower alley... "

"How much time do reckon all this is likely to take?"

"... And, about half-way down *that*, in a sort of alcove in the spatial wall, you'll become aware of a presence, which will offer you various special experiences and then crystallise into an elderly lady."

"Right."

"Do not ask it where the nearest convenience is."

"Why?"

"Because, if you do, it will give you a load of long tedious directions, and you'll simply end up back in front of it, where it will warn you in a roundabout way not to listen to it anyway... "

"What you mean in a nutshell is: Don't bother!"

"Exactly," the elderly lady replied with a cackle, and de-featured back into the zone of space.

"Of course," she called out invisibly, "of course, if you'd turned the wrong way after the Third Startling Turbulence of Breelginar, you'd have come back into the explanation somewhere else... "

Joe looked round for somewhere closer to relieve himself. He realised he'd better be careful where he did this. You might easily find yourself upsetting some unseen and highly sensitive being.

A humanoid-looking type came into view in a way that looked as if he was simply turning sharply sideways from somewhere invisible. "If I were *you* I'd just do it on the other side of that asteroid," he said. "That's where I usually go for a slash, and no one's complained yet."

Joe looked around him and spotted a largish pumice-type rock some way off. He drifted over to it and solved his problem.

The humanoid type, who'd been looking discreetly in the opposite direction, turned to greet Joe again as he drifted back towards him.

"By the way, my name's Voinkg," he said.

Joe had a sudden uncomfortable feeling, "*Voinkg-The-Grim*, Eater of Beings and Phenomena?"

The humanoid's face took on a weary expression, "You've been talking to that old bag," he replied curtly, "don't pay any attention to *her*!"

Joe eyed him uneasily. "So how come you got that name? Are you saying she just made it up?"

"She saw me one day having haddock and chips, and gave me that title." He thought for a moment. "Well, I suppose if *occasionally* having haddock and chips makes me a grim eater of beings and phenomena, then that's what I *am*, particularly from the haddock's point of view. Now, If she'd spotted you having a pee behind that space-rock, she'd probably have called you The Ghastly Inundator of Asteroids, and warned other travellers to stay clear of you. She's got a label for just about everything that's gone past her. The strange thing is a lot of beings think it's all true, and never realise they're going to end up on her list too!"

Joe felt that he might as well be getting along. He thanked the humanoid for his advice. Then, making what seemed a special effort of the will, he somehow managed to change the direction and speed of his drift, so that he was steadily leaving Voinkg behind.

A bit after that, though, he felt the line of his movement change again, as if his detour was being corrected. This gave him a feeling that maybe he was travelling on some kind of pre-set course.

Suddenly there was another brief speed change and a new correction, as if a collision-avoidance manoeuvre was happening. It was soon clear to Joe that dodging a crash was exactly why his course *had* changed.

A tiny point of light seemed to be moving along the path he'd been on, and it seemed he was now travelling parallel to it. The point grew very slowly until, though it was still quite small, he saw that it was a separate piece of space with, in the nearest part of it, what looked like the front end of a spaceship.

He felt he could easily reach out, pick it up and bounce it in the palm of his hand. But, since his course had been changed in order to avoid it, he thought the best thing would be to keep his eyes on it and see what happened.

As the spaceship was growing larger quite slowly, Joe thought that, in the dimension – or whatever – it was travelling in, it was still some way off but moving very fast. He began to make out what seemed to be portholes in the vessel's side, and what looked like some kind of spaceline logo on its tail.

***

Eelag tinkered nervously with the insides of his text-message handset. The ghastly being had done its best to total it. But he was still desperately hoping to get it working again. Maybe, at least, he could turn on its receiver mode.

Doubts about his dealings with the debt-collector were making his screwdriver-hand jumpy, and his recent trussed-up experience hadn't done any of his other body parts much good either. He was feeling twitchy all over.

He peered at the graunched handset. It looked as if he'd managed to get the receiver unit working, but the sender part was knackered. He looked up for a moment towards the far edge of the beach. Even at this distance the face of Zunddertokk's henchman looked horribly triumphant.

Eelag had expected him to head back to his boss straight after he'd got what he wanted. But for some reason the foul creature had chosen to take a break on the edge of the sea first. All things considered, Eelag thought, it wasn't really surprising. After all, it was one of the most beautiful beaches of the entire Level.

But, even though the sun was shining strongly again, he saw the henchman couldn't sunbathe properly. Whilst he'd seemed able to spread and shrink his accompanying storm whenever he wanted, it was clear he couldn't switch it off completely. A tailor-made cloud was soaking his body in drizzle.

A large bird with colourful, translucent wings spiralled towards the beach, extended its brilliant organ-pipe feathers, and played itself down with a fine rendering of Three-Berry Blues.

Eelag watched the bird's graceful landing, and thought about Shloomger, and what he might imagine was happening on the beach. He wondered, too, how his friend would react when he found out the debt-collector had got what he'd come for.

***

Joe guessed, from the speed it seemed to be doing, that the spaceship would suddenly grow huge, whoosh past him and disappear into another point of space. But it continued to grow at a steady rate. After a short while it changed to a new, curved course. At first it seemed to be heading outwards and away, but then began spiralling inwards towards him.

By the time it had drawn alongside, it had grown to the size of what he took to be some form of bulk-tour space-cruiser. As far as he could tell from looking through the portholes, there were enough cabins for a couple of thousand varied creatures of more or less humanoid-size, as well as what looked like a series of suites, ballrooms, dining areas and conference halls.

One of the conference halls was fully lit, and packed with an audience of varied creatures. He heard an announcement being made over the hall's PA system. "And you see, on your left, a chance example of Golden Rule Fifteen… "

Joe saw the ship tilt slightly, as the passengers surged to the portholes to get a look at him. "… And a Gilt-Edged Diploma-of-Unsurpassable-Merit to the first of you who can tell me, without looking at your folders, what that rule is… "

There was a burst of what Joe took to be theatre-organ music. A low, green slimey light splurged round the interior of the conference hall, and seemed somehow to seep out through the space-cruiser's hull, condensing into a cloud around it. Projected on the cloud was the image of a multihybrid creature, that Joe thought was probably a composite, travelling-version of some planet's entire range of species.

Under the image, banner headlines proclaimed the diploma-winner as *Sprinkishik The Complete, Spacetime-share Sales Champion for the entire region of Sub-Lamina 2s4!*

The trainer's voice continued, "Congratulations *Sprinkishik*! Golden Rule Fifteen is… Well, let's hear it from *all* of you who were nearly there on the buzzer *with* him."

There was a loud chant from inside the ship, "*Never let any unforeseen sales_opportunity go by!*"

"… So let's *do* it, folks! *Invite him in!*"

*

Joe stared at the trainee and asked himself how creatures got themselves into such head-banging, no-hoper assignments as this one. "Look, forget what you just heard on that mega-hype-course," he said slowly, "and tell me if you *really* think that here – wherever here *is* – I'm going to buy *life insurance* from you or anyone else!"

A voice struck up quietly behind the trainee. "Remember Rule Seventeen," it murmured, "*overcome initial customer resistance to concept*!"

"Er.." the creature tried, "while you might not think *now* that it's worthwhile, because you're not convinced the insurance company will be around to pay out… "

"Stay *positive*!" whispered the voice behind it.

The trainee pressed on. "What I mean is you're probably… er… "

"Not 'probably', '*Clearly*'!" said the voice.

"Yes, of course, you're *clearly* really saying to yourself that it's a good idea, but… "

"No 'buts'! '*And*'!" corrected the voice."

"Sorry, *and* that you'll take out our mega all-cosmic-risks policy at *some* time in the future… "

"Don't forget the *eye contact*!" the voice prompted.

"Which eye do I use?"

"*All twelve* of them, for Larnipp's sake!"

"Right. So, at this very particular moment, *Joe*, my company is making you this *unrepeatable* offer at a *specially* reduced premium... "

"Go away!" said Joe.

The creature went away.

It was replaced by the next entity in the queue, an unenergetic energy-salesbeing from Sub-Lamina 2RSJ.

Joe took a sip from the cup of free whatever-it-was he'd been handed when he'd agreed to come on board, and wondered how he'd ever let himself become Client of the Evening. Then he realised it was because he'd always wanted to see the inside of a spaceship.

The ship struck him as a mix of channel ferry, motorway service-station and conference centre, though he'd never before come across a solar-tanning saloon that offered inter-dimensional access to the sun of your choice.

He glanced at the line of varied beings, each of which, in its particular way, was going through its notes while it waited to meet its sales opportunity.

"Look, just how much longer is this going to take?" he asked a badge-encrusted trainer. "I have to get away soon. I think I'm travelling on some kind of course myself, but I'm delighted to say it's not *this* one!"

"Now, if you'll just answer a few questions about the cost of your energy-consumption over the last payment period," the trainee creature murmured, "there's no sweat. I'll take my time over reading them to you. I mean you don't *really* need to tell me anything, but if you'd *like* to, I *suppose* I can get around to making you a better offer some time... "

Joe turned to the trainer again. "Right! That's *it*! I'm out of here *now,* either via the space-exit or through the walls, if I can make it!"

"Ever thought about a set of matching travel cases?" said a polka-dotted centaur half-way down the queue. "The deluxe range self-redirect if they get lost."

Joe stopped himself suggesting it should climb into one and demonstrate.

"Or an inter-cosmic money belt?" suggested a fifty-valve invertebrate behind the centaur. "It'll print off notes from over four billion denominations at any point within Lateral 2D5... "

"Nope."

"... And extrude a range of Inter-Universal charge-cards for those awkward moments... "

"I *said*... "

"It'll even arrange credit for its own purchase... "

"Thank you, and *goodbye*!"

The Multiple Heads of Training came over. "On your way out," they said in harmony, "maybe you'd like to pass through our duty-free sales area... "

*

Joe looked back at the receding spaceship till it had become the tiny point of light he'd first seen. The point made a sideways turn and disappeared.

For a while his speed of drifting seemed to increase, as if the time he'd spent on the spacecraft was somehow being made up. But eventually he slowed. He sensed a few slight jolts, as if a series of fine course-corrections were being made.

Then he thought he'd stopped moving, but he couldn't be sure. Maybe he'd imagined it. And maybe he'd also imagined the thin, sort of pencilled, line that had suddenly appeared in front of him and then vanished. A smell of peppermint seemed to have come and gone too.

The space around Joe re-loaded itself moments later with more lines, some of which were linked up. The peppermint was messing about too. One instant it was there, the next, it and the lines had gone. Then the scent and the lines came back again, and this time they had some music behind them, but just a snatch.

With each fade-out-and-return, more lines appeared,

with fuller shadings inside them. And – every time – Joe could here a bit more music. It seemed to be in a kind of multi-stereo.

Now a part of the area within the lines had almost filled itself in, and Joe realised it was a standard lamp. Nearby, other items were growing more solid. Between them, and behind them, were moving shapes.

The peppermint was vaguely back, mixed with furniture polish and chopped shallots. For a moment it seemed to Joe that he was breathing down the wrong end of a pair of nostrils. Then the smells somehow sprang into focus.

It was clear he was arriving somewhere. Up to now he'd thought of turning up in places as something you did in one go. Even after rough journeys, destinations had always presented themselves ready-made when you got there. But this one seemed to be reaching out to him piece by piece.

It was a tough job getting his mind and body round the experience. He decided the best thing was just to let it happen.

CHAPTER 23

Boontrak was more confident he'd made progress. He'd started to think about how he might leave the cave. He knew he had a huge amount of energy stored in its rock walls, and he had the feeling that if he could get some sort of big encouraging push he might just be able to break free. But he knew that, for the moment, it was still a dream. Maybe it always would be.

He'd have liked to have some sun in the cave, but a giant boulder just outside the entrance blocked it out. It was never *really* dark or cold, though. His intrinsic power acted as a combined night-light and storage heater.

Reflecting on things generally, he supposed there were probably beings around the various Levels of Existence who were a lot worse off.

There are, of course, beings who are far *better* off, and who realise that things have gone generally well for them. But there are some who, though having heaps going for them, such as three square meals a day (or the cosmic equivalent), huge travel opportunities and plenty of spending money, make it their mission to journey around moaning to others that existence is in fact unmitigated misery.

One of the problems for an Upper-Leveller who's become stuck on one of the lower levels is the near certainty that sooner or later one of these beings will drop by for a one-way 'chat'.

Proorong Sproondip's reputation as a gloom-spreader, for which he'd been awarded a commemorative puke-splat on the Walkway of Dejection in Nurbb, had led to regular warnings of his whereabouts being a major selling feature in navigation systems used by a good many Upper Levellers.

Since Boontrak was a sitting duck, there was something inevitable about Proorong's arrival. This sense of the inevitable was something Proorong liked to rub in as soon as he turned up anywhere.

He installed himself in Boontrak's cave without waiting to be asked. Through the folds of fog-skin he was accustomed to wearing, he started the 'conversation' he believed Boontrak must have been looking forward to for a very long time.

"*This* isn't much of a place!" he said.

***

The waitress finished polishing a piece of wall panelling nearby, and turned round, clearly surprised to see someone at the table. She stopped munching her peppermint and grinned at Joe.

"Must have been quite a fancy dress party!" she said.

Joe looked around, and realised he looked different from everyone else in the place.

For a start, the clothes of the other people in the pub-café had another style. It was as if they had been made individually for them on some kind of loom exactly the shape of the person's body, and had then tuned themselves perfectly to their wearer's way of life. As the people moved, the clothes seemed to know exactly what they were going to do, and to move a micro-instant before they did.

Joe reflected on the place. Wherever he was in existence, this looked like a relaxed, easy-going part of it.

He saw that the standard lamp next to the table where he was sitting had completely filled itself in. He reached out a finger and pinged the shade. The vibes that came through his fingertip told him there was no other lampshade like it anywhere.

He noticed that the music had also become complete, and that there was something very unusual about it.

It seemed to be producing itself through all the objects around the room, including the lampshade. Joe had no idea how it was doing it, but it was as if every piece of furniture, picture, cup, bottle, – even every beermat – was being called on at moments to make parts of the sounds.

"Would you like anything?" the waitress asked with a cheering smile.

Perhaps because of the fire he'd come from – and the fact that his spaceship drink hadn't fully quenched his thirst – Joe found himself asking for water.

He smelled cooking happening somewhere, and realised he was feeling hungry. The idea of hot food so soon after the blaze didn't appeal to him. He tagged some basic bread and cheese onto his order, plus a beer as a chaser for the water.

The water tasted as if the café's boss had a brother-in-law who owned some very special mountain spring, and when the bread and cheese came it woke a hidden bread-and-cheese-dedicated corner of his soul that seemed to have been waiting for it for ever.

And the beer stirred memories of events in a pub he remembered had been called THE BEND IN THE SKY.

He tried very hard not to think about Riska, and told himself the best thing would be to find out where he was, because that would be the first step in getting back to her.

He drank his beer and ordered another.

"Funny," said the waitress, "it was quite a while ago, but I remember there was a bloke in fancy dress as well, sitting exactly where you are now."

She stopped and thought for a few seconds. "I don't think he was from round here. He had a sort of… different outlook on people. And he was asking strange questions."

It seemed to Joe she was drawing on deep reserves of being positive about people.

"*Yes,*" she continued, "I think *that's* probably the best way of putting it. A different *outlook*. I remember he seemed to have a lot of steaming anger in him, the poor man. I don't suppose you've come across him?"

"You never know," Joe murmured, "you can meet people like that sometimes." He searched for a way of finding out where he was without seeming a total looney. "I mean, maybe he was a bit stressed because he wasn't from round *here*."

"Yes, dear, I expect you're right," she said.

The beer had soothed Joe's dry throat. Speaking was getting easier.

"Maybe he'd got *lost*," he suggested, "and sort of wandered in here. It can happen to a lot of people... ", he cast around in his mind for some sort of example, "I mean, only the other day, I was looking for a bank, and found I'd walked into a betting shop."

Joe could see the woman was looking at him carefully.

"You're not from round here either, *are* you?" she said gently.

And, before Joe could answer, she'd had to move off to serve another customer.

***

"Now I come to think of it," Proorong observed, scanning the stones around the cave, "the longer I've been here, the worse you look... "

That, Boontrak thought to himself, was the only worthwhile statement the fognoid had made since he'd turned up!

"Pity you didn't get in touch with me," the visitor said, slightly hurt, "I could have dropped in a lot sooner. Still," he de-darkened his tone marginally from Abyss-Setting -74 to -73, "I'm here *now*, anyway, and unless you get better quickly, which seems very unlikely, I'll know where to come and find you, so we can have more of these little chats."

Boontrak minded at the entity that he needn't bother, and that perhaps he should be getting along now, as there must be a great many other beings – a long way away – waiting to listen to him. But if the fognoid had picked up the message, it was clear he wasn't paying attention.

“Looks like you’ve been in some kind of collision,” Proorong went on, “travelling too fast, probably, and ignoring safety requirements!” He swirled his mist-coat disapprovingly. “Of course, you’ve only yourself to blame. You can’t say that power-brain of yours, the one that’s spread around the walls now, didn’t have good navigation facilities. But most likely you weren’t using them! I’ve seen too many cases like that! Why, only the other day… ”

And Boontrak knew somehow that he was dozing again.

***

Joe was intrigued about what, apart from his ‘fancy-dress’ clothes, told the waitress he wasn’t a local. He saw she was heading over in his general direction again.

“What makes you think I’m not from round here?” he called out as she passed.

She laughed. “Well, there’s the way you keep staring at things, like at people’s clothes and the ripple-races in the ceiling that those customers were watching earlier. It’s as if you’ve never seen anything *like* them before.” She gave him a closer look, “and you *do* seem to have been travelling a bit recently… ”

Joe peered at the reflection of his face in the copper edging of the table and saw the smoke-stains on his forehead.

“And, of course,” she continued, “the bit about the ‘bank’ and the ‘money’.

Joe tried to sound sensible, but realised he was starting to gabble. “Well… I mean… I know a lot of it’s done automatically now and with cash machines and all that… ”

He saw she was looking at him a good deal more carefully. Maybe it was time to settle up and move on.

He asked for the bill and, without thinking, pulled some money from his pocket. The waitress looked carefully at the note in his hand, as if she thought he was trying to show her a picture of something.

"Well, it's what I normally use for paying," Joe said with a friendly laugh, "where I come from… " He looked around to see if anyone else was dealing with their bill at the same time, and saw, a few tables away, a small, slightly cuddly-looking animal make its way in through an open window. It settled on the arm of a customer who had just got up to leave. The man stroked the creature briefly, ushered it quickly down from his arm and across to a nearby waiter, and left.

The best Joe could make of it was that, as well as this being a ceiling-ripple sports pub, it was some kind of hamster-racing outfit too. He got up. Within a few moments a small group of the animals had arrived and installed themselves on his shoulder. He followed what the other customer had done, and guided the creatures onto the tray the waitress was holding.

She thanked him, and gave him another thoughtful look. "I know!" she said, "you're an actor, just come from dress rehearsals. And you're still sort of playing the part you've been practising, *aren't* you? I had a friend who did that. It used to take him hours sometimes to get out of his role."

"Well, not exa… "

"And you must have met that other fancy-dressed bloke. Maybe you're trying to copy him. *He* asked me about 'paying the bill' too!"

"Can't say I… "

She stopped and looked at Joe in a kindly way. "Mind you, you're being far too nice if you want to imitate him properly. He was a lot more impatient. In fact he rushed out without settling up at all."

Joe saw his chance. "Acting's *fun*", he said cheerfully, "and *you* look as if you could do it brilliantly! By the way, I'm Joe. What's your… "

"Ochania," she said, and gave him a warm smile.

Joe sat down again. "Well, Ochania, why not give it a try *now*. Let's pretend I really *have* come from a long way away."

She giggled, and glanced around the pub quickly. "Alright, just for a bit… "

***

If it hadn't been that she wanted desperately to get back home and find Joe, Riska would have liked to stay a great deal longer with the man in scrambled space.

His sudden changes in appearance had taken a lot of getting used to. In fact she wasn't sure she was really used to them yet. But their talks had been fascinating.

It wasn't clear to her how he managed to do it, but he seemed able to keep a hold of memories imported from the various characters whose heads he'd borrowed, and his guest limbs had also given him useful skills.

He was, for example, a dab hand at the piano, as long as the hand he was using at the time happened to fit the keys. And when it came to cooking, even though it might be the spike-helmeted head of a Statically-Charged Warrior Of Thrutt that was staring at the stove, his 'piments doux farcis' and his 'omlettes aux fines herbes' came out a treat.

As for general handyman tasks, he was a master. Of course there were occasional difficulties, like the time he'd been holding a water stopcock closed with the thumb of a shark-surfer from the pulsing oceans of Borarnscheen.

When the hand had suddenly vanished, Riska had done her best to help him deal with the cascading water. After a few tricky moments, a long-nailed replacement had turned up, clutching an orange silk handkerchief that had been just the right size to block up the stopcock.

But it was the man's talent for recalling things that had been happening in all sorts of areas of existence that intrigued Riska most. Admittedly he didn't usually have the full story on particular events. His accounts tended to be based on short glimpses or sensations of the action, along with descriptions or hearsay that his heads had picked up from conversations with others. But since, occasionally, heads limbs and other body parts returned by way of an encore, he could sometimes add sequels to his tales, and even tails to his sequels.

He, too, would have liked her to stay longer. He tried not to think about how he'd feel after she'd gone. Though his various parts in other lives kept him busy in a piecemeal kind of way, this was the first time he'd ever known what it was like to be at home with somebody else there.

And Riska was much more to him than just *somebody else*. He'd become really fond of her. But he knew, even when he had the torso of a Gnarlian mammoth-wrestler, or the arms of a boulder-hurling asteroid-deflector from the outer planets of Thrannik, that he stood no chance. Riska had spoken to him a lot about Joe. So he'd decided the best way to put his own feelings for her into practice would be by doing what he could to bring the two of them together again.

***

Joe frowned in a puzzled way. "I *see*. So you mean you don't have to go out and *get* money. The money comes and finds *you*."

The crowd of customers that had gathered round the pair were enjoying the dialogue. Ochania's answers were so natural that many of them simply assumed Joe was from some small island on the other side of the planet.

"I don't know what your word '*money*' means", she said, "I suppose those fladds do what you call 'paying the bill'."

"*Fladds*?"

"Yes. They come when they want to."

Joe realised this would need far more time than he had. So, in the hope of finding some way back to Riska, he switched away from the subject and hurried the talk on to travel, and how to start doing it. Farankeglook – if he'd heard its name right – was fascinating. He asked Ochania a few basic questions about it. But it was clear now that she was feeling the need to press on with her work.

"Look, it's been a good laugh," she said after a few more moments, "but I have to get on now."

Joe thanked her. "Well," he said, turning to the crowd, "if anyone *else* would like to help, just for a minute or so... "

A man who looked like one of the pub-café's regulars said, "Of course, if you want to know about Farankeglook, and a lot more too, one of the best people to tell you is Arbeeshius Fnoog. He's the wisest man I know!"

There were murmurs of agreement from the people around.

"Arb, he continued, "knows what's *what* and what's *where* on Farankeglook. He's always pleased to meet new people and explain things." The man got up and put his arm on the shoulder of another customer. "Glenth here knows where Arbeeshius lives. I'm sure he'll be happy to take you to see him."

***

Ked had a strange feeling, standing near the man who was feared on Thrarrxgor almost as much as K*rargxt himself. He was struck by how insignificant Sculpin looked, compared with the giant 3D projections of him that had appeared in the hangar roof-space.

The Chief Engineer was clearly unimpressed by the bland non-alcoholic drinks and the grovelling patter Bernie had been giving him. He turned away from him to meet the staff who were standing close by, causing severe bouts of trembling amongst some of them.

Ked was just outside the grim introduction circle. But he could see Sculpin would soon be coming to Shloomger who, unlike many others, seemed remarkably laid-back. It cheered Ked up, as what he and Shloomger were about to do was as high-risk as it could get.

He was distracted by a hand-wringing announcement from Bernie that Mr. Sculpin would soon graciously re-open the newly 'up-graded' Intervenor by carrying out the planetary annihilation he'd mentioned earlier, after which a buffet would be available with further complimentary K*rargxtko drinks.

*

"Looks like that could be freshened up a touch," Shloomger said breezily, looking at the glass in Sculpin's hand, "or, if you'd rather, I've got something else a bit more interesting."

Sculpin gave Shloomger a glance that would have frozen anyone else in the hangar. He was startled to find it had no effect at all, and became curious. "What do you *mean*?"

"Special cocktail-mix. Best way is to try it and see."

"You're not seriously suggesting… "

"Ah, yes, of course. Security considerations! I quite understand. Could be poisoned, you think. Oh well, never mind."

"If *you* test one on yourself first, maybe I could give it a try," Sculpin muttered, surprising himself.

"Right. Fine. Well, if you could give me just a bit of time, I'll get one ready."

*

Joe stood next to Glenth on the terrace outside the pub-café. The breeze hum-strummed through the bamboo shades above the tables, and played over Joe's face in a way that made clear it wanted to be breathed.

He inhaled deeply a few times, and then drew an even longer lungful as he took in the view.

It was, it occurred to him, like standing on a giant surfboard.

The terrace of the pub-café was on top of a range of hills that ran down ahead of him towards a green plain, and the wind-streaks in the grass below made Joe feel that the terrace – with him on it – was on a wave racing for the beach, ready to curl and break any second.

He noticed that, though there were plenty of houses tucked into the hillsides, they fitted in so well with the shape of the land that they might almost have grown out of the ground itself.

He could see there were roads too. Well, *some* kind of roads.

As something shot past in front of the pub, it occurred to him that his thoughts about surfing weren't so way out.

The whizzing-by had happened so abruptly that he hadn't had a chance to take it in fully. He tried to recall exactly what it had been. A few seconds later a couple of other zooming shapes shot across his view and vanished round the corner.

Joe was just turning towards Glenth to ask him about it, when he saw he'd picked up what looked like a longish surfboard. It had some kind of convex lozenge shape on its underside, but he couldn't make out how it worked.

"Sorry," Glenth said, "I didn't ask you. Perhaps you'd like us to use yours instead."

"Er, no, *yours* is fine. As a matter of fact I'm not, sort of familiar, with any of this."

His companion looked at him in a surprised but patient kind of way. They made their way down to the 'road'. Joe saw that it was in fact one of two parallel roads. Glenth put the board on the edge of what looked like some sort of acceleration lane. Then he stood on it at the back, and beckoned to Joe to position himself at the front. Joe saw him take a small handset from his pocket and play on it deftly with his thumb.

There was a deep, powerful murmur that seemed to come from some way back. Joe looked over his shoulder and saw the surface of the road behind them rise into a wave. He watched the wave race towards them, and hoped it was Glenth who'd be steering, as he hadn't a clue what to do himself.

He felt the board lift under his feet, slightly at first. Then it kicked up sharply, and the acceleration pitched Joe backwards. But some kind of compensating force coming up through the board re-balanced him.

It was like nothing he'd done before. The nearest he'd got to this was a cliff take-off with his hang-glider into a force four. And to think, here, you got this every time you went down the road for a pint!

The floor of the board nudged him into a good lean-angle, and they banked into a right-hander. As they straightened out of the turn, Joe, who was back into the thrill of having his face speed-rubbed by the wind, saw that this had just been for openers. Till now, all they'd been doing was riding the road's start-up lane.

He wondered how long it took to pick up the art of switching waves. He could see his companion was handling it like someone born to it. Glenth fingered the handset, nonchalently manoeuvring the board with his whole body. He also seemed to be using the pressure of the oncoming air to fine-tune the steering.

They edged towards the centre lane. Joe looked over his shoulder and saw the road behind them build into a seriously powerful wave. It was some eighty feet away and closing fast...

CHAPTER 24

Boontrak woke with a start, and wished he hadn't yet. His visitor was still there. He wondered whether, at the entity's core behind the fog, some kind of black-hole and gloom-pit duo might be orbiting each other. The being's flow of misery-gutting was so continuous it had to be re-charging itself from somewhere.

Proorong seemed, in his way, to notice Boontrak was paying slightly more attention, because he included the fact seamlessly into his jabbering.

"... And of course there's no excuse for the behaviour of these *wastrels*! *Antisocial's* what I call it. Oh, I see you're a tiny bit more alert now. I thought for a moment that you'd drifted off *completely*. Not, of course that you could switch off *for good*! Not someone from *your* Level. I suppose you'll just have to go on existing in your sad comotose state for ever... "

The prattle suddenly stopped. The mist-cloak swirled around the being in a way that made it wonderfully clear it was preparing to leave.

"Ah!" Proorong muttered self-importantly, "I have just detected, at a considerable distance from here, another wretch in need of my comfort and advice."

Then he added the only cheering words of his entire visit.

"And so," he said, "I'm afraid you'll simply have to get by without me."

***

Joe was busy still trying to get his head round the whole experience of dry wave riding. He and Glenth had been up on a high roller in the fast lane for a while now, and this was *wild.*

On top of the heart-thumping accelerations and the mind-blowing speeds, he was impressed by the way Glenth could casually turn and drift the board around the wavelanes. He was also intrigued by his use of the handset to call up specially shaped big-beaster roadwaves at just the right moment, like ribbon-twist turners for banking round long bends, sharp front-risers for fast braking, and huge racer-cliffs for overtaking on the straights.

And, as if all *this* wasn't enough, their route had taken them through country that roared its beauty. They'd shot across bridges over death-drop canyons, plunged -in what seemed glass tunnels – under the floors of rivers, climbed through high grasslands, and scooped mist off the edge of a mountain that Joe would have liked to share a large piece of time with.

At present they were travelling along the centre line of a valley.

Ahead of them Joe could see that the landscape was becoming more wooded.

Glenth leaned forward slightly so Joe could hear him more clearly over the sound of the wind, and shouted, "It's not far now!"

*

Joe looked back towards the wave-road in the distance and guessed they must have walked a quarter of a mile or so by now. It had taken him a little while to get used to firm ground since Glenth had eased the board off the road, had parked it next to a bush, and had led him along the path.

"Fnoog lives at the top end of the valley," his fellow-traveller said, "just the other side of the Writing Trees."

"Sorry, didn't quite catch that... "

Glenth smiled. "I was saying he lives fairly close to here."

The path led them to the edge of a small forest, and for a while it seemed content just to skirt the woodland. Then suddenly, without warning, it plunged inside.

The route twisted around so much, Joe felt at times they must almost be coming back on their tracks. But he sensed, from changes in the light, and the smells and sounds of the forest, that it was taking them further in.

It grew steadily darker, and the moment came when Joe realised the forest was running things completely. As if to make the point it became even murkier. Tough bouncer-type branches leaned over the path, and Joe half-expected a timbery voice to ask what business he was on and then to tree-root-him back the way he'd come.

But the casual way Glenth was pushing on, and the fact that he seemed almost on nodding terms with some of the heavier branches, made Joe more relaxed. He had a sense they were being let through. He wondered where exactly they were going.

At last he noticed that, here and there, the place was becoming more open, and that sunlight was breaking through to the woodland floor.

Glenth said he would go off and have a sleep nearby. He pointed to a grove of trees ahead. "I think you might like to go and stand there for a while," he said.

***

"Well, here we go then!" Shloomger chuckled and poured a powdery-gungy mixture into a couple of glasses, then stirred it vigorously with the catalytic mixer-stick from the pack Eelag had given him, "This one's a Ram's Reviver."

Sculpin watched the mixture expand into a liquid and change colour rhythmically, slowly at first, then faster.

Just as it seemed to have gone through its full range of colour shades, the cocktail switched to a burst of kaleidoscopic patterns, after which it paused and became transparent. Then, in the centre of each glass, part of the liquid drew itself together into a perfectly sculpted, but mercifully scaled-down, version of a super-breasted reliever from Rock Planet Rynktor.

"How long did it take you to learn to put one of those together?" Sculpin asked.

Shloomger thought for a moment. "Dunno," he said, "six million years maybe."

"An amusing reply," Sculpin said curtly, "and what is the special *technique* for producing those effects?"

Shloomger reflected briefly. "They say it's the ingredients but – you know – *I* think the secret's in the way you stir it." He paused. "But some say it's the way you *drink* it that makes it really special. I suggest we start on the blue bit first."

They had moved away from the crowd so as to carry out the sampling undisturbed. If anyone had been standing nearby, they would have noticed, as the two took up their glasses, that the colours had reappeared in the drinks, in new changing patterns.

Sculpin looked at Shloomger warily. "After *you*," he said, tight-lipped. And, as Shloomger was about to take his first sip, Sculpin suddenly swapped glasses with him.

Then, following Shloomger's tip on drinking-technique, he worked his way, from blue, through the other colours.

As Sculpin tried the different tastes and sensations, it seemed to him like being in moments from other lives, ones he'd have traded for his own without stopping to think about it.

Then, as he came up for air, a translucent flash-fizz shot from both their glasses and combined itself into the hologram of a mercilessly *bigger* version of another super-breasted reliever from Rock Planet Rynktor.

And Squid saw that she was definitely beckoning to him.

"Well," Shloomger said to him, belching slightly, "maybe there's just time for a second one... "

*

Ked made his way as discreetly as he could towards his objective, and trod on a mechan rat. It screeched metallically and turned to pincer his ankle. He jerked his foot away and moved on. Fortunately, in the hubbub of chatter and food preparation, no one seemed to have noticed the noise.

He ran through his tasks in his mind. The first one was a piece of teamwork with Shloomger. All he could do was hope things would come together alright on *that*. As to the second one, there was a chance he might be able to manage it, but it was more complex. And getting to grips with the system procedures could be difficult. The third task could be even trickier. He might have to hand over to Shloomger on that later, but he'd have a try at it anyway.

He turned to the first job he had to do.

***

Joe stood on the woodland floor and looked up. There was something very special about this place. The trees here were different. The tops of their branches seemed somehow rooted in the sky.

During the walk through the forest the silence had been overwhelming. But here, after a while, he became aware that there were sounds all round him. He supposed the reason he hadn't heard them before was that he hadn't been listening.

When he noticed the first sound, close by, he couldn't tell exactly what it was. It was as if something was scratching gently over a surface, pausing, then moving again.

As he listened more carefully, trying to pinpoint it, he realised the sound was coming from a flower on a branch of the tree nearest to him.

It was a large flower. Its outer petals were a couple of times the size of his hand. He was surprised to see that, anchored to the underside of the bloom and curving up over it, was a slim sort of tendril. Following it with his eye, he saw that the tendril reached over the edge of the flower, and that its tip was touching one of the petals.

He saw, too, that the tip of the arm was working its way across the petal. As he looked more closely, he could see that it was marking it with a beautiful script.

Whether it was because his face had brushed some part of the bloom, or because it sensed in some other way that he had been looking at it, the flower opened itself out fully, and let out a long, whispering sigh.

Joe looked up at the other branches around him and saw that, on them too, were other flowers. And he realized that the sounds he had been hearing were coming from the whole of the grove. All the trees were writing on their flowers.

He couldn't be sure whether it was because the sounds from the flowers were building into each other like waves or whether something else was making it happen, but after some moments he knew that a single rhythm had come alive in the wood and was humming through the air around him. And he realised that he was dancing to it.

He couldn't tell how he recognized the feeling. Perhaps in his dreams he'd danced with spirits. He sensed he was dancing with them now.

After a time, in its own natural way, the dance brought itself to an end.

A petal was lying on the ground in front of him. He picked it up and put it carefully into his pocket.

He saw now that the floor of the grove was covered with fallen pieces of flowers. He wanted to stay longer and pick up more of them, but it was getting late.

He walked a short distance from the wood, and then found himself turning round to listen to the sound of the trees as they wrote.

He couldn't recall afterwards how long he had stood there. From time to time winds sprang up around the grove. Gusts tore at its edges and jeered at it with stings of cold rain. But still the trees went on writing. Still their petals fell unflustered to the floor.

Sometimes a bird would pick one up and fly away. And Joe wondered what would become of that piece, whether anyone would ever read its words, and whether the trees would ever know.

But still they went on writing.

***

"And *this* one's a... ?"

"Lagoon-Lapper."

"Ah, *yes*", Sculpin tried to hold his eyes steadily on Shloomger, "that's it! Yes, you told me a moment ago! You must give me the recipe. And for the others too."

Shloomger noticed Sculpin had said 'must', in a much looser way than usual. He hoped he was judging things right. "Certainly, Sir. I'll make an appointment with your secretary for a mixing demo. Then your staff will be able to knock these drinks up on demand. But of course, I'll need an authorising letter from you to fix the appointment. He took Sculpin's empty glass. "Well, maybe you'd like to try another, Mr. Sculpin. How about an Android's Afterthought?"

Sculpin was intrigued by the rainbow corona that had formed round Shloomger. But, glancing across the hangar, he saw that everybody had one. For a quarter of a second he tried to think carefully. "Alright, but make it the last!" he murmured, "there are things to be done."

"Rightho Squid. You don't mind me calling you Squid, do you? A *last* one then!" Shloomger paused. "Ah, by the way, there's one thing I should mention about *this* cocktail. Its special effects don't work when it's near some kinds of electronic stuff, like protector cards against the Viewer and the Intervenor and the Transporter," he put his arm on Sculpin's shoulder to steady him, "they *block* out the drink's energy, you see. So, if you could just remove them first, so as to get the real benefit of it... ”

Sculpin swayed against him slightly, reached inside his collar, dragged off a wire-chain necklace with a set of metallic cards on it, and handed it to Shloomger with a distant casualness, as if off-loading his coat to a doorman.

Shoon put it carefully out of reach and moved back to Sculpin. “Right, in a sec I'll run off the letter for you to sign. But first I'll mix you that drink.”

*

Bernie was becoming even more nervous than usual. He'd never seen Sculpin so relaxed and convivial. That security operative next to him at the edge of the hangar had tied him in conversation far too long. He watched in amazement as he saw Sculpin sign a paper the operative had just handed him.

The time-readout in Bernie's ear implant told him the schedule was slipping. On the other hand, the last thing you did on Thrarrxgor – and it *would* be the last – was to suggest to Sculpin that he should get a move on with *anything*.

He chose the easy option of mingling with the crowd and waiting for Sculpin to call the next shot when he felt like it.

***

Joe turned and looked back at the path that had led them away from the writing trees. The last traces of the forest were disappearing. Glenth pointed to a gate in a hedge a short way ahead of them.

“That's the entrance to the place where Arb generally hangs out,” he said casually, “Arb hasn't exactly retired, but he's kind of *settled* there for the moment to do some research. He's chosen it because a few odd things have happened there.” He paused, and stared for a moment at the gate. “Of course,” he added, “it might just be chance that they happened there, but they certainly seem to have been rather odd.”

*

Arbeeshius Fnoog sat on the lawn and contemplated the spot of ground where he had witnessed three very strange happenings. He had thought about the spot, on and off, for many years.

He had done a lot of other things in between his contemplations, including giving lectures on unexplained phenomena. But he had returned frequently to this place, not only because he wanted to try and work out fully what had happened, but also on the off chance that something new and unusual might take place there yet again.

The first strange event had occurred when, as a young man, he'd been sitting on that particular piece of ground thinking about a girl he'd met at a dance a couple of days earlier.

He'd been so taken up in his thoughts that he'd scarcely noticed a sleepy numbness in his right hand. He remembered later that it had felt loosely as if his hand was somewhere else as well as being there on the end of his arm. It was only some minutes later – when he'd felt a sort of tickling in his palm – that he'd been surprised to find his hand filled with hundreds of small seeds.

He'd absent-mindedly put them into his trouser pocket, with the idea of looking at them more closely later. But, shortly afterwards, he'd set off for a brief walk and, as he got to the edge of the forest, he'd felt a sudden urge to sneeze. Pulling his handkerchief from his pocket he'd spilled out the seeds. The breeze had picked them up and scattered them over the ground nearby.

He'd often wondered where the seeds had come from, just as he'd wondered later about the items that had arrived in the next strange event that had taken place.

***

"I thought, Squid, you might like to see how impressive you look – I mean *are* – when your image appears up there in the roofspace."

Shloomger took Sculpin's glass, emptied of its cocktail, and put it back on the tray with the others. "So if you'd like to step over to this area, where we can focus on you for just a moment… "

He guided Sculpin by the shoulder to a space on the hangar floor onto which a pink guidance circle had just been projected. The Chief Engineer took his place and looked up vaguely into the roofspace.

If he actually saw his expanded image, it was only for a very short time. This was because, to minimise drawing attention to the event, Shloomger remotely closed the giant image a fraction of a second after it had appeared. After that, projecting a new image of Sculpin would have been impossible anyway.

This was because Sculpin was travelling out of Thrarrxgor's universe on a finely honed pulse generated by the hangar's Transporter Beam.

*

Bernie left the crowd and came over. Shloomger could see he'd reached super-agitation state.

"Where *is* he?"

"Where's Who?"

"*Sculpin*! Who *else* do you think I meant?"

"Ah, well… yes. Well, he's gone off for a bit."

"Gone *off*? *Where*?"

"Well, I wouldn't like to say, exactly." Shloomger threw a glance at the door of the Executive Lavatory.

"Well, how long… ?"

"Your guess is as good as mine."

"And what about the destruction of that planet?"

"Well, I think it'd be better to wait till Sculpin gets back before thinking about that, really. I mean, one never knows how he might react. It might make him very angry if he found out you'd gone ahead without clearing it with him first, don't you think? After all, *he's* the one who's supposed to be *doing* it isn't he?"

Bernie gave him an intensely irritated look and walked off to re-join the crowd. Shloomger watched him go, then turned on his heel fast and set off out of the hangar. He had to get on with his next task very quickly.

*

Ked lifted his hands away from the Transporter Controls. He'd been impressed at the way, when Shloomger had sent off Joe and Riska, he'd fixed all the Transporter settings *remotely* from the Switcher Desk. Though Ked was actually *sitting* at the T. desk, he was finding his job very tricky.

Still, he told himself, at least he could work uninterrupted. No one had noticed him at the desk when he'd sent Sculpin off, and nobody was looking now. The teams seemed to have turned their backs on the operational side of things while they socialised with other staff. And, apart from the desk where *he* was, all the desks were deserted for the moment.

Anyway, there were still two tasks he had to do. They weren't going to be easy. But what the *heelgritt*!

He returned his hands to the controls, and got ready for the next one.

***

The worktable of Arbeeshius's study, in the house overlooking the lawn where he sat, was covered with a set of tools, measuring instruments and manuals. These were the items he'd acquired some years before, in the *second* unexplained event.

Arb had also happened at the time to be sitting on the spot of ground at which he was now staring, when he had realised that his whole left arm had gone to sleep, rather in the same way that his hand had done during his earlier experience.

He'd thought, a bit later, that the whole of him must have dropped off to sleep for a moment too. This was because, when he'd decided to shake his arm about and get it back into working order, he'd found that the crook of his elbow was cradling a collection of equipment and manuals he'd never seen before.

He'd looked around to try and catch sight of whoever might have delivered them, but had seen no one.

In the days that followed, he'd carefully studied the books and the other items, and so had become the only expert, in the whole of Farankeglook, on wave-roads and how to build and work them. It had given him great pleasure to share his knowledge with others and to introduce this clean, new and exciting transport system to various parts of the planet.

Arbeeshius paused and thought about the third strange event that had occurred. One day, not long before, when he'd been standing contemplating the place of the first two odd happenings, someone had brought a person to see him. Arb had thought him very unusual. This was because the visitor was rude and bad tempered, something the people of Farankeglook were not familiar with.

The man had told him that he had come from somewhere that he didn't want to talk about, and that he now wanted to go *back* to. He had also said that he'd somehow missed the departure time for his return.

He'd mentioned he'd been told that Arbeeshius was an expert on transport, and that he'd come to see him in case he needed to make some sort of alternative travel arrangements.

Arbeeshius had told him he might be able to help him travel *around* Farankeglook, but this didn't seem to satisfy the man at all. In fact he'd muttered about Arb's world being blown up very quickly if he didn't jump about and help him.

This was something the kindly man of Farankeglook had not understood, since he'd always tried to help people if he could. Nor could he fathom out why anybody would want to set about blowing up worlds.

Arbeeshius had done his best to make some polite conversation, during which the man had let slip that his name was Dangle. The fellow had also muttered something about his transport probably having been remotely rescheduled anyway, and about his being likely to start his return journey soon.

And then, standing – as it happened – on the very spot that Arbeeshius had been contemplating earlier, the man had vanished.

Arb looked up and saw Glenth approaching with a visitor. He noticed that the tall young man was dressed in clothes that were unusual for Farankeglook, a bit like the clothes that man Dangle had worn.

The young man walked over to him and happened to stop and stand on the spot that Arbeeshius had been contemplating. Then the young man smiled, said "Hello, my name's Joe," stretched out his arm to shake Arbeeshius's hand, and vanished.

CHAPTER 25

The sweat poured from Ked's forehead, ran down to the tip of his nose-pendant, and fell in a fine stream onto the Transporter control board. He moved his head back to redirect the flow away from the link-wires. Short-circuits, especially through his body, were the last thing he wanted.

Tracking Joe to exactly where he was, and then pulling him away, had been a head-grinder of a task, particularly as Ked had been using the tricky *fast-find-and-return* procedure.

And, after he'd managed to do *that*, he'd realised he'd made a deadly mistake by setting Joe on a default-course, identical to Hepkin Dangle's old one, which meant he was heading directly to Thrarrxgor and into *K*rargxt's* debriefing Room. Then, when Ked had tried to correct *that,* he'd made another cock-up which had looked like being as terminal as the first one. Bringing Joe back to his original departure-point had seemed a good idea, till he'd found out that Joe had been seven feet above the ground and hurtling straight at it.

He told himself he could at least *try* and relax now. His last correction had adjusted Joe's journey so that he'd be slowed to zero speed and delivered at ground level. And he calculated that he should, in fact, be arriving very soon.

Ked finger-drummed the air. He had to get on fast with the *next* task. And that would probably be even tougher.

He made his way quickly over to the deserted Intervenor Desk and sat down in front of it. Since Shloomger was still away he'd have to make a start on his own at what they were planning to do. He concentrated totally on the control board.

Because of this, some time later, he didn't hear the sound of the teams returning to their work. And he was taken completely by surprise when a chorus of angry voices asked him what the *grintz* he thought he was doing.

***

"About your getting home," the man in scrambled space said one day, over breakfast, "I've thought a good deal about it. And, as far as I can see, the best way is for you to shake the right hand at the right moment."

Riska grinned at the mesh of the bee-keeper's headgear. "That's the story behind a *lot* of people's success. But what exactly did you have in mind?"

He peered pensively at the ceiling for a few moments through his faceguard. "Er, perhaps I wasn't putting it as clearly as I might. What I mean is that you have to wait for the right hand to come round... " he paused reflectively again. "Well, it *could* of course be a left hand which turns out to be the right hand. ... What I'm trying to say is the right *sort* of hand... "

Riska nodded patiently, and asked him to continue.

"I get this feeling," he said, "it's sort of automatic. But, just before I get a new head or hand or... " he coughed, "... or *whatever*, I have a kind of *sensation* of what it's going to be."

He glanced down at the cramponed mountaineer's boot on his right foot, and spoke softly in an almost confessional way. "Sometimes I'm even able to, sort of, *fast-forward* till I get the hand, or whatever it is, that I'm looking for."

He gave her a determined look. "So, when next I get the feeling there's a suitable hand from Earth about to come up, particularly one from near where you live, then I'll tell you... "

A young hippie face suddenly grinned at her under its double daisy-chain coronet. "But, of course it'll have to be from a time that's the right sort of *now* for you *too*. Anyway, when it arrives, all you have to do is hold on to my hand firmly till it leaves. I'll do the rest."

Though Riska thought the plan sounded ingenious, she wasn't entirely convinced. "I thought you generally ended up importing things, rather than sending them back," she said, glancing round at the kitchen hardware.

"Depends if I want to hang on to them, really." He stopped, upset about what he'd just said. "I didn't mean I wanted to get rid of *you*. You *know* that, don't you?"

Riska told him that she did.

"You see, it's just I *understand* that you want to go, and this is the best way I can think of."

He lapsed into silence for a few seconds. "About that business of returning things. Well, I've sometimes been able to send some of them back later, but only if the hands or other parts that brought them turn up again. It takes a fair bit of concentration, though." Absent-mindedly he moved a falcon from his right wrist to his left arm, and pushed the daisy chain a little higher up his forehead. "And sometimes I make mistakes, and send body parts back loaded with things that came from somewhere else."

"That can cause a bit of a shock, I should think," Riska said.

"Yes, I suppose so." He paused thoughtfully. "Actually, I once did a re-direction *deliberately*. There was an executioner's axe that turned up one day, so I put that in a scrap-dealer's hand, and replaced it with a rubber one from someone on a carnival float."

Riska stared into the blue eyes peering from under a Viking helmet. "So, to summarise, the idea is I shake hands with a person on Earth more or less around the time and place I left it."

"Yes, that's broadly it. But for reasons I won't go into, it'll be a day or two *after* you left, or thereabouts. And I'll try to arrange it so that, when you do, the person's not far from where you live."

"So it'll be a goodbye-hello handshake," Riska said in a sudden swirl of mixed feelings.

"Yes, that's it."

"And will we... "

"... Ever meet again? I don't know. I hope so."

***

"How did you get up here without being stopped?" Thyghnia Thrubb eyed Shloomger suspiciously. His badge might show he had a security job, but it didn't give him clearance above floor three, let alone to Sculpin's private office.

"Ah, yes. Well, as a matter of fact a lot of people *did* stop me on the way," Shloomger said brightly, "and they were all particularly keen I shouldn't get any further than their control zone." He stretched his arm forward and handed her a piece of paper. "But when I showed them *this,* they let me through to the next zone till... well, here I *am.*"

Sculpin's secretary took the paper and started reading it.

"It's a document, signed by Mr. Sculpin," Shloomger said helpfully, "instructing you – after that bit about the cocktail-mixing demonstration – to give me, immediately, the temporary destruction-exemption that Mr. *K*rargxt* signed for K*rargxtus3b22c4r. That's the planet Earth."

The secretary looked at him coldly, "It may surprise you," she glanced back at the paper, "... *Shoon*, that staff in Mr. Sculpin's secretariat can read. But I assure you that I *can.*"

She passed the letter through a machine on her desk, "Well, the equipment has verified that it *is* Mr. Sculpin's signature," she observed, clearly disappointed, "even though it is close to the limits for... " she glanced at the monitor readout "... for '*wobbliness*'. So, if you wait for a moment, I will bring you the document." She gave Shloomger an even colder look. "And, as far as the appointment for the mixing of *cocktails* is concerned, I will discuss the matter personally with Mr. Sculpin before contacting you!"

"Certainly! Excellent idea," Shloomger observed, "*just* as you say!"

A section of the wall self-melted into a doorway, and the secretary passed through into Sculpin's office.

*

After what seemed to Shloomger a very long time, Thrubb returned. The wall fused itself back together. Shoon looked at her carefully. He'd wondered if there had been a problem getting the document Marlin had told him about, but concluded she'd probably simply decided to keep him waiting.

She handed him the paper. "I'm not quite sure why you need it," she said as Shloomger got up to leave, "seeing that the planet concerned has probably been destroyed by now, or is just about to be."

"What do you mean?"

She gave Shloomger a couldn't-give-a-toss look. "Some time before you arrived, I contacted the Hangar Operations Manager – er, *Bernie*, I believe he calls himself – to check *where* exactly Squid... er... *Mr. Sculpin* was in his schedule..."

She paused, as if considering whether the matter was worth spending any further seconds of her time on, "He told me things were on hold, as Mr. Sculpin was temporarily unavailable. He asked me if I thought Mr. Sculpin would be *really upset* if the planetary annihilation went ahead without him. I said I was sure that, with so many other things to do, Mr. Sculpin wouldn't mind at all... "

Shloomger reached instinctively into his pocket for his K*rargxtko-issue hologphone, and then remembered that its core had been slowly and painstakingly removed by the guards on the floor 2 entrance barrier.

He turned hopefully to the secretary. "Do you mind if make a call from one of your office phones?"

She looked at him as if disappointed he hadn't dropped

spontaneously dead. "I suppose you may, *Shoon*... if, of course, you have a sufficiently high security clearance code to enter into the system before making the call."

"Could *you* make it for me, then, and tell Bernie to stop the annihilation?"

The secretary waved four heavily-armed guards over to the desk, "These members of staff will now show you out of this office, *Shoon* !"

***

"Let's hope it's simply 'Au-revoir'," the man in scrambled space said.

Riska held onto his hand very tightly, the way he had explained.

"I won't forget you... " he said. He paused for a moment while his other hand put down the piece of pastry dough it had been holding, reached to her cheek and brushed away a tear. "I hope you'll remember me. Though, if you do, I'm not sure by which face it'll be."

"I will, and by *all* of them," she said.

Then, before Riska knew what was happening, she, and the hand she was holding, were whirling around in black velvety space.

***

Joe watched the picture of the burnt-out building assemble itself piece by piece.

The first things to prise their way into his consciousness were the arc lights. Then, as the image began to fill in further, he could see there were workmen putting up heavy-duty fencing around the site. The calf of his leg felt damp. He moved his hand to it, and realised he was lying in a puddle.

He stared at the blackened wall above him. How much time had passed since he'd fallen off it?

Where was Riska?

He got to his feet and broke into an air-gulping run towards the shell of the building.

***

Shloomger was glad that, though it was as mortal as anyone else's on Thrarrxgor, his body was reasonably athletic. He sprinted down the last of the corridors leading to the Hangar, took a short cut in through a side door, looked up and saw an image of the planet Earth suspended in the roof-space.

"Blow it up!" Bernie's amplified voice shook the hangar walls.

There was a pause.

"I said *Blow it up*!"

The image increased slightly in size.

"No! *Bigger*!"

Shloomger let out a brief gasp of relief, then sprinted towards Bernie, who was seated on the main control platform, and waved the document at him.

"Stop, Bernie!"

The Ops Manager didn't seem to have noticed Shloomger. Then suddenly, as he swung his head round towards the Intervenor team to give the annihilation order, he caught sight of Shoon.

"What the... ?"

"It's from *K*rargxt*!" Shloomger shouted, waving the paper even harder, "Destruction-exemption for K*rargxtus3b22c4r! *Stop the whole thing!*"

*

Shloomger sat at his security operative's desk and watched Ked shift uncomfortably on the machine box that he'd dragged over to serve as a kind of couch. "So how did you talk your way out of it?"

As he asked the question, Shloomger's eyes were drawn to the tattoo now completely covering Ked's face. Since they'd begun speaking it had 'progressed' from running a set of spectacular colour-changes, to morphing through a wild image-library, and then moving on to a series of cartoon video-clips. Shloomger noticed that now it seemed to be entering a '3D' stage. Ked's skin seemed have begun building itself into a model of Thrarrxgor city.

Ked gave a dry cough. "The one thing I had going for me was that the whole team was keen to get the annihilation over. So once I'd spieled that I'd been closing the Intervenor because a fault had turned it on, they didn't ask for any more details." He paused, clearly reflecting on some painful experience. "But, all the same, they didn't seem very keen to discourage their female whiplash-supervisor from making an example of me for not having cleared it with her first!"

"Ah. Yes, I see." Shloomger paused. He looked closely at Ked's facial skin, which had now moved on to do an impression of feeler-stud waves surging across a fairground palm-reading machine. "What *you* need is *this*!" He handed Ked a cocktail that he'd been too busy to finish.

Ked took the glass shakily and started sipping. The sip slid seamlessly into a slurp, then a series of major gulps. After a serious exchange of ideas with the liquid he re-surfaced. "You see, it's not the whiplash experience that's been getting to me," he rasped, "I simply sort of *braced* myself for that! It's how close I got to killing off that bloke Joe in the first place."

Shloomger sensed the tattoo was beating a retreat. Ked's face seemed to be staging a recovery.

"Ah, the *regrets* have been muscling in, eh? Maybe you'd better have a drop more."

"You see, Shloomger, I nearly *did* it."

"But you didn't."

"Well, no. I didn't."

"And you whooshed Sculpin away."

"Well, I suppose I did *that*."

"And you got Joe back home."

"Yup, that too."

"And your kerfuffling about with the team on the

Intervenor Desk held back the Intervenor start-up just long enough for Earth to be saved."

"Well, now you mention it, Shloomger… "

"And our next step is to try and mess up the Intervenor well and truly, isn't it?"

Ked took another pull of the cocktail. "*Yup*, that's what I was trying to start when the Intervenor team came back."

"Right. So let's junk the regrets and get on with junking the Intervenor, eh Ked?"

"Yup. Right! In fact, spot *on* Shloomger!" Ked blew a kiss at the go-go dancers waving from the rim of his glass and stared for a moment into the hangar space above them. "But how are we going to do that? Won't those people at the Intervenor Desk be wise to any new shots at getting into the machine?"

Shloomger sat back in his chair and put his hands behind his head. "Look, I may be wrong, Ked, but it seems to me that things have just kind of *changed* round here, at least very temporarily."

"Meaning?"

"Well, in an outfit like K*rargxtko, when someone turns up waving a piece of paper that has the life-and-death signature of the MAN HIMSELF, it tends to have an effect on the way people respond to you. I noticed that with Bernie. After he'd stopped the annihilation and then double-checked K*rargxt's signature, he seemed, well… "

"Grovelling?"

"Almost, I'd say. So, to enable us to sort out that task you were so harshly interrupted in, it will probably be useful if I *ask* Bernie if we can have access to the Intervenor to run a few checks on it." Shloomger chuckled quietly. "I'll tell him it's so we can *reassure K*rargxt that his instructions have been complied with*. I don't suppose Bernie's likely to object… "

***

The megastar had met a lot of people during the evening. But then, he reflected, one always *did* at London film premières. And he'd shaken hands so many times that his arm seemed to have gone to sleep.

Standing near a large floral display in a quieter part of the reception hall, he wondered if perhaps the whole of him might also have nodded off for a split second, because he didn't recall having seen the arrival of the beautiful woman who was holding his hand with such confidence.

He realised his arm, and the rest of him, were now very much awake and highly agitated in a very positive kind of way.

"Goo," he said.

Then he noticed he'd stopped speaking.

He tried again.

"Goo," he repeated.

"Hello," said Riska.

She was wearing the self-designing Alpanaskro dress that had been given her just before her journey.

"... d evening," the megastar achieved, "haven't we met before? I have the feeling we've somehow been in touch... "

"Yes, we have, in a way," Riska said.

"I'd just like to say I'm altogether... "

"Yes I'm pleased to see that you are now."

"... happy... "

"And I'm pleased about that too... "

"To have met you. In fact, if you would like to... I mean, if you were perhaps free some time... "

Riska smiled. "Well, as a matter of fact, I must go and find my boyfriend now."

"Ah, er... yes – I quite understand. It's so easy to lose oneself in places like this... "

Riska smiled. "Goodbye. Shaking hands with you has meant more to me than you can know."

"I was just about to say the same. Goodbye."

As people turned to look at Riska, as she walked across the reception hall and out into the night, many found themselves wondering where the beautiful woman had got her designer pastry-flour make-up.

CHAPTER 26

"Do you think this'll work?"

In the quiet that had fallen on the hangar since Earth's reprieve, Ked heard his voice echo from the wall's, and hoped none of the staff had been listening. He went on in a whisper, "It's a tough call, Shloomger."

Shoon paused in his data-keying and checked a readout on the Intervenor Desk where they were sitting. "Yup, this stage *is* trickier than the stuff you were doing before you got stopped." He turned back to the keyboard. "But If I'm right this should wrap the job tighter than a takeaway from the Black Hole Boogie Bar."

"The *what*?"

"Just a joint I've called into sometimes."

"Say, I've never heard of that! Have *you* got *around*, Shloomger! From what you said, I picked up that you'd *cruised,* but that sounds *far off*, man."

"Yup, a fair bit," Shloomger said modestly, and glanced at the readout again. "And about getting this job properly done, it's good you *were* stopped, because I hadn't thought it through enough before."

"So, how'll *this* be better?"

Shloomger looked at Ked thoughtfully. "Well, before we knacker *this* machine, we have to make any other Intervenor machines in K*rargxtko dependent on it first. Prototypes, spares, the *lot*. Plus of course any other Viewers and Transporters they've been building."

"So when *this* blows they'll *all* crash?"

"Exactly." Shoon checked his work. "Well, that seems to have done it."

Ked tugged nervously at a bunch of starched hairs serving as a micro-beardlet on his left jaw. "And K*rargxt won't be able to get them working again, or have *new* ones made?"

" I doubt it. It looks as if Sculpin kept all the key secrets to himself. I reckon he knew the moment he handed K*rargxt the tricks of the trade he'd have an extremely nasty accident."

"And Bernie and the staff here couldn't do it?"

"No, Ked. As far as I can make out, Sculpin kept things so tight that Bernie and each person down the ladder just did the job they'd been given, without understanding properly how the machines or the system worked."

"So, once we've skrittzed *this* machine, and everything that's linked to it crashes, then K*rargxt's power to do anything beyond Thrarrxgor has gone too!"

"Yup, as long as Sculpin's away."

"And it doesn't look like *he'll* be coming back soon!"

"Well, not for the moment, anyway, Ked."

"You mean he *could* make it back to Thrarrxgor?"

"Well, there *are* ways and means to do that sort of thing. But I think it's best if we concentrate on what *we* have to do right *now*, eh?"

"Right, Shloomger."

"And, what we have to do *now* is *nobble* this thing completely – processor core, nodes, switches, wires, the lot! Then we get out of here."

Shoon reached into his pocket and drew out a blaster pistol, dragging with it a half-eaten sandwich, which fell to the floor. Ked watched him slide the weapon out of sight under a file of papers.

"Where did you get *that*, man? There's a total ban on bringing in anything like that without special clearance!"

Shloomger coughed lightly. "Oh it's just an item I sort of borrowed from Bernie's office desk while he checked out K*rargxt's signature. We'd gone in there after I showed him that document, you see, and... "

Ked looked up. "Well, you'd better use it on the machine fast Shloomger. I've just seen one of those supervisors looking over here kind of *extremely* impatiently. In fact she's going over to talk to Bernie *now*."

"Er, right... " Shloomger moved his eyes carefully along the edge of the control panel. He pressed his finger against a catch, lifted the panel-cover and swung it upwards on its hinges. Then he slipped his hand back under the file of papers, grasped the pistol and put his weapon-hand deep into the well of the machine.

Ked looked across the hangar again. He could see Bernie talking to the supervisor.

"Shloomger!"

"Yes, Ked?"

"Look, I seriously *suggest* you get on with blasting it *now*! Some of those people are about to head over here!"

Shloomger scanned the innards of the machine and selected the first components for blasting. He flicked off the safety catch and pulled the trigger. Nothing happened.

"They're coming this way, Shloomger!"

Shoon checked the safety catch again, then looked at the whole of the gun carefully. "I say, Ked. It's got a yellow plaque on the top with a funny sort of symbol on it. It looks like... "

"They're *coming*, Shloomger!"

"... Like a pistol, a small circle and a hand... "

Ked turned looked at the gun, and groaned, "*Drunnged gritts*! I *missed* that. I should have *seen* it... "

"Seen *what*?"

"It's ring-protected, Shloomger! The authorised carrier wears a code-ring that's only for them and the gun. No one else can work the thing. It's *useless* to us!"

***

"Do I have to tell you *again*? They did a *full search* after the fire! Rescue, Forensic, the *works*! And they found *no one*!" The security guard glared at Joe, "And my orders are *nobody* comes onto this site, *whoever*, *whatever*! *Right*?"

The guard's colleague came over. His mouth started edging towards a quarter-smile, as if he might be about to play the softy in a nasty-guard/slightly-less-nasty-guard combo. Then the quarter-smile self cancelled and defaulted to '*Drop Dead*!' setting.

"Look, mate, if she'd been around here, don't you think they'd likely have found some kind of *remains*? Though I suppose," he added, brightening a good deal, "it's always possible that, with the heat of *that* fire, a body could have been so totally… "

"Look, your *best* bet", the other guard cut in, in a tone that implied he was doing Joe an immense favour in telling him,"is to contact the local hospitals and the police. Maybe *they'll* know something."

*

"You're sure? You're *absolutely certain*? *Nobody*? No record of anyone *at all*?"

Joe closed the call.

He got up, walked over to the window of his flat and stared at the night sky. Outside, the city breathed its life-sounds.

A numbness invaded him.

He tried to understand. But he could not. He tried again. He tried to understand how people, trains, the city, the world, could go on without her. Didn't they realise they couldn't? Didn't they *know*?

And it was *his* fault. If they had never met, she wouldn't have been on that building with him…

He looked at the stars, faint against the city's glow. And he said out loud:

"If all those were mine and this world too, I would give them up to have you back, Riska."

She slipped her arm around his waist.

"I let myself in," she said.

***

The group of supervisors walked back across the hangar towards Bernie's office. What had looked like being a short and terminal encounter with them had simply turned out to be a long, unpleasant discussion.

It was clear neither they nor Bernie had any idea what K*rargxt wanted done now, and since Shoon had recently been up to Sculpin's office, they were playing things carefully. Apparently Bernie had tried to contact K*rargxt's secretary to find out whether her boss could order Sculpin out of the executive lavatory. But she was 'unavailable'.

Shloomger looked at Ked. "And now," he murmured, "we need a swift alternative to the blaster."

They looked at one another for ideas.

On the floor nearby, a circle of mechan rats moved in towards the half-eaten sandwich, then backed away slightly as Coot began tapping his foot nervously. Ked noticed the noise they'd made, and looked down. Shloomger's gaze followed his.

"Maybe, if we threw the sandwich into the machine," Ked suggested, "the mechans would jump in after it, short the switches and burn it out."

Shloomger shook his head. "I don't think they'd get up into it that easily. The machine and the desk are too high, and it looks to me as if it's designed to be mechan-unfriendly, even with the covers off."

Ked was feeling desperate. "Maybe we could try to catch a few and sort of *drop 'em* in... " He glanced at the sprinter claw-wheels on the mechans' limb-shafts, "... Well, yup, perhaps we don't have time for that. Anyway," he glanced at Shloomger, "I've kind of got, like... *allergic* to the idea of killing things."

"You're not the only one," Shoon said quietly.

Coot searched around frantically in his mind for a solution. "So, what the spragg *do* we do, Shloomger? When

Bernie finally gets through to K*rargxt's secretary and they work out that Sculpin's missing, that crowd'll be back here in seconds... "

There was a sudden surge of noise around the hangar walls. Ked saw that Bernie was pointing at them and waving his arms around.

"Looks like it's just happened," said Shloomger. He looked up at a series of power cables dangling above the machine, all of which seemed to be linked to a fragile junction box, and pointed to one of them. "Well, if we're going to try and short this thing out *seriously*, I think *that's* the one to go for! Now, if I can just get up on your shoulders, Ked... "

As Shoon leapt up and made an all-or-nothing grab at one of the cables, he noticed, in the corner of his eye, that Bernie and the supervisors very clearly disapproved of the idea.

Ked had spotted it too. He saw, as Shloomger got both hands onto the cable, orang-outan style, one of the supervisors take out her pistol and fire. The beam just missed, and blew a man-sized section out of the hangar wall. She re-aimed at Shloomger's swinging body and, this time, her aim was perfect.

It was so perfect that, if Shloomger had been where she thought he'd still be, the beam would have blown him away completely. But an instant before the woman squeezed the trigger, he was already dropping back down towards Ked and the machine, released by a broken junction box, his hands gripping the insulated part of a loose and extremely live cable.

Some of the others had been on the point of firing, but, as their aim followed Shoon down onto the machine, they hesitated, swung their pistols away from it and ran at the two of them instead.

Ked saw the fall had winded Shloomger. He grabbed the cable, thrust its severed end through the control panel hatch, and pushed it hard down against what looked like a significant-looking set of components. The tremendous bang, and the smoke that began to pour out through the hatch, confirmed exactly how significant they *had* been.

It was clear to Shloomger, as he clambered down from the top of the control desk, that, now they'd achieved their objective, it was very much the moment for them to leg it. And, since the opposition was about twenty-five feet away, a quick bolt round the back of the burning machine looked like a good first step.

He grabbed Ked by the shoulder. "I'd say it's *this* way. And then out through that newly-crafted hole in the wall!" As they turned Shloomger reached down, picked up the sandwich and flung it onto the floor in their pursuers' general path.

It worked well. As they came round the side of a large components crate, the three leading members of Bernie's group tripped over the mechan rats that had begun swarming around the food. The next two fell over *them*, and Bernie somehow fell over all five of them.

Ked saw him activate some kind of handset, and heard sirens start up throughout the hangar. It gave him the idea of calling Grux. He pulled the remote from his pocket and keyed into it.

Then he and Shloomger sprinted for the gap in the wall.

***

Not far from the cave, strobed by bursts of sunlight through the cloud-race, dust devils spin-tangoed amongst the boulders. Beyond the rim of the hollow in the ridge, a lone grassblade cut its song through the dry wind. It wasn't a cheerful song, mainly about being blasted by gales and waiting to be eaten by the next passing goat.

The agent spirit was undeterred. "You'll *love* this one!" it enthused.

The client spirits were sceptical. Baygroon, who seemed to have appointed himself as spokes-spirit, was furthest from liking it. "Has to be *dark* in there, man! See that fat stone in the entrance?"

The agent glanced at his notes. "Secluded, with protective features against the elements, this elegant, geologically sculpted residence… "

"*Cave*, man! It's a *cave*!" Spirit Seelib muttered. He turned to the others. "I *told* you that irrealty bureau's useless."

The guide continued. "Yes, a cave *maybe*, but a cave with *potential*! Think of the space… "

"*All* caves have space! That's what caves *are*!" Seelib felt his spectral pressure rising. He'd been warned about how close he could get to materialising if he didn't take it easy. "That's why we made with your *cave* tour. If we'd been after something smaller, we'd have asked for your *cranny* list!"

"Are you referring to our portfolio of bijou nooklets, Sir?"

"*Whatever*!" The spirit turned to the others in the haunt. "Anyway… lets *case* this *rock-hole*. It can't be worse than the others!"

"And… " the agent added, "… a feature that makes this cave particularly outstanding… "

"How can a cave be *outstanding*?" objected another spirit, "that's the opposite of what a cave *is*. Kinduv *in-crouching* I could maybe accept, but… "

The agent resumed, "Let me simply say that a further advantage of this residence is that – apart from the occasional bear and bat – there's only one occupant, and *he's* simply spread-out wall-covering and no trouble at all. When my colleague slipped in some time ago, he was fast asleep."

"Like, what's '*Some time ago*'?" one of the group asked, "he might just have been *resting*. Maybe he's agressive when he wakes up. Has your colleague been in recently?"

"Well it was, as I say a while ago, but she said she felt good *vibrations* inside the place… "

"*Okay*!" Seelib cut in. "*Drop* the spiel! Let's just *see* the pad, man!"

*

The Fangster slid quietly from its slot in the K*rargxtko Exec. Beast Park and locked onto the tightest route to Ked. An Upper-Grade Limo-Beast snarl-snapped at him as he cut through its reserved drive-space. Grux side-clawed round it and sped out of the park.

The maze of roads and barriers inside the K*rargxtko HQ complex made straight-lining impossible, but the Fangster was skilled at slicing off as much as he could get away with.

The signal seemed to have come from a point somewhere on the far side of The Hangar. As there had been no repeat command, Grux headed for the closest road to it, and prepared to look out for his master.

Ked and Shloomger scrambled through the gap in the hangar wall. To avoid making himself into a target nicely framed by the hole, Ked swung to the left along the outside of the building. Shloomger followed him. The management inside had clearly glimpsed which way they'd turned as they'd gone out, because two new guess-blasts blew out sections of the hangar wall just behind them.

Ked pulled Shloomger down into a shallow drainage ditch just below one of the external hangar supports. "Chances are they won't aim here!" he bellowed into his ear, "if they do, they'll likely bring a large piece of the roof down."

"Ah, but do *they* know that?" Shloomger shouted, "it's a double-skin wall, and they can't see that pillar from the inside!"

As if to prove the point, a blast took away not just a piece of the wall, but a large and clearly vital part of the pillar too. Its severed upper section began to sway precariously. The shooting didn't resume. Instead, they could hear a different set of sirens starting up.

"That's the evacuation signal!" Ked shouted.

Staff who'd been near the the damaged area started pouring out through the blast holes.

"Bernie and the others'll soon be out too, and then they'll have us in direct line of fire!" Shloomger shouted. "Let's get out of here!"

Grux was still sore, in some places severely, from his clash with the ferals. But it hadn't slowed him. His claw-wheels snatched and held, as he pulled a wild turn into the Hangar service road.

The Fangster had heard the first wall-blast while he was still half-asleep in the Beast Park. So, when Ked had called him, he was alert for some kind of trouble. The new blasts had made him ready for more.

He knew he was off-bounds. This part of the road network was only for Service mech-beasts. He'd infringed round here before, and got away with it, but it was risky.

He slowed and scanned for his master.

Crawling along a narrow ditch, trying to keep out of sight, when the ditch is only an inch deeper then *you* are, is tricky at the best of times, and purists would say that, if you're having to do it at all, it's *unlikely* the times are going to be the best.

As well as staying below ground level, Ked was contorting himself trying to drag the remote from his pocket as he guessed at the distance to the main ditch near the service road.

"How much further do you reckon?" Shloomger shouted from behind him.

"Dunno. Maybe thirty feet!" Ked worked his wrist straight so he could operate the remote. "Question *is*, will Grux come by before the K*rargxtko Mechbeasts do?" He pressed the remote.

Grux could see three vicious K*rargxtko Security mechbeasts coming towards him. The new signal he'd got from his master showed Ked was somewhere close by.

The Fangster focussed on the ground ahead, to the right of the stretch of road between him and the oncoming mechbeasts. He sniffed out Ked, and someone else. But the other beasts were nearer them. He swerved onto the roadside and raced over the ground towards the two. As the Fangster vaulted a main ditch it caught sight of its master in one of the smaller trenches that ran into it, and fast-clawed round to the left of the two, sending a shower of flayed turf down on them. Opening one side of his passenger section, he scooped them in with his shopping-loading accessory, and bolted off on a fast route round the end of the Hangar.

Glancing back, Shloomger saw that the entire staff contingent were standing outside the building, watching the smoke from the machine pour through the blast holes. The roof was beginning to sway.

Moments later, Grux felt the ground-shock come through his claw-wheels as the structure fell in on itself.

Shoon surveyed the scene through the Fangster's rear window. "Well," he murmured, "top marks to those trigger-happy supervisors for that total demolition job!"

Ked stared through the Fangster's side-window. For a moment he was silent. Then he took a long deep breath and searched for what to say.

"Dungtkers' Grits!" he muttered, "Dungtkers' *Grits*!"

CHAPTER 27

The Predictions Manager looked at the soothsayer hopefully. "Thruke says there'll be a big rise in prices soon. What do you reckon?"

Ora stared into the time pool for a moment."Well there's *one* thing that inflation has going for it."

"What's that?"

"It makes it cheaper to live in the past."

Proyn drummed his fingers. Working with seers was testing his patience to the limit. "Look, I want more stuff from you Ora. The guys in the dealing room need to use a lot of paper *fast*."

She smiled. "Must be a *real* panic if it's hit *all* of them. Or is that bug going round again?"

"Not *that* kind of paper Ora! It's *special*. Thruke says it's just been 'written.' Some sort of debt they can buy things with. And the company's got heaps of it!"

"Well if it's that 'near-money' I just pre-saw, tell them they can use it like I *thought* you meant!"

Proyn stared at her. "You want me to say *that,* while the firm still *has it*? Are you joking? I have to talk it *up*. If I told Thruke those assets he's got are duff, I'd be out of here in an hour with my private items in a shoe box!"

Ora glanced at the "If"corner of the pool. "No. If you told him that, it'd be *Eight minutes*. And in a *jam jar*."

The manager's face twitched. "Look, do you have *anything*? Something to give those guys an idea what to buy right now?"

"I can't make stuff up Proyn. I've got my professional standards! All those forecasts I gave you last week came out right." She gave him a serious look. "Take the one about the diamond asteroid heading for that planet populated by super-voles."

Proyn shifted on his seat. He had to hand it to Ora. She hadn't simply spotted the two bodies were on a collision course. She'd topped that with her prediction of the battle that had taken place between the Inter-Vole Asteroid-Deflection lobby, backed by insurers and rare-gem stock-holders, and the 'Voles-Say-Bring-It-On' pressure group that had been hurriedly set up by diamond-buyers across the planet.

"Well, how about some of your *earlier* things? Have you got any updates on *those*?"

Ora looked at him. "You *really* think you could ring extra mileage out of them?"

"Well, we can *try*. Did you get anything more on the threat from that bloke K*rargxt, the one with the list of worlds and stars to blow up?"

Ora's eyes searched the pool. "Now, where was *that* when I last saw it? ... Maybe somewhere near the birth of that quadruplet-universe system on Level 4? Let's see now... "

Proyn tried to jog her memory. "And K*rargxt was planning to waste that bloke. What was he called? *Joe*, wasn't it?"

"Yup." Ora tried to concentrate.

"And that planet he was on, *Earth*, was going to be destroyed?"

"Yup."

"So things can get grim on Sub-Lamina 2k16 by the sound of it."

"Yup."

"Do they ever get any chance of an upgrade there? To immortality?

She went on staring into the pool. "Yes, I heard people on Earth, *did* get an offer."

"Where from?"

Ora pointed upwards silently for a moment, then looked at her boss straight in the eyes. "From The Top Of The Very Top Level, and I'm not talking about the outfit we work for here."

"You mean… ?"

"Yup. And I heard that the One who took the offer down to them got treated apallingly, and executed, as if He was some kind of criminal."

Proyn looked at her in amazement. "What happened *then*?"

"He came alive again, said goodbye, and went back home."

"And is the offer still open?"

"I heard it is."

There was a pause. Proyn drew in a deep breath. "Maybe we can stop for a bit," he said.

*

"Thanks for the food." The Predictions Manager closed the lid of Ora's sandwich box and stood up. "Let's forget about markets and all that stuff. Do you think you'll be able to find any news about Joe and his friends, and about K*rargxt's plans?"

Ora rubbed her eyes and looked into the pool for a long time. "None of it's very clear, Proyn. But, as far as I can see, K*rargxt's destruction programme seems to have been halted. Something to do with a key staff member having gone missing… "

"Great!" There was a crash as Proyn sat down on her sandwich box. "Oh, sorry!"

"… And equipment being knackered!"

"Ah… Right. Yes."

"Of course that doesn't mean the threat's gone completely."

"No, I suppose not. If K*rargxt got his act back together, that whole business could start up again fast."

"Yup." The clairvoyant shifted her attention nearer to the pool bank. "And I like the resignation letter you're going to give them next week, Proyn. Very nicely worded."

"What are you talking about, Ora. I'm not thinking of... "

"And you know what Proyn?"

"*What*?"

"After you've left, you're going to be very happy."

***

Ked pulled the Fangster through another claw-burning turn that shot them off their city-exit route and onto a rough track. Shloomger was sorry his body hadn't been warned about it.

"I doubt the K*rargxtko mechans'll follow us in. It should be safer for us here," Ked shouted, almost impaling Grux on a pointed piece of scrap-iron. "This is a real labyrynth! I know, because – in between other part-time jobs – I used to drive a dumper mech-beast out this way when I needed money for studying."

"And in between the *sludge-ponds*, I hope!" Shloomger shouted, as the Fangster sidewaysed down a tapering soil-bridge that separated two pits.

"No worries. Grux knows it too. I've often brought him down here for a bit of... exercise."

"But don't these ponds flood and sort of... change shape and size... ?"

"Well, yup. Quite often, in fact... " Ked clutched a grab-handle as the Fangster three-sixtied a couple of times, hydroplaned round a missing piece of the soil-bridge, splat-slid through a clump of rushes, and scrambled out of the swamp. "... But he tends to manage okay."

*

Shoon looked back at the maze of mud-track, marsh, vegetation and scrap metal they'd climbed away from. "Here'll do, I think," he said.

It wasn't the first time Ked had looked at Shloomger as if he'd gone completely mad. He'd realised the first time that he'd been wrong. But now he was having new doubts. It was as if Shloomger had announced he was embarking on a career as a professional looney and intended to go right to the top.

"Look, are you skrit-grittz sure about this, Shloomger? I know I said it's mainly no-go for K*rargxtko police, but there's nothing here for you to *survive* on!" He waved a hand at the rising ground ahead. "The further out there you go, man, the *wilder* it gets!"

He turned and pointed at the swamp behind. "And if you want to get back to Thrarrxgor on your own through *that*, you'd better *forget* it Shloomger! I didn't tell you, but there are things in those ponds – *feral mechan* things – I wouldn't want to see a *picture of*, let alone get anywhere *near*!"

Shoon looked at him in a kindly way. "Thanks for the advice, but I've decided to head for home and take my chances with pursuers *there*," he gave Ked a friendly pat on the shoulder, "and if it means being chased around *here* before I leave, I'll test my luck out on that too."

"But how'll you get home from *here*?"

Well, I'm sort of about to fix a *rendez-vous*, and I reckon the sooner I do it the better." He looked back at the swamp, "So, now we're out of *that* stuff and on better ground, I think it's the moment to be on my way… "

Ked gave Shoon a long look. "Well, if you're *set* on it, I'll not stop you. But take care of yourself."

"I will. Now, to change the subject, what are *you* planning to do Ked?"

"Oh *I'll* make out okay. I'll take Grux further round the edge of Thrarrxgor City, get him to work up his best camouflage job, and then we'll creep back into the less visited parts of town, go to ground somewhere. Grux and I have got used to surviving."

*

Shloomger moved his feet around to get used to the firm soil after the wild marsh-ride. He reached in through the Fangster's window and shook hands with Ked.

To avoid syrupy farewells they took leave of each other fast.

Shoon watched the Fangster turn and head back through the swampland towards the edge of Thrarrxgor city. He stood thinking for a time, then reached into his pocket and took out his text-module. It would be getting dark soon. But, before he contacted Eelag, he had another message to send.

***

"There's nothing like a good crêpe!" Marlin pushed back his empty plate.

"Thanks for finishing the cooking while I was upstairs. I hope my kitchen equipment isn't too old fashioned for you."

Joe hung up the frying pan and glanced round the room. "No it's fine. Most of it's a lot more up-to-date than my stuff."

Riska poured Marlin another coffee. "I was going to ask you if your device is still working okay. But it must be, if it picked up Shloomger's message."

"Yes, it got it clearly. It was good of him to send it. I imagine he must still have a fair amount on his mind at present."

" So the threat from Thrarrxgor's over?" Riska asked.

Marlin considered for a moment. "Well, the danger was really from K*rargxtko and the man at the top of it. But, now his deputy's gone and his hardware's wrecked, I think we can breathe more freely. At least, we can as long as he can't get his plans back up and running."

"And you'll be able to keep an eye on that?" said Joe.

"Well, the K*rargxtko network's still operating, and if my device goes on functioning okay I should be able to, er... *access* data from it." Marlin mused for a moment and reached under his dining-room table to give Spanger a piece of food. "But I think, now things seem to have quietened down there, I should be able to spend a bit less time monitoring Thrarrxgor and more on developing my spatial/temporal transporter."

"The time machine, you mean?" Riska said.

"Well, yes, if you want to call it that," Marlin murmured. "Anyway, to wrap up our discussion of how things have gone, I'd say that – all in all – they've turned out fairly satisfactorily, apart of course, from the dreadful mad axeman incident, the gas depot explosion, the flash flood at the seaport, and the fire… "

"And the fact that Joe's new job went up with that too," Riska added.

"Well, yes," the old man smiled confidently at Joe, "but I'm sure, with your abilities and experience, you'll soon land another one."

"I'll leave my *recent* experience off my CV," Joe muttered, "or it'll be goodbye to all job prospects for ever!"

"On this planet at least, I suppose," said Riska. She stopped twiddling the fork she'd been holding. "Marlin, what's likely to happen to Ked and Shloomger?"

Quilldragon got up, wandered over to the window, and looked out at some new cat-scratches on a log in the garden. He frowned. "I'm really concerned about those two. Life's going to be tough for Ked. And I think Shloomger's in danger. I don't know where exactly he was *from*, but – as far as I could tell from his messages – he didn't seem to know much about Thrarrxgor."

"And there's nothing we can do to help them?" Joe asked.

Marlin turned and looked at them. "No, there isn't, I'm afraid. I don't know that it'll do them much good, but we could sort of *think* them our wishes for good luck."

"Yes. Let's do that," Joe and Riska said in unison.

The three of them fell silent for a while.

At last, Quilldragon came back over from the window, gave them both a warm smile and held out his hand. "Well, it doesn't look as if I'll need to call on your help again," he said brightly, "at least, not as long as that character Sculpin's away from Thrarrxgor. But I hope we'll stay in touch."

Riska and Joe shook hands with him and said they wanted that too.

Marlin hand-ruffled his beard. "Thanks for everything you've done. By the way, what are your plans *now*?"

Riska smiled. "To get away for a bit."

"Yup, *together,*" Joe said.

***

S 2 E: Hope all well at your end. Some time since were in contact. Job completed here, so now wish to return. Please instruct machine to locate me and transport me back.

*

S 2 E: Hope got message ok. Currently in spot not best to stay in long. Swamps on one side (plus hostile authorities in city beyond) and wild country on other side. Would appreciate swift arrangements for return.

*

S 2 E: Counting on you receiving this. Situation getting tight. Night falling fast now and some very nasty-looking creatures leaving wild-country and heading for swamps. Problem is, am on their route. Rapid transfer from here requested.

*

S 2 E: Would be useful to know if you got my recent transmissions. Are you able to reply? Options for survival diminishing. Creatures mentioned are in fact some sort of feral mechans, and clearly pack hunters. No apparent way to deter them. Suppose could try singing. Please initiate immediate removal as requested.

*

S 2 E: Singing not success. Only good point is voice maybe better than I thought, as mechans not repulsed. Major bad point is they now forming close circle and moving in.

Instant extraction and return from here essential.

*

S 2 E: Well, then I suppose it's Goodbye. Goodbye, Eelag.

***

Eelag hit the 'Recall' button for what he calculated was the thirty-fourth time, and checked the instructions again. This new version of the transporter programme he'd installed was a mind-tangler to use.

As far as he could tell, he'd done the first part of the routine correctly, just as he had done in his test-runs after Shloomger had left. Sending and recalling items to-and-from other Levels had worked fine then. But on the other hand, as it had involved things like deckchairs and sunshades, which didn't re-immortalise themselves, this had made it a lot easier. If he could have done it now, he'd have brought Shloomger back straight away as a mortal and let him re-immortalise once he'd arrived. But this transporter device didn't seem to allow for that. Shloomger would need to re-immortalise the precise instant he was beamed away from Thrarrxgor.

He glanced down at his graunched messager and took in a sharp breath as he read Shloomger's latest text. He wished the module's transmitter function was working. Then, at least he could have let Shloomger know he was trying.

He put his hand to his forehead. Well, if *this* latest try hadn't worked, it'd all be over very soon.

He got up and checked the horizontal bin-like contraption

again. Before he'd left, Shloomger had commented that it looked like the offspring of a mating between a total-enclosure sunbed and a giant sandwich-toaster. Eelag thought his friend's description seemed pretty much spot-on.

He heard a sound above him and looked up. A large, beautiful bird, which had been soaring over the beach for a good part of the morning, did a couple of gentle spirals, played a completely new variation of Coral Calooba on its feathered tail-tubes, and prepared to touch down.

When, afterwards, Eelag reflected on the event, he couldn't remember whether he'd spotted the wrongly-set switch just before the bird landed on it, or just as it did.

In any case, the weight of the bird tipped the switch to the correct position. A series of lights came on.

Eelag and the bird watched another of the lights throb on and off.

"Looks as if that's done it," he muttered. The bird made what seemed like a satisfied cooing sound, and flew up into a thermal.

The light continued throbbing for a while. Then there was what sounded to Eelag like a drawn-out kind of thud, a bit like when he'd test-recalled his portable solar barbecue – only louder and heavier.

There was a beep. A bright green light came on just above the hatch-handle.

Eelag undid the lock mechanism and lifted the hatch.

***

Maybe it was because Proorong had gone, or maybe it was because he really *was* getting stronger. Whatever the reason, Boontrak was beginning to feel a good deal better. And now, for the time being at least, he had some interesting companions.

He gazed benignly at his new cavemates. "So you've closed the deal okay?"

"Yeah, but a short lease, to start with," said Prarf, who –

as far as Boontrak could make out – seemed to be the main admin. spirit in the group.

"So are you from around here?" Boontrak led on, by way of polite conversation.

"Sort of," Baygroon muttered, "but only after we drifted into the area. Got turned out of where we were before."

"Oh? Why was that?"

"Sank into some *soft* rocks, man. *Pink* and *sweet*!" Baygroon giggled, "cave was full of them. Whaywhawoo! Real *nice*!" He whirled round and spirit-grinned to the others. "We got *whooahwayeezey*, man! But the locals – the *spirit* locals, not the bears – *they* didn't like us. And they moved us on. *Man*, were they a *real mean* bunch of ghosts!"

Boontrak tried to search the local knowledge part of his brain. "Don't think there's anything like that here… "

"No worries! No spoil-spooks in *this* cave," Baygroon laughed spiritedly, "we checked before we signed!"

There was a brief silence, and then Boontrak said, "I suppose you're not into seven-dimensional poker, or else *fifteen* if you prefer?"

There was a very much briefer silence while the spirits gaped, in their way, in disbelief. Then one said, "are you telling me you've got a fifteen deck *here* in the cave?"

Boontrak, who hadn't thought of this as anything particularly special, said in fact he *knew* he had, as it was one of the factory-installed games he'd recently found while running a damage-check on the most basic elements of his brain.

He added that he, himself, wasn't specially into playing it, but would be happy to project the deck for their use, in return for a bit of conversation.

And suddenly, there were even *better* vibes in the cave.

CHAPTER 28

"*Bralzted Krooblytes*!" Eelag stared into the interior of the apparatus. After some moments' trying to work out what to say next, he said "*Bralzted Krooblytes*!" a second time.

Shloomger, who had been staring back at him since he'd opened the hatch, decided the best thing to say was probably, "Hello Eelag!" and did. After a second or two he added, "you seem to specialise in leaving this recall business to the very last."

Eelag looked in disbelief at the remnants of Shoon's gear. Tooth-torn wasn't the term. It was clear that whatever beasts had attacked him had simply looked on his clothes as a form of appetiser pastry-shell.

Shloomger waved aside his offers of help. "Can't understand why you really need to use this bin," he said, climbing out of the machine, "I'd have thought your system could have swift-beamed me back to a point of your own choosing, like a comfortable deckchair or something." Shoon stretched and took a few deep lungfuls of air. "Mind you," he added, "I'm not complaining. It's extremely good to be back. Things were getting terminally tight. Those mech-beasts must be seriously disappointed with their catering arrangements at the moment."

"I'm afraid that, once I'd sent you out using the bin, I couldn't switch to another return method, Eelag muttered, "and, up to now, the bin's been bit easier to use… " He stopped. His friend was looking around. The gypsy knew there was no way he could hide the fact that things here were seriously different.

"There's been a big storm here, Eelag. A real klonker, I'd

say. I can see you've started to clean the place up, but it must have been a serious face-washer."

"Er, yes, it *was*, really. But, on the other hand, it was a rather *local* kind of storm, in its way."

"*Local*?" Shloomger looked at the shambles around him. "Well, if it was '*local*', I get the feeling that whatever did this must have hung around for quite a time!"

"Well, as a matter of fact... "

"And, how about *that*?" Shloomger pointed to a downtube from the bungalow's guttering. "Must have been *some* storm to put a figure-of-eight knot into *that*!"

"Shloomger, there's something I have to tell you... "

"... And just take a look at *this*!" Shloomger paused, realising Eelag obviously *had* taken a look at it. "The entire contents of your museum of travel mementos have been turned out and flung around outside higgledey-piggeldy! Well, I know a good many of the sculptures *were* a bit like that already, but it looks as if pieces from a scrapyard have been having a *wrestling match* and, somehow, they've all *lost*! How did *that* happen?"

"I had a bit of a problem, Shloomger... "

"Bit of an understatement, I'd say, Eelag... "

"It wasn't just the storm, you see. I mean, the storm was a sort of *accompaniment* ... "

"Well, if it was the accompaniment, Eelag, the singer must have been amazingly powerful to get his voice heard through *that*!"

"He *was*, Shloomger."

Shoon realised that something very serious had happened to his friend.

"I think you'd better tell me all about it, Eelag," he said gently.

*

"And this *henchman* character wanted you to tell him where I was, so he could drag me off to Zunddertokk."

"Yes."

"And you didn't tell him."

"No."

"That was very brave of you, Eelag."

"Well, I don't know. I just… "

"It *was*, Eelag." Shloomger scanned the stretch of beach around his friend's home, and reflected on just how horrible the visitation had been. "What I don't understand, though, is how you managed to get him to *leave*." He paused for a few seconds. "I suppose he *has* actually *gone*."

"Oh yes, he went eventually. But he didn't seem to be in any hurry. Not even when I'd given him what he wanted."

"But how did you do that, if I wasn't *there*… ?"

Shloomger saw that Eelag was clearly embarrassed. The gypsy got up and walked over to the small part of his bungalow that was still more or less intact. After a few moments he came back holding something. He sat down and looked at his friend.

"I *had* to do it, Shloomger. It was the *only way*," he handed Shoon the item he'd brought out, "it's your chequebook, the one for your Inter-Level Bank account. It was in the bag of things you left here before you set off. I couldn't use your credit module. I didn't have the code."

Shoon took the chequebook and glanced at the last completed stub. " 'Pay … *Zunddertokk…* '," he stopped and looked at it closely. "Ah! *Well*! There's no amount written on the stub. And anyway, as I wasn't *there* to sign it, you couldn't have… "

Eelag shook his head sadly. "I left the amount blank on the cheque too, Shloomger. And, well, I *forged* your signature. You see, I managed to convince the henchman that, though you were away somewhere unknown, you'd left the cheque for me to give to Zunddertokk, or any of his staff, if they happened to drop by."

Shloomger looked at him admiringly. "When did you get a chance to forge the cheque? I mean, he must have been keeping a fairly close eye on you."

Eelag gulped at the memory. "Well, yes he did. But after

I'd relented and he'd untied me, he went off to raid the kitchen. I suppose he must have been quite hungry… ”

“And you nipped into the living room and did the necessary.”

“Yup. In fact I had just a bit more time than I'd thought I would. I saw afterwards that he'd cleaned out the entire fridge. And the freezer too. And he seems to have got completely the other side of those twenty giant cheeses I had in the storeroom.

“And then you gave him the blank, signed cheque.”

“Yes, I knew that, with Inter-Level exchange rates being so volatile, and allowing for inflation, Zunddertokk would insist on the amount being left open… ”

“Not to speak of Inter-Level differences in time… ”

“*And* those, of course… ”

Shloomger gave Eelag a look that breathed his friend a deep, warm, emotional gratitude. “And so, Eelag, you have saved me,” he said quietly.

“Well, maybe for a *while*, Shloomger, but the moment's going to come when… How can I put it?… ”

“When the cheque – with whatever huge sum Zunddertokk has written on it – is going to bounce.” Shoon smiled at his friend, “It's alright, you don't need to be embarrassed. There's no way any cheque I wrote for Zunddertokk could really do anything else. In fact, I'm surprised that henchman accepted the cheque at all. He can't have been the brightest.”

Eelag shook his head. “No, he certainly didn't seem very gifted in the brain zone.”

Shloomger considered carefully for some moments. “The principal problem, I suppose, is that the cheque's likely to bounce as far as here, with Zunddertokk holding it firmly when it comes. And the principal *question* is: *When will that happen*?”

He stopped and looked at the unclouded sky. “It's possible it *could* take quite a lot of time before he turns up, maybe at least as much as has gone by since I took out that loan. After all, you know what these Inter-Level bank transactions can be like.”

Eelag brightened a little. "I suppose you could have a point there… "

Shloomger resumed, "Of course one never knows. Maybe it'll be sooner than that," he grinned at the gypsy, "but anyway, as far as I can see, I'm no worse off than I was before."

He looked out at the waves rolling in on the sea. "And, you know, the funny thing is that I've rather got to like this "Never-know-when-it-might-happen" thing. It's something I picked up from being mortal."

Shloomger fell silent for a moment, and watched the birds soaring above the beach. Then he turned to his friend and grinned again. "You were right about *real* travel, Eelag. It makes you look at life sort of *differently*."

***

A large bubble of sun-warmed air lifted itself from the field that had been its nest, and climbed skyward. Around the rim of its launch site, new air surged inwards to take its place, tugging at the clover and drag-bursting the dandelions' seed-clocks.

Hundreds of feet above the soil, moving across the valley in the windstream, what seemed to be two eagles spiralled steadily upwards on higher bubbles of rising air. It was only an occasional glint of sunlight, reflected on an airframe as they turned, that would have told a distant eye that they were not birds.

The pilots were not yet high enough to see sufficiently far, but, beyond the hills in the distance, brushed by the changing patterns of sun and cloud-shadows, was a campsite where Joe had once stayed. And beyond that – and still out of sight for the moment too – was the pub where he and Riska had first met, and which had a strangely drawn sign above its door that read

THE BEND IN THE SKY.

***

And at the same moment – with allowances for turbulence in space, time and a great many other things – at a place far away, on a different Level, an entranced silence settled on an audience around a large field.

This was because the band had just begun to play

The Six Wild Moons of Glondor.